MY SCOTTISH EMPRESS

BY
KAREN A. FAY

PublishAmerica
Baltimore

First printing

Hardcover 9781456067267
Softcover 9781456067250
PUBLISHED BY PUBLISHAMERICA, LLLP
www.publishamerica.com
Baltimore

Printed in the United States of America

Author's Dedication

To Patrick, Nicholaus, Rebecca, Bennett, Emmi, and Devon; Always follow your heart because dreams really do come true. Without all of you I would never had the courage to write.

Acknowledgements

My husband, who helped with spelling and critiquing.

My daughter, Rebecca for her wonderful help with the computer and also her wonderful ideas and words of advice.

Synopsis of *My Scottish Empress,* a novel by Karen A. Fay

Imprisoned by her family's secrets, which have controlled her life, Abigail Fox is determined to become a single, financially independent merchant in the early 1800's. However Pirates, England and a powerful Scottish Laird named Gabriel McKenzie have other plans for her.

Ready to embark on an adventure of a lifetime, Abigail sets sail for England where she is planning to operate a shipping company. On her arrival she is arrested for crimes she did not commit and sentenced to a life in Debtor's prison. She is soon sold and forced to work off her debt as a cook and servant in an English Manor where she is introduced to Gabriel.

Intrigued with this voluptuous American and her past, Gabe forcibly returns the reluctant Abigail to his home in Scotland. Gabe soon discovers that Abby is hunted by Black Dog, a notorious treasure seeking pirate, and vows to protect her against the constant threat of abduction. But as well protected as Gabe kept her Abby was finally kidnapped and forcibly take out to sea.

Will Gabe's love for Abigail triumphantly free her from her abductors or will he lose her to the lifetime of secrets that have kept her imprisoned

My Scottish Empress is a whirlwind of emotions that will capture the heart of the hopelessly romantic historical reader through seduction, suspense, romance, danger and a touch of humor.

MY SCOTTISH EMPRESS

PROLOGUE

"Anna, your daughter is going to be the death of me yet. Do you know what she's done now?"

"Now John, calm yourself. It just cannot be that bad," Anna replied.

"Bad? Your daughter was just walking across the barn roof. Do you know why? Well, she thought it quicker than walking around the barn on the ground."

"She is only seven, John. We must be patient with her," Anna encouraged her very upset husband.

"Do you have any idea what she did yesterday? Your beautiful little daughter was hanging upside down from the tree in the middle of town, with her skirts over her head. If she had not had those bloomers on you made her wear, she would have exposed herself to the entire town and God knows what else," John sputtered.

"John, she is just a child and that is normal for a child to do," Anna explained, trying not to giggle at her irate husband.

"Anna, we have eight children. Eight wonderful, well behaved children and then we have Abigail. She is far worse than all eight of them put together."

"She just needs more attention, that is all and we just don't have the time to give it to her," Anna replied.

"You are not bringing up that subject again, are you?" John asked with raised eyebrows.

"Well, it would solve our problem, John, and her grandfather is so lost now that his wife has passed away. He would give her the constant attention she needs we are unable to give her."

"Her grandfather is a salty old sea dog who has the most colorful language I have ever heard. He can cuss better that any three men put together. Your daughter will come back talking and acting like a gutter snip."John replied with his hands waving in the air.

"Abigail's grandfather is a retired, well educated sea captain who is keeping himself busy designing and building ships at the docks. Abigail is a little girl but more than that she is a child. He will let her be the child she so needs to be. It is only for the summers and when she comes back I will be ready with a bar of soap to wash those dirty words out of her mouth and we will resume her lessons you so want her to have. You, John, will have a break and so won't the rest of her brothers and sisters."

"You will miss your baby, Anna."

"Yes I will but she is so like I was at that age and she doesn't need to be tamed and molded into a woman, she needs to be a child and her grandfather will give that to her."

"I can't hit her again," John said lowering his head. "It just breaks my heart every time I take her to the wood shed. If she would only cry out, I would know I was making some difference, but she won't. She just takes my punishments and then turns and looks at me with those big tears running down her cheeks, not saying a word. I give up, Anna, we will try it your way. Send word to Abraham and I will bring her to him the end of the month but if this doesn't work I swear, I will lock her in her room until she is twenty years old."

"Oh John, you will not and you should not make threats you do not intend to keep. I am very proud of you. Abraham will be so pleased," Anna said smiling at her husband.

At the end of the month, John and Abigail Fox set off to Boston to the ship yards, where her grandfather, Captain Abraham McDough was waiting.

For the next nine years she would return each summer to be with her beloved grandfather. She learned everything he could teach her about ships and the sea. She spent the summer wearing britches and climbing the rigging hanging upside down from the boom.

There wasn't a single knot she couldn't tie or a map she couldn't read. Abe would take her out on maiden voyages of ships she had helped build. Abigail had her own tools and very strict rules placed on her by her grandfather. She learned to take orders like the ship hands and swim like a fish. Abigail's grandfather expected a lot from her and she never disappointed him or she would not be allowed to accompany him sailing.

Abraham had groomed her to be a true sea captain with the abilities to take over and run a well managed ship. During the days, Abigail would work alongside the old captain but at night he taught her to love the written word and smoke a pipe, much to her father's dismay and play the violin and drum.

In the fall she would return home inland and spend the winters resuming her lessons, math, history and literature from her father and music, cooking and art from her mother. And every fall Anna Fox would wait impatiently for her daughter's return with open arms and a very large bar of soap.

CHAPTER 1
Starting Over (1800?)

She sat in the office area of the bank only two day after her husband's death collecting what was left of her inheritance. Roy wasn't even buried yet and the debtors were everywhere. Mr. Pinkerton, the bank manager had been given the difficult task of executor. It was he who decided; Abigail must sell everything and pay off all debts without asking her. It was the law then; women were not allowed to own their own land.

The day after her husband's death, an auction was arranged without her knowledge. Everything including her land, house and livestock was auctioned to the highest bidder. Her clothes where the only possessions she managed to take from her home of twenty three years.

It didn't surprise her that the new owner was the nephew of Mr. Pinkerton, the snake, or that the price she received for her property was much, much less than the actual value. Her friends and neighbors became more interested in what they could steal from her in the auction than being friends and bidding at a fair price.

So now she sat at the bank, clutching a small brass key, waiting for Mr. Pinkerton to finalize the paper work and return to Abigail what was legally hers after everything was paid off.

The First Riverton Bank was a one room establishment with one small teller window on the far wall, a large walk-in vault on its left and a small business area, designated by a three foot wooden railing surrounding it. It always reminded Abigail of a paddock where animals were held waiting for slaughter. There was a large ornate desk for Mr. Pinkerton and a well padded chair just behind it. Abigail was sitting in the front of the grotesque desk on a wooden chair without a cushion.

It was a common practice of Mr. Pinkerton to wait on male customers first and leave the ladies to wait until he was good and ready to assist them. Sitting in the office area only heightened the anticipation of what was coming to Abigail in the hands of the devious bank manager.

The bank had been exceptionally busy today, partly because of the auction but also because of the cattle dealers who had drifted into town ready to sell their stock. Mr. Pinkerton was in his glory with all the new money coming into his establishment and also it gave him ample excuse to make Abigail wait. And wait she did, for hours.

Finally, when all the men had left the bank and only the women were left standing in line, Mr. Pinkerton entered the office area to finish the business with Abigail. By now, Abby's temper was reaching the boiling point. She had all she could do not to reach across his desk and put her foot in his face but she wanted this done and finished today, so she'd never have to deal with The First Riverton Bank ever again.

She was sitting looking across at the infamous Mr. Pinkerton who had no intention of looking up at her. She was an inconvenience to him now. He had legally robbed her from well needed inheritance, and helped to make her homeless. He could no longer weasel anything else from her and was more than willing to get rid of her permanently.

Finally he looked up at Abigail through thick half glasses that rested on the end of a very large bent nose. His long fingered hands were crossed on his thin chest over a very well tailored black suit. The smell of heavy sickening cologne permeated the air just as he began to speak through very large horse like teeth. "Your husband was not a very wealthy man and did little to provide for you in the case of his death," he spit out as he ran his thin fingers through his slicked back greasy black hair. "I took it on myself to treat you as a charity case and manage your finances to the best of my ability for a small fee of course, taken from your remaining funds."

"I was under the impression, sir that the judge ordered you to deal with the estate," Abigail said through gritted teeth. "You had no intention of helping me until you found a way of gaining your own wealth with the auction."

"You will hold your tongue woman or I will keep you here on display in this office until I see fit and charge your account for every minute you are in my establishment. Do I make myself clear?" Mr. Pinkerton growled.

"And let me make myself perfectly clear, Mr. Pinkerton, if you charge me one more undeserved fee, or keep me here one minute longer than is absolutely necessary, I will tell the town about your little interlude at the brook near my house with a certain Mr…"

Before she could continue, Mr. Pinkerton rose and forced her to stop with an expression of anger and disbelief that anyone knew of his dirty little secret.

"I see," Abigail said smiling up sweetly, "that we have come to a pass road. May we continue this farce so I may leave?"

Mr. Pinkerton sat slowly back into his fully stuffed chair and began to fumble nervously through the papers. Abby just waited for the next trump card that she was ready to play. Mr. Pinkerton had been nothing but miserable to her and her children since she moved here twenty three years ago and it was more than high time he felt a little of what he dished out.

She was not about to let him humiliate her in front of the remaining customers. Nor was she going to take any more of his condescending attitude. Roy, her husband had never been a good business man, he had contributed little to support his family and it was because of him that she was now homeless. He was an abusive father and an even worse husband who took extensive business trips returning with only the smell of a woman's cheap perfume on his clothes.

Abigail was glad she was finally free of Roy and the land that kept her here. She was finally free and ready go back to where she was the most happy. Tomorrow she would bury the husband she was forced to marry and make plans to go back to the sea but for now she would give Mr. Pinkerton what he deserved.

Abigail had little expectations when it came to Roy's finances and expected little to nothing and she was not surprised. Mr. Pinkerton was very loud when he announced to Abigail the total of the estate, making sure all remaining customers heard her personal business. Gossip spread like wild fire in Riverton and Mr. Pinkerton was one who wallowed in dispersing peoples' hardships to whoever would listen. "That concludes our business Madam. Would you like me to escort you out?" Mr. Pinkerton asked through gritted horse teeth.

"Not so fast, sir, we have one more piece of business to discuss," Abby said with the sweetest smile she could give him. "There is the matter that goes with this," and she held up her brass key and an account number. Mr. Pinkerton's face went a nice shade of green. "You?" He asked, mortified.

"Yes, it is me and has been for twenty three years. Now go and get my box and my nest egg." Then she added in her very own condescending way, "and be quick about it if you know what is good for you. I have put up with enough from you this day." The bank manager did what he'd been ordered and returned with a very old nautical looking box.

"Are you sure you should take that out of safe keeping?" Mr. Pinkerton asked, acting nervously as if someone was watching him from the back room.

"Why, are you planning on stealing this from me too? You have used my box to keep your bank alive all these years without knowing it was mine. You will not be much of a bank now that it is gone. Hopefully you will be able to pay all those people back their money they think is in your bank."

Then she turned to the ladies still in the bank waiting for their turn. "If I were you, ladies I would take what funds you have in this bank and leave with it before the town discovers there are no funds left and Mr. Pinkerton is the crook everyone thought him to be." She opened her box and quickly counted the funds inside and quickly examined the contents. "Looks like I have all that I came for. Have a nice day sir." And with that she walked out of the bank with a large smile across her face leaving Mr. Pinkerton to deal with ten very frantic female customers all demanding their money at the same time.

Abigail's husband had contributed little through the years to support her or their family but her grandfather had. After he died, Abigail was his only heir. He left her well and with very definite orders on how to spend his money, orders which she had followed to the letter. No one knew she had an inheritance from her grandfather and that was the way she wanted it.

Even her three sons and daughter had no idea that the funds which kept them alive all those years were from their great grandfather not their worthless womanizing father. Even Mr. Pinkerton had no idea. All dealing had been in writing. Abigail was very good with numbers, doing business in writing was a sure way to keep tabs on Mr. Pinkerton. It also made it impossible for him to steal from her.

As Abigail started to leave, she couldn't resist announcing her future plans to the lady costumers and, of course, Mr. Pinkerton. "I will be leaving very shortly. I have plans to return to Boston, where I spent my summers as a child and open a business there. Good day all. It was nice knowing you." With a sweet smile and a nod of her head she left carrying an old nautical looking box and a brass key.

As she started down the street a middle aged woman followed her from the bank. She was not much taller than Abby, very well dressed with a distinctive Boston accent and very similar to Abigail's coloring. "Excuse me, madam; I could not help over hearing you and Mr. Pinkerton at the bank. I was not trying to eavesdrop but the bank is so small it was hard not to."

"I completely understand," Abigail answered with a smile. "How can I help you?"

"It is I that can help you, madam. After hearing what transpired in the bank it would not be very Christian of me to not offer my help."

"I am in no need of charity, madam, thank you for your kind offer but I will be just fine, especially after I reach Boston."Abby answered politely.

The lady's face turned red. "Oh, I have made a real mess of this, madam. I would like to start over."

Then she reached out her hand to Abigail and said. "My name is Elizabeth Shaw. My husband Niles and I are from Boston. We had business in town with the cattle dealers which will be concluded at the end of the week. I was hoping that you might consider returning home with us in our coach. My husband doesn't like to ride inside.

He prefers the outside and his stallion. So that leaves me alone inside the coach for the duration of the trip. Don't misunderstand me, I love accompanying my husband on these business trips but I get board always talking finances and investments. Once in a while I would like female company, especially on the long road to Boston. I would be so grateful to you if you would except my offer and join me on our trip home."

Then Abigail extended her hand and said, "My name is Abigail Fox now. I refuse to use my husband's name from this day forth. It is so nice to meet you. I can't promise I can accompany you, but if I finish all the final tasks I need to do by the end of the week then I would love to. After all it is the only Christian thing to do," and then she giggled.

"Abigail Fox, I can tell we are going to be very good friends." Elizabeth said with a smile.

The two ladies said there farewells and last minute instructions and went their separate ways. As Abigail walked away a strange feeling came over her, the feeling that somehow she would be ok no matter what happened. It was the most peaceful feeling and it was at that moment Abigail knew she would survive and make it on her own.

The next day, Abigail stood in the rain with her four grown children listening to the minister give Roy his final send off. There were few mourners for Roy and not one tear shed, maybe because of the rain or maybe because he spent so little time in Riverton or maybe because of who he really was. It didn't really matter to Abigail anyway. At the end of the service, the people that were there threw a flower in on his coffin now lowered into the dugout grave. Abigail threw the last letter he had received from one of his many mistresses.

The little family returned to the town and stayed at the hotel. Their family home had been sold. Ellery, her eldest, twenty two was now an accountant for a large men's clothing store not far from Boston. Stephen and Daniel, twenty one, her twins had just received commissions on a sea vessel sailing to Europe.

Hannah, now twenty, was working as a school teacher in a private girl's academy, also near Boston. All her children were doing fine, starting their own lives, following their dreams just as Abby had taught them. That is why she was shocked at the negative response they gave her regarding the business she had intended to open in Boston.

Ellery had insisted in escorting her but Abby was determined to be independent and not a burden on her children. They had their own lives to live and so did she. Abigail was free and on her own with no one telling her what to do and no one depending on her. Plus she knew it was the right move for her and she was going to follow her heart. Grandfather's money was still there to help her but she would have to be very careful investing it because once it was gone there would be no one to fall back on.

In less than one week, Abigail lost her husband, her home, her land and now was saying good bye to her children but the feeling of peace and happiness was so strong she could not deny it. At the end of the week Abigail Fox joined Elizabeth and Niles Shaw on their journey back to Boston.

Her four children came out the morning she was to leave to say their last farewells and made Abby promise she'd send word immediately on her arrival in Boston.

The Shaws turned out to be very nice people and Elizabeth and Abby quickly did become very good friends. The coach was more elaborate than any carriage or stagecoach Abby had ever ridden in which made the trip even more bearable. Elizabeth and Niles had two business stops to make which delayed getting to Boston but Elizabeth insisted on paying for Abby's rooms for her inconvenience even though Abby would not hear of it. In the end Elizabeth won out and Abby received free room and board. The trip to Boston was turning out to be a very exciting adventure, one she wished she could have shared with her children but for now she would just hold these memories to be shared at a later date.

It was well into the third day on the road when Elizabeth finally asked the question that Abby was dreading. Elizabeth had been in the bank that day and had overheard Mr. Pinkerton announce the sum of coin that Roy left her. It was only a matter of time before she would want to know Abby's plans.

Abby was a very clever intelligent woman. She knew enough not to trust anyone when money was involved with the exception of her children. So when Elizabeth casually dropped the subject, Abby was very careful not to disclose what she actually had to invest. "If I may be so bold as to ask you about how much you would like to invest," Elizabeth asked point blank. "I know it is none of my business but Niles has many contacts on the docks and he could be a real help to you finding the right investment. Of course he would need to have a rough figure from you to give you the best advice." Abby knew better than to look a gift horse in the mouth and so it was then and there that she decided not to spend any more time with the Shaws than she had too.

It was very late on day three, when the Shaws reached their Boston home. Elizabeth insisted on Abby spending time there until she had suitable living arrangements. Although Abby was reluctant, a few days would not matter and Abby finally did talk to Niles about her projected investment. Niles was quick to call her attention to a number of fine businesses on the wharf. He even offered to introduce her around, but still Abby was not about to trust anyone she had known for five days with a decision as important as her finances.

CHAPTER 2
WELCOME TO BOSTON

It was early morning when Abby awoke to meet her first day in Boston. The window to her upstairs room overlooked the city street. As she looked out her window to the street below she was greeted by the passing street vendors calling out their wares. There was a funny little round man with a bright white apron pulling his cart full of bread and rolls. Then there was the flower woman with a torn red dress carrying a large basket of fresh cut flowers in every color imaginable. Black hacks worked the street ready to pick up their first paying fair for the day. There was a mother holding tightly to a very active little boy's hand scolding him for his behavior.

Abby could smell the sweet smell of bread baking from down stairs and hear the clop of the horse hooves as they passed by the town house. The street was full of activity and she was missing it all stuck in this house. Quickly as she could she washed and dressed for the day. It was the first day of her new life and she was not going to miss a minute of it.

Abby never guessed at age thirty nine that she would find herself a widow and alone in Boston getting ready to begin her first real adventure. It was like she was seven years old all over again, full of excitement and anticipation, traveling to Boston with her father to stay with her Grandfather for the summer months. She had to smile when she thought of how many times her poor father asked her to sit down. By the time they had reached Grandpa's house her father was holding on to the back of her waist band trying to keep her from jumping out of the wagon.

That same wonderful feeling crept over her and she was out the door of her room and running down the stairs as fast as her feet would allow. Elizabeth had promised to take her around Boston this morning but woke with a bad headache and was not able to get out of bed. Abigail could not wait another second; she was out the door and standing in the street smelling the many scents of Boston.

Then out of the blue she smelled it, the familiar smell of the ocean. It was as if she had returned home, the only thing missing was her grandfather. Before she could think what she was doing, Abby was walking alone down the street not paying attention to any danger that might be walking behind her. As she rounded the corner, she recognized where she was. It was the same street her grandfather walked each day to the ship yard.

With the wind blowing in her honey blonde hair she tightened her cloak and walked the way to the ocean. It was as if her grandfather was walking beside her holding her hand and smoking his pipe. She was home again and it felt so good. Just two more streets and she would be down at the docks. Turning the last corner, she stopped dead. There it was the shop where she helped build the ships and there in the hopper was a new boat beginning to take shape. She wanted to grab her britches and her tools and get to work.

Abby smiled to herself when she thought about her tools and her grandfather ordering the work for the day. He always assigned jobs to the workers and never forgot to give Abby one as well. Abby looked down at her hands, they were not the child hands she once had. They now were hands of a thirty nine year old woman who was a little rounder than she should have been. As she looked into the window, she saw her reflection, not the skinny little blonde headed girl but much older, rounder blonde with the same smile she had when she was seven.

Never in her wildest dreams did she think she would be standing in this very spot again. A man passed her smoking a pipe and Abby felt her Grandfather standing next to her. A tear slipped out of her eye as she thought of that kindly old man and how he had made her summers wonderful. A strong gust of wind blew her hair loose from the tie into her face redirecting her attention down toward the ocean.

She turned and walked down to the docks where the sounds were so familiar. Boston was not like it was when she was a child, it was very dangerous to be walking alone on the docks especially if you were a woman, but Abby was so distracted by all the familiar sounds and sights that she was oblivious to the danger that had been following her since she left the town house.

There in the harbor, were ships of every size and shape. Abby could name each kind and what their cargo must be. She loved to look at the hundreds of masts jetting up into the sky with their sails tied up and their rigging flapping. What she would give to sail off on one of those vessels, far away and not just a day trip. England or France or Italy would be just fine she thought to herself with a little giggle.

Then a pungent smell of dead fish surrounded her nose. As she stood looking at the ships the nauseous smell kept getting stronger. Instinctively, Abby started to move away from the smell but to her surprise it kept following her. She started to walk a little faster but the smell was getting worse. In the corner of her eye she noticed the reflection in a window, of four foul men looking directly at her from behind.

Realizing she was in trouble, she started to look for help but she had drifted into an area no self respecting person would be seen in. Moving faster but still trying to look as if she had not seen her assailants, Abby tried to find a way to escape. She could hear the footsteps of large men coming up from behind her. Panicking, she started to run. Her skirts blew in all directions with the strong southerly wind coming into the harbor; her hair was completely free of its tie and blowing wildly around her head.

She was alone and scared and being stocked with no help in sight. How could she have got into so much trouble the first day? Abby could hear her father's voice saying, "*Abigail, when are you going to use that head of yours and think before you react*." Think, she kept telling herself. Don't stop, find an answer. The sound of footsteps lessened. Abigail turned to look over her shoulder and gasped. Two of the men were gone; the other two were close behind her.

As she turned back around, the sight of the missing two men was right in front of her not fifty yards away. They had circled around her, sandwiching her between them. There was no escape. The ocean was on her right and unoccupied shops on her left. It was too cold to swim but she was going to chance it until she heard men's voices arguing on her left which drew her attention away from the swim.

Five feet in front of her and to the left was a door with a very shiny gold knob. A light was coming through the window just beyond the door. She needed to make it to that door but her assailants were almost upon her. The footsteps coming from behind were slamming down just behind her heels and the men in front were reaching for her. She ducked and grabbed the knob, turned quick and pushed as hard as she could as a hand gripped her shoulder from behind. The door swung back, hit the wall and bounced back to hit the hand clutching Abigail's shoulder with enough force to cause the hand to release.

Abigail stumbled into the room causing enough noise for the arguing men to stop and look out into the waiting room. The four foul men saw the two shop keepers and turned and walked away as if they had done nothing wrong, but they did not go too far. Abigail was still their target and they were not going to give up that easily.

She noticed that the biggest man wore a green coat with patches all over it while the other three, wore the same black coats and britches with wool hats pulled way down over their foreheads. They had frightened her enough to leave a lasting image of their faces in her mind forever.

The two men from the office just looked out at Abigail and then went back to their heated discussion without acknowledging her in the least. She straightened her skirts, fixed her cloak and tried to make her hair look presentable. Shaking from her fright, Abby needed to sit down and get back some of her composure. The only suitable chair was next to the office door the shop keepers were in. Patiently, she waited for a chance to talk to the men and waited and waited. She began to think of Mr. Pinkerton and her anger started to rise but she was stuck, she could not leave and they did not seem to want to even talk to her. So she did what she could, she listened to the men's argument.

"The only thing we can hope for is to take on a partner, someone who will resume the office in London and buy into the business here in the colonies," the first man said.

"Do you see any one banging down our door to buy into this business?" The second man said sarcastically. "We are in big trouble and the bank is not going to wait any longer. Tomorrow they will foreclose on our ships and we will be ruined."

"We have to wait for Niles Shaw. He said he would help us with a solution and he was supposed to return today."

The two men continued their worthless discussion. Why they continued in this manor without a solution in sight was beyond her. They argued about the debt they had to pay. The time they needed to pay it in and even who was going to deliver it to the bank but when they started to talking figures Abigail's hopes began to rise.

These men knew Niles, they needed a partner, they needed funding and they wanted someone to go to London. This was her chance to sail again, the opportunity to have a business and it was in her price range. She tried not to listen. Abby looked around the office, at the old dusty faded Victorian couch near the front window with a brick replacing the broken leg. She tried to focus on the tattered fabric of yellow silk and brocade. When that didn't work, she looked at the painting on the wall of a rough sea and a three mast ship sinking beneath a large overpowering wave. That could be a sign, she thought to herself. This could be a disaster. Take your time, think this through but she could not keep her mind focused on anything but what the two men were arguing about.

She stood and walked to a small table with out-dated charts laid out on it. They had been very carefully laid out over the dust still on the table. Everything in this office was peculiar, from the outdated charts to the dusty faded furniture to the painting of a sinking ship on the wall.

Finally she decided to make her presence known. It was most rude of these two to completely ignore her especially seeing her enter the building. Were all men like Mr. Pinkerton when it came to business? I am not stupid, Abigail thought. I am educated, very good with figures and can sail a vessel as good as any man. Then she stood up, looked directly into the gilded mirror and whispered to herself, "Stop being a coward Abigail Fox. You march yourself right in that office and take the bull by the horns." Then she nodded to herself, turned, straightened herself up and walked to the open door.

"Excuse me, sirs. I have been waiting for over thirty minutes. Do you have so much business that you can afford to ignore mine? If you are that busy than, I will bid you good day and go somewhere that will take me seriously. Niles Shaw has given me more than one establishment to visit today and I will not waste any more of my time here listening to you worthless arguments."

Then she turned and walked out into the waiting area. As she reached the door she received the reaction she was hoping for. "My apologies, madam, my partner and I have acted very rude. Please accept my humble apology and do come back in so we can discuss your business." As Abigail looked out the door she noticed and smelled her four assailants still hovering around the lamp post. She slowly shut the door and turned around.

"Very well, Gentlemen, I will give you five minutes."

The tall thin man bowed graciously to Abby and motioned her to the office. Once inside he offered her a very comfortable red velvet chair with doilies on the arms to hide the worn fabric. The tall thin man took his place behind the black mahogany desk while the bald man sat next to her in the matching red wobbly velvet chair that made a thumping sound each time he moved.

The office, like the outer room was run down. The plaster walls were painted a dingy yellow and the dark red curtains that hung in the windows needed a good washing. The portrait that hung on the wall behind the thin man was that of a sea captain baring a very strong resemblance to the man in front of her. The thin man took a moment to clear his desk of unneeded papers and then he began to speak.

"Let me start by introducing myself and my partner. My name is George, George Webber from a prominent house in England and this is Jon, Jon Washburn also originally from England and this is our business The W&W Shipping Company. We ship to ports all over the world but mainly Europe these days, much more profitable. Our company has three sea faring vessels which are, at the present out to sea except one which is currently anchored in the harbor."

Abigail listened to George as he talked about the business and what they were currently shipping for cargo. As he talked she had time to actually look at the man. He was very homely, she thought, with a very high receding forehead, slicked back black thin hair and a wide red colored nose. His lips were thin exposing a mouth full of crooked teeth. A long neck with a large Adam's apple made him look even more undesirable. She wanted to ask him if he was married. Waking up to that face each morning was enough to frighten any person out of slumber.

Jon was just the opposite. He had a round face with very pink blotchy skin. His suit was well tailored to fit such a heavy man and he smelled of too much cologne. A white handkerchief, he held in his left hand which he would use to wipe the sweat from the top of his bald head. These two men resembled salt and pepper shakers. They went well together but did not match.

Then it was Abigail's turn to speak, "Pleased to meet you Mr. Webber and you too Mr. Washburn. The reason I have come here today is because I was interested in investing in a business of my own. But after hearing your long conversation, I have not ruled out a partnership if the right deal could be made. My husband just died, you see, and I have been left a rather large inheritance which must be invested in a business by the end of the month or it will be donated to the church. My husband had a sick sense of humor. He believed a woman was not capable of running a business and felt his money would be put to better use in the church. I have every intention of making him roll over in his grave." Then she smiled at the two men waiting to see what kind of a reaction she would receive from her well made up lie. Mr. Washburn broke out into laughter and Mr. Webber just looked amused.

"The way I look at it sirs, you will be doing business with my husband's funds but I hold the purse strings."

"Please, madam, call me George. We must not be on such formal terms if we are to become partners. May I call you Abigail?" Abby just nodded affirmatively. He then brought out papers to talk real business. The meeting lasted the rest of the day ending with an inspection of the vessel they anchored in the harbor. To the amazement of the partners,

Abby inspected the ship from top to bottom, making note of all needed repairs to become sea worthy for the ocean trip to London.

She gave her list to the captain with orders to see to all the repairs by the end of the week or lose his job. When back on land, Abby said, "My grandfather taught me well when it comes to ships. If we are to finalize this deal, sirs, I want just my name to that vessel. I also want my choice of captains. The one you have now has not kept the ship in good condition. I will not tolerate a ship in such poor regards."

Both men looked surprised at her but did not refuse her. Abby knew how much they needed her funding. They were not about to refuse her a thing. If the partnership was to dissolve, Abby wanted to walk away with something. She had no intention in staying with these two men for long, but for now she needed their contacts in London. She also needed that particular vessel, a full cargo by the end of the week and that would be easier said than done.

The three walked over to the Bank of Boston where they met a man similar to Mr. Pinkerton. He had the same kind of suit on, tailored to fit perfectly with the same shoes and condescending attitude. It did not take Abigail long to get his undivided attention however. By the time the three walked out of the bank, Abigail was a full partner of a shipping company.

Her inheritance was almost depleted but she would be fine after she sold the cargo in London and she still had her nautical box. That she would not touch until she absolutely needed to. For now she would just let the partners think they had a very wealthy partner with unlimited funds and she would keep her secret that she was actually maxed out and would be leaving the partnership as soon as possible.

Elizabeth and Niles were very thrilled with her dealings the first day and extended their invitation for her to stay at their town house until her ship would sail. Abby also took up Elizabeth's offer to go shopping for proper London attire. It turned out that Elizabeth was very familiar with all the shops in Boston and bought more for herself than helped Abigail.

At the end of the shopping day, however Elizabeth insisted that they visit just one more shop. She found a lovely powder blue satin gown for Abigail with pearl buttons and French lace adorning the sleeves and scooped neck line. Abby loved the gown but felt it a little too extravagant for her taste but Elizabeth insisted she look her best when she reached London. With the dress, went a lovely, but not practical set of little blue satin slippers, definitely made for inside wear and very little walking but very fashionable. Abigail never had a pair of shoes that would not last more than a year but she must look and act the part of a wealthy business woman so she bought the satin slippers.

The next day she found a cargo to take to London quite by accident. A ship in the harbor which was scheduled with cargo destined for London had extensive damage due to a storm at sea. So the ship was not seaworthy to sail to London without repairs first. Abigail made arrangements to deliver the cargo in its place.

The last thing on her list was to notify her children of her success and let them know she would be gone for a few months and not to worry. Niles had offered to get the note to her children but she found a couple heading that way and they offered to take it for her instead. For some strange reason Abby did not trust Niles. She did not want him anywhere near her children or even to know where they were. Giving her note to the complete strangers seemed like the right thing to do for some strange reason. All was going so well. Tomorrow she would find a new captain and sign on her crew and by the first of the week she would be off to sea.

She stood on the deck of her new ship inspecting the repairs she had ordered when a white haired man boarded her vessel. At first he did not see her on the upper deck and just stood on the main deck and looked around. It only took a second look from Abby before she recognized one of her old friends from her summers with her grandfather. She was speechless. Abby could not believe he was still alive and in such good health. Martin VanHause was a deck hand when her grandfather was a captain. He was always a good humored man with blonde curly hair, now very white and very pink skin. Abby was allowed to work with him on occasion. He was the one that taught her all the nautical knots and here he was as if he had never left the ship.

Abigail came down the steps of the helm to greet her old friend. He had not seen her since she was sixteen, the year she married Roy and the year her grandfather died. She never expected him to recognize her but to her surprise he did. At first he said nothing but just stared into her eyes. Then a big smile came across his face and he walked over to greet her. As if she was still a child, he picked her up and swung her around just as he had done when she came to stay with her grandfather. Martin had a very thick Swiss accent which sounded like music in Abby ears.

"Marty is that you?" Abby squealed as she was being swung in a circle.

"Ya, ya, girl it is I," Martin replied.

"Are you here for the captain's position?" Abby asked hopefully.

"Ya, girl. Do ya know the owner? And what in the devil are ya doing on this ship without an escort?" Scolding her as if she was seven again.

"I'll have you know, Mr. VanHause that you are talking to the owner of this vessel and I am too old to have an escort," Abby said teasingly.

"You? Ah, your grandfather would be so proud."

"So what do you want to talk to the owner about?" Abby asked hoping it was to hire on as the captain.

"I need a job girl," Martin answered with a big smile.

"I have need of a deck swab," Abby said teasingly.

"The only deck swab around here is the little girl who grew up to be an owner of her own ship," he answered. He sounded just like her grandfather when he said that. It was as if someone had just turned the clock back twenty years.

"Well the only other position available is the captain. Are you up for the job?"Abby asked hopeful.

"I should turn you over ma knee for even asking that question, girl. You may be older but you can still be spanked," Martin said with a teasing smile on his face.

"Does that mean you will take the job?" Abby asked, praying for a "ya" from him.

"Ya, with two conditions; one that I don't have to share my captain's quarters with you and two, that you play chess with me every night that you are on board."

Abby looked up with tears in her eyes and jumped into his arms. "I have missed you so much, Marty."

"You, my dear are the only one that has ever called me Marty and you can only call me that when we are alone, Martin or captain in front of the crew."

"Yes sir, Captain Martin, sir." Abby answered with her hand at her forehead in a salute.

"Now show me my quarters and what you want me to do."

CHAPTER 3
Turn Of Events

Abigail didn't sleep at all last night. Her things had already been moved on board her ship which she renamed The Lady Fox. Captain Martin insisted she stay on land while the ship was being loaded. He was sure she would not get a wink in with all the noise. Abigail was much too excited to sleep. She spent most of the night pacing the floor in her room. In the morning she left for the docks before she could break her fast.

Martin had a man waiting for her in a hack in front of the Shaw's house. She thought she was too old for an escort but Martin would not let her come alone regardless of how she felt. By the time Abby boarded, Captain Martin had already had a meeting with her partners and had checked the cargo twice. He was not too impressed with The W &W Shipping Company and he was going to have a very serious talk with Abigail as soon as they were out to sea. He also was suspicious of her friends, the Shaws.

Abby received last minute instructions from George and Jon. They insisted she unload cargo before she visited the London Office and they also reminded her she would be responsible for business in London. They made her promise she would tell the harbor master that she was the one in charge in London and responsible for all business arrangements. Abby thought it was strange that the harbor master would be involved for a quick cargo delivery but she was determined to do whatever necessary to make this business work. London was another country and they may have different rules that she wasn't familiar with but was not about to question her partners yet. She would talk to Martin about it as soon as they were out to sea.

The Lady Fox raised anchor with the tide and off to sea as scheduled. Abby felt just like a child again. She could not stay in one place long enough to warm the floor board under her feet. Captain Martin couldn't help but smile to see Abigail act with such excitement. Finally he couldn't stand her restlessness any longer and gave her work to do. She became a deck hand just like in her earlier days and she didn't complain a bit. A good day's work meant a good night's sleep.

The Captain had brought a few surprises into her cabin that she was not aware of, one being her grandfather's old charts and his sea jacket. A warm quilt for her bunk and a small desk he nailed to the floor with a journal to write in. And finally a heavy rain coat for those rough wet days at sea.

After dinner the first night, Abigail and Martin enjoyed their first game of chess in twenty four years. He was surprised when she beat him without his help. She was surprised when she entered her cabin that night to find the little gifts Martin had left her.

Abigail slept like a baby with a warm fuzzy feeling that everything would work out alright. Martin had always treated Abby as his daughter and Abby had always looked at Martin as her second father. Now that her father and grandfather were dead, Abby felt even closer to this wonderful old man.

She woke to the sound of strong winds off the port side. On entering from the lower deck she found most of the sails at full mast and the ship sailing at full speed. "Your late, girl. I could have you flogged for that," the Captain teased. "Just for that it will be two chess games tonight and this time I won't let ya win."

"Thank you for my surprises," Abigail said as she went to find some food. On days like this, when the wind was strong and moving in the right direction, the captain like to stay at the helm. When Abigail finished her morning chores, she joined him but before she could say what was on her mind, Martin broached the subject first.

"I need to talk to you about your partners and before you tell me it is none of my business, I am making it my business. They are not to be trusted. There is something wrong here, I can smell a rat or two. I have not lived sixty years with my head in the sand. You have always been the child I never had, I am not about to lose you after just finding you again. And, I know you like the Shaws but Niles has the same air about him as your partners, I don't trust him or her either."

"I was hoping you felt the same as I do," Abby answered with a small guilty grin. "Every part of my body warned me about the Shaws and the partners but I wanted this ship so bad. That is why I insisted my name be the only one attached to this vessel. Martin, if something happens to me when we get to London. I want you to promise me you will take her out to sea. I won't be able to get out of trouble if my ship, my only source of income, is impounded."

"Do you think something is going to happen to you?" Martin asked ready to protect her.

"I would be a fool if I didn't," she answered with her head bent down.

"Then why are we going to London? We can sail to another port and still sell the cargo."

"I think my partners have made many enemies and I am not sure going to another port will be any safer than London. The cargo has nothing to do with the partners or the Shaws. It came from a ship damaged in the last storm near Boston. The captain of the Lady Mary was looking for a ship to take his cargo. The partners acted surprised and upset that I had filled my ship. They really wanted me to go empty so I could get there faster," Abby said.

"Then we should be very careful," Martin warned.

"The partners wanted me to get rid of the cargo fast for some reason. I am thinking that the port authorities will be on the lookout for the W & W Shipping Company. So I plan to avoid telling anyone I am affiliated with them unless I absolutely have to. That is the reason I changed the name of this vessel. Hopefully it will buy us some time." Then Abby looked up at her captain and said, "Martin I am sorry I got you into this mess. I hope you won't hate me."

"Little girl, I could never hate you, throttle you, yes but never hate you, and if you were seven years old I'd have you across my knee right now."

"Marty, I just had to have this ship, look." And then Abby moved some rigging hanging off the nearest mast to reveal her grandfather's mark. "See, it is grandfather's ship, one he designed and help build."

"What is the mark just below his?" Martin asked with a twinkle in his eye.

"Alright, I admit it. It is mine. The very first ship I worked on with him," Abby said looking a little guilty.

"My husband was next to no good. He rarely ever brought home funds from all those extensive business trips he would take. I really don't know what he thought we lived on; certainly not what he gave me. It was my grandfather's box that put food on my table and clothes on my children's backs but more than that, I could buy books for them to learn. We did not have a real school in Riverton and I could not afford private school. My only option was the books grandfather left me and the ones I bought. No one knew of that box, except me. It took care of us just like this ship will take care of me now."

"We have a few weeks before we reach London. We will have plenty of time to plan our strategy but for now take the helm and make me proud," Martin ordered. Abby smiled and jumped to the task.

So for the next two weeks, Martin and Abby worked out their plan. Abby made Martin promise to take care of the ship regardless what happened to her and to follow her plan. The captain of the Lady Mary had also given Abby more ports to go to after London. Martin would finish the voyage, making the appropriate stops and then return home or come back to London if that was where she was going to be. If Abby was arrested, which was a possibility than Martin would return in a few months with the funds she needed to free her. What was important was to keep the ship and not let the authorities impound it.

For now it was just smooth sailing and now and then getting a sailor to pose for her sketch book. Chess in the evening with Martin and while she was on the sea she was going to do nothing but enjoy it.

The Lady Fox entered the London harbor on the exact day scheduled. Her cargo was the property of a very wealthy lord who had made arrangement to have dock space for unloading. Before they could tie the ship off, the lord was on board inspecting his precious cargo. Wagons were lined up at the dock waiting for his orders and he wasn't about to wait another day for his property. After only being in port for three hours, the Lady Fox was empty with the cargo paid for and ready to become seaworthy again. Abigail was thrilled with the thought that they might be able to leave as fast as they came but at the last minute they received an unexpected visit from the harbor master demanding Abigail's presence at the court house.

He would not leave without Abigail, although he did give her time to change into suitable attire. Thirty minutes later and many last minute instructions for Martin, Abigail left with the harbor master and three armed guards and two men from her ship as escorts. The Lady Fox was ordered to anchor out at the far end of the harbor and wait for the next instructions by the harbor master but Martin did not anchor, he just went out to sea.

At the court house, Abigail stood waiting for her name to be called from a long list the bailiff held. She had worn the ornate powder blue gown with the pearl buttons and the French lace and the fashionable blue satin shoes which were only good to stand in and nothing else and her grandmother's diamond earrings.

The room was crowded with every kind of person imaginable, from lowly peasants to well dressed noblemen. The judge sat in a very high desk looking over the entire room. His gavel slammed down hard on the desk signaling the bailiff to call the next name. One by one, Abigail watched as each accused walked into the roped off area then onto the wooden podium in the very center of the room.

A tall railing encased the podium which reminded Abigail of a small cage an animal was put in just before slaughter. The more names that were called the more Abigail got sick. Her knees were knocking and she was having a very hard time to breathe especially with all the cigar smoke. Abigail's men never left her side even when her name was finally called. She walked into the roped area and the up into the podium. The railing was so high that the judge could not see but the top of her head sticking out.

"You in the cage," the judge ordered. "Stand up so I can see you." When the judge realized she was at full height he ordered a stool for her to stand on.

"Abigail Fox, you are the representative of The W & W Shipping Company. You have been accused of fraud, extortion, failure to pay outstanding debts, and assault with a deadly weapon. What say you, guilty or not guilty?"

Abigail's mouth dropped open when the charges were read. "Sir, this is the first time I have heard of these charges. I was not aware my company has done any of these things."

"Guilty or not guilty, madam?" The judged asked even more forcefully.

Abigail did not know what to say. Surely her partners were guilty and they knew what they were sending her into before she left for London, the snakes. So she answered for herself, "Speaking for myself and only myself; Not Guilty your honor. I have only been involved with this company for one month, I cannot speak for them. I have very little knowledge of their affairs here in London and have come to see what I can do."

"Are you a full partner in this company?" The judge asked.

Abby knew that if she said yes she would be responsible for their crimes but there was no way around it, she was a partner. "Yes, your honor."

"Are you here to pay the debt?"

"I am here to make an arrangement but cannot pay everything at this time," Abby answered.

"Do you have any idea what your company owes the good business men of London?"

"No, sir, I have no knowledge of this."

The judge motioned the bailiff to give the bills to Abigail to look over.

When Abby first looked at the bills she just gasped. This could not be possible, no one could owe this much. She quickly added the figures in her head with penalties and tax added on and just stood there. Finally she said. "I had no knowledge of this when I became a partner. This information was not divulged to me. This is more than the whole company is worth and five times more than I can pay. Surely I cannot be kept accountable for debts that were concurred before I was part of the company, your honor. But I will do everything in my power to try and pay off this debt over time. I just need time, your honor."

A little round man stepped out from the crowd and spoke loudly, "We merchants have waited over ten years, your honor, and we want justice now."

Abigail turned to the man and said, "I am very sorry this happened to you sir but I cannot be the scapegoat. I have not wronged anyone. My only crime is to have stupidly invested in the W & W Shipping Company. This company had cheated me as well."

The room broke out in a rage demanding that Abigail pay for the company's crimes. The judge slammed the hammer down demanding silence. When the crowd quieted down he spoke. "It is the law, madam that the responsible parties are the names on the business. Your name is on the document making you a responsible partner. It is too bad that you had to deal with these criminals. The court recognizes that you had no action in these events and because of that I will be as lenient as I can. However justice must be served and you are to pay the price."

Again the hammer went down to silence the crowd. Abby could feel tears swelling in her eyes. "I sentence you, Abigail Fox to the debtor's prison where you will stay in solitary confinement until your debt is paid or your note bought which will enable you to work off your crime."

At that moment two guards entered the podium and grabbed Abigail. One put her hands in irons and the other shackled her ankles. The crowd was loud with insults and cheers as they led her away. The two guards walked on either side of her guiding her down a long haul leading to the back of the court house.

Two doors, side by side were pushed open allowing the three to walk out into the alley together. The jail wagon, already full of standing people, was opened to allow Abigail to be pushed in by her two guards. One of the guards found it necessary to reach up under her skirt and squeeze her large bottom. "Best get use ta it my lady. Ya will get much more than a pinch in that prison," said the guard than he shut the door to the wagon and laughed.

The sound of a whip cracked and the wagon took off. A turn to the right and then to the left and the wagon was going down the busiest street in the center of London. The man to her left hollered, "duck," as a rotten tomato sailed into the wagon striking a woman next to Abby.

Than another one and the wagon was the target of every rotten piece of food that could be thrown.

Not one person made it through the line of fire without getting hit. Abigail looked down at her powder blue dress to see stains of tomato, squash and watermelon. The French lace had been ripped when the guard helped her into the wagon and the blue fashionable slippers were already tearing. She glanced at the crowd just in time to see her two escorts pass by. They nodded at her in acknowledgment and then turned and disappeared into the crowd.

By the time the wagon reached the prison, Abigail was soaked in smelly spoiled food. Fearful they might take her earrings; Abby carefully slipped them off and hid them in the waistband of her dress. The wagon door opened to a large shirtless guard with a whip in his hand. "Only the women get off here," he shouted. Abigail was the first to get off with a jerk and a fall into the mud. The large guard picked her up and pushed her toward the door of the prison.

There was a small room just as she entered. Another guard was waiting on the other side of the room. "Line up here," he hollered. Five female prisoners lined up in front of the guard waiting for their instructions. He walked slowly in front of each one inspecting each woman. "You are going to make the guards real happy," he said to the young woman next to Abigail. "It's too bad you are so old, you would have been more fun than her," he said pointing to the woman on Abby's left.

"Who is Abigail Fox?" A voice said from behind her. Abby turned around to face a tall thin man. "I am," she said waiting for the worst.

"The judge liked you lady. He gave strict orders you are not to be touched and to keep you by yourself. You will come with me." Then he turned and started to walk down a long dark corridor. Abby limped along, the shackles irons digging into her ankles and the chains making chinking sounds as they dragged on the stone floor.

They came to a stairway leading down to the lower levels of the prison. The lower they went the darker and smellier it got. The stairs and walls were all made of cut grey stone with a torch lighting the way every twenty feet or so. Cries of women came out through the cell doors as they passed. Pungent smells of human excretions and mildew permeated the hall.

Finally they reached the bottom floor of the prison. At the very end of the hall was a single door. The guard walked Abigail to it and using a key to open it. "Your new home pigeon," he reached down and took her cuffs off but left her shackles. "We don't want ya to think ya can run now do we." He pushed Abigail into her sell on to moldy hay on the floor. She rolled over to see the door close behind her. "It is too bad the judge won't let ya be touched. Ya have good breasts ripe for the squeezing," the guard said hissing a laugh as he left.

Abby looked around. Her cell was completely dark with no windows. She felt around to see how big the room actually was. She found a chamber pot, still half full and a ripped blanket. The wailing of a woman came to her attention. It seemed to come from the cell closest to the stairs.

Abigail sat quietly for hours listening to the cries and moans of very unhappy women. At six p.m. the door opened. "Bath time Pigeon," and a bucket of cold water went flying into her cell, drenching Abigail from head to foot. Then a tin cup of water and a plate of broth were left on her floor with a spoon and a stale roll.

Each day was the same. A guard would make the rounds in the morning. Sometimes he would empty the chamber pots but most of the time he won't. At six p.m. sharp the only meal of the day was served, always the same broth and one roll and a tin cup of water.

As bleak as her surroundings were Abigail never gave up hope. She would not let herself believe that this was what her life was to be. Martin would come for her some day. Although the debt was so great she could not fathom just how he would be able to pay it. But he was her only hope and she would not give in to despair. Thirty days passed and still no word.

Abigail passed the time by telling stories to the women in other cells each night just to have something to do but she also listened. The women in these cells were scheduled to hang but there was rarely a woman hanging so their fate was to sit and rot and be tortured by the guards.

In her six by six foot cell, Abby found out more information about her partners than she wished to and also any other London gossip. She was amazed about how much information she could obtain from just sitting and listening to the guards talking as well as her fellow prison mates.

On her sixtieth day the routine changed. The guard did not come down for his morning inspection. Something was up. The women stood impatiently at their doors trying to see someone coming.

A light started to drift down the stairs. The woman in the end cell began to scream in fear. The guards had used her daily until she went crazy so now she was alone in the dark with the other five women. The light came into view. Two men came walking down the hall carrying a lantern. Closer and closer they came to Abby's door. She heard the key turn in the lock and the door opened. A tall tin man stood in the door way holding the lantern high to light her cell. Abby had been in the dark for sixty days and the light hurt her eyes. She could not see anything.

Then the man spoke, "Damn, I was hoping she was younger. I certainly can't use her as a whore but it is too late the deal is done. I cannot change my mind now." Then he addressed Abigail. "My name is James. I am your new owner. You will not be a whore but I can still get some good use out of you. Come with me now and don't dally."

Abigail grabbed her blue satin shoes and slipped them on. They were barely stitched together and followed the man up the stairs and out of the prison. It was a cool day and raining hard. Abigail was so happy to see the light after sixty days she didn't mind the rain.

James walked to the hack waiting and started to climb in. Abigail started to lift her skirt to get in when James said. "What do you think you are doing? Luggage rides up there," and he pointed to the top of the carriage. She hesitated for a moment trying to figure a way up there. The driver did not offer any assistance and the footman was still holding the door for James. She started to climb when a large hand gave her backside a big push. Abby landed on top of a trunk and just caught herself from falling off the other side but lost the first of her worthless blue satin shoes.

In a very quiet voice the footman said. "Grab hold, lass. It is a long way and I donna want you to fall off." Abigail looked back at him in surprise. "You're Scottish?" she asked.

"Aye, Why?" he answered. "My grandfather was from Scotland. He was a McDough." Then she thanked him for helping her up on the carriage. He nodded at her but said no more. She understood talking was not allowed and she didn't want him to get into trouble.

The rain was warm and wet, a great combination to get the stench of the prison off her. It was not the same as a bath but it sure felt good. If she had had a bar of soap she would have used it right over her dress. She put her head back and smiled up at the rain. When she opened her eyes the kindly footman was enjoying watching her with a grin on his face. She noticed him watching her and smiled back at him. It felt so good to smile and be wet and in the light. Abigail raised her arms over her head enjoying the moment. A big hand reached out and grabbed her ankle. "Hold on lass, ya are having too much fun," the foot man said shaking his head and still grinning at her behavior.

"This feels so good. It's as if I died and went to heaven," she said in a whisper not to call attention from the driver or James. The kindly old foot man just smiled back at her. What she didn't notice was the driver had looked back over his shoulder and was also smiling at her as he drove the horses on.

It took the coach most of the day to get to its destination, a lovely large white manor with black shutters. Abby watched in amazement as the manor came into view. They entered the property through two large stone abutments connected to each other with an elaborate iron archway encasing the name of the estate, Restitution. Abby remembered thinking this to be an odd name for such a beautiful property.

A long drive directed the carriage toward the house, edged with large oak trees. The carriage pulled up in front of the manor under a wooden canopy resting on four stone abutments resembling the two at the entry gate. Abigail sat on the trunk waiting for instructions. The old footman jumped down and opened the door for James to exit the hack. Abigail started to make a move but the footman looked up quickly and shook his head. So Abby just stayed and waited, at least the hack was under cover from the rain but she was still very wet.

Without acknowledging Abigail, James walked into the manor and four servant men came out. Abigail was helped down by the footman and then the trunks were taken down and brought into the manor. The strangest thing happened next, the hack and the two men drove off disappearing to the back of the house leaving Abigail unguarded, standing alone. Her hands and feet weren't in irons. She was free to go.

Turning around she began to walk back down the road the hack came in on. No one was around. Her first impulse was to just run as fast as her feet would carry her, but she was not sure that this was what James wanted which could result in her death. If she walked leisurely and they stopped her she could explain she was just looking around and wasn't aware of the boundaries. If she made it to the front gate, she would run for dear life and freedom.

Slowly she strolled down the lane looking around as if she had all the time in the day. It felt good to walk and stretch her legs and the air was clean and crisp, not anything like the smell of the prison.

From the corner of her eye she saw some movement coming from the wooded area just outside the gate. A chinking sound caught her attention next, acknowledging her suspicions. Armed men were hiding in the woods waiting to hunt an unarmed helpless middle aged, larger than she should be, woman. What kind of place was this? Do they use prisoners as game to hunt? Abby's instinct took over, she reached the gate and turned and slowly started to walk back to the manor without looking at the woods.

When she reached the overhang at the house she sat down out of the rain and waited for someone to tell her what to do. As she suspected, James rode up from behind her on a very large muscular black stallion. She sat on the edge of the abutment with her back facing James not turning to acknowledge his presence.

He rode up to her and stopped his horse directly in front. Glancing up she looked directly into his eyes. He was dressed in a riding jacket and britches with high black boots. His dark brown hair was slicked back from the rain. A whip hung from off the back of his saddle and a riding crop was held in his right hand. Abigail was not about to give him any satisfaction, so she looked up at him and said, "Would you please tell me where you would like me to go so that I can start to work off my debt or am I to just stay out here and be ignored."

James looked furious. He dismounted. A man came up from behind him handed him a walking stick and took the reins of his horse. Abigail tried to look oblivious to what just happened. She pretended her walk was innocently done just to kill a little time while she waited. "You have a beautiful home," she said with a tiny grin. "I took a walk down to the gate and back. Are those oak trees that line the drive?"James just grunted and said, "follow me." He started to walk toward the barn.

Abby just followed, watching from the corner of her eye, the men filing in from their hiding places in the woods. What is this place, she thought to herself. They reached the barn and James took her to a small red wooden crate box. It was about six feet wide by six feet long by four feet high almost the same as her prison cell but much shorter. "Welcome to your new quarters. It is not the same as the dungeon you were in but it will do, I am sure."

Then he opened the door and motioned for her to enter. Abby hesitated for a moment. James took his cue and raised his walking stick slapping it across Abby's back. She fell to the barn floor on her hands and knees. Then James kicked her backside projecting her forward into the doorway of the crate. "Crawl, you bitch," James ordered. "This crate is your new home. It is for the animal you really are."

Abby refused to cry out or acknowledge James' insults but crawled slowly into the crate. The door slammed shut behind her and then she heard the padlock securing her prison. She sat up to see her new surroundings. A small cot was at her right with a chamber pot just under it. The floor was covered with a thick amount of fresh hay. The slats were spaced about an inch apart giving light to the inside of the box. She backed herself to the far wall and waited for James to finish his orientation.

"I will tell you once woman, you will follow my rules or pay my price. I own you and you will do whatever I tell you. Do I make myself clear?" Then he added, "It is too bad you are not younger, you would have made a good whore. But maybe there is still a chance." Then he laughed as if he had made the funniest remark ever. He however was the only one that found his remark humorous.

Abby was left alone still in her wet dress shivering. Her fashionable shoe was ruined. The stitches that were left had let go in the rain leaving her barefooted and the once lovely powder blue gown was stained beyond recognition. Her pearl buttons were gone and the French lace in shreds.

She sat with her knees curled up under her chin and she finally wept after sixty days of imprisonment. The prison had not been able to break her but this crate was worse than the dungeon and the sting across her back let her know what kind of a life she would have here. Terrified that this was the beginning of the end, Abigail wept like a small child.

Then a familiar voice came through the slats. “Come now lass, it’s not that bad is it? I brought ya some food and a bit of water.” Abby looked up through tears and saw the kindly old footman, looking at her through the spaces in the slats.

“Donna be shy now take the food. Ya will need your strength. Tomorrow is another day. Now take that wet dress off and put this on. It will keep ya warm.”

The footman pushed a plate of food through the slats and then squeezed a soft dry shift in next. Abby took the food still sniffing and the shift and slid back onto the wall of the crate. “Thank you,” she said softly.

“Ya very welcome lass. Sweet dreams. I will not be far.”

He stood and turned to walk away when he heard, “Wait, I don’t even know your name,”Abby said still sniffing through tears.

“It is William, lass. Pleased ta meet ya Abigail Fox.” Then he tipped his hat and gave her a sweet grin.

“Same here William, and thank you again.”

Abby slipped her wet dress off and put the dry shift on. It was clean and soft and smelled of fresh heather. The plate of food was the best she’d had in a very long time. She ate every bite then looked to see if anyone was watching then licked the plate clean. Exhausted, Abby curled up on the cot and went to sleep.

CHAPTER 4
Living At the Manor

Abigail woke to the sounds of the barn door sliding open. The horses in their stalls whinnied and stomped in the anticipation of their morning meal. She could hear men's voices and hay sliding down a shoot from an upper level of the bar to be fed out. Abby knew how the horses felt, her stomach was growling with hunger as well. Hopefully, William would remember to bring her something. Watching through the slats, she could see the men walking down the long walk between the horse stalls. They were speaking of an important Scottish Laird who would be coming to visit in the near future and which stalls they would be using for him.

Then the door of the barn opened again and the chatter from the barn men went silent. It was James and his walking stick. The men kept working and did not look up to acknowledge him. There was a general fear which swept the barn the moment James entered.

Each man moved along concentrating on the job at hand. Abigail moved to the back of the crate hoping he was not here for her. She watched as James moved down the walk, inspecting his horses as he went. He knew them all by name and stopped and greeted each one. They were his pride and joy and he treated them much better than the men that took care of them.

"The Laird is due to arrive on Saturday or Sunday. I want the barn ready for him and his men. There should be about twelve or thirteen of them. I want their horses well cared for. Do not disappoint me men." Then he turned toward the red crate. "I have unfinished work to do," he sneered.

Abby could see him coming closer through the spaces in the slats. She kept moving back but the wall of her small crate would not let her go any farther.

He bent down and looked in at her. "I see you have made it through the first night. It is now time to officially orient you to the way of life here."

The key went into the lock and a click sounded. The door opened and James looked into the crate. "Well, what are you waiting for? Come out and meet your fate."

Abigail came out cautiously waiting for another slap across the back. She stood up for the first time since he had put her in there. She was a little stiff and shaky from not eating this morning.

"Time for a bath," James ordered, "Come with me, I need some morning entertainment." Abby followed him as he walked outside to a water filled trough just in the back of the barn. He stood in front of it with his arms folded holding his walking stick in one hand and a bar of soap in the other. It was a cool day with a breeze blowing across the paddock.

The sun was out but there were too many clouds to get any heat from it. "Well, what are you waiting for? Take that shift off and get in your tub."

Abby walked to the side of the trough and waited. "Do you need some help?" James asked almost laughing at her expression.

"No, just a little privacy, please," Abby answered.

James breathed down hard. "I have given you an order. I thought we got this cleared up last night. But I was obviously wrong. That will cost you a good slap on your naked back."

Abby stood twisting her hands together in front of her. Slowly she started to unbutton the shift. James was enjoying her discomfort. She lifted the shift over her head and dropped it along side of the trough. Naked, she held on the side of the trough to balance herself. She lifted her leg to climb in. At that moment, James slapped her back with his stick knocking her into the icy water head first. She came up with a gasp. James was there to hold her down.

"Before you may rise my dear I want to watch you bathe. I will tell you when you can come out."

Abigail sat in the freezing water, her teeth already chattering from the cold. James handed her the soap, "Now let's start by washing your breasts." James watched in amusement as Abigail obeyed his every command. When he tired of his game he ordered her to get out. Cautiously she climbed out hoping not to get hit again.

By now she was shivering so she could barely stand. James bent down and handed her the shift. Abigail quickly put the shift back on. "Follow me." he ordered and started back into the barn. Abby did as she was ordered. She was too cold to feel humiliated but she would be as soon as she stopped shivering.

In all her thirty nine years she had never hated anyone as much as she hated this man this minute. It showed on her face. "Yes, you are going to hate me," James stated. "I truly look forward to our next encounters. I am your owner and you are my slave. I have the right to do whatever I want to you and no one will lift a finger to help you." He then walked toward the manor.

Leading her around to the back of the manor to the kitchen, where he entered with Abigail following. Like the barn men, the kitchen servants never lifted their heads to acknowledge them as they entered the room. She felt the same fear as she felt in the barn. Abigail was still dripping wet from her bath and just wanted to run to the large fireplace on the adjacent wall. Her hair was drenched and uncombed and the shift she was wearing was wet from her skin and her feet were bare and as cold as ice.

"Olga," James shouted making a few of the women jump. A very round older woman looked up from her dough and walked over to James. Her head was bent never looking up at him. "I've brought you the help you asked for. I expect no problems when the Laird arrives now." Olga just nodded her head but said nothing.

A woman was washing the floor next to James on her hands and knees. She was trying to move as far away from him as possible without him noticing. He did notice however and like Abigail the woman on the floor received a walking stick across her back. Are all these people prisoners like me, Abigail wondered? James reached up to strike her again when Abigail gently nudged his arm causing him to drop the walking stick. The woman scurried out of the room before he had a chance to hit her again.

Abby moved to the fire, so he would not blame her. A puzzled look came over James' face when he looked around to see how he could have dropped the stick. He had suspected Abigail but she was facing the fire and not anywhere near him to have hit his arm. The other servants just kept their heads down and continued their work. Without a word, James picked up his stick and left the kitchen.

As soon as the coast was clear the servants relaxed and welcomed Abigail properly. "My name is Olga," the round woman said in a very thick German accent. "I am the head cook hear over there is Pete. He is the butler and over there is Mary the one you saved from the stick." Then she added, "Mary is from Scotland."

Abigail smiled and said, "It is so nice to meet you all. I haven't met too many friendly people since I landed in London." The whole kitchen started giggling when they heard Abby's accent. At first Abby was taken aback but then she realized what they found funny when Pete asked, "Where did ya get that accent, lass?"

Abigail had to smile back, "My grandfather was a sailor, my father was English, my mother was born of Scottish parents but she only lived in the colonies. I was born and brought up in the colonies. The accent you hear is from all those people combined." Then she giggled which made everyone in the room giggle too. Abigail had a laugh that would bring joy to anyone. It actually made people want to laugh too.

"What do your friends call you, Abigail?" Olga asked.

"Abby, they call me Abby," Abby answered with a slight blush.

"Abby, I think we are going to all be good friends. Just watch those lessons YA?" Olga replied with a grin. "Now what can ya do?"

By the end of the day Olga knew exactly what Abby could do. She could cook and cook very well. Olga was thrilled, she had plenty of help serving and cleaning but what she really needed was someone who knew her way around the kitchen. Abigail chipped right in making a wonderful vegetable dish. Then she made garlic mashed potatoes which seemed to melt in your mouth. Even James told Olga how good the potatoes were.

The new friends worked until late in the day, way after dark. Abigail was tired but it felt so good to have something to do. All those days in prison alone in the dark were like hell on earth. Abigail worked long and hard never stopping and never complaining. The last dish was washed and wiped when James entered the kitchen. All were silent.

He pointed to Abby, "Time to go back to your quarters, woman." Abby knew too well what that meant. With him he brought a young man who wore a uniform like a guard. "This is Wayne," James said. "He is your personal guard. He will see to it that you do as you are told. Any trouble from you and he will enjoy enforcing a lesson or two. You will sleep in the barn like the animals and wear the chains when not in the house. Run and I will personally kill you."

So he was going to kill her yesterday, Abby's instincts had been right again. Leaving would be harder than she had thought but she was not about to rule it out. For now Abby would work and fit in as best she could, and not give James too many opportunities to inflict lessons.

Wayne proved to be a man of little intelligence who talked too much and slept even more. He knew something about everyone and was more than willing to share what little knowledge he had. By the time he had walked Abby to the barn she learned every bit about the manor and its inhabitants and the Scottish laird that everyone was talking about. Wayne proved to be a cruel person who enjoyed having power and inflicting pain. Abby had to be very careful around him. He was always looking for a reason to hit her.

Each night he would put the irons on her and lead her to the barn where she would spend the night with the rats. It was the third night when she woke to something biting her. She screamed and woke William. He came out of his room and spent the rest of the night next to the side of the crate. Abby was terrified.

Did James intend to feed her to the rats piece by piece until there was nothing left of her? It certainly felt like that. Each time he saw her he would ask if she liked her sleeping arrangements. William was always there if she needed a friend and he would even stay up and watch for the rats so she could sleep in peace. He took a real chance. If James found out he was helping her, he would be severely punished. But still he would not let her be alone if she needed someone.

During the day, she would work in the manor. Little by little she was introduced to the rest of the staff. The downstairs help were very nice but the upstairs maids were a little cold. Then there were the whores. As it turned out James was a very powerful business man. It was he who the partners had robbed. The W & W Shipping Co. owed him more than ten men could pay back. The reason Abby was there was to get the partners to England so James could have his revenge.

The manor was used as a business endeavor. James would wine and dine his business associates. There was nothing he wouldn't do to provide his guests with anything they wished just to clinch a business deal. This included bed partners. It turned out that James would buy the notes of the convicted debtors in prison. Then he would bring them to the manor and force them to work. The young women were forced to be James whores, the men were the butlers, stablemen, grounds keepers and so on. Every servant James had working for him came from the debtor's prison. He employed the guards like Wayne to keep the prisoners at the manor.

Anyone who did not fit would become one of the hunted. James had clientele with unique tastes. Hunting an unarmed person was much more sporting that hunting a deer. The prisoners had no rights. James could do as he wished and there was no ramification for it. He was doing his civic duty to rid the country of riff raff and the king was one of his best supporters.

James insisted that Abigail send a note to her partners asking them to come to England to her aid but when she refused he condemned her to the rat filled crate until she did. Abby was determined not to send anything back to the colonies. She did not want to take the chance that her children would discover her fiasco. For all they knew she was in England enjoying the adventure of her life and she would stay a prisoner for her entire life to keep them from finding out.

She was also leery of her partners. It was not beyond them to get her children involved making them their next innocent victims. She was going to protect her children at all costs. James would never get her to write that note, ever. So at night she fought the rats and in the days she served them.

James was even more vicious than usual these days. The Laird would be here in a few days and James was determined to make his stay perfect. Both James and the Laird had a lot invested in this business venture and both had a lot to gain from it. He would not fail and God help the person who did not do his or her job properly.

Every nook and cranny was cleaned twice and every bed made up and ready for the important guests. Olga was instructed about the meals she was to serve and Abby was to assist her in any way. Even the servants where given new uniforms to wear. Abby even received a pair of shoes, a little too big but at least they were shoes.

CHAPTER 5
The Laird Arrives

Abby worked long days. She did everything she could to stay out of the crate. Wayne would hound her from dinner on until she would finally give in and went back to the barn. He usually was so angry by the time she settled in that he would teach a lesson or two on her back. Wayne was lazy preferring his long hours of sleep. In his eyes, Abby worked too long.

If she interfered with his sleep, she paid the price. But Abby would rather a hit than a bite, so she would deliberately bait Wayne just to catch him off guard making him stay up way past his beloved bedtime. Most of the time he was so tired that he would lock her in and then leave.

Friday was one of the days the laird was scheduled to arrive but he sent word that he was delayed. The staff had worked another long day and still the laird had not arrived. It was well past 10:00 p.m. And Abby still had the hall to mop. She took her time as usual to make Wayne stay up a little longer. She began to whistle as she mopped which made the job easier. The acoustics in the hall where exceptional and as she whistled she began to sway and soon she was scrubbing and dancing at the same time not paying attention to the audience collecting at the doorway of the hall.

She twirled around her mop as if it was the most gallant dancer at a formal ball and she was the princess at his side. She scrubbed and whistled and continued her chore until she finished her floor. Her song incredibly finished at the exact time the floor was finished and as the well mannered princess she was she curtsied to her well trained partner thanking her mop for such a wonderful dance.

At that moment a round of applause erupted at the entrance of the hall surprising Abigail causing an unladylike sound to fall from her lips. Thoroughly embarrassed, she turned to face her unexpected audience. There standing at the doorway were thirteen kilted men watching her dance with the mop. She was mortified and her red face showed it. She did the only thing she could think of, she bowed with the grace of a queen acknowledging the applause. The Scotsmen smiled at her but said nothing. Finally the biggest one said, "Good evening." Abby stood in silence. Then he said in a thick Scottish accent, "I am the Laird Gabriel McKenzie and these are my men. I think we were expected."

"Please to meet you Laird Gabriel McKenzie and his men," Abby said politely.

Gabe smiled when he heard her accent as well as did his men. She certainly caught his attention with her whistling and the way she swung her hips as she danced. He was not about to let her leave without finding out just who she was.

"And ya are?" Gabe asked.

"I am…. just leaving with my dance partner here to find you someone who can welcome you better than I can. Please make yourselves comfortable until I can find someone." And with that she picked up her mop, the bucket and scooted out the side door of the hall.

"Gabe, the lass refused to tell ya her name," Joseph, his first in command teased.

"Aye, I noticed that. Well I will have ta find out another way won't I," Gabe answered with a grin and a twinkle in his eye.

Almost immediately servants entered the hall followed by James. Food and drink were brought in and the laird and his men were given the proper welcome that Abby promised. But there was no sign of the lovely lass that had sweetly welcomed them with her unsuspecting whistling and dancing. Gabe was intrigued with this woman, from her age to her strange accent. He would find out more about her. She was not the usual servant James owned.

Abby watched the windows from outside of the hall. They were all lit up as she was escorted back to the barn. Under her skirts she had a plaid given to her by Mary the woman who was washing the floor on her first day. She was so thankful for Abby's help with James, she insisted Abby take her plaid. "It will keep the rats from biting ya. Rats donna like wool," Mary told her. "Just donna let anyone see it or they will take it away from ya and punish ya and me for having it."

Abby had been so moved with her gift that she reached out and hugged her, nicely surprising Mary. Even though the life at the manor was hard, Abby had managed to build good friends. Olga, Mary and William were proving to be the family she didn't have in England. She laid down in her crate completely covered by Mary's plaid. Abby fell asleep thinking of her children and the handsome laird she had just met.

It was the first night in a long time; Abby had slept through the night. The plaid did the trick; the rats did leave her alone. She woke to the door of the barn, sliding open. Quickly she rolled off the cot and stuffed the plaid under it pushing some hay in front to hide it. She looked through the slats to see the laird and James entering the barn. Abby pushed back in the crate hoping Wayne would not come after her while the laird was still in the building.

James was showing the Laird his prize mares. Gabe had a stallion that James wanted to use for breeding and they were trying to work out the details. It was decided that James would bring the mares to the laird's house in the fall.

The men were deep into their business discussion when Wayne walked in. As usual he was half asleep but today he woke up real fast when he saw James. James also woke up when he saw Wayne and wondered why Abby was still in the crate at this late hour. He excused himself from the laird and took Wayne outside.

Abby could hear James hollering at Wayne from inside the barn. She couldn't help but giggle to herself, a very well deserved reprimand. Abby slipped into her uniform and waited until Wayne came to get her. Moments later, Wayne came back into the barn carrying the irons. Gabe watched as he went to the red crate. Surely there must be a very dangerous criminal inside that crate, Gabe thought to himself. He was curious enough to see just who was inside. Positioning himself, in a stall just out of sight but where he could see very clearly, Gabe watched Wayne open the door and demanded the occupant to exit.

The surprise on Gabe's face when Abby walked out was well hidden from behind the wall of the stall. He wondered what she did to merit such treatment. He watched as Wayne cuffed and shackled her. This also surprised Gabe. He saw no resistance from her and heard no anger either. She just stood patiently while Wayne put her in irons. Then Gabe watched as Wayne took his anger out on her. Three hard slaps with a stick across her back was her punishment for the reprimand James had just given him. He blamed her for taking too long last night which caused him to oversleep. To Gabe's amazement, Abby said, "Wayne you are just going to have to take longer naps during the day so you can keep up with this grueling pace."

Wayne lifted his hand again but Abby said, "Now don't you tire yourself out Wayne. Hitting me again might prolong my getting out tonight." It worked. Wayne lowered his hand and pushed Abby in the direction of the house.

James returned just after the two had left. Gabe couldn't help but ask questions about the crate. "It is not like ya ta use such harsh punishment on a woman James," Gabe stated.

"I know but it is all I can think of to make her write a letter to her partners. Can you believe she is a partner in the W & W Shipping Co.?"

"Her?" Gabe said in complete surprise, knowing very well of the shipping company's reputation. "I canna believe she could be involved with those scoundrels."

"Well, actually she had nothing to do with any of it. She just had bad timing. She is as much a victim as we are. They took her inheritance, convinced her she was a partner and sent her to England where she was convicted of their crimes and sentenced to prison. It was my good friend Judge Sherman who contacted me to see what I could do to help. I was way up in the highlands when I got his message, which is why she stayed in prison as long as she did."

"James ya know she is innocent and ya still treat her this way?" Gabe asked appalled.

"Truth is, I really like her. She is good-natured despite her situation and the rest of the staff never says a word against her. I especially like how she picks on Wayne. For now I must not show her favoritism but if she is no use to me I will have to kill her. I will really regret that. She will run, she has already tried and when she runs she will give me no choice," James continued. "I would like to keep her for myself in London, but she hates me now and I have no answer for her but I am up for any suggestions you can offer."

"Maybe there is another way," Gabe encouraged.

"Maybe, but for now I want your word, other than talking to her, you will not interfere," James asked with a look that said he would take nothing less.

"I will give ya until I leave. If ya haven't found an answer for her by then, than I will not stand by and watch an innocent woman harmed," Gabe said giving him the same look. "Especially that one," and he nodded in Abby's direction.

"Then we have come to an agreement?" James asked.

"Aye, for now," Gabe answered, and then he asked. "What is her name?"

"Abigail Fox."

Gabe smiled inwardly to himself. This hound dog is just about to tree himself an innocent Fox.

The next day James, the Laird and his men went off leaving Abby to work as usual while Wayne, her guard slept under the lilac bush. When they returned back to the manor, the Scots all entered the hall and waited for James and Gabe to come up from the barn when Abby came in, running at full speed carrying a very wet dripping sponge in her right hand. She gave them a sweet smile but said nothing and did not break her stride. Finally stopping at the far window, she opened it and hurled the sponge out as hard as she could, hitting Wayne under the lilac bush and just missing Gabe as he rounded the corner in front of James. Gabe looked up just in time to see Abby shutting the window.

The Scots watched as Abby turned and ran out of the hall just as fast as she'd came in with her skirts flying in all directions. Joseph went to the window to see Abigail's intended target crawl out from the bush soaking wet from the direct hit of the sponge. Gabe stood by the corner watching as well. Wayne was cursing and spitting, still half asleep, trying to figure out how and why he got hit with a wet sponge. Then as innocently as can be, Abby came walking around the other corner holding a large basket of freshly picked vegetables acting as if she'd been in the garden all the time.

As James rounded the corner by Gabe, he saw Abigail with the basket and Wayne guarding her. Gabe had all he could do not to laugh, but up in the window of the hall a small group of Scots were laughing their fool heads off. Abby had deliberately waked Wayne so that James would not catch him sleeping. Gabe could not understand why she had saved her guard who was always so cruel to her.

Abby rounded the corner walking right past James and Gabe without a single acknowledgment and into the kitchen followed by a very wet angry Wayne. Gabe had to see what she was up to so he told James he'd be just a moment and would meet him in the hall. Gabe followed Wayne to the kitchen but stayed back enough to hear the conversation but still out of sight.

"You little bitch," Wayne shouted as he entered the kitchen. "You hit me with that sponge and you will pay dearly for that."

Then Gabe heard Abby shout back. "Oh! no I won't. In fact you will never hit me again. I saved your sorry hide and you know it. If I hadn't thrown it at you, James would have caught you sleeping again. I think he threatened to cut something off, if he caught you again, am I wrong? What was it?" Abby pretended to think knowing very well what he had intended to cut off. "Was it your balls, Wayne?"

Wayne backed out of the doorway into Gabe's view followed by a little spit fire of a woman pointing her finger at him threatening him within an inch of his life. "You ever harm me again and I promise, on all that is holy, that I will make sure that James catches you and gives you the punishment your worthless hide deserves. Now get out of my sight before I change my mind and tell him right now." Wayne turned without saying a word and ran toward the barn. Abby stood in the kitchen door laughing so hard she had to hold her stomach. Gabe stepped back so she couldn't see him. He whispered, "Well done lass, well done." Then he went to the hall to find the other men. He had to make sure they kept her secret from James.

Through the dinner meal, Gabe found himself recalling the flying sponge and the stunned look on Wayne's face. He found himself smiling and when he looked at his men they were doing the same thing. Gabe and the Scots had never seen anything so funny.

It was Abby's turn to serve the dining room this evening. As she entered the hall, she was greeted with more smiles than usual from the Scots. None of them let on that they knew what she'd done but they gave her the funny feeling they knew something. It was Gabe who finally confirmed her suspicions when he asked, "I seem to have a sticky spot here by my plate. Might ya have a nice wet sponge ya can toss my way?"

Abby gasped and turned three shades redder than usual and answered, "No sir, I don't but I can get one for you if you would like."

Gabe just nodded his head and smiled. He had her in the most uncomfortable position, like a cat stocking a mouse. "Later on this evening", Gabe said in a teasing kind of way. "I'll be needin' something from the kitchen. Will ya be there ta help me, Abigail?" Gabe knew he had her on the hot seat and he was enjoying making her squirm. As she looked around the table all the Scots' eyes were upon her.

So she answered him as sweetly as she could. "Why yes Laird, it just so happens that my guard has given me permission to stay as long as I need to in the kitchen from now on." She smiled at him in a way to let him know she was in complete control. Gabe and the Scots broke out in laughter but never let on just why. Abby excused herself and left the hall as fast as she could before James became involved.

Later on that evening Abby was just finishing in the kitchen. She was alone while Wayne waited out in the yard for her. Not paying attention, as usual, she started to whistle as she washed the last dish. Gabe had come into the kitchen not making a sound content to watch her very round backside sway to her tune. As she turned to put the last dish in the strainer she saw Gabe. She squeaked from the scare he gave her. She looked at the Laird and lowered her eyebrows and said, "You need to stop startling me liked that. You are going to make my heart stop."

Gabe raised his eyebrows at her and said, "Ya make my heart skip a beat every time I see ya these days."

Abby wasn't sure exactly what he meant by that remark, but she was hoping it had something to do with Wayne."Is there something you wanted, Laird?" Abby asked as nicely as she could still leery about his actual reason for coming into the kitchen at such a late hour.

"Well that depends on what ya are offering, lass," he answered.

At that Abby turned in a huff and started toward the kitchen door which led out to the yard.

"Oh, now donna get ya feathers ruffled. I was only teasing," Gabe said as she was about to flounce out of the kitchen.

"Around here, sir, those kinds of remarks are taken quite literally. I suggest you choose your words more carefully," Abby said with a frown facing the door with her hand on the knob.

He was surprised that he had insulted her. That was not his intention. He wanted a nice visit with her with no strings attached. So he said, "I'm sorry, lass. I dinna mean ta hurt your feelings." Abby just stood facing the door and did not turn around.

"I'm making a mess of this. If it is all right with ya, may I please start over again?" Gabe asked.

"I have some pie just out of the oven if you are interested," Abby offered with her back still facing him.

"I am but only if ya have a seat with me, I would like ta talk ta ya."

Abby went to the warming ovens where she had the pie and Gabe sat at the table in the center of the kitchen. He watched as she cut a generous piece for him and placed it in front of him.

"OH, wait, I forgot the cheese."

"Cheese?" Gabe asked.

"Yes cheese," then she recited a little poem; "Apple pie without the cheese, is like a kiss without the squeeze." She placed the cheese down beside Gabe and sat on the opposite side of the table.

"Ya are no havin' any, lass?" Gabe asked as he dipped into his piece. The pie was just the right temperature and the flavor was better than any pie he remembered having. "Did ya make this, lass?"

"Yes, do you like it?" But before he could answer she added, "Is there something wrong with it? I can give you something else if it is not to your liking."

"Relax, lass. There is nothing wrong with this pie. I do like it very much and I would of told ya that if ya had given me a chance."

"Looks like my turn to make a mess out of things." Then she looked right at him and asked, "Is it alright if I start over?"

Gabe just smiled at her. "I have not come to make ya nervous or talk ta ya about what happened with Wayne today. But seeing how we are on that subject. That was the funniest thing I ever saw. Ya are lucky it was I rounding that corner and not James, although I think he would have seen the humor in a flying sponge."

Abigail blushed like a child being caught with her hand in the cookie jar. Gabe noticed her uneasiness. He also noticed everything about her. He was fascinated with her. There was just something about this woman who refused to give him her name. He loved the honey color of her hair and he enjoyed her eyes as they changed colors. They seemed to be green when aroused and hazel when calm. He was infatuated with this woman from the first moment he heard her whistling in the hall. Her round figure was precious, not too thin or round. She had the most enticing voluptuous breasts, just right for big hands to gently caress. But it was that bum that he enjoyed the most. How she would sway it as she whistled. He wanted to just reach out and squeeze it. He wondered just how old she was and where she was from. Her accent was fresh and a bit hard to understand. He even enjoyed the little bantering she gave him. Woman never refused him. He could have anyone he pleased at any time from young to old. He was laird and that was his privilege but this woman refused to answer a question. She surely would never enter his bed willingly.

Gabe found her most refreshing, impish and charming. He would have to talk to James about her again. He wanted her whole story and most of all he wanted her.

Gabe finished his pie, and asked for some ale. Abby went to fetch it for him. He watched her leave and return never taking his eyes off of her. When she placed the goblet down in front of him he reached for her hand and smiled up at her. "Thank you," he said.

She pulled her hand away from his and said, "You are welcome Laird." She could not ignore that hand that touched her. He was huge, well over six feet tall with broad shoulders with a narrow waist and hips, long muscular legs and a good size foot. She could put two of her feet in one of his boots. But it was his hands that caught her eye now. They, like him were huge. He had long fingers and a large palm. When he touched her, the heat of his hand seemed to shoot right through her.

This was the first time she had a chance to study his face. He was gorgeous with bronze skin and slight lines around his eyes, high cheek bones and a smooth complexion with a straight, slightly wide nose which fit his face perfectly. He had just shaved giving him the scent of cinnamon and spice making his lips just right for kissing. And when he smiled he had deep dimples in his cheeks. She loved his laugh, full, booming and uninhibited. Abby could have stared at him forever until she realized what she was doing. Feeling her face getting hot again she turned away from him.

Gabe smiled at her and said, "Do ya see something ya like, lass?"

"I am sorry, sir. You keep catching me off guard. I am not usually so bold," she blurted out.

"You haven't answered my question," Gabe teased not expecting an answer.

Joseph, Gabe's second-in-command entered the kitchen at that point, saving Abby from an embarrassing moment. "Abigail, do ya have some of that pie for me?" He asked. Abby nodded and motioned for him to take a seat. Five minutes later, Colin and Simon entered the kitchen. Soon Abby had a table full of Scots eating her pie and cheese and drinking ale.

Gabe watched as she interacted with his men, she would not take any bantering from them and returned their teasing with bantering of her own. Abigail did not seem intimidated by the room full of men but enjoyed them instead.

James entered the kitchen and Abby went silent. She backed away from the table and stood at the wall waiting for her orders. When James saw all his Scotts having fun he sat down to join them. Abigail made sure that they had everything they needed and slipped out the side door of the kitchen to return to the crate for the night.

After that night, the Laird made it a nightly occurrence to visit the kitchen but he mentioned to his men that he wanted to visit with her alone. Each night she would have a treat ready for him. "Just in time," she'd say when he entered the room. "I need a taste tester is anyone else coming this evening?" When Gabe told her no, she'd say,

"Well then you will just have to do." Secretly she wished he would be alone. He was becoming her highlight of the day. Abigail would scold herself after she went to her crate. "*Keep away from him*," she'd tell herself. "*There is no future for you with him or anyone ever*." But her heart would not listen.

Finally she decided that a moment was better than an eternity alone. Her fate had been sealed by her partners. Damn them and damn England and Damn Gabriel McKenzie and most of all damn James.

Abby was beginning to feel that escape was her only option. Even if she was killed trying to escape, it would be better than living in hell at the Manor for the rest of her life. Each night in that rat infested crate made her decision more certain. She would wait for the Scots to leave and then she would run. One way or another it would be an end to this slow torture. Being eaten alive by rats was not as appealing as running for freedom.

This particular night Gabe stayed longer than usual. "Sit down lass and talk to me."

Abby looked surprised. Sitting at the same table with a guest was not allowed even if it was in the kitchen and after midnight. But Gabe would not take no for an answer. "Tell me about your husband," he asked half expecting a direct "no".

To his amazement she didn't say no but, "You first. Tell me about your wife."

"Fair enough, but if I tell you about Anna than you will tell me about your husband. Is it a deal?"

"Deal," Abby agreed.

"I married Anna for the clan. We needed the land and the alliance with her family to survive. I met her the day I married her. Oh, I knew of her but I never had the pleasure ta actually meet her. She was a beautiful red head with green eyes, just like my Emily. Tall and thin, very willing to share my bed and give me as many children as I wanted. But she had little interest in the children once they were born. She was a good woman but we had wet nurses for her and nannies. I did not love her when I married her but I grew ta love her even though she was not a good mother. For the most part I think we were happy. She died from an infected wound she got on a nail. It was a year of suffering before it finally took her. Even amputating her leg did not stop the infection. It was a sad day but I was glad her suffering was over. That was four years ago now."

"I'm sorry Gabe," Abby said sincerely.

When Abigail thought he was finished she shared her story with him, a story she had told no one even her children.

"My grandfather and both my parents died when I was sixteen. I was the baby of the family of nine children, the black sheep in their eyes." And she blushed but continued on. "I had many offers to live with one or another but the thought of living with any of them was not something I could ever see myself doing. Believe it or not I was so different from them. So when Roy asked me to marry him it seemed like a good idea. It seemed like the right thing to do at the time. My brothers and sisters agreed with the match even though he was a lot older than I was. I was not given the option to refuse him either. They just marched me to the first priest they could find and the deed was done, no questions asked."

"How much older?" Gabe asked interested.

"Well I was sixteen and he was thirty six, twenty years. My family felt I needed someone older who was more stable and could put up with my imperfections. Roy was a traveling salesman. At first I was thrilled to think I would be traveling and seeing the country, but that was not what happened. Shortly after we were married, he brought me to Riverton where I lived until he died. In order to collect his inheritance he needed a wife and it was required in the will that I live their or it was to be donated to the church. He had inherited a small farm with a house and barn from his aunt. It was not in good repair but I still had my tools. My grandfather was a ship builder. In the summers I would live with him. He taught me well and it was a good thing because Roy was helpless when it came to anything except sales and I don't think he was very good at that either because he never brought much back for us to live on.

At sixteen I lost three of my family, married and became pregnant. When I was in my seventh month Roy took his first business trip and didn't return until Ellery, my first son was six months old. He left again just after I was pregnant with my twins and did not return until after they were born.

I remember being so proud of them, they were so cute, but Roy was furious. He had a plan and they were not part of it. One boy and one girl was what he told me I could have and he did not want any more and he really did not want them but he told me he did. But I did. I wanted a dozen, that was why I was so happy with the twins because it gave me two more than he wanted."

Gabe sat smiling at her as she talked about her children. He could see how much she loved them and what a good mother she really was.

"I was not allowed to contact my family ever. I was alone when I gave birth to the boys. I really wanted a girl so we tried again and again he left before Hannah was born. I was thrilled she when she was born but it meant no more children for me. After Roy found out I was pregnant for her he never touched me again."

"Ya mean he never bed ya again?" Gabe asked.

"Well that too. He never touched me ever in any way. I was not allowed to touch him or kiss him and when we slept he'd put a pillow between us so I couldn't touch him. I really don't think he liked sex." Then she changed her mind and said, "I don't think he liked having sex with me any way." Abby looked up at Gabe and saw the look in his eyes. "I'm not stupid, Gabe, I know those business trips where not what he led me to believe. I found many things that confirmed my fears. Especially the day he died.

At the cemetery, the day we buried him, everyone there threw a flower into his grave. I threw in the last letter from his mistress signed with a big letter E." There was a moment of silence and then she added, "I taught my sons well. They will never have a lonely wife. I could not kiss my husband but I certainly could kiss and hug my children and I did every single day."

Wayne came into the kitchen at that point and very politely asked if she was ready. Abby just walked away without saying another word to the guard holding her hands up to be cuffed and shackled. Before she left she put a chunk of bread into her pocket. She saw Gabe watching her. "It's for the rats. They don't bite as much if I feed them a little first." Gabe watched as Abigail hesitated before Wayne took her out for the night. He waited until she was gone and slammed both fists down hard onto the table and then left the kitchen.

CHARTER 6
Soup Anyone?

The next day, Abigail was working in the kitchen when a large carriage pulled up the drive. The staff was required to meet James' new guests as they arrived. Abigail stood next to Mary and Olga and William watching the grand entrance of the carriage and the guards coming down the road. By the looks of the carriage and the many servants, there was a very important wealthy person inside. James left with Gabe this morning and was not here to greet this guest which is what started the first set of events.

Lady Jennifer Black, a loud, rude, spoiled, obnoxious, excuse for a woman came out of the carriage appalled from the lack of her host's presence. She threw her first tantrum, one of many, hollering at her staff as well as the entire staff of the manor. She even had the horses nervously stomping around and ready to bolt. William had to help her footman to calm the beasts down.

Nothing pleased her. She had brought so much staff and luggage the manor could not accommodate her, especially with the Scotts in residence. Lady Jennifer demanded four rooms just for herself and another twenty rooms for her staff. She wanted the Scotts to be thrown out until she found out who the Scotts were. Then she calmed down and tried to be a little more agreeable but that did not last long. After cooking all day, she changed Olga's menu and wanted a full band to entertain after dinner. She even had music she wanted played, one being a fast march with a snare drum. The staff were frantically trying to meet all her demands but were failing desperately especially with a snare drum.

James would not be pleased if he came home to a house with an unhappy guest. Needless to say the staff were all upset and working as fast as they could, including Abigail, Mary and Olga.

Lady Jennifer insisted on the march being played after dinner even though all the musicians that were needed to play this piece of music were not available.

William the footman volunteered to play the horn or the snare drum but he couldn't play both. Finally Abby said, "I can play the drum." All the musicians looked and said at the same time "YOU?" Abby blushed and said, "Yes and very well actually." It was unheard of to have a woman playing in a band especially a drum. They could be in more trouble if she was discovered playing.

So Abby gave them her idea. "Let me wear a jacket, the britches and the hat. I will stuff my hair up in the hat and pull it down low so no one will see my face. If I stand in the back of the first row, no one will even know I am there but they will hear the drum, William can play the horn and that will be all we need to complete the band and to please Lady Jennifer. James will also be pleased. If you stand near the door I can sneak in without being seen and leave after the number is played."

They all agreed it might work and handed Abigail her music, her drum and sticks. There were so many notes on the pages it was hard to see the staff, but Abby did not even flinch when she saw it. The other musicians were very happy with her reaction. Abigail spent the rest of the day banging on a pot in the kitchen getting ready for her first and only performance.

"How did ya ever learn to play the drum like that?" William asked after he heard her beat the pot.

"My grandfather," Abby said with a smile. "He thought I had too much anger when I was a little girl and I needed a way to vent it so he gave me a drum to bang on when I got angry, which was most of the time." Then she started to giggle. "It back fired on him, however, I was pretty good and the men on the docks let me play with them. The tourist loved to see this little girl hitting a drum with the other musicians and would reward us handsomely. It didn't stop with the drum either, I played as many instruments as they would let me. My grandfather was very pleased and allowed me to play when and where I wanted. But his favorite instrument was the violin and he would request it all the time."

James finally returned just before dinnertime to a house full of changes thanks to Lady Jennifer. The staff could not believe how James handled her. She was polite and agreeable, not at all like the villainess she portrayed earlier. He even was looking forward to the entertainment she had arranged after dinner.

The hall had been setup as she requested, and the seating arrangements made. Gabe was seated to Lady Jennifer's left and James to her right. The dinner came out perfect and then it was time for the band. The men all filed in carrying their instruments, wearing white jackets with gold buttons and white britches with a gold tassel hanging down from the knee and a very tall white hat with a gold brim in the front. The tall hat was held on under their chins with a gold braid. Gabe noticed the front row stopped and stood while the back row filed in blocking the men from view. He could see just the tops of the hats of the second row except for one very short musician. Inconspicuously a box was brought in for the short musician to stand on.

Gabe watched as the back row got into position carefully hiding the short musician from anyone's view. From where Gabe was sitting, he could see the box and two tiny feet standing on it. If he didn't know better, those little feet belonged to only one person that he knew of.

Without saying a word he got up and strolled over next to the entertainers. Carefully, he looked down the back row of the musicians to confirm his suspicions. There perched on a small wooden box was Abby dressed like the other men in britches with a drum strapped over her shoulders and sticks in her hands ready to play. She was concentrating on her music and did not notice Gabe looking down the row at her.

Her hat was way too big and she was having trouble keeping it from falling over her eyes. Her britches were tied on with a rope and she was in her stocking feet. Gabe had to turn away before he started laughing. He knew she was up to something but he never thought that she would try this kind of thing.

Dressing in men's clothing was a punishable offense. If she got caught she could have her head shaved. Gabe went back to his seat and waited for the music to start. Lady Jennifer had to get up and make a long speech about her find and the music she was so proud of. Finally it was time to play. The music started with a long drum role. Abby did not disappoint the other musicians or the audience.

Then the others joined in with a foot stomping march made to get the blood pumping. Soon the audience joined in clapping and tapping their feet ending with a standing ovation. Gabe watched as the men of the band stood shoulder to shoulder while the inappropriate musician made her quick exit before she was discovered.

While James and Lady Jennifer congratulated the musicians, Gabe slipped out the side door hoping to catch Abigail in her britches. By the time he made it to the kitchen, Abby was back in her servant's uniform pretending nothing had happened.

"What is this?" Gabe asked pointing to a white band jacket and a tall white hat lying on the table.

"An extra uniform," Mary said trying to protect Abby.

"Where are the britches that went with them?" Gabe asked suspecting that Abby was still wearing them.

The three women just looked very guilty. So Gabe said, "If the person responsible doesn't show me those britches, by the time I count to three…… I will have to talk to James." Then he started counting "One……two……" Before he could get to three, Abby lifted her skirts to expose the missing britches.

She bowed her head expecting to be reprimanded when Gabe said, "Well done, lass, very well done. I enjoyed your concert and your secret is safe with me." He smiled at her and left the kitchen before the women had time to react to the compliment.

Lady Jennifer decided to have a formal dinner the next night demanding all the guests to come in formal attire. Even the servants wore different uniforms with white gloves and powdered white wigs. One of the serving wenches slipped and hurt herself and was unable to serve the dinner. Abby and the other women thought that James was a little too rough when teaching her a lesson and her slipping had nothing to do with her injury.

James specifically requested Abby to take her place. He had been lapse in Abby's lessons recently and he was about to change that in front of all the guests.

As the night before, Lady Jennifer had made the seating arrangements. She had planned for James to be on her left and Gabe on her right, but Gabe had other ideas. He made the excuse he needed to talk to James. James understood his meaning and offered Lady Jennifer the seat on his right and Gabe sat on his left. It was very obvious that Lady Jennifer was after husband number three and Gabe would have no part of it. She was not happy with the rejection and was not about to give up so easily.

Gabe had eyes for one woman and she was coming into the hall in a new black uniform with a frilly white apron and white gloves carrying a kettle of soup and a ladle. He had to laugh to himself when he saw her. She was the only one who was not wearing a white wig.

Abby stood at the entrance of the hall waiting for James to signal for her. She was instructed to stand behind the head table until James raised his hand for her to start serving but for now she just had to wait until he motioned her into the hall. The soup was extremely hot and very heavy. Abby had all she could do to hold on to it. Finally, James noticed the servants ready to enter. He also noticed the absence of a white wig on Abby's head.

His anger rose giving him one more excuse to teach her a lesson. Mary and Abby were the first servants to enter the hall. Abby carried the scolding soup and Mary struggled with an overly filled tray of hot rolls. Abby took her place at the back of the head table as instructed while Mary walked to the front of the head table placing the rolls in front of James. When Mary set the tray on the table, one of the rolls fell off and rolled to the floor.

One of James' prize Keeshonds, which were always in the dining hall jumped up and stole the lost roll. Another hound challenged him and a quick tiff erupted between the two dogs resulting in loud growling and barking which disturbed some of James' guests.

James became furious with Mary's clumsiness. He stood and raised his walking stick striking her across the face. All the guests went silent. An uneasiness came over the entire room as they waited to see what else James was about to do. Mary put her hand on her cheek and bowed her head with tears falling down her face.

Abby saw her opportunity. James really did raise his hand. That was supposed to be his signal and Abby was not about to let Mary get hit again. So she scurried to James' side while he was preoccupied with the dogs and Mary.

James did not see Abby at his side but the Laird was watching her like a hawk. As James stood with his hand still raised reprimanding Mary, Abby filled his bowl to the very brim with the scalding soup. Then she slowly positioned his bowl directly under his raised arm. Backing away from the table she waited for James to sit down. The Laird watched the drama unfold but said nothing.

The next string of events seemed to move in slow motion. As James began to sit down, his raised elbow, came down into the center of the scalding bowl of soup, causing him to flinch, emptying the entire contents of the bowl into his lap, and severely burning his most sensitive man part. He jumped up again bellowing in pain, trying to back away from the table but Abby was ready with an extended foot causing him to trip and fall backward hitting his head and elbow on the stone floor.

Dazed from the fall James did not see Abby scoop another full ladle of scalding soup and dump it in his crouch, burning him a second time. Everyone at the table was watching the fighting dogs except the Laird and Mary who were watching Abby and James.

So not to be discovered, Abby moved away quickly to the other side of the table and resumed serving her very hot soup ignoring the dogs and James' calls for help.

James started to come too just after Abby moved away. He was too dazed to have seen what she had done. Screaming in pain, the servants came in and helped James to his feet and out of the hall. They brought him to his chamber where his personal physician could attend him.

Abby never looked up or acknowledged James in any way but continued to innocently serve the soup. Everything happened so quickly that the guests did not realize why James was carried out. Only Abby, Mary and Gabe knew the real reason.

Mary was still standing at the head table with her hand holding her bruised cheek. Abby caught her attention and motioned for her to leave the hall while she finished serving the soup.

Olga was in the kitchen when Mary entered still holding her cheek. She quickly put a cold cloth on Mary's face while listening to Mary's version of what happened in the hall. Olga sent the other serving wenches up to the hall with the next course, hoping to help Abby.

The last table Abby served was the head table which should have been served first. So Abby wasn't to upset when Lady Jennifer scolded her for her incompetence. She was hoping Lady Jennifer would help prove that she was nowhere near James when he was burnt. She finished serving her and moved to the Laird. "Soup Laird?" she asked looking guiltless.

"Aye, lass," he answered with a grin and then added. "In my bowl please."

Abby's eyebrows shot up in disbelief. He knew. She stopped what she was doing and just looked at him. Her guiltless expression changed to one of complete fear.

Gabe reached up and took her hand. "Relax, lass. He had it coming," he said in a whisper. Abby looked into Gabe's eyes, she nodded and gave him a grateful expression then left the hall as fast as her little feet could carry her.

James didn't leave his chamber for the next two days which delayed the business dealings with Gabe. A little frustrated his trip was prolonged, Gabe decided to ask James if he could have Abigail for the day for his personal use. Gabe knew if he asked him to take her for any other reason, James would have denied him. As it was James was thrilled he could get what he wanted out of her after all.

Far behind the manor, on the top of the back hill sat a house which James called his special cottage. The whores would speak of it often. They told of the mirror over the bed and the copper bathtub for two. There was a huge feather bed that seemed to swallow one up as soon as it was laid on. The house itself was only one room with windows overlooking the ocean. A true lovers retreat with a large stone fire place which James would only let used by his most special guests. When Gabe asked for Abigail, James was quick to offer his special cottage as long as he wanted to use it.

It was not Gabe's intention to bed Abby but if he could get her approval he had every intention of using the special cottage as it was meant to be used. He wanted her, not just for one day but for as long as he lived. He needed a few more answers especially about her partners and her family before he could put his plan into action.

Gabe had figured out a way to help Abby but he still had to convince James and that was not going to be easy. Plus Abby was not going to like any part of his plan, which is why he was not about to give her a choice. If all worked the way Gabe wanted, Abby would be pardoned and her property returned but most of all she would have her freedom. Hopefully she would not choose to leave him but it was a gamble he had to take.

At day break, Abby was awoken by the barn door sliding open. Gabe came in alone and saddled his stallion. When he was ready, Wayne opened Abby's crate and took the irons off of her. "You are going to make the Laird happy today," Wayne said with a disgusting smile on his face. "He requested ya special. So ya best make him real happy if ya know what I mean or ya will pay the price when ya return. It won't be me that punishes ya but I will sure enjoy watching." Then he laughed spitting through his yellow teeth.

Standing at the door was Gabe holding his stallion's reins. Wayne had to push Abby over to him. She had no intention of going anywhere with him. Gabe noticed her reluctance and said nothing but went over, lifted her over his shoulder and carried her to his mount. Wayne rolled with laughter as he watched Abby kick and squirm to get free.

With one quick thrust, Abby found herself sitting on his horse and then a second later, Gabe mounted with one graceful leap. She tried to slip off but he caught her and sat her hard on his lap. He snaked his arm around her waist and gave her a quick squeeze and said, "Behave Abigail. I will not tell ya again." A gentle nudge and the stallion was off in a slow canter and then a full gallop. Abby just hung on for dear life. Gabe rode like he was born on a horse. His seat never left the saddle. His hands were gentle on the reins and the stallion was powerful. He never seemed to tire.

"Where are you taking me?" Abby asked with a nervous voice. Gabe did not answer but squeezed her waist a little harder.

"Maybe we should slow down a bit. Your horse seems to need a rest," Abby said next. Gabe ignored her again and just urged his horse to go faster. He could tell she was very uneasy with this situation and he was enjoying watching her squirm.

"Does James really know you have me? I cannot believe he gave you permission to do this," she said trying to pretend she was angry. "I think we should go back so I can hear it from his own lips."

Gabe was smiling. She was trying every trick she could think of to get out of bedding him. But he was not about to take her back until he was good and ready. He needed some answers from her and he was determined to get them even if he had to keep her at the special cottage for a week.

Next she tried to lean away from him to loosen his grip. Gabe couldn't believe that she had every intention of jumping at a full gallop. "Ya are acting like a spoiled brat who won't go ta bed at her bedtime."

"I am not," she said crossing her arms in front of her and pouting.

"Oh, Aye ya are and I have a lot of experience with how ta treat a brat. Do ya wish ta find out what that is?" Gabe asked firmly.

Abby put her head down and said nothing. She settled down and rode along with him. He gave her a gentle hug and rode on. It took another hour to reach the special house. Abigail just rode with him. Gabe was hoping she would give in and they would have a good day but he wasn't counting on it.

When they stopped in front of the cottage, Abby asked, "Can I ask if this is our destination or will I be accused of being a spoiled brat again."

"Ya may ask and it is. Time ta get down." Gabe dismounted and then reached for Abby.

She crossed her arms and announced. "I am not getting down and I don't care if you think I am a brat."

"Suit yourself, lass. We can do this the hard way if ya prefer it."

"I prefer you take me back to my homey crate right now," Abby demanded.

Gabe was not about to play this game. Before she could protest he lifted her off the saddle and over his shoulder and carried her into the house. A little man came out from the barn and took Samson to his stall in a small barn just left of the cottage. Once in the house, Gabe walked over to the huge bed and tossed her into the middle of it. The bed did seem to swallow her up and the more she moved the deeper she sunk until she said, "I am stuck and I cannot get out." She crossed her arms and lowered her eyebrows into a little pout that reminded him of his little five year old, Emily.

Abby did not want to look at Gabe so she looked up at the ceiling. She squealed in surprise to see herself looking back. Gabe broke out into laughter as he watched her completely helpless.

"Are ya ready, lass?"

"Ready for what?" Abby asked still squirming to get free of the bed.

"For what I have planned for the day," Gabe said with a smile.

"Could you please tell me exactly what you have planned and what you are expecting me to do with you all day?"

"I am waiting for ya ta settle down and I will tell ya," he said with raised eyebrows.

"Fine," Abby said and she stopped squirming and listened.

"First, I have no intention of bedding ya unless ya want me ta."

"Really?" Abby asked completely surprised.

"Really, I brought ya here because I need some truthful answers and I wanted ta be alone ta get them. I thought ya might be more willing ta answer them if we were alone. But I feel ya owe me for not telling James about the drum and especially the soup and the wet sponge. When we return, James will ask me what I liked best about ya and I will not lie ta him. He will know."

"Just what's that suppose to mean?" Abby asked with a nervous expression.

"I want two physical things from ya. One, I want a kiss, and not just a little one on my cheek. A kiss full of passion is what I want and I will take nothing less. Second, ya will allow me to touch ya naked breasts or ya naked ass. Ya will choose which one I can touch for as long as I want with my hands."

"And if I refuse to decide?"

"Then I will choose, both."

"This sounds like 'forcing' to me Gabriel McKenzie," Abby said looking surprised at his demands. "And what questions do you have? I mean nothing to you. You have no right to interfere and I'd thank you, not to."

"Are ya a wee bit nervous, my sweet?" Gabe asked with a huge smile. "Surely I'm not as bad as the rats in ya crate."

"Well the rats in the crate have yet to ask me for a kiss or to feel my ass," Abby said with her eyebrows lowered and her arms crossed. "Fine, kiss me and let's get this over with so I can get out of here," she finally said.

"No lass, not like this. I told ya I will not force ya and I mean it." Then he changed the subject, "Ready ta break ya fast?"

Leaving her still stuck in the feather bed he went over and started a fire. He took out a couple of sweet rolls that were left for them on the table in a basket. But when he went back to the bed he found Abby sound asleep. She looked so beautiful. He did not have the heart to wake her so he removed her shoes and covered her with the quilt and went out to talk to Colin, the man who took care of his horse on their arrival.

Colin was one of his men. Gabe wanted him to be ready in case he needed to send word back to the manor. Then the two men carried in water, enough to fill the two person copper tub. There was a large kettle hanging over the fire which was used for heating water. It would take some time to heat enough water to fill that tub but Gabe was determined to give Abby a good day despite her protests.

.................She was sitting up high looking down at the wolves circling under her. In the distance she could hear the sound of men coming in her direction. She tried to cover herself so they would not see her. They were planning to hurt her. The men stood just under her beating a helpless well dressed gentleman while she watched, unable to help and hoping they did not see her. Then he look up, seeing her and ready to kill her.....................................

Abby started to scream and scream unable to wake from her dream. Tears came down her face and she thrashed back and forth as if trying to get free. Gabe rushed to her side taking her in his arms. He gently talked to her to get her to wake. When she opened her eyes and felt

Gabe holding her. She jumped and pushed herself away from him as if he was the one in her dream. It took a few seconds before she got her bearings. Tears still came down her cheeks and she had the look of terror all over her face.

This was not the first dream she had like this. They were coming more often and each dream was worse than the one before. Still breathing hard from fright, Gabe tried to calm her down, "Abigail, wake up lass. Ya are dreaming. Ya are safe, wake up."

Abby finally realized where she was and tried to look away from him. "Lass, talk ta me. What is it?" But Abby only shook her head, no. She reached up and threw her arms around him and asked, "Please hold me. Just hold me for a little bit and then I will be alright." Gabe scooped her up in his arms and carried her over to the fire. He sat down in a large overstuffed chair with her in his arms. She curled up in his lap and trembled uncontrollably.

When she seemed to calm down he asked, "Do ya have these dreams quite often?"

"Not dreams, Gabe, just one dream. The same one over and over and each time it gets worse."

"When did it start, lass?"

"When I was in prison, I haven't had one like that since I was a little girl. I really thought I didn't do that anymore," Abby confessed.

"Do what lass? What is it?" Gabe asked very concerned. He noticed her apprehension and said. "Today, I get the answers I want, lass, and ya are going ta tell me."

"I don't think you will understand," Abby whispered.

Gabe took her hand and said, "I promise, whatever ya tell me will not go any farther than this room. Does that help?"

"I don't want you to think badly of me and after I tell you….. Well… I don't want you to fear me." And before she would let him answer she began her story.

"When I was a little girl, the dreams were so bad that my father use to sleep with me. I remember waking up to three people holding me down. My mother and father had no idea how to help me so my father went to see Old Joe."

"Who was Old Joe?" Gabe asked curious.

"He was my father's best friend. Old Joe was a real Indian shaman and a horse whisperer. To the Indians, a shaman is a holy person, one that can heal and has visions. The visions were believed to tell the future. Sometimes they were warnings and sometimes they were blessings of things to come. Old Joe believed I had a gift. He called it the gift of sight. I never believed it was a gift at all. To me it was more like a curse. Old Joe would tell me not to fight the dreams but to let them come to me. If I would accept it, the dreams would help me. It was right after my father talked to him that Old Joe took me into the mountains. We spent two months up there and he worked with me and my dreams."

"So ya are having a vision?" Gabe asked.

"Yes," Abby answered fidgeting with her hands as if trying to decide if she wanted to tell him her vision.

"Tell me, lass. I donna want ya ta ever not confide in me. And I do understand, my mother was like ya."

Abby got misty eyed and said, "Someone is going to die and I think I am going to witness it."

"Do ya know who?"

"Not yet but I am sure it will come to me." And she put her head down.

Gabe felt so bad for her that he said, "Come here lass." And he hugged her like a little child.

"Is there something I can do for ya, lass?" Gabe whispered in her ear.

"You are doing it. I just need a hug." Then she lifted her head and looked into Gabe's eyes. She threw her arms around his neck and said, "I'm not very good at this, I will need some help and she pressed her lips against his. He was soothingly warm and his lips smooth against hers. She felt him rub her back and pull her closer to him. Then he opened his mouth and encouraged her to do the same. His tongue entered her mouth causing rippling sensations to go all through her body. She mimicked his actions with her tongue exploring his mouth. He made love with his tongue and she did the same. She hugged him more and encouraged him to give her more.

A little groan from the back of her throat let him know she liked what he was doing. His big hands slipped down her back and held her bottom. Slowly he massaged her in circular motions stopping to gently squeeze now and then. He tasted delicious and he was so warm that she didn't realize that her skirts were up past her waste. His warm strong hands were now on her naked skin. Tingling sensations rippled through her one after another.

She wished the kiss would never stop. Before she could protest he had loosened her top and pulled it down exposing both breasts. With one hands still on her bottom he held her naked breast stroking the nipple with his thumb. Abby arched her back to give him more room. Her breast was larger than his hand which made him smile while his tongue still probed her mouth. Then she realized what he was doing and quickly pulled away. She sat in his lap with one of his hands on her bottom and the other still caressing her breast.

"I'm not so sure we should be doing this," Abby said looking into his eyes while he still caressed her.

"Ya donna like what I am doing, lass?" Gabe asked refusing to stop.

"No, I mean yes but I cannot do this with you I am not a whore."

"Do I make ya feel like a whore?" Gabe asked still enjoying her reaction to his touch.

"Not really, I just cannot do this with you or anyone especially you."

"Why not?" Gabe asked surprised she stopped the kiss.

"Because you'll take something I have no right to give," Abby said pushing his hand off her breast. She stood up fixed her gown and walked over to the window and looked at the ocean.

"What will I take, lass?" Gabe asked following her to the window. Abby just put her head down and didn't say anything. He turned her around to face him. "Answer me Abigail," he demanded.

Abby kept her head bent and whispered, "My heart."

Gabe put his arms around her and hugged her but did not ask anymore of her.

The rest of the day he asked his questions. She answered each one without hesitation. He was very interested with what happened at the Riverton Bank.

"Did ya see Elizabeth in the bank?" Gabe asked.

"No, but my back was to the people so she could have been there I really don't know. She told me she was and I believed her."

"Donna ya think it is funny that a strange woman just showed up outside the bank just as ya left offering ya a ride ta Boston? Did ya have your grandfather's box with ya?"

"Now that you mentioned it, she just showed up. I did not see her come out of the bank. She must have been waiting for me outside already and yes I was holding the box."

"What was in the box Abigail?"

"Truth is I don't really know. My grandfather had some books for me which I took out and some gold coins which kept my children and I alive and clothes on our backs. I never opened the documents on the bottom, but I am sure Mr. Pinkerton knew."

"Why did ya not open the papers?" Gabe asked surprised.

"They were written in my grandfather's handwriting. All I could do was cry when I looked at them. Plus, I didn't want Roy to take what was there and lose it like he lost everything he owned. No one knew who the box belonged too. All the transactions I made were by correspondence only and I led Mr. Pinkerton to believe I had a spy to watch him so he could not cheat me. I used it more than once so he believed it. It wasn't safe for me to remove the box until Roy's death."

"Where is the box now, Abigail?" He asked with his eyebrows lowered convincing he suspected something.

"It is safe. I made sure of it before I left Boston," Abby said getting a little nervous. "No one can get to it but me, not even my children." Then it was her turn to ask questions. "Gabe what are you thinking. Please tell me."

"I think ya are in a lot of trouble and not just with James and England. Ya stumbled into something and whatever is in that box has a lot to do with it. I also think ya should not trust Mr. Pinkerton, Niles, Elizabeth Shaw or ya partners or the four dock men who chased ya into the W &W Shipping Co. in the first place. Prison saved ya life and so did James by taken ya here. Promise me ya will not run."

Abby bit her lips together and did not answer him.

"Abigail Fox, if ya run he will kill ya. Ya cannot make it. He wants ya ta run. Donna do it," Gabe pleaded.

"Death is better than a crate for the rest of my life Gabe and right now death is looking really good," Abby whispered.

Gabe turned her around and slapped her bum hard. Then he turned her back around to face him and said, "Donna ever talk like that again. Death is never the answer. There is always hope."

"Not for me there isn't. All I have to look forward to is paying a debt I had nothing to do with, spending the rest of my life waiting on strange people and living a very lonely life. I am not stupid Gabe. James is planning to kill me if I run or not. At least I have a chance if I run. Not much of one but it is better than nothing and it is much better than being eaten alive by rats."

"I want ya ta promise me ya will not run." Then he said again slightly shaking her, "Promise me Abby. I want ya word right now."

Abby bit her lips again and then said, "I promise I will not run while you are in residence at the manor but that is all I can promise."

"Very well, I will accept your word."

The water was finally hot for a bath. "Time for ya bath, lass."

"Oh no, I do not want a bath. I don't like taking cold baths and I will not take one today," Abby protested. "I hate that trough behind the barn and I hate taking a bath while that Wayne watches me. I won't do it and that is final."

Gabe rose and picked her up again and carried her to the bath he had just prepared. He pulled her skirts up and stood her barefoot in the warm water.

"It is warm?" She said with a big smile.

"Aye, now do ya need me ta undress ya or can ya do it yourself?"

"Turn around," she ordered.

"Nay, ya still owe me and I am cashing in," Gabe said with a big smile.

"Fine," Abby said sputtering. This was the first hot bath she had received since she left the colonies and she was not about to give it up just for a little privacy. She lifted her gown over her head and hurled it at Gabe's head and quickly sat down to enjoy her tub. Abby watched as Gabe started to undress. "What are you doing?" She squealed.

"It is a tub for two and last count there is only one in it. Now shove over or I will sit bare ass on top of ya," Gabe teased.

"You wouldn't dare!" Abby said covering her face with her hands to hide her embarrassment.

A splash told Abby to push over quick before she was sat on by a very large Scottish laird. Abby slumped down into the water to hide her bare body, but Gabe only teased her more. "Donna trust me Lass? Am I going ta have ta sit ya on my lap and wash your backside?"

"Gabriel McKenzie if you as much as come an inch on my side I will get out."

"Then ya can sit up so I can look at ya big beautiful breasts and I will promise not ta touch this time."

"Fine, but you stay over there and I mean it," Abby said, with her eyebrows down and pointing her finger at him as if he was five years old.

"Aye, ma I will be a very good boy," Gabe said laughing.

After dinner, Gabe had all his answers and ordered Samson to be brought from the barn.

Abby was looking at the ocean one last time before they went back. "It was a wonderful day. I haven't had such a good day in many months, thank you."

"It would have been a lot better if ya had let me bed ya," Gabe teased.

Abby giggled and then stood on her tip toes and kissed his cheek. "I really don't want to leave."

"First I have ta force ya here and now I have ta force ya to leave. Ya are just a spoiled brat and I should turn ya over my knee and paddle ya back side," he teased.

"If I am spoiled, Laird it is your own fault. Now kiss me once more and I will leave without a complaint." Gabe reached down and kissed her long and hard and left her wanting more but satisfied with his kiss.

Gabe helped her on Samson and mounted but this time they walked slowly back to the manor. He kept his arm around her waist. Now and then accidently let his thumb lift her breast. Abby did not protest.

CHAPTER 7
Sing For Me

The next day two Scottish messengers left the manor. One went to see the King of England and on to the King of Scotland. Both carried messages from Gabe.

Gabe went to the kitchen to have his late night rendezvous with Abby, but she was already gone. It was the first time that she did not wait for him. They had such a wonderful day at the special cottage. Gabe could not understand why she was avoiding him, so he marched out to the barn to find out.

The door slid open with a big bang startling the horses and Abigail. Even William came out of his room to see what happened. Abby could see him coming straight at her through the slats of her crate. She backed up against the back wall hoping it was far enough to be safe.

"Abigail Fox, what are ya doing in there with me waiting for bits ta eat?" Then he called Wayne. "Get ya sorry ass out here and let her out so she can take care of my needs now." Wayne came out laughing at Abby. "Now ya are going to get what ya deserve and more to ya," Wayne said as he unlocked the door of her crate but Abby did not come out.

"Come out here now Abigail or I will come in there and get ya," Gabe demanded.

"Go away Gabe. I am done for the day," Abby said from the back of the crate.

Gabe bent down and crawled in, grabbed her ankle and dragged her on her backside out of the crate. Still holding her ankle he said,

"Are ya going to walk back ta the kitchen with me or will I have ta drag ya back by ya ankle?"

Abby stood up and without a word held her hands up so Wayne could remove the irons. With a huff she walked out of the barn followed by Gabe. She walked as fast as she could to stay in front of him so she didn't have to walk by his side. She rounded the corner of the manor and entered the kitchen by the side and slammed the door in Gabe's face before he could follow her inside.

Gabe entered the kitchen by kicking the door right off the hinges. Abigail was at the counter getting something for Gabe to eat when she felt him grab her arm and drag her out of the kitchen and up the stairs to his room. He threw her inside the room, shut the door then locked it and slid the key into his kilt. Every occupant of the floor came out of their rooms including James to see Gabe and Abby go into his chamber. James was thrilled that Abby was making such a good impression on Gabe. With their eyebrows raised the occupants returned to their rooms quietly all except Lady Jennifer who slammed her door and then threw her water pitcher shattering it all over the floor, water and all.

Abby stood and faced Gabe waiting for his next move. He stepped forward and she stepped back. "Abigail, take that gown off and get into that bed now," he ordered.

"I will do no such thing Gabriel McKenzie," Abby said in complete defiance.

"NO? Do ya need some help Abigail? If I help ya I promise I will rip it off your back." He took one more step forward and Abby flinched. She pulled her dress off and threw it at him in a huff leaving her standing in front of him in her shift. "That too, Abby," he ordered pointing at the shift. Abby's mouth dropped open in surprise. "Gabriel?" Abby said getting ready to run.

"Do I need to count ta three? One……Two……..Three." Abby slipped off her shift and ran naked, jumping into his bed and pulled the quilt up over her head. Gabe smiled as he watched her round bottom flying into the center of his bed. He went over and sat down on the edge of the bed leaning directly over her with one hand on either side of her. "Abigail?"

"Yes?" She answered still buried under the quilt.

"Ya can come out now."

Abby took a few seconds and slowly she peaked out dropping the quilt to the end of her nose still holding on to the top edge.

"The next time ya try ta avoid me for no reason, I'll drag ya naked through the manor and up ta my room. And from now on ya will sleep in my bed naked until I leave. Do ya have any objections?"

Abby just kept the blanket high and said, "No and where are you sleeping?"

"In my bed, naked as a jaybird with my arm around ya holding one of those big beautiful breasts in my hand and ya bum pulled in against my groin." Abby flipped the quilt up over her head and said nothing.

"I thought ya'd see it my way." He stoked the fire, took care of his needs and stripped down blowing out the candles and slid into bed. He reached out and pulled her over to his side of the bed. He rolled over on his side and dragged her in close to him. Gabe fell asleep holding her breast and whispered, "Sweet dreams, my sweet." Then he kissed her on the top of her head.

Abby waited until she thought he was sleeping and whispered, "You too Gabe, thank you for saving me from my crate." Gabe smiled and continued to pretend to sleep.

When she woke the next morning, she was alone but she had warm water to wash. He had picked her uniform and shift up off the floor and carefully draped them over the back of the chair. A bar of rose smelling soap rested on the dry sink and one red rose rested in her shoe. Tears flooded her eyes. How she was going to miss him when he left.

She entered the kitchen late to a frazzled group of servants. Lady Jennifer was on a rampage barking orders and insults causing a mass frustration throughout the entire manor. She had the staff cleaning frantically in all directions even James' whores chipped in to help. She was throwing whatever she could, smashing priceless crystal and ruining works of art. Behind each mess she created was a servant quickly cleaning.

James, Gabe and the Scotts had left early this morning for their last business venture. Gabe was planning to leave Monday morning and James intended on concluding all business by Saturday. Both men were very pleased with the way the visit had turned out and had already scheduled anther business venture this time next year.

Today they had some racing stock they had to pick up and some brood mares which James would deliver in a few weeks. All went well and James wanted to celebrate with dinner and entertainment that evening but Lady Jennifer had the staff going in circles and the dinner would end up simple rather than elaborate as James had requested.

James was still upset about the soup burns he had acquired last week and was out for revenge. Mary and Abigail were on his lesson list. Even though James could not blame the two ladies for his burns, he was suspicious. James' physician announced to the staff that his burns would completely heel with no side effects. Abby felt a little disappointed with the announcement. She did not wish for his death but she was hoping he would be out of commission for a little while longer. It was a nice break from his lessons especially for his favorite whore who was walking around these days with a big smile.

Today was the first day since James' accident that he left the manor. Abby was hoping for a wonderful productive day but Lady Jennifer had put a stop to that by making each of the staff miserable from inside and outside the manor, even Wayne was complaining about her.

Olga, Mary and Abby were hoping she'd settle down by supper. James did not need any extra help with his lessons. Tonight would be extra stressful as it was. Both Mary and Abby had been ordered to serve again by James. The two women suspected James was out for revenge and they were one of his targets.

Abby was instructed to serve the stew and Mary was to bring in the rolls. As before Abby stood at the entrance of the hall waiting for permission to enter. She looked around to see who was present and spotted her bedmate, Gabriel in deep conversation with the villainess, Lady Jennifer. How she would like to dump this whole pot of stew on her head and there Gabe was smiling at her.

Abby didn't understand why she was so angry to see him talking to Lady Jennifer. He would be leaving in two days and Abby would never see or hear from him again. She kept telling herself to forget him but her heart would not listen. Then she heard her name called very loudly. James had been signaling her but she had been in such deep thought that she was not paying attention.

Both the women walked together up to the head table. They gave each other a "*be careful*" look. Poor Mary, as soon as she placed the rolls down on the table James stood ready to hit. "Those rolls are unacceptable," he bellowed and started to raise his walking stick. "The rolls are overcooked and way too large." Just then Abby came to her rescue. "They are supposed to be like that, sir. If you will kindly have a seat, I will show you."

Mary gave Abby a look. "What are ya doing?" she whispered. "Watch and play along," Abby whispered back.

Abby looked to Gabe hoping he would help one more time. Of course it might mean he would get to rub her bottom again. "May I serve you first, Laird?" Gabe nodded.

James took this opportunity to throw an insult, "I think you have been serving my guest very well already, I'm told and not with stew," then he snickered. Some of the other guests also joined in with his humor. "Maybe when the Laird is gone you will warm my bed and make me just as happy," James provoked.

"Would you like me to bring some soup with me James, sir?" Abby said with a smile and the Scots began to laugh, but James became angry. Ignoring him she reached for Gabe's trencher and took a hot roll from Mary's tray. "May I borrow your knife Laird, please?"

"I bet you'd like to use that on me, Abigail," James interrupted again.

"Well sir, a knife is just so messy. Honestly, sir, I prefer the element of surprise."

She took Gabe's dirk and cut the top off the roll. Mary watched pretending to know what she was doing. The rolls were way over done and when Abby opened it up the insides where very sparse. She scooped what was left of the inside out onto Gabe's trencher. "See, we now have a bowl." She used her ladle to fill the bread bowl full of stew and then sprinkled the bread from the inside over the top. Finally she leaned the top piece she cut of first against the soup bowl and handed it back to Gabe. "The roll must be large enough to accommodate the stew. But more important they must be cooked hard or the stew will seep through. You can dip the top piece in the stew and then break and eat the sides as you go."

Gabe noticed Abigail's hand shake a little when she handed it back to him. Then she turned to Lady Jennifer and said, "Lady Jennifer would you like a bread bowl or prefer stew in your trencher?" Before she could answer, Gabe said, "Jenny would love it in a bread bowl. She likes ta try new things, donna ya Jenny." Joseph took Gabe lead and said, "Mary pass me one of those rolls. I will try a bread bowl too." Abby smiled at Gabe and moved on to James. "I'm sure you will have a bread bowl, correct, James, sir?"James nodded and said, "Very clever woman. Where did you learn such a thing?"

Abby continued to serve moving as far from James as she could but still answered. "Where I come from it is a common practice to use bread for bowls. Soup works if it is thick but stew is much better. The more inexperienced cooks are given the rolls to bake. They are very good at over cooking them." Then she moved to the rest of the Scotts. James watched as Abby addressed each one by name without hesitation.

It angered him to see her smile at them and the way they interacted with her. He was in a foul mood all of a sudden even though the day had been most profitable for him. Gabe watched James watch Abby and tried to start a conversation with him, but it didn't work.

"Abby," James called. "You seem to be entertaining my guests very well with your stew bowls. I think, because you seem to be so good at entertaining, you will sing for us after dinner."

Abby tensed and gritted her teeth. Gabe noticed her reluctance. James continued speaking after seeing Gabe enjoying his stew in the bread bowl. "After you finish serving, you will sing for us all."

"Wonderful," Jennifer said in reply. "I love local talent."

Abby was not about to sing for anyone especially James and Jennifer. So she said sweetly, "Oh sir, I am not a singer. My voice is that of a bullfrog. I will surely hurt your ears and the ears of your guests. My mother always said I had just one note and that one was wrong." Then she smiled sweetly and finished serving the last bit of stew.

She picked up her kettle and turned to exit the hall. "Abigail," James called. "We are waiting for your serenade." James refused to let her leave the hall. He motioned for Wayne. Gabe was getting annoyed with James but said nothing. Abby however was ready for him.

She made a large bow and then a curtsied. Seeing an empty stool at the end of the table, she pulled it slowly across the floor, making as much noise as she could with it hoping she would annoy James a little more. She jumped up on the stool and again took a bow. She cleared her throat as loudly as she could, making the most disgusting noise possible. Then she raised her arms and started to sing as loud and off key as she could muster, carefully not forgetting a single word to her long drawn out song. James began to heckle her, laughing hysterically. The laird's face showed no emotion nor did the rest of the Scotts. The other guests sided with James calling insults and laughing. But this was Abby's plan. She began to laugh with them at herself agreeing with the insults and adding some of her own. She was not about to let James embarrass her or humiliate her. Instead she worked the room.

Gabe and the other Scotts watched as Abby brought the entire room to her side. They actually enjoyed her terrible frog voice singing and joined in to help her, mimicking her frog voice. Abby was sure by the time she finished, James would never ask her to sing again. Bowing gratefully to her new fans and waving her hands in appreciation, Abby jumped down from the stool and ran out of the hall, leaving a standing ovation and approving applause. As she was leaving she turned to take one more bow and noticed all the Scotts where standing and applauding as well.

The next day was Saturday and the Scotts were preparing to leave. James had ordered food for their long journey which Abby, Mary and Olga were making when James came into the kitchen. Mary was bent over cleaning up a spill when James slapped her across the back for her clumsiness with his walking stick.

Abby ran to her side and took the next blow just as Gabe came into the kitchen. James' hand rose again to hit Abby when Gabe asked to speak with James in private. He was forceful enough in his request that James lowered his hand and followed him out of the kitchen without another word.

Abby, Mary and Olga listened as James and Gabe argued from the study. Gabe was not giving in to his demand but the women could not hear what he was wanting. James tried to counter but Gabe would take no other offer. They went at it for hours and when they came out James went off alone and Gabe went for a long ride.

Abigail had had it. She could not take any more. The hit on her back was very painful and Mary was crying uncontrollably. She was also discouraged and upset with the Scots' departure on Monday. Abby knew that she had promised Gabe not to run but she could not take anymore.

The rats in her crate where getting braver. Abby was not able to keep them from biting her. Even Gabe could not keep her out of the crate all the time and what would happen after he left. She was exhausted, lonesome and death seemed so much better than the manor and she was losing Gabe. Abby decided to make her move. Tomorrow she would steal the keys from Wayne and leave.

Maybe with the confusion of the Scots' departure, Abby would have more of a chance. Tomorrow would be her first day of freedom or her last day on earth. Either way it was something she was looking forward to. Gabe did not come down to the kitchen that night and Abby spent another night in her crate.

Wayne came and got Abby before 4:30 a.m. By 7a.m. Abby noticed Wayne looking for a hiding place to take his normal morning nap. She gave herself a few words of encouragement to get her nerve up and slipped out of the kitchen without being noticed even by Mary or Olga. Quickly and as quietly as she could she combed the area just behind the manor to find a sleeping Wayne. She was in luck today. He had chosen the lilac bush just fifty feet away and his backside was facing out with the keys protruding just out of his back pocket.

After looking around, to see if the coast was clear, she lowered to her hands and knees and reached under the lilac bush for the keys in Wayne's pocket. With one quick pull she loosened the keys lifting them out of its tight hiding place. Wayne did not move, even when one of the keys got caught on the edge of his pocket. He just kept snoring and making weird hissing sounds. Abby rose to her feet, checked to make sure she was alone and hurried back to the kitchen after she slipped the keys into her waistband.

Olga and Mary were still in the pantry, when Abby reentered the kitchen. They did not notice that she had not been there. Abby felt bad deceiving her friends but she could not take the chance of involving them in her escape or it would mean their deaths as well. The next thing to do was to hide the keys. Wayne would search her first when he noticed his keys missing. Then he would spend the rest of the day trying to find them. She smiled to herself when she thought she'd be free of Wayne for a whole day and after tomorrow the rest of her life, however long that might be.

When the two ladies came out of the pantry Abby went in to hide the keys. In the back, on the top shelf where some wood was missing. Abby placed the keys just out of sight. Easy to get in a hurry and undetectable unless you knew it was there.

The bells sounded for chapel. Abby jumped when she heard them. She didn't realize it was so late. James had a service every Sunday morning regardless of who was in residence. It was mandatory for the staff, "*the sinners*," to attend each and every Sunday. There was no excuse for absence or tardiness. Severe punishment would be inflicted on any one who did not take Sunday service seriously.

James had designed and built his very own chapel. The floor was his pride and joy. It was a mosaic of the Garden of Eden all hand laid with various kinds of marble. The arched windows that lined the sides of the chapel where handmade stained glass, each different and each as beautiful. A fresco of heaven had been hand painted on the ceiling. The altar was made from white marble held on the backs of four white marble cherubs. A golden candelabrum hung over the altar with a large ornate cross suspended from it.

Every inch of the chapel was beautiful even the pulpit used by James' own personal priest in residence. James would not have any benches or chairs on his mosaic floor. Everyone needed to stand even his guests. His servants had to stand in a roped in area. Abby was surprised he had not put a sign in front of it that said "sinner's section." She hated Sundays. They were always the same with the long drawn out sermon directed at the roped in area occupants. Abby knew how many stones it took to make the angel Gabriel's head and how many candles were in the candelabra. She spent every minute in the chapel thinking of anything else. The Angel Gabriel was her favorite and today she said goodbye to him.

There was also one more debt she had to pay before she left and she started to look around the Chapel to find the people she needed to pay back. Standing in the rear, just on the other side of the entrance stood the Scotsmen, all standing together. Carefully she left the roped in area and went to the back of the chapel. When the pipe organ started playing, Abby hurried to the backs of the Scotts and wedged her way in between Joseph and Gabe.

Both men looked down in surprise to see her standing there. But she refused to leave and kept her eyes pinned on the backsides of the Scotts in front of her. The pipe organ started to play her favorite hymn, Amazing Grace. Abby started to sing just loud enough for the Scotts to hear her. The rest of the chapel also started to sing. One by one the Scotts stopped singing so they could listen to the angelic voice coming out of their midst. Eyebrows rose as each head turned to see who was singing so beautifully.

Abby could sing and sing well. Her voice was soothing and easy to listen to. If James had even suspected she could sing like this he would have never tried what he did in the hall the night before. Gabe and Joseph smiled down at her as she finished her song. Abby had sung just for them a true serenade to say thank you for all they had done and also a goodbye.

When the song ended, Abby slipped to the back of the chapel and then to the roped in area again. Later when the music played again, every Scotts head turned at the same time to see if Abby was singing but what they saw was Abby deep in thought not paying any attention to her surroundings. At that moment Gabe knew she was up to something.

When the service finally ended, Abby started back to the kitchen. As she started to leave the chapel she noticed Gabe talking to James and they shook hands. Whatever they had disagreed upon the day before had been obviously resolved. She hoped Gabe wouldn't be to upset with her escape, but she just had to leave and today was the day. Abby never broke her word and she would try to leave about the same time as they did but she could not wait another day. With any luck he would not hear of her escape at all.

Abby slowly walked down the long hallway from the chapel trying to work out the last minute details of her escape in her head. She had planned this for months and did not want to make any stupid mistakes. Her heart was light and she had her warm fuzzy feeling again. Everything would be fine and she was happy.

She took a deep breath and encouraged herself to get back to work. The kitchen was just in front of her but she didn't want to go in. She wanted to run now but she had to keep her head. Then coming up from behind her, were James and his walking stick. Abby quickly scooted into the kitchen where Wayne and two other guards were waiting for her. Mary and Olga were standing in the corner hugging each other and crying. Abby was confused. What was happening here?

Before she could talk, Wayne held up a new set of irons and said, "Hello Abigail, I have some very good news for ya. Ya have been sold. Now be real good and put on your new jewelry." Abby started to step back. "No," she screamed and turned to run but James was there and caught her before she could take two steps. She turned and kicked him in the groin and then started to run again as he doubled over in pain. "Get her," he ordered. "And put those chains on her."

Abby made it to the door but there were more guards waiting for her. She found herself held roughly by four guards, each holding on to one appendage. Abby put up a good fight but ended up with the shackles and hand irons on anyway and a few hard kicks in her belly. "You're lucky you got just kicked, bitch," James said through gritted teeth. "You should have received much worse but I promised your new owner I would not damage you."

Abby looked up through teary eyes and ask, "Who?"

"That is none of your concern. You have cost me dearly and I am most relieved to get rid of you. I feel I got the better end of the deal. If it was up to me, however, I would have killed you. Your days were numbered. This deal saved your sorry excuse of a life. And I will get those partners of yours with or without you. They will wish to be dead when I finish with them."

Then he turned to the guards and said, "Put her in her crate until her new owner claims her. I want two guards on her at all times. It will cost you your lives if she escapes."

Mary and Olga were still in the corner hugging each other. "Find her gown she came in. She leaves the same way she came. If you cannot find it than she will leave naked and you are not to feed her. She is not mine anymore. Let her new owner take care of her."

The four guards carried Abigail out to her crate. Wayne opened her door and she was thrown in. She rolled and hit the back of the crate hitting her head hard. When she woke the door was opening and her old blue dress flew in at her.

Wayne took the cuffs off long enough for her to slip her old dress on and as usual, he watched her strip down and then dress. Her head was aching and her stomach was sore from the kicks. Abby laid on the hay curled up crying nonstop. Finally, the other guard felt sorry for her. He bent down and tried to console her and when Wayne gave him a hard time about it, the other guard hit Wayne knocking him on his backside. "What has that sweet woman ever done to you to make you treat her like that?" The other guard said to Wayne. Then he turned and bent down looking into the crate at Abby. "Come now, little one, it is not that bad. I don't know who bought you but I know who ever did will treat you better than James. He is the worst."

Abby just kept crying but said, "thank you" through sniffs.

Then the guard tried to cheer her some more. "Don't worry, little one, you can have my supper tonight. I always liked your cookies you'd send to us guards late at night. I will really miss that." But there was no consoling her. She had lost her chance to escape.

The guard was true to his word. He did give his dinner to her but she could not eat much so she gave it back to him. Wayne would not stand anywhere near the guard, which actually made her smile. "Thank you for hitting Wayne for me," she whispered. "I've wanted to do that very same thing for a very long time."

"You are very welcome, little one. I'll do it again if I get a chance." Then he gave her the kindest grin she ever saw.

Just after dark, Abby had another visitor, William. "I came to say goodbye, lass."

"I will miss you, William," Abby said.

"Ya never asked me my last name."

"I never did ask you," Abby realized. "Please, tell me what it is?"

"Aye, McDough." Then he smiled.

"Did you know my grandfather?" Abby asked excited.

"Aye, I did. He was my cousin and so are ya. I am very proud ta have met ya."

"Me too, William," Abby answered reaching through the crate to touch his hand.

"I know who bought ya, but I canna tell ya. I want ya ta be real good ta your new owner. Ya will be treated very well." Then he kissed his fingers and touched Abby's hand that was sticking out through the crate and walked away.

Just after midnight she had her last two visitors, Olga and Mary. Abby tried to give Mary back her plaid but she wouldn't take it. The three friends said their goodbyes and Abby told them where she hid the keys. Mary decided to throw it back under the lilac, hopefully for James to find.

It was the longest night in her life. She tried to get some sleep but the rats had other ideas. James had not told her when she would be going. It could be days before the new owner came to get her. All she could do, was wait. Waiting was harder than any prison she'd been in so far.

CHAPTER 8
I AM TAKING YA HOME, LIKE IT OR NOT

Abby woke to the sound of male voices coming toward the barn. As they came closer she could tell from the Gaelic spoken that it was the Scotts. Both her guards stood up in front of her crate to prevent any more visitors. Abby's guards were given strict instructions not to allow any visitors. Letting her see her three friends was a very big risk for the guards. They could lose their jobs or be severely punished so when they stood their ground this morning, Abby wasn't upset with them. She was grateful for the few visitors that she was allowed to have and she didn't want the guards to get into trouble.

The Scotts, however never even looked in Abby's direction. They just came in talking and laughing amongst themselves, preparing for their departure. Their horses were saddled and one by one they left the barn. Abby tried to see her last glimpse of Gabe but could not see him. She heard his laugh, however. Slowly she scooted to the back of the crate and waited.

About twenty minutes later, James came walking into the barn. Abby sat up and watched as he came over to the crate. He bent down and looked at her through the slats. "I am going to miss seeing you in this crate, Abigail." Then he stood up and ordered the door opened. "It is time woman, your new owner wants you now. Come with me and do not give me any trouble."

Abby crawled out of her crate trying to conceal Mary's plaid which she wore under her skirts. The new shackles were much tighter than the other ones causing her ankles to bruise badly. The chain that tied her ankles together was also much shorter making difficult to walk. James was not very patient with Abby. He kept pushing her to make her go faster. As she reached the open barn door he pushed her hard making Abby lose her balance and tumble to the ground. The hand irons pinched as she landed and blood spilled out from her wrists.

The guard that had been so nice to her the night before reached down and helped her up. He then took her under the arm and helped her walk. The other guard came over next and took her other arm and lifted her off the ground that so she would not have to walk bare foot through the barnyard. James did not discourage their help and Abby whispered "Thank you," to them. With James pushing her from behind and the two guards helping her from her sides, she did not pay attention to who was standing in front of her waiting to take her away. Before she knew it, she was set down in the midst of the Scots and their horses. She became a little nervous to be that close to horses while she was barefoot and tried to step back, but the two guards held on to her arms.

No one said anything. Abby just kept looking for the stranger who was taking her away. She really did not want the Scotts to see her in her filthy ripped gown. She was really hoping they would have left before she was taken away. It was then she realized her gown wasn't dirty. Someone had bleached it and removed all the stains. It was completely clean just a little faded and all the rips and tears mended. She looked down to see a patch here and there in white linen. Abby wondered who had done this for her and where did they get the fabric. James would not approve of such a thing.

In the grassy area next to the kitchen stood her three friends, Mary, Olga and William, waving. She had to look twice at them. Olga's apron was at least eight inches shorter than Mary's and William's shirt was out of his kilt, the shirt tail had been cut off. Abby looked down at her gown again and smiled. They had cut some of their clothes to mend her gown. Looking over at them she mouthed, "thank you."

"Are you ready to take her?" James asked from behind Abby.

Then Gabe walked around a little mare that he had been adjusting her saddle and said, "Aye."

Abby gasped, anger filled her from top to bottom. “You?” She shouted at Gabe. But he did not answer. He just finished fixing the little mare’s saddle.

“Take those irons of her now,” Gabe ordered.

“Are you sure Gabe? She will run,” James said as he motioned to Wayne to open the cuffs.

“That is none of your concern James, now is it?” Gabe answered still not looking at Abigail.

When the irons were released Gabe said, “Thank ya James for our accommodations and stay. I will see ya in a month?” Then he shook James hand. He turned and grabbed Abby’s arm and started to lead her over to the little mare. Abby tried to fight her way free. “No Gabe No, Please NO!” She shouted.

Gabe only held onto her arm and pulled her over to her new mount. She skidded her bare feet in the dirt trying to stop him from pulling her. He got tired of her tantrum and picked her up and plopped her down hard on her horse. “Promise me ya won’t run Abigail,” Gabe demanded as he adjusted her stirrups noticing her bare feet and the bruising from the shackles. He also noticed the plaid she had hidden under her skirts but said nothing.

“I will not promise anything. Now let me go,” Abby snorted.

“Oh, is that the way ya want it. Alright than, listen real well. From the moment I bought ya. Ya became a member of my clan. I will not treat ya any different then I would anyone else. My word is law. Break my law and I will punish ya. Don’t make me do that, Abby. I guarantee ya will not like it.” Gabe handed her the reins then said, “If ya run, I will track ya down and I will not stop until I have found ya. If I have to drag ya back kicking and screaming I will. Ya are mine and I will never let ya go. So the sooner ya get that through ya head the better it will be for all of us.”

“You should not have interfered,” she snapped angrily at him.

“Abigail, I guess I dinna make myself clear enough. If ya run I will find ya and when I do I will lift ya skirts and strap ya naked back side until ya canna sit down for days. Now, I will not tell ya again. Ya will ride behind me. There will be no complaining and no whining, none, and you will stay up with us. Do not slow us down or I will throw ya over my horse's rump with ya ass in the air and ya head and feet danglin' at his sides." He turned and with one leap mounted Samson and motioned to the Scotts to ride. James watched as they disappeared from view over the hill side, Abby right on Gabe's tail.

Abby tried not to cry but the hurt was too much. She had lost again. Today she was going to be free or die trying. Instead she was in a new prison with a new owner and drifting farther from home. The chance of her ever returning was getting slimmer with every minute that passed. Damn Gabriel, he should have not interfered. Damn her partners and the debt they put on her shoulders. Damn James, England and now Scotland and damn that box her grandfather gave her. It is what started this mess to begin with. The secrets it contained caused the life her grandfather had to live and now it was running hers.

She had lied to Gabe when she said she had no idea what was in that box. She knew very well. Her grandfather had been very careful and had shown her all of its contents and explained the secrets it contained. He made her promise to do three things and she would be safe for the rest of her life.

Coming across the ocean was the first promise but the way things were going, she would never be able to complete the other two. Her time was quickly running out. It would only be a matter of time before the treasure seekers would be hunting her, which is one of the reasons she did not want Gabe's interference.

Without him knowing it, keeping Abby was putting himself and his clan in great danger. She was going to have to run. She had no choice. The risk was too great if she stayed. Oh how she wanted to stay. Gabe had stolen her heart that day in the special cottage despite her efforts to stop it but she could never allow herself love like she wanted.

After talking to Gabe that day she realized that she was already being hunted. Mr. Pinkerton must know what was in her box and although he wasn't going to pursue her, she was sure he'd hire someone to. The Shaws and the partners all wanted her to go to England and pushed her to make a quick decision. But it backfired on them.

Changing her vessel's name did not fool the authorities at all. Abby was sure that her partners and the Shaws were having her followed.

In a very odd way, the debt of the partners actually saved her life for a while. Prison was the only place where they could not get to her. It also prevented Abby from leading them to the one thing they wanted—the secret which was in that box. She was sure they would get to her soon and force her to tell them the whereabouts of the box and reveal the remaining piece of the puzzle. Abby feared for her life, her children's life and the McKenzie clan, especially Gabe.

If Abby had not been arrested the day she arrived in London, she was sure that they would have followed her and taken what they wanted and eventually kill her. And all that her grandfather and his ancestors before him, had tried to preserve would be lost all because of fortune hunters.

Gabe rode for hours, never stopping and never slowing. To Abby's surprise, her little mare kept right up and never slowed. Hour after hour they rode. Conversation was minimum and only between the men and in Gaelic. Abby rode between Simon and Joseph just behind Gabe. By the time late afternoon came, Abby was just about done. She had not had a bite to eat or drink for twenty-four hours and she hurt from one end to the other. Her feet were freezing from her bare skin resting on the metal stirrups. Abby was hungry, tired, in pain, sore and cold. If she was allowed to complain, she certainly had enough to complain about.

Joseph kept careful watch on Abby as they rode. He noticed her shifting in the saddle but only thought it normal from the long hard ride. Then her flapping stirrups caught his attention. Her feet were missing from her stirrups; in fact her feet were missing all together. He could see her skirts flipping from side to side but he could not see any sign of her feet or legs.

In Gallic he called to Gabe to stop a moment and check on Abigail. When they stopped, Gabe turned Samson around and looked right at Abby disgustedly. Joseph pointed to the empty stirrups. Gabe's eyebrows rose and a look of complete shock went across his face. Abby just looked straight ahead not acknowledging Gabe in anyway, biting her lips together trying to contain her anger. "Abigail, where are your feet?" Gabe asked trying to stay as calm as he could. Abby just kept looking forward, gritting her teeth with no intention of answering him. Gabe cleared his throat and asked again. "Abigail?"

Through clenched teeth she said, "At the end of my legs?"

Joseph turned his head to hide his smile and the other men did as well. Gabe had his hands full with this woman and his men loved to see him surprised by her defiance.

Gabe said nothing but nudged his stallion forward. "Why are ya riding like that, lass?"

"Because, I am not allowed to complain or whine," Abby sputtered.

Gabe was trying to have a little patience with her so he said, "Alright, would ya mind telling me why ya are riding like that? Ya have my permission ta complain."

Abby was fuming by now and physically miserable so she took him up on his offer. "There is not one part of my body that is not hurt, hungry, wet or cold. Sitting on my feet is giving me some comfort to one part of my body and if you do not give me a break real soon, I swear I am going to burst." The men had all they could do to contain their laughter. Gabe gave them a dirty look and said something to them in Gaelic that Abby did not understand.

Abby sat looking straight ahead and refused to look at Gabe. He dismounted to help her get down but she would not let him touch her. Slowly she straightened out her legs and dismounted on her own, mumbling to herself. As she started off to the woods to attend her well needed needs, Gabe called, "Donna be long or I'll come and get ya."

To his surprise he heard her say just loud enough for him to hear her, "I'll take as long as I Damn well want to."

The men were out of control with laughter. They started teasing Gabe with questions like "Can we tend our needs before we burst too, Laird?" and "I'm going ta take my damn time too." It was then that Gabe realized that he had pushed them a little too hard. Even his men let him know this it in a nice way. He had been so focused on the events of the day and Abby's reluctance that he had overlooked the needs of his men and Abigail. He and his men had broken their fast but he was sure that James did not feed her. A little guilt came over him about her treatment. He even suspected that she had not eaten since the early the day before.

Gabe watched Abby return from the woods, hobbling and still mumbling to herself. She walked past the other men and mounted her horse without Gabe's help. Before she could cross her feet under her bottom again, Gabe had gone to his saddle bag and took out a clean pair of wool socks and a biscuit that Mary and Olga had given him as well as a clean shirt.

"Give me ya foot, lass," Gabe ordered gently and he slid a sock over her tiny foot. He smiled to see the heel of the socks end half way up her leg and the rest, way over her knee. Walking around to the other side he slid the other sock on. Then he gave her his shirt. "Put this on, it will help."

Abby took it and did not complain but she still looked miserable. Next he handed her the biscuit. In a soft voice she said, "thank you." Then she added out of the blue, "I didn't steal it."

Gabe looked up at her confused, "what?"

"The plaid under my skirt, I didn't steal it."

"It is no concern of mine," Gabe answered coldly.

"Well it is a concern of mine and I want you to know I did not steal it. Mary gave it to me as a gift. I had to hide it from James," Abby explained.

"I told ya, I donna care," Gabe answered sharply.

"Well I do care," Abby said not letting this topic go.

"Why?" Gabe growled back.

"I don't want you to think badly of me that's all," she said softly.

"I donna think bad of ya lass. Now, eat ya biscuit. We need ta keep moving if we are gonna get ta the inn by dark."

Abby started to curl her feet up under her again when Gabe ordered, "Keep those tiny feet of yours in those stirrups or I will tie them in." Then he mounted and they took off as fast and as hard as before.

It was a few more hours of hard travel before they reached the inn. He was to meet someone there tonight and he did not want to miss him. Abby was so tired by the time they reached the inn that she went straight to her room then to bed and fell asleep.

The little room she was given was between Gabe's room and Joseph's, allowing them to keep an eye on her. It had a small bed just big enough for her with a clean warm quilt. A wash basin stood on a small table and a chamber pot was just under her bed. She washed and undressed quickly then crawled into the bed not even tending to the fire. Before her head hit the pillow she was asleep. When Gabe came up to get her for dinner, he found her fast asleep and did not have the heart to wake her. Instead he tended her fire and kissed her cheek then left Abby alone to sleep.

In the morning Gabe had to wake her three times before she would get out of bed. The last time he had to threaten to douse her with water. When she finally stumbled down to break her fast the men were already saddled and ready to go. As she walked past Joseph and his honey colored mount she said, “Your horse has a loose nail and it is digging into his frog. He wants you to fix it for him.” Then she kept walking not noticing the surprised look on Joseph’s face.

Then she started to walk past Samson to her mount and he bolted out of Gabe’s grip lunging at Abby. Gabe let out a yell but Abby never flinched and let the lose stallion come right up to her. She gently held out her hand and Samson put his soft nose into it tickling her. The next thing she did was reach up and tightened the side strap holding the bit by one notch but not the other side. She pulled down on the bridle centering it in Samson’s mouth. The nose piece, she loosened next. She refastened it around the outside of the side straps rather than under them like Gabe had. “What are ya doing ta my horse Abigail? I donna like anyone fooling with him,” Gabe said in a scolding voice.

“Your horse is cutting molars and the bit is hitting the sensitive area. Haven’t you noticed him throwing his head each time you tried to turn him?”

Gabe had to admit she was right but he had to know. “How did ya know that, Abby?”

Abby looked surprised Gabe would ask her such a question and answered, “he told me.”

Both Gabe and Joseph were having a hard time believing her explanation until she started to walk to her own mount. Samson began to whinny at her. Abby stopped and said, “You are very welcome Samson.” It was as if they were talking to each other.

“Abigail, come back here,” Gabe ordered. “What did ya do ta my bridle?”

Abby went over to show Gabe what she did but before she could explain, Samson bent his head down to her and nuzzled her cheek.

Abby giggled from the soft nose rubbing her cheek and then rubbed Samson's big neck, "Oh, you big softy you." Then she showed Gabe what she had done. "The nose piece on the outside of the side straps will help keep the bit from hitting those sensitive molars." Before Gabe could say anything, Joseph called, "He does have a lose nail. I dinna notice it when I checked his hoof. The nail slid in when his hoof was raised. Thank ya Lass. Ya save my horse from going lame. I suppose he told ya, right?" Abby just gave him a smile, shrugged her shoulders and then went to mount her own mare.

"The next two nights we are spending outside. Make sure ya keep up, lass," Gabe said when Abby finally mounted her mare. Abby just nodded and then yawned, still having trouble waking up. The bed felt so good last night and it was warm which made sleep easy for once. Her belly was full but her backside and legs were very sore from the ride the day before.

Scotland was so beautiful everywhere and Abby tried to keep her mind on the landscape and not her hurting muscles. When she thought they were not paying attention, Abby would curl her cold feet up and under her bottom but not for too long.

When she was a little girl, she would ride sitting on her feet. It would make her father angry. He would punish her by forbidding her to ride for a whole week when he caught her. So she would wait until she was far from the farm and then ride like she wanted. She smiled to herself when she remembered how she rode as a child and she was still doing it.

"Don't think for one moment, lass that I donna know how ya are riding behind me," Gabe said as they rounded a large knoll.

Abby dropped her feet down and picked up her stirrups and did not do it again. Gabe smiled to himself. Her behavior was so defiant but he was enjoying his new challenge.

Like the previous day, the group road non-stop for the whole day, never stopping or slowing. Just before sundown, Gabe finally stopped and gave the order to make camp. Each man worked to get ready for the cold night to come. Each had a job and went about doing it. Abby offered to help but no one would allow her to interfere with their duties, so she walked a little and stretched her legs.

She had every intention of leaving and she needed to test her boundaries. Each time she tended her needs she would take a little longer. She was farther from England, but she could still get a ship from Scotland and maybe it would not be so dangerous.

Abby kept trying to get her hopes up and figure out her next move but these Scotts were smart and even though she was not in irons they knew exactly where she was and what she was up to. Her only chance was to catch them off guard, then she could slip away unnoticed, but for now she would just keep trying different little things to see what they would let her get away with.

This time she had stayed in the woods a little too long as far as Gabe was concerned. When she turned to return, he was standing not three feet in front of her. Without saying a word he grabbed her by her arm and pulled her back to the camp. She thought he was just going to bring her to the fire, but instead he walked right past the fire and over to the bed that was made for her with pine boughs. A plaid had been stretched over the top of the boughs and another one draped over tied branches making a wall to protect her from the wind and rain.

"Good night lass," Gabe said then started to walk away.

"Now?" Abby asked surprised.

"Break my rules and ya will be punished. Tonight ya will not have ya supper. Ride with ya feet under ya ass tomorrow and take too long in the woods and ya will not eat for one whole day." Then he turned and walked to have his supper. Abby crawled into her bed with her stomach growling in protest. Truth was she was very hungry. She lay down with her back facing the fire and listened to the men as they talked to each other while they ate. It wasn't too long before her eyes closed and sleep over took her.

.....She could hear the wolves. They were all around. She could feel their breath from behind. She needed to run, she needed to find help, safety, but the branches were everywhere pulling on her skirts keeping her from getting to her full speed. Howls came from the front now, turning to the left she sees a large tree with low branches, running now, running as fast as she could, they were right behind her and to the side. They were everywhere and the tree was just a few feet away. Jumping, she grabbed the first branch and swung her feet up onto the

next branch. Something was pulling on her skirt. She could hear as wolf growling pulling on her. She screamed and pulled her body up on the branch as hard as she could but the wolf would not let go. She could hear the skirts ripping as she pulled her body up into the tree higher. The wolves where circling and lunging at her, their white teeth inches from her face, screaming she fought with her hands pushing the black wolf away from her skirts. Pulling on the higher branches she was getting out of reach but they continued to jump at her and missing by inches. Stop she screamed let me go. They kept circling and growling, than their attention shifted to male voices coming closer. The pack moved out of sight but she could still see them from her tree. Climbing higher, she needed to get away, sensing danger she feared these men more than the wolves. Darkness had come but the moon lit the grassy area just under her. Looking down she could see the men. She could hear the sounds of flesh hitting flesh, the moan of pain, and the sound of fabric ripping and the sight of male naked legs lying on the ground motionless. The wolves were returning, then he saw her. He is coming. He was grabbing her, stop, let me go…………………

Blood curdling screaming came from Abby's bed. All the men jumped from their slumber. They grabbed their swords and ran to her aid, expecting to find an animal attacking her, but what they found was Abby in the arms of Gabe still sleeping screaming at the top of her lungs.

"What is wrong with her?" Joseph asked Gabe as he watched Gabe try to stop her from thrashing. "She is dreaming," Gabe answered. "Help me hold her down so she doesn't hurt herself." The men watched as Simon, Joseph and Gabe held on to her. She was trashing so hard they had all they could do to hold her down without harming her. "Is this because ya sent her to bed without her supper?" Simon asked trying to avoid being kicked.

"Nay, Wayne told me she had many dreams like this that was why he was always so tired. She'd keep him up all night. He complained about it all the time," Gabe answered keeping his eyes directed on Abby. He watched as she began to cry still fighting and screaming. "She is almost through it," Gabe said. "Wayne said she'd start to cry and it would wake her up."

Abby woke to find three Scotts holding her down and the rest watching her in disbelief. She jumped at the sight of all of them watching her.

"Wake up lass," Gabe said softly in her ear. Abby turned and looked at Gabe through tear filled eyes.

"I'm awake. Let me up," Abby demanded.

The three men let her go and she jumped up and backed away from them.

"Abby, ya are safe lass. It was only a dream," Gabe said holding his big hand out for her to take it. Abby was still suffering from the effects of the nightmare and wiped her eyes and said, "I need to be by myself right now. I am sorry you had to see that. It is not my fault. I'm fine now. Sorry I woke you all." She turned and ran into the woods, her skirts flaring out as she went.

When she reached the shelter of the trees she dropped down to her knees and cried uncontrollably into her hands. Shaking, she kept going through the dream in her mind. Then she started to chant softly like Old Joe had taught her and rocked back and forth. The Indian way was to chant which always calmed her. That was the worse dream yet and the actual event was coming soon. She could never see who was on the ground and she feared it was one of the Scotts.

A big hand reached down and gently touched her shoulder. Abby jumped and turned to see Gabe. "Did I take too long again?" She asked through tears. "I just can't go back yet, I am still too upset." Gabe did not answer her but bent down and picked her up from the ground. He carried her like a baby in his big arms. "Shhh," he whispered. "It's all right." Abby turned her head into his chest and cried some more. Gabe did not ask what the dream was this time, but took her back to her tent. He laid her down next to Joseph who was already lying on her bed. Then Gabe laid down on her the other side. He covered her with his plaid. The two men moved closer sandwiching her gently between them. Gabe put his arm around her and just kept telling her she was fine and to go back to sleep. The warmth of the two men and the feeling of safety finally allowed her to go back to a restful, sound, uneventful sleep.

When she woke in the morning, the camp had been completely broken down. The horses all saddled and the fire put out. They had let her sleep as long as they could before waking her. The man they called Cookie, handed her a biscuit and a hot cup of herbal tea. "What is this," she asked after she took the first sip.

"My mother would give this same tea ta me when I was just a lad after I had a bad night. It used ta help me. I thought it might help ya too," Cookie answered.

"Thank you," Abby said with a slight smile. "Did you have a lot of bad nights?"

"Aye, but that was after my father died. I must say they were not as bad as what I saw last night."

Abby just lowered her head. She really did not want to discuss last night at all. Instead she concentrated on getting away. Today she would make one more extended stop in the woods. She was hoping they were feeling bad for her and would allow her more time. The more time she could get alone, the more of a lead she'd take when she ran. Hopefully it would be enough to get free of the Scotts.

The day was colder and much windier than any day so far. The threat of rain was in the air. So when Abby asked to stop the Scots were not happy. They were even less happy when she took a long time coming back. If she could just get them use to her long exits, they would not realize she was gone. It was such a slim chance but one that she was planning to take.

Because of the weather, Gabe decided to make camp early. Abby knew if she was too long again tonight it would mean a missed supper and no food the next day, but she had to keep this behavior up. As she entered the woods she stumbled on some red raspberry bushes ready to pick. What a great idea she thought, she would have a great excuse for taking so long and they would not be to upset with her. It was so important that they did not suspect anything was wrong. That would be her only ally for escape. It was Abby's intention to get the men to think she was in the woods taking her time but she would be long gone. She was hoping the next time she was taking too long they would just think she was picking berries or something like that and not come to look for her until it was too late.

So she picked berries and ate as many as she picked so it wouldn't hurt so much if Gabe made her miss dinner again. She filled her plaid and then decided she needed a well deserved bath. Looking around, there was no sign of the Scots. She quickly undressed and jumped in. The water was freezing she wanted to scream out but she did not want to attract attention this soon. When she finished her bath, without soap, she came out of the water and dressed, happy that they still had not come to look for her. The sun had just broken through the clouds spilling warmth on the grassy area near the water. So, Abby decided, seeing how she was not being missed yet, she'd lie down and enjoy the sun, but it was not long before she fell asleep unaware of the time.

She woke feeling cold. It was as if the sun had gone down behind the trees. When she opened her eyes, the sun was still out. It was just behind thirteen angry Scots watching her sleep. As she looked up at them trying to act as innocent as she could she looked into scowling faces, folded arms and the silent treatment.

Trying to make it better, she showed them the berries she'd picked for them but that didn't work either. She received her answer she was looking for. She wanted to know just how long she could stay out of sight before they would come after her and the answer was not this long again. She was going to have to figure another way to leave. This was definitely not working and she was about to pay the price of her insolence.

Gabe motioned to his men and Abby felt two sets of hands reach down and pull her to her feet. Without saying a word they escorted her back to the campsite. Abby thought for sure she would be taken to her bed area, but they took her over to Gabe's saddle bags where Gabe was already waiting. He bent over and pulled out a length of rope, measuring about ten feet. Abby stood facing Gabe while the two Scots held onto her forearms. Gabe tied the rope snugly around her waist, not explaining what he was up too.

When he was sure the rope was secure, he dismissed the men with a quick nod. Abby just waited for his next move. "Come with me," he ordered, holding on the other end of the rope giving her a little tug as he walked away from her. She felt like a dog on a leash. Abby could not understand what he was doing but it was not long before she found out. He stopped by a nearby bush and raised his kilt and started to relieve himself right in front of her. She was so appalled she turned her head. She couldn't believe he would do such a thing in front of her like this. She tried to walk away but he held tight to the end of the rope.

It wasn't long before she understood just what he was up to and she did not like it in the least. "Your turn, lass, do ya want me to help ya hold up ya skirts?" Gabe said after he finished his need.

Abby's mouth dropped open. She was not about to relieve herself in front of him like he just did in front of her. "I am not about to do such a thing in your presence," Abby blurted out.

"Suit yourself, but I am not coming back to the woods until morning and if ya have to tend your needs before then, well ya will relieve yourself in front of the men."

"I will do no such thing. You will have to let me go by myself."

"Nay, lass. Ya cannot be trusted by ya self. We already tried that, remember. I am not about ta leave ya too long alone so ya can run. I am not stupid. I know just what ya were trying ta do."

"If I promise not to take too long from now on can I have a little privacy?" Abby asked half expecting the answer.

"NO and donna ask again. Now relieve ya self or I am going back ta camp dragging ya behind me," Gabe ordered.

"Fine," Abby said. "Could you at least turn around?"

"I will watch ya or hear ya and if ya donna wants me to watch ya than I need ta hear ya because I am not dropping this rope," Gabe said raising his eyebrows as if in a chess game. "What is ya decision?"

"You want to listen to me urinate?" Abby asked.

"No, I want ya to sing while ya urinate." Gabe watched Abby's face drop in complete surprise. "Take ya pick, but ya best get on with it because I am leaving in two minutes, ready or not."

Back at camp the men stopped what they were doing to hear "Amazing Grace" coming out of the woods. They had to smile at each other. Gabe was making progress. A few minutes later he returned pulling Abby at the end of the rope.

Through the rest of the night, they took turns holding Abby's rope. She was not allowed to wonder any farther than the length of the rope. As she suspected, she was not allowed dinner. So she sat and watched them eat, her stomach growling loudly. Finally she asked to go to bed. "Ya may sleep anywhere your rope can reach," Gabe said with a sickening smile across his face. That was when she noticed the men had not made her a bed area tonight. Gabe reached over and grabbed a plaid and tossed it to her.

Abby laid down right where she was sitting and covered herself with the plaid then pulled the rest of it over her head. She reached down under her skirts and pulled the plaid out that Mary had given her. Sitting up she laid the plaid out on the ground Gabe had given her and used Mary's to cover up with. "That plaid," Gabriel asked, "where did Mary get it?"

"She told me it was her family's colors. I think she called them her clan. Why?"Abby asked from under the plaid.

"I was just wondering," Gabe answered giving his men an approving look. They had all recognized that plaid. It was the colors of the Murray clan which bordered on the McKenzie land. Gabe and the Murray laird were very good friends and Gabe knew that Laird Murray had been looking for his daughter for years. Gabe thought he'd recognized her but wasn't sure. Mary was a lot older and much thinner than he'd remembered.

His plan was to tell Murray of his find and let Murray deal with James. But for now, Abby was his main concern. How was he to get her for his own? He thought she was beautiful even for her age. She was a bit voluptuous but for some reason, Gabe found that pleasing. He loved her wit and sense of humor and her forwardness. He wanted to experience her laughter as well as her temper. She was so different from any woman he'd ever known. Abby was the first woman since his wife's death that truly interested him. But for now he would have to act indifferent for a while to see how she'd react to his six children, the highlands and the rest of his clan. If she'd do half as well as he'd suspected she'd be his by Christmas.

She woke the next morning up tight against Gabe's back. Somehow in the night she had rolled next to him. He was always so warm and it was cold, but still she should never have done that. She rolled over to get a little distance between them and then felt a big hand come over her stomach and pull her close to him again. "Good morning, lass," Gabe said while his eyes were still shut. "Ready for a trip ta the woods?" At that moment, Abby was brought back to reality. She was still on a leash and Gabe held the end. He stood up and tugged on her rope. "Come lass it is time ta take our leave."

Abby wondered what he would do if she refused to get up, so she rolled over and closed her eyes. Gabe could not believe what a little brat she could be. So he decided to treat her like one. "Abigail, I will count ta three. If ya are still on your back by then I will put ya over my shoulder and carry ya ta the woods and not just watch but I will hear ya sing while I hold ya skirts up. One.....two.......Three," Abby had almost made it but not quite. She found herself dangling over his shoulder while he walked to the woods. The men at camp smiled at each other as they heard the morning rendition of a shaky Amazing Grace coming from the woods.

The laird did not teach his lessons like James but he got his point across. By the third day she was getting very annoyed with her leash and the silent treatment.

"How long are you going to keep me on this leash?" she asked Gabriel.

"As long as I want ta," he answered not looking at her.

"I didn't run I was asleep," she sputtered.

"Really?" Gabe answered in disbelief. Abby's temper was rising by the second.

"If I wanted to, I would have been far away by now." Then she added when he did not comment, "I can walk away from you whenever I please and all you will be able to do is watch."

Gabe raised his eyebrows with the expression of "*don't even try*" written across his face.

"Alright lass," he said through gritted teeth. "Ya just do that if ya can and I will be pleasantly surprised." Then he cleared his throat and lowered his voice and his eyebrows and said, "but if ya do, I will find ya and ya will be punished. Ya will not like being strapped lass. I guarantee your bum will hurt for at least two weeks and ya will not sit for at least one and it will be a whole month before the bruising goes away."

Abby's eyes opened wide. She glared directly into his eyes and said, "Sounds like a challenge to me."

"Take it anyway you want lass," he said. "Just remember, ya will be the loser. Donna tempt fate. Ya will not like what ya get."

CHAPTER 9

The Fox Is On The Run

The next day they reached the town Gabe was planning to visit. He had to finish a transaction with a fellow laird here. They had plans to stay two days if all went well. In the middle of was an inn that Gabe would inhabit when he was in town. It was always clean and the food was very tasty and plentiful. The men needed a good meal in their bellies for they would be on the road for a few more days until they reached the next town. The innkeeper was given strict rules when it came to Abby. One was the location of her room. It was to be facing the outside market place with Simon in the left side room next to her and Joseph in the right side room. Gabe would be directly across the hall.

Abby felt like a "*Fox*" in a cage. Her room was lovely, clean and the bed soft and comfortable. It had a small fire in the corner and a wash basin on the table in front of the window. She was looking forward to spending a night in a bed rather than at the end of a rope sleeping on the cold ground. Abby was hoping she would be taken off her leash soon or at least while they were in the town.

She had been given her own room, so she thought this to be a good sign. But she was wrong. Gabe had no intention of letting her off the leash even to sleep. "Ya know the rule lass," Gabe said when she mentioned sleeping in her own room tonight. "Ya may sleep anywhere in the length of the rope."

"But it won't reach the room across the hall from you. Didn't you rent that room for me?" Abby asked hoping he would give a little just this time.

"I rented the room and ya may use it if the rope goes that far. Ya will not be out of my sight, especially in this town. And I will not let ya off your leash for one moment."

That did it, Abby had had it. She was leaving and leaving today. She sat in her room looking out the window at the marketplace. Simon sat in the chair holding her leash. Her answer was out there and she had to find it. All she needed was a way to distract them just long enough for her to leave unnoticed.

Abby's heart pumped fast as she skimmed the market place from her window. She had just a few minutes before Gabe was taking her down the street on her leash with Simon and Joseph. Before they left the inn she would know what she was going to do. "Abigail, Simon," Gabe called from the bottom of the stairs, "It is time to go." Simon gave Abby a playful tug on her rope. "Ya heard him, lass."

"Yes, I heard him. I just wanted to say that I will miss everyone and thank you for everything," Abby said waiting for his questions.

"Planning on going somewhere?" Simon asked with raised brows.

"I told you I would let you know when I was going and I have decided it will be today."

"Are we supposed ta watch ya leave?" He asked sarcastically.

"You can if you want," Abby said as she started out of the room.

By the time they reached the bottom of the stairs, Simon was fuming. "Gabe, did ya know that Abby, here, is leaving today and we are ta watch her walk away?"

Gabe looked at Abigail waiting for her explanation. Abby just picked her chin up and said, "Are you three coming, I cannot wait all day to leave." She started to walk out of the inn but Gabe took hold of her leash and gave it a good tug.

"You are acting like a child, Gabe," Abby said not turning around to look at him.

"I told you I would give you notice of my leaving and I am sick of being on this leash. Are you going to take it off?" She asked with hands on her hips.

"NO," Gabe said with a big scowl across his face and giving her a very warning look.

"Then I just cannot stay another day," Abby sputtered.

Gabe stood up and said "Ya first, lass. I donna want ta be disappointed."

"I aim to please," Abby said and flounced out of the inn dressed in her faded blue gown with patches here and there. She was in her bare feet, tied at the waist by a rope held by Gabe walking from behind. It was the most embarrassing moment of her life. Even worse than riding through the streets of England in the prison cart dodging spoiled vegetables. Just breathe, she told herself. You can do this. It will work.

The foursome started down the street of the market place which was lined with every kind of vendor imaginable. Gabe walked directly behind Abby with an extra strong hold on the end of the leash with Simon to his left and Joseph to his right. They stopped at a booth here and there as they walked down the row. Abby tried not to look. She didn't have any funds so looking at beautiful fabrics and shoes would only make her feel worse. Instead she watched a couple just down the row on the left.

A very round woman and what looked like her husband were selling very large fish a few tables down the way. From where Abby stood she could not tell just what kind of fish they were handling. Gabe was a large man but this man was at least a head taller than him with fists the size of cannon balls. They had a table next to the crowded walkway and a flat bed wagon parked just behind the table filled with fish. As they sold a fish, the man would toss another one to the ground from the top of the wagon. His round wife would bend over with her backside protruding out into the walkway, pickup the fish and flop it on the table.

As Abby watched the couple work, she noticed the woman hit a passer-by from time to time with her rump as she bent over. The couple never stopped working. He would toss and she picked it up. As Abby watched the couple, Joseph leaned down and whispered, "Simon tells me ya are leaving today. I bet my horse's honey colored tail that ya won't make it fifty feet."

Abby looked up at Joseph and said, "I will take that bet sir."

Then Gabe gave her a little push toward the fish selling couple. "Keep walking lass," he ordered forcefully.

"I just want you to know that your rescuing me from James is well appreciated and I promise I will do my best to pay you back," Abby said to Gabe while walking in front of him.

"Just remember my promise, lass. I will punish ya if ya run."

The three men knew she was up to something but they were sure she would not be able to get too far so they were not too worried. Still they were watching her like hawks.

Timing was everything. She had to get to the fish couple at the exact right time or it would not work. Carefully Abby watched the couple, adjusting her timing as she walked so she could arrive next to the fish woman when she bent over.

The man in the wagon tossed the fish to the ground. The round wife bent over to pick the fish up at the exact moment Abby reached her. Abigail reached out and grabbed the fish woman's bottom and gave her the hardest pinch she could squeeze and then continued walking. The fish woman let out a loud yell and screamed in Gaelic as she stood holding the large fish to look into the face of her assailant.

As she was told, Abby kept walking so when the fish woman turned around she was facing Gabriel not Abby. She angrily swung the fish she was holding hitting the unsuspecting Gabe across the head assuming he was her assailant. The man in the wagon jumped down to protect his wife. Swinging his cannon ball size fist, he hit Gabe square in the chin right after being hit with the fish. Both Simon and Joseph came to the aid of their Laird. None of the men had any idea why this couple, were attacking them. They were forced to protect themselves and they did.

A full blown brawl broke out in the middle of the street, knocking over tables and involving innocent bystanders. Gabe, Simon, Joseph and the fish man were surrounded by angry town's people trying to break up the fight. Abby kept giving her leash little tugs until she had the entire rope wound up in her hand. She was free to go.

Turning away from the brawl, Abigail walked away, down the street and turned the corner looking back to see her Scotts and the fish man being carried up to the Magistrate. It was against the law to fight in a public place resulting in a night in the stockades. As Abby had promised, she would leave and they would not be able to do a thing about it.

Abby had earned her freedom but she could not get far barefoot or in her faded patched gown. As she turned the corner she found a small cobbler's shop. When she opened the door a bell rang to announce her entrance. She wasn't surprised at the expression on the shop woman's face when she laid eyes on Abigail.

Reaching into the waistband of her skirt, Abby pulled the only thing of value she still owned, a set of diamond earrings she had hidden there when she was in the wagon going to prison. When she had been arrested in England she had sense enough to slip them off her ears and hide them in the waist band of her gown. She was not about to lose her grandmother's earrings to the debtor's prison or James and she was not about to lose them now but they would give her something to bargain with.

She needed to shop. She needed shoes, socks, and a heavy warm cloak of some sort to keep her warm and if she could swing it a new gown. All this would take very convincing acting. Abby planned to get all she needed and still have her grandmother's earrings tucked safely in her waist band.

"Good morning madam," Abby said hoping to get the shopkeeper's attention. "I do apologize for my ghastly appearance but I have been robbed." The shopkeeper gave her a disbelieving look but Abby continued, "I have come all this way from the colonies to paint a portrait of your king. However, I was overpowered by thieves who stripped me of my clothes, my escorts and stole my wagon with my portfolio and my paints, leaving me naked on the side of the road. A kind Scottish woman felt bad for me and gave me this gown. I stand in front of you today looking to purchase a pair of shoes with the only thing left I own." And she reached in her waistband and pulled out one of the earrings, "this diamond earring. Would you be interested in bartering with me?"

Abigail must have made some kind of impression because the shop woman took the earring and examined it. "It looks real," the shop woman said surprised.

"Looking the way I do, I understand your reluctance to barter with me, kind woman, but if you would like, I will wait here while you go to the jewelers to get it appraised. I passed one not two doors down if

I am not mistaken." Then Abby gave the shop woman a convincing smile.

The woman excused herself and went in the back to talk to the cobbler, her husband. Sitting on the floor, playing with hand carved wooden horses sat two little boys with the resemblance too remarkable not to call them brothers. They sat in front of the hearth oblivious to the customers that walked in and out of the shop. Looking around, Abby found just what she was looking for, a piece of chalk and a piece of cold charcoal she took right out of the fire. When the woman returned, Abby asked her for a piece of large parchment the cobbler used to wrap the new shoes in. Then the woman gave her the parchment without question and was off to the jewelers to get the earring appraised leaving Abby to sketch the two little boys playing.

They were playing so intensely that they paid little attention to what Abby was doing, but the cobbler came out to check on his sons and was thrilled with Abby's delicate drawing. When the cobbler's wife returned with the earring, the cobbler called her to the back. Abby could hear them discuss the drawing and the earring.

While they were in the back, a lovely older woman stopped in to pick up her order. Abby's back was toward the lady. She too was fascinated with Abby's creation and found herself watching her as she worked. Abby took the opportunity to tell her sad made up story convincing the lady that she had been robbed and was in need of shoes and new garments.

While Abby was talking to the lady, the cobbler's wife came out from the back room. "We are ready to make an offer," the shop woman said. "What shoes are ya interested in?"

Abby pointed to a small pair of boy shoes sitting on the top shelf full of dust. The cobble's wife automatically protested. "No lass, them are boy's shoes and much ta small for ya." Abby only smiled and said, "I would really like to try them anyway unless they are an order for someone. I am in need of a good pair of sturdy walking shoes and those look like they will do just fine."

Then she lifted up her skirts to show the woman her tiny feet. "I have never seen a woman whose feet are this small. They may fit after all," said the cobbler's wife astonished.

While Abby waited for the shop woman to get the shoes down, the older lady whispered, "Donna pay more than one coin for those. They were an order and the man never came ta pick them up and that was two years ago."

Abby tried the shoes on and they fit perfectly, a little wider for a thick pair of socks to fit in. "They fit ya. Wonderful," said the cobbler's wife. "Maybe a buckle would make them more feminine. What do ya think?"

"I am not really interested in fashion, madam. What I want is sturdy shoes for walking. How much are you asking for these?"

The cobbler walked out from the back room and answered her question from behind her. "We want ta trade those shoes for the drawing ya just did of our sons."Abby was thrilled but she tried not to show it. She needed a pair of socks as well.

"I am sorry sir," Abby said with a sweet smile. "I need this drawing to show the king. As I told your wife I lost my portfolio and I have no example of my work to show your king. I cannot possibly sell it." Then she said adding a little gravy to the pot. "I will never get such a beautiful set of boys to sit and pose like this again. They are too special. My drawing will surely convince the king to hire me to paint his portrait."

"How about a buckle?" the wife urged.

When the cobbler saw she wasn't budging he said, "And three pairs of thick wool socks?" Abby was just about to take the offer when the older lady said, "I bet if ya offer her three coins so she can buy a new gown she'd take the offer." Then the older woman looked at Abby and winked.

Abby finally left the cobbler shop with her diamond earrings, one pair of boy's shoes with a buckle, three pairs of hand knitted thick wool socks, three coins and a promise to draw a portrait of the older lady's husband. "My name is Harriet," the woman said as they left the shop. "I live just down the road and I think I have a lovely gown that will fit ya just fine." By the time Abby finished the drawing, she had added a thick warm cape, a pair of gloves, a wool hat and a green wool gown. Harriet and her husband were thrilled with the likeness Abby drew.

Abby did not put the gown on. She had another idea but she did ask Harriet's husband to escort her past the stockades. He offered Abby his arm and the two of them went walking back up the walkway toward the stocks and the inn.

He was a lovely man about the age of her father if he had lived. Abby enjoyed his stories and his humor all the way up the walk. They passed the fish lady still stewing about her husband's unfair treatment and the broken tables that had been ruined in the fight with the damaged merchandise. As they reached the top of the walk, Abby had a clear view of the stocks and the four men occupying them. As they came closer Abby's escort met someone he knew and started a conversation with him which gave Abby the opportunity to talk to Gabe, Joseph and Simon.

As she walked up to them she hesitated. The looks they were giving her made her feel very uneasy. Still holding the rope in her hand she said, "Would you like me to leave your rope at the inn before I leave?" All three men never said a word. They were beyond furious and if they could get out, Abby was sure she would not be the happy one standing.

"Well," Abby said with a smile, clearing her throat nervously. "I will be leaving now right after I say goodbye to the other men. Have a good night?" Then she remembered Joseph's remark about his horse's tail and said, "Oh, Joseph, I will be taking you up on your offer to cut your horse's tail off. I will need it shortly." Then she turned and grabbed her escorts arm and walked back to the inn. Abby thought she heard Joseph growl as she was leaving but she was not sure.

"Gabriel," Joseph whispered in a very low voice. "We are going after her are we not?" Then Simon said, "Gabriel, I am going after her with or without ya."

Gabe turned his head as much as he could in the stock and said, "OH, we are definitely going after her. I am sure I will need ya help. We will not be making this mistake again and I promise ya that woman will pay my price dearly."

As Abby reached the inn with her escort, she noticed the innkeeper's wife loading a wagon in the back. She said her thank you and goodbye to her new friend and went to see what was going on with Ella. Abby made sure there were no Scotts from her party in the back of the inn before she went to talk to her. "Ella what is wrong?" Abby asked.

"My sister is having a baby and the girl I hired to go with me is nowhere to be found. She is most likely up in the hayloft with that new stable boy," Ella sputtered.

"Can I do something to help?" Abby asked hoping she would say yes or at least offer her a ride out of town.

"Only if you can deliver a baby," Ella answered still loading the wagon with supplies for her sister.

"Well, I have had a boy, a girl and twin boys on my own and I was alone each time I delivered. Plus I have assisted in many births back home in the colonies. Will that do?" Abby said with a big grin.

"Twins? Ya had twins by yourself?" Ella asked in surprise. "Get your stuff. Ya are hired."

"I need to tell the men that I am leaving with you. I will only be a moment." Abby put her new cloak and socks in the wagon threw her new gown over her arm and ran out to the barn. She looked to make sure no one was in the barn before she entered and heard the stable boy and a guest up in the hay loft. Smiling to herself, she reached for the large garden shears hanging on the wall and went down the walk to find Joseph's honey colored horse.

"Sorry old man," Abby said to the horse as she cut fifteen inches of hair off the tail. She stuffed it in her pocket and tied the rope around her waist again. Running to the inn, she opened the door and pretended to say goodbye to Gabe. Then she turned and asked Dougal to lead her up to her room. "Gabe ordered me to stay alone in my room for the rest of the day and night until he can deal with me later. He asked me to ask you to stay outside, in the hall as my guard until he returns in the morning," Abby lied.

Dougal never argued with her but believed her. She handed the end of her rope to him and walked to her room with him just behind her. "Dougal, I have a real hard time getting to sleep without the window open, but then I get cold and wake up. Would you mind coming in my room in an hour or so and shut the window for me? And Gabe said to tell you to all stay at the inn until he returns."

"I can do that, lass and ya can keep this rope in ya chamber with ya. I am not about ta sit here and hold onta it the entire night," Dougal said not suspecting a thing.

Abby went into the room and began to work. First she took her faded gown off and laid it on the end of the bed. Then she took the extra quilt off the bed, folded it and stuffed it under the blankets to make it look like a person sleeping there. She took the horsetail out of her pocket and laid it on the pillow, burying the end of the tail under the blanket to make it look like her own hair gently laying there. She slipped her diamond earrings from the waistband of her old gown and put them on, then dressed in her new gown. Taking her rope, she opened the window and carefully slipped out onto the roof inching to the chimney at the back of the inn.

Abby was thrilled that Dougal did not want to hold on to the rope. She had planned to climb down the tree from her window but using the rope around the chimney to slide down to the ally below was so much easier and quicker.

Ella was just about ready when Abby came around the corner. "Abby," Ella said. "We are going ta be up all night. Ya take the first nap and then I will wake ya in an hour or so and I will take the next nap. Ya can drive the wagon, right?"

"Yes I can and a nap sounds very good to me." Abby jumped up in the back of the wagon and covered her whole body up with her new cloak, hoping she would not be seen by her Scotts. She could not believe her luck. Sleeping in the back of the wagon would let her escape without a trace or trail to follow. Abby's heart was so excited. She was finally free. She would do what she set out to do when she left the colonies, take care of that damn box if Martin had not done it yet. But she was not going back to England. She would find a boat out of Scotland and use her earrings to book the passage and maybe hook up with Martin.

Abby was sure Gabe would not be able to find her. Her heart was breaking but she could not have love until she was sure that she completed her grandfather's wishes and destroy the remaining documents in that box. Until then she would be in danger and would endanger the people around her and she would just have to be happy to have known him.

As the wagon went in front of the inn, Abby heard Colin say, "Have a good trip Ella. Do ya need someone ta go with ya?"

"No Colin. She is in the back of the wagon taking a nap. We will be fine." Abby was so worried that she would have said her name but Ella just said "she." Abigail breathed out a large sigh of relief and then closed her eyes and went to sleep.

Ella woke Abby up about two hours later and then Abby took over. Ella's sister's house was easy to find, right on the way. So Ella lay in the back under Abby's cloak and slept. Abby kept busy imagining the look on Dougal's face when he discovered he was guarding nothing but a horse's tail and Joseph when he found his beloved honey colored horse tail missing. She hoped that Gabe and Simon and Joseph would forgive her but she was sure they would not. She feared that the inn keeper would tell Gabe where she was so she planned to leave right after the baby was born. Abby had made it this far and there was no need to take unnecessary risks. She was free and she was going to stay that way.

Just before dinner, the two ladies reached their destination. They were greeted by a very worried Thomas, the expectant father and eight little boys. All twins ranging from ten to four years of age. "Your sister has had all twins?" Abby asked surprised.

"Aye," Ella answered. "And I am sure she is having another multiple birth. Thomas has decided not to have anymore even if they do not get their girl. Kate wants a girl so bad. Thomas agreed to try until they got one but he doesn't want any more than ten children."

"Wow," Abby said. "Five sets of twins. They are the luckiest people I've ever known." The two women smiled at each other and headed upstairs where Kate was waiting already in labor.

Ella took Abby to a room at the end of the house. As they went down the hall, Abby looked into the opened bedrooms, four little rooms with two beds in each room with a handmade quilt on each bed. The last room had two cradles waiting for the new arrivals.

Kate was a beautiful woman with deep blue eyes and auburn hair. Her round belly was definitely full of babies. Abby and Kate became good friends right away especially when Abby told her about her full grown twins and all the pranks they pulled. Between contractions

Abby kept Kate's mind busy with funny stories. Ella was very glad she had come to help.

Labor went fast after midnight and soon it was time to deliver, but Kate was exhausted and unable to push. Thomas paced the hall outside the room while Abby kept encouraging Kate. Ella started to look worried. This was taking too long and not at all like the other births. Kate started to look funny.

"I need to put my hand in and see what is keeping her from delivering," Abby said to Ella. With a nod from Ella, Abby reached in to find a big baby blocking the birth canal half turned. She tried to turn it but the umbilical cord was wrapped around its little neck. "Don't push Kate," Abby ordered while her hand was still in her womb. "I think I almost have it." One more minute and Abby was able to loosen the cord. The baby turned on the next contraction and slid into Abby's hands. She handed a round baby boy to Ella just in time to catch the next boy baby as he left the womb. The two ladies tended the babies while Kate took a few minutes break but the pains started again.

Abby ran to the see what was happening and found a third baby but it was wedged up under Kate's rib cage and Abby had to go in again. A little tug and Kate's baby girl was born. She handed her to Ella but the baby did not cry. Kate was bleeding too much and the women had to tend to the mother. They worked together and finally did get the blood stopped.

Then Abby asked where the little girl was and Ella motioned under the bed. Ella thought the baby was dead so she put it under the bed and helped Abby. It took the two women together to stop the bleeding. When Ella told Kate her little girl did not make it, Kate broke into uncontrollable screams and cries. She woke the entire house of boys with her wails.

Abby grabbed the baby girl and ran down the stairs and out into the cool night. She sank to her knees on the grass and tried to remember what Old Joe taught her. She pinched the little girl's nose and gently blew into her mouth pushing softly on the little chest. Over and over she breathed into the baby's mouth calling to Old Joe to come in spirit for help. Something told her to look in the baby's mouth; she could see tissue lodged in the back of her throat. Abby tipped the baby over and hit her on the back gently to see if she could dislodge the blockage.

It was just blind luck that it came out a little, just enough to let Abby reach in and dislodge it with one finger. Then she tried to breath into her mouth one last time and this time the little girl took her first breath and wailed the most beautiful cry Abby had ever heard. "Thank you Old Joe," Abby whispered and wiped the tears out or her own eyes. "Come little one. Let's bring you to meet your new mother and father." Abby stopped in the kitchen and washed the little girl and then wrapped her in a small blanket and went up to Kate's room.

When Abby walked in carrying the bundle, Ella verbally attacked her. "How dare ya bring a dead baby to my sister Kate. What kind of an animal does such a thing? Take her out of here this minute." But Abby refused to go. Instead she said, "Kate if you don't want this beautiful little girl, I will take her." Thomas jumped up ready to throw Abby out of the room when the baby started to cry in her arms. Abby smiled at Kate and then gave her their only daughter. Kate lay in bed holding her triplets all healthy and doing well. "I'm so sorry Abby," Ella said after she saw the baby move and heard her cry. "I thought you......." and she could not finish what she wanted to say. She just put her head down and cried in her hands. Abby reached over and hugged Ella.

"Okay, you three are going to bed and get some sleep and I am not talking to my new triplets," Thomas said with a smile. Kate, Ella and Abby did not argue but gladly crawled into their beds and slept. Abby had wanted to leave right away but she was exhausted so she planned to leave first thing in the morning.

***

Gabe slammed the door open to the inn bellowing to his men. Dougal looked down from the upstairs where he was still guarding Abby's room and Joseph's horse's tail.

"Where is she?" He yelled followed by Simon and Joseph. The men looked surprise at his question and even more at his anger.

"What is wrong?" Colin asked jumping to his feet.

"Gabe, she is up here. I have been guarding her all night just like ya ordered," Dougal said.

Gabe ran up the stairs three at a time. He slammed open the door of her room to find what he thought was Abby sleeping in bed with her honey colored hair draped on the pillow. He stomped across the room and pulled the blankets down. Dougal was shocked along with the other men crowded in the little room. There in the bed was a quilt carefully folded to resemble a person sleeping, with a bunch of loose horse hair draped on the pillow.

"This canna be," Dougal exclaimed. "I saw her come into this room and I even closed her window for her. I never thought anything was wrong, even her gown is here."

"Where did this hair come from? Did she cut her hair?" Cookie asked from behind Gabe.

"Looks like a horsetail to me," Simon said sarcastically looking directly at Joseph. Without saying a word, Joseph ran out of the inn to the barn where he found his short tailed horse.

All the men could hear him yelling from the barn. She had cut his horse's hair just as she said she would. If Abby had been there that moment, no one would have stopped him from inflicting bodily harm on her.

Then Simon looked at Dougal. "Congratulations ya prevented a horsetail from escaping."

Gabe left Abby's room and ordered everyone to the dining room where they could all compare notes. Abby had to have made a mistake and Gabe was going to find it and then find her. Gabe told the other men about the events at the market place right down to the stocks.

"Abigail Fox told us she was leaving. She told us when she was leaving and how she was leaving. I almost think she wants us ta find her. She even told Joseph she was going to cut his horse's tail off. I want that lass and I will be the one that takes care of her punishment. Do I make myself clear?" Then he looked directly at Joseph, then Simon, then at Dougal and the rest of the men. They all nodded in agreement.

"Now, there are thirteen of us and one of her surely one of us saw something that can help."As Gabe finished that question, the inn keeper came in thanking Gabe for allowing Abby to go with his Ella to Kate's house. All the men stood in silence with the most sinister smiles on their faces. "Hounds," Gabe said, "looks like we have found our *Lady Fox*."

The next thing Gabe did was send a man up to Thomas' house to check on the ladies. He had strict instructions to stay out of view.

"There is no need ta hurry after her. She will not be leaving Kate and Thomas' house for a few days. But in case that she does leave sooner, she will go to the ocean and follow the coast to a port. She went in the only direction I would have never looked, north and we will not lose time finding her. But for now we need ta get the business taken care of and then we will leave. It's time to split up." Then Gabe gave them their orders. The next morning they were off to catch their honey haired colored *Fox*.

***

Abby woke to three little boys staring directly at her. "Do ya think she is alive?" The first little boy asked inching closer to the closed eyed awake Abby.

"Maybe she is a witch," the second little boy said.

"Do ya think we should poke her ta see if she bleeds? Witches donna bleed," the third little one said.

Abby had all she could do not to laugh or open her eyes. The first little boy came as close as he could and put his face almost touching Abby's. She could feel his breath tickling her nose and she started giggling. All three boys jumped back just as their father caught them in a room they were forbidden to be in.

"Ya three better march ya little backsides out of here before I decide ta tan all of ya for disobeying me," Thomas ordered. "I am so sorry Abby please accept my apologies. I'll see ta it that they donna bother ya again."

"They are fine and they did not bother me, but I think I still need to convince them I am not a witch," Abby explained followed by a little giggle.

"What? They called ya a witch? Now I really am going ta tan all three of them,"Thomas barked.

"Not while I am here you don't," Abby said in protest.

Kate was in her bedroom resting and the triplets were all asleep and doing well, even the little girl. She was so much smaller than her two brawny brothers. They must have given her a hard time in the womb but now she was making up for it. When she cried, the whole house knew it. Abby loved seeing this incredible family and it made her miss her own more, which reminded her of what she needed to do today….. *RUN.*

There was a knock on the door and Thomas went to open it. For a brief moment, Abby panicked but it was a false alarm. Two townswomen entered carrying a basket of gifts and offered to stay and help. Abigail decided this would be a good time to leave.

"Ella," Abby said. "It looks like you have enough help now and I think I should get back to the inn and my escorts."

"No need for that, lass," Thomas joined in. "Gabe sent a man up here yesterday. He said for ya ta stay here and they would be joining ya in a day or two."

Abby's eyes opened wide. They knew where she was. All she could think was leaving and leaving fast. She kept telling herself not to panic. They haven't caught me yet. She still had a chance, a slim one but a chance. Abby had to think of a good excuse to leave so they wouldn't worry or wonder where she went. Think, she kept telling herself. Finally, she said, "I hope you don't mind, but I really need a good stretch of a leg. It is so beautiful here and I would just like to take a long walk."

"I'll go with ya, lass," Thomas offered.

"You are needed here. I won't have it. I will be fine. Just point me in a direction that I can't get myself in too much trouble," Abby said, smiling as innocently as she could.

"If ya go west about an hour ya will find the coast and if ya turn south from there and walk a good two hours ya will find the ruins of the old castle. No one ever goes there anymore. It is quite safe for a good 'stretch of a leg'," Thomas said.

"Well don't worry about me." Abby tried to ease his fears. "I still may walk back toward town and meet up with them. I just need to follow the road. I can't possible get lost."

"Ya be wary of strangers. Ya, hear, lass," Thomas warned.

"I will," Abby smiled. Then she said her good-byes and headed south in the direction of town. When she thought it safe to double back, she turned and went west to find the coast. Gabe might look here for her, but she did not know the country and the coast would at least lead her to a port. With a little luck, she would come to a port where she could get passage back to the colonies without going back to England and before Gabe could catch up with her.

Don't get discouraged she kept telling herself. It is a big country. Finding me would be like finding a needle in a haystack. Truth was that Abby loved Scotland and the McKenzie men. She had become very fond of Gabe even though she tried not to. Part of her wished they'd find her and then the other part of her wanted to go home. Abby's mind raced as she walked. The faster she walked the more she thought. She kept remembering Gabe's warm hand on her naked breast. How it had felt so wonderful and how she wanted more.

In all the time she had been married to Roy never once had he touched her breast. Don't be stupid, Abigail Fox, there is no future with Gabriel McKenzie, she scolded herself. Alone is your future and you just will have to accept it, just like you accepted the responsibility of the box. Besides if Gabe did find me, she thought to herself, he would never forgive me for putting him in the stocks. I certainly sealed my fate with Gabe that day. It was the choice I made and I must live with it, no regrets now. Then she said "Just keep walking" out loud as if she needed to hear her own words of encouragement.

Her mind kept going back to the house filled with eleven children and two happily married people. Thomas and Kate were so blessed. To be loved and to love, how wonderful that must be. Those children had two parents that loved them and cared for them. How she had wanted that for her own children.

Stop this thinking, she told herself. Concentrate on where you must go. When she looked around she was in the midst of very large trees. She had no idea how she had drifted in here or where she was. Hopefully she was not going north again. She had walked way over an hour and the ocean must be close by now, but she could not hear, see or smell it. The worst part was this feeling of being watched. Keep walking, she told herself, don't stop now or you'll be someone's supper.

The forest started to get darker the farther she went. All she wanted to do was go back but someone or something was behind her and she could feel it. The forest started to become thick with underbrush and walking became harder as the brush pulled on her skirts. Through the corner of her eye, she saw a figure dart by her. It was much too fast for a man but not too fast for a wolf. Abby began to look for the nearest tree she could climb. Running seemed to be a good idea just now and the sooner she ran, the better. About fifty feet in front of her was a magnificent tree full of low branches just waiting to be climbed. Abby lifted her skirts and ran for dear life feeling the brush scratch her legs. As she ran she realized her dream was coming true and she was trying not to panic.

She reached the bottom of the tree just as she heard the sound of something coming up fast behind her. Reaching as high as she could, she grabbed a low branch and pulled herself up to safety at least for the time being. She frantically climbed the tree, pulling with all her strength, escaping the growling wolves at her heels and scrapping the inside of her legs from the rough bark. It wasn't quite like climbing the rigging on a ship but she could still do it. When she reached a safe height, she sat down on a sturdy branch and looked down at her would be assailants. Five very mean hungry wolves circled the tree hoping to get a chance for an easy meal. Abby was not about to oblige them. She would just sit and wait them out, but time was her enemy as well now. These wolves were not helping her escape from Scotland and Gabe might be too close for comfort. She waited for the next part of her dream to take place.

Abby was stranded in that tree for more than two hours before the wolves decided to hunt elsewhere. Climbing down, however would wait until she was sure they would not come back. It was getting dark now. She had little sun left in the day. It would be wise if she just stayed here for the night and then start fresh in the morning. Abby was tired, hungry and very thirsty but she could not risk the danger of the woods in the night to satisfy her needs. Propping herself against the tree trunk, she tried to get as comfortable as she could hoping she'd not fall in the middle of the night.

The night seemed to last forever. Sounds were amplified letting her fears takeover. She finally did drift off for a few hours but was awakened by male voices. Quietly she watched as four men dragged a poor soul just into her view but not right under her tree. Helpless, she watched the four men beat the other until there was no movement. They stripped him of his clothes and personal belongings. Abby was so afraid she could not move.

One of the men wearing a green jacket with patches took out a long knife and stabbed the helpless man to death. The sight of a man being murdered in front of her eyes made her sick to her stomach. She started heaving uncontrollably while holding her hand over her mouth to muffle any sound which might alert the thieves.

One of the thieves heard a sound and looked in Abby's direction. "Oh, please make them go away," she whispered to herself. But the man with the green jacket started walking toward her tree. Abby pulled her legs up trying to keep her hiding place undetectable. He slowed down as he reached the tree looking from side to side but not looking up. Abby watched as he continued to find just where the noise came from. As he turned his head, Abby recognized him. She knew his face but was not sure where she'd seen him. She lightly gasped which made him look up.

Abby drew her legs up higher hoping it was too dark for him to see her. But he did see her anyway. He called to his buddies to come and get the witness. As he started to climb the tree, a loud howl came from the right. The man in green said, "Let's get out of here before the wolves smell that blood. Leave the body, the wolves will take care of him."

"What about him?" The second pointed at Abby. *(Good, she thought, they can't see my face.)*

"Leave him. We'll look for him in the morning. He can't go too far tonight with those wolves," the man in the green said in a deep raspy voice.

The four killers left, leaving Abby alone in the tree to watch as the wolves come to claim the slain man's body. Tears filled her eyes as she turned her head from the view of the feeding wolves.

Abby waited until all was quiet. The wolves were gone and she could not wait any longer. Slowly she worked her way back down the tree looking for any sign of the wolves or the four men. As she reached the ground, she saw something shinning in the morning sun. She walked over to find a man's ring. It was heavy yellow gold with a huge red stone. Abby thought she saw the man bury something while looking her way. It might be a ruby but she did not think she had seen one so big. The ring had carvings etched in the side that looked like words in a foreign language but she was not sure the exact one. This must be the ring of the man they killed, she thought. It looked so familiar. Abby decided to take it with her. Maybe someone could identify the ring and the man that died such a horrid death. Maybe she could remember where she saw the ring before.

The sun rises in the east and sets in the west, Abigail reminded herself and then she walked away from the sun as fast as her legs would carry her. Find the ocean and then follow it home. She ran as far as she could then walked trying to keep her pace up. When she tired, she reminded herself about the four killing thieves which gave her more strength to continue. When the sun was over her head she rested by the ocean. She had finally found it. A ray of hope filled her body with happiness. Keep going she told herself, ignore the hunger and you are not too tired. The sun was now in her face, time to go south.

By the end of the day, Abby had blisters on her feet and chapped lips from the ocean wind. She looked for a safe place to spend the night but there were no large trees only scrub bushes. *(I need a place to hide.)* She was far enough from the woods now for the wolves not to be a threat but she was more concerned with the four killing thieves. Abby was at her end. Sleep had evaded her for two nights and she just couldn't go on any further. Her only hope at this time, was a hiding place, somewhere dry and warm, a shelter from the wind, a hole in the ground would do nicely.

Abby crawled under the big bush next to a small lock away from the wind of the ocean. She dug herself a hole with a hard piece of bark, big enough to lie in and then cover herself with leaves. With some luck, she could sleep and not be found. Exhaustion set in, Abby had just enough strength to lay her plaid in the hole, crawl in, cover herself with her blue and green plaid cape and then cover that with leaves. Covering her head was the last thing she did, hoping she had covered herself well enough not to be discovered. Sleep was almost immediate.

***

Gabe reached Thomas' house the first thing the next in the morning. Thomas came out to happily greet his friends and show off his new healthy triplets. After congratulations where extended and the story of the triplets birth reminisced, Gabe asked for Abby.

"She's not with ya?" Thomas asked. "She was going to meet ya. I watched her walk back toward town."

"Ya didn't tell her how ta get ta the ocean, by any chance did ya?" Gabe asked.

"Aye, I did. But if she changed her mind, she would have ta go through the woods and there are wolves in there. Ya donna thinks she's in trouble do ya?" Thomas asked concerned. "That lass saved my Kate and my little girl."

"We'll find her Thomas, don't worry. She's only hours away and on foot. We can catch up with her this morning. Ya take care of those babies. I'll send word."

Gabe and the men mounted their horses and then he gave the men their orders. "We split up. Joseph, take three men and go through the woods toward the ocean. If she is in trouble ya will find her there. If ya make it ta the ocean and have not found her go south and find me. Simon, take two men and go back ta town. Make sure she has not doubled back. If ya donna find her there meet me at Bess' house. The rest of ya come with me. We'll go straight ta the ocean and then south, she won't be much further than that."

CHAPTER 10
The Hounds Are Hunting

She woke in the morning to men's voices. Carefully she peeked out from her hiding place hoping it was not the killers. All she could see was a handful of Scottish men wearing kilts, but she could not see any more than their hems. She was relieved it was not the killers and almost sure it was not Gabe because they were few in numbers. *Stay low and wait out your time. They will leave soon*, she thought.

Her morning needs were becoming necessary. She strongly hoped they would move on soon. She kept her head low and watched the shadows of the men as they kept looking on the ground. What were they were looking for she wondered. She wished she could see their faces but she did not dare raise her head any higher. The man with the big black boots kept walking toward her bush and then back. He was talking in Gaelic and very low voice. *Why, are they whispering, she wondered,* she wondered.

"Colin, do ya see that bush behind me. Try not to look right at it."

"Aye, Gabe. Why?" Colin asked.

"Watch the leaves under the bush, tell me if they move," Gabe ordered.

At that moment, Abby took another look.

"Aye, Gabe. They just moved."

"Looks like we have just found our little *Fox*," Gabe smiled. "Now we need ta encourage her ta come out of her very clever den. Aye, Gentlemen?"

Abby watched as the man with the big black boots walked back toward her bush. "*Damn him*," she whispered. Her needs were getting much stronger. If they didn't leave soon she would burst. Abby heard him stop right next to her. She laid there motionless, hoping he would just leave. Then she heard water running. *Was it supposed to rain*, she wondered. The sky was clear, she thought but she didn't dare check with that man standing right over her. Abby was sure she could hear water falling. Then a warm wet feeling began to saturate her back. A pungent smell followed.

Abby put her hand over her nose. The smell was sickening and she was getting wetter by the second. It was then that she realized what he was doing. In all bloody Scotland, this would be the bush he chose to relieve himself. *How utterly disgusting*, she thought. Then her gag reflex took over.

"We will stay here all day men," the man said in English with a strong Scottish burr. Then he added, "If ya need ta relieve yaself, use this bush and only this bush."

Abby was getting real nauseous and panicking. More warm pungent urine was coming down into her hole. Tears puddled in her eyes from the strong smell. She wanted nothing more that to run and take her chances but she didn't quite dare.

"We are going ta take turns urinating on ya lass, until ya come out," Gabe said.

A tiny voice came out from under the leaves. "Is that you, Gabe?"

"Aye and it is Colin's turn. What are ya going ta do, stay in there for more or come out and take what is coming ta ya?"

"I'm coming out," Abby said in a defeated voice.

The men watched as the leaves lifted and Abby quickly scurried out from her handmade pit dripping wet with pungent male urine.

"Very clever, lass," Gabe said through gritted teeth. "I'm impressed and surprised. I never thought ya would get this far." Abby starting taking a step backward, hoping she could still get away.

Part of Abby was so relieved that it was Gabe that found her but his threats were promises. She was out of the frying pan but she was now into the fire.

Before she could take another step, he reached out and grabbed her arm. He swung around and started pulling her toward the small loch. Before she could protest, she was flying through the air finally landing in the very cold water with a huge splash. She stood gasping from the cold water to the sounds of the men laughing at her.

"It is time for a bath, lass," Gabe ordered, throwing a bar of soap at her. "Take as long as ya wish but ya'll not come out until ya smell like a rose."

Abby stood there with a horrified look on her face. "Are you all planning on watching?"

"Aye," they all said at once.

Abby turned her back to the men and folded her arm in complete protest.

"Do ya need my help, lass?" Gabe asked through laughter.

He started to take a step forward as if to come in and help when Abby said shivering, "I am more than capable of bathing myself, th-th thank you."

"Very well then, ya can start by removing ya gown and washing it. When it is clean ya can throw it ta me," Gabe ordered.

Abby could not believe what she had just got herself into but the water was so cold. She had minutes before she would freeze to death. Turning away from the men she lowered into the water and removed her dress. Washing it as fast as she could and still getting it clean of men's urine she hurled it back at Gabe.

"Now the shift, lass," Gabe ordered.

Again, Abby turned her back and removed her undergarment leaving her stark naked in the black freezing water of the lock. Without turning she washed her shift and threw it over her shoulder at Gabe. Then, she washed herself.

Before she could come out, Gabe called, "Donna forget ya hair, lass."

Abby was shivering, so by now that she could no longer feel her feet.

"Time ta come out before ya catch ya death, Abigail," Gabe said.

"Please th-th-throw me a plaid?" Abby asked not turning around.

"Nay, lass, if ya want a plaid ya can come and get it."

Keeping her arms folded over her breast, she turned staying deep in the water. To her surprise, Gabe was the only man still on the shore holding a plaid out in front of him. Abby couldn't stand the cold anymore. She had to come out and fast. Walking out of the water, naked, still trying to hide some of her with her arms she reached for the plaid and Gabe stepped back.

"Not funny, Gabe, give me th-th-the plaid," she barked through chattering teeth.

"Turn around lass and I will put it on ya."

Abby was so cold she rolled her eyes and turned around exposing her generous backside to Gabe. A warm plaid came across her shoulders. Grabbing it, she closed it around her freezing body.

"Dry yourself off, lass and then put this on."

Abby turned and saw Gabe standing behind her with one of his spare shirts and another plaid in his hands. She looked for her extra socks and shoes but they were gone. "The men took them. They are waiting for us with the horses. Ya will not need them today."

Abby quickly wiped herself dry and started to put the shirt on. "Wait, ya back is still wet. Let me help." He didn't wait for an answer but started to wipe her back dry. Then to Abby's surprise, he wiped off her bottom and the back of her legs. He took his shirt back and slipped it over her head and tied the strings. Then he wrapped his plaid around her waist and tied it on with the rope he had used for her leash. Reaching around her, he lifted her up in his arms and carried her up to the waiting horses with the plaid hanging way over her tiny feet. He carried her as if she was a fragile flower. She felt no anger from him but a warm feeling of safety.

The men made comments about her new dress and how nice she smelled, all in good humor. They seemed relieved they found her and that she was unharmed.

Gabe put her up on his horse and then swung up behind her with one easy leap. He picked her up and rested her on his lap with her legs dangling over his right thigh. The plaid covered her naked feet from the cold. She felt another plaid come across her sandwiching her between it and him. Abby was wrapped up in his arms as if in a cocoon warm and safe. At first she stiffened trying to not touch him but soon his warmth won out and Abby relaxed in his arms.

"Rest ya head on my chest, lass. It's time ta sleep." Abby did not argue with him. It had been three days since she had really slept or ate. The rhythm of the Gabe's horse and the warmth of his body was more than she could fight. Sleep overtook her.

On the way back to Gabe's to Bess' house, they stopped for a few moments to let Thomas, Kate and Ella know that they found her and she was fine. Abby never woke but slept through the entire visit. As Gabe turned to leave Thomas saw him give his sleeping passenger a gentle kiss. Thomas smiled at Kate, "Do ya think our Gabe has found someone ta share his life, Kate?" Thomas asked knowing what the answer was.

Gabe met up with Joseph and the other men, but Simon was still unaccounted for. They would meet him at Bess' house. Joseph was thrilled when he saw her. He and the other men had come across the remains of an unrecognizable person in the woods half devoured by wolves. Joseph was hoping that Gabe had found her alive. He was sure dreading giving Gabe bad news.

Abby finally woke about mid-afternoon. She had not moved a muscle since he had rested her in his lap. When he felt her squirm, he asked, "feeling better?"

Abby, still very groggy just nodded, yes. Then he added, "we will be riding another few hours before we get ta the house. You'll have a bed for two nights, but then we will have ta camp the rest of the time."

Abby just rode quietly in his arms. He felt so good and she felt so miserable. Guilt was taking over. She regretted putting him and his men in the stockade. Abby felt like a failure. Her attempt to get home was a disaster and now she was moving farther away from home, the box and still a prisoner. Things couldn't get much worse. She was wrong again.

CHAPTER 11
It Is Hard To Say I'm Sorry

The little group reached their destination just before nightfall. The house they were to stay in was about a half mile away in plain view. Gabe pulled his horse around and stopped. "Joseph, take the men down to the house, tell Bess we will need supper and rooms for two days. I'll be along shortly."

Joseph looked at Gabe with a worried look. "I can stay if ya want Gabe."

"Nay, I need ta do this myself. I'll meet ya at the house."

Reluctantly the men left Gabe and Abby behind. Gabe turned Samson toward the woods and urged his horse on until he found a little clearing in the middle of a glen. There were three large boulders in the middle of the grassy area and a small pond just on the far side of the clearing. Gabe dismounted and then reached up and took Abby down. "Go tend ya needs, lass. I'll wait for ya here."

Abby was thrilled she could relieve herself in private and pleased that Gabe stayed back just so she could tend to herself alone without her leash or singing Amazing Grace. She quickly finished and hurried back not to make him wait. With a big smile on her face she said, "how was that, not too long, was it?" Gabe was sitting on one of the boulders with one foot up on the rock and the other on the ground. His arms were crossed and he had a serious look on his face which alarmed Abby. "Is there something wrong?" She asked half expecting the answer.

Gabe took a long hard breath and then stood up. "Let's get this over with, lass," he said.

As he unfolded his arms, Abby noticed he wasn't wearing his belt but had it folded in two in his right hand. "Get what over with?" Abby asked stepping backward.

"Ya know very well what, lass. Let's not make this harder than it need be."

Abby stepped back again. "I think I've been punished enough, Gabe. You do remember pissing on me and throwing me in the freezing loch."

"Aye, I do remember but I donna thinks ya have been punished nearly enough. Do ya know what the punishment is supposed ta be for lewd conduct in a public place?"Gabe asked.

"Yes, it is one day in the stockade," Abby answered confidently.

"Nay, lass it is dismemberment. Simon, Joseph and I should have had a hand cut off."

"They really cut hands off in Scotland?" Abby asked shocked at his statement.

"The woman ya pinched couldn't tell the judge for sure that I was the culprit. So, he decided to just to punish us for brawling in a public place. Thank God, I knew the judge well. He knew I was not lying."

"I don't know what to say, Gabe. I'm so sorry. I really didn't know that. It is so different here, I am so sorry," Abby said sincerely.

"Me too, lass. I am not looking forward ta punishing ya but ya broke my rules and it's my job. So let's get this over with so we can get ta the house and put this behind us. I think fifteen straps will be a fair punishment."

"I don't think that is a fair punishment at all. I said I was sorry and I think that is enough. I am not about to just let you hit me and that's final."

"Well lass that doesn't surprise me in the least. Ya have not made this easy since we left James'. So let me explain what will happen if ya fight me." He started to walk toward Abigail. "I'll take both ya hands and pin them ta ya back. I'll put ya face down on that boulder and strip ya of that plaid. Then I'll lift the shirt tails and strap ya naked ass thirty times. And I will not stop after that until ya ask," Gabe explained through gritted teeth.

Abby was not going to let him touch her. She turned and started to run even though she had no shoes on. Within three strides Gabe had caught up with her. Like he said, he twisted both her arms behind her back and held them there with one big hand. He pushed her over to the boulder and forced her brutally down on the rock scraping her right cheek and bruising her cheek bone. She felt the rock scrape her skin and a little trickle of warm liquid dripped down her stinging face as her head slammed into the hard rock. She felt her plaid falling from her waist and then the shirt tail rising over her bottom. She kicked and squirmed but he was way too strong.

He rested his knee on her legs to keep her from moving. Then she heard the first sound of his belt slicing through the air and then felt the sting of the strap as if slapped across her tender backside. She wanted to scream out in pain but she was not going to make a sound. The second lash hit with just as much force as the previous one, causing tears to start to puddle in her eyes. Still she refused to make a sound. She clenched her teeth together and got ready for the next blow. Gabe was very good at using a belt. He'd done this before, making sure not to land on just one spot. Tears ran down her cheeks in a constant stream while she kept count of each blow. The only reaction Gabe received from Abby was a flinch as the belt landed on her tender hide.

Abby counted fifteen. She was hoping he would stop then. By the time Abby counted twenty five, Gabe did not feel her flinch any more. She just lay quietly face down on the boulder not moving or fighting in any way. At the twenty ninth blow, Abby could not take any more. As it struck her backside she let out a tiny whimper. Then Gabe heard, "Please stop". The final slap crossed her bottom at the same time Abby said "Please, Gabe." She felt her arms release and his knee raise off her legs, the shirt tail landed over her bruised buttocks.

She curled her arms up to her head and buried her face in them and cried uncontrollably still shaking from the pain. As if he knew she needed a moment, Gabe left to tend his horse. When he returned she was still lying over the bolder shaking and crying.

"Time ta leave Abigail," he ordered in a very emotionless tone.

Abby pushed herself up and turned around looking for the plaid to drape around her legs. When she could not find it, she looked up at Gabe through a much scraped, bruised, teary eyed face. He was holding it. She reached out for it and to her surprise he gave it to her. She wrapped it around her waist and waited for her next order.

"We walk from here," he said. Abby just started walking, her bare feet feeling very tender from the rough terrain. It wasn't long before the skin was ripping off the bottom of her feet but still she did not complain. She just kept walking and silently crying.

Gabe never said a word to her or acknowledged her bare feet but walked along side of her not forcing her to go faster. They reached the inn about an hour later. Gabe opened the door and was greeted with a big hug and kiss from the woman he called Bess. Without saying a word to Abby he went up the stairs to his room leaving her standing alone on the porch.

"Come in lass," Bess said with a warm smile.

But Abby said, "my feet are bleeding. I don't think I should come in because I will track blood through your house." She raised the plaid and showed her feet.

"Oh lass," Bess said in a concerned voice. "Stay there I will be right back."

Two minutes later she came back carrying a pair of garden clogs. "Here put these on for now, I am sure they are much too big but they will get ya ta your room where I will tend your tiny feet."

Abby gave her a very weary smile and did as she asked. Bess led Abigail up to a small room at the very end of the house. It was clean and had windows on two sides. There was a small bed for just one person with two extra quilts. The fire had already been lit and it was cozy in the room. There was a small table with a wash basin and a pitcher filled with clean water. A bar of soap rested in a small dish just this side of the basin and the chamber pot was under the table.

"Gabe requested this room for ya. Ya should have what ya need and I will bring up a bath tomorrow. Now have a seat and I will look after those feet."

Bess noticed Abby's hesitation. "Oh, did he use the strap on ya girl?"

Abby just nodded.

"Alright then, lie on the bed and hang ya feet out so I can see them. That will work better anyway," Bess ordered.

"You don't have to do that, I will be fine," Abby said politely.

"Lord girl, where did ya ever get that accent? Now ya donna argues with me now. I think ya have been through enough tonight."

So, Abby lay face down on the bed and wiped the tears as they fell and let Bess tend to her cut feet. After Bess left Abby washed and then removed his plaid and shirt and crawled on her belly in bed and cried herself to sleep. When she woke it was way past noon, a tray of food had been left on the table and the curtains opened. Even though she had not had her supper last night, she still did not feel up to eating. Her feet were swollen, her bottom hurting, her cheek stiff making it difficult to open her mouth. Even her arms ached from being bent behind her back. All she wanted to do was lie in bed and not move. That is exactly what she did. She listened to the chatter of the men in the hallway between her naps but did not leave her room the entire day.

Just before dinner a knock at the door woke her from yet another nap. In came a large tub and men carrying buckets of hot water. Abby buried herself under the quilts and waited for them to leave. She had never seen any of them before hopefully she would not have to meet them again not dressed. After they were gone, Abby slipped into the tub and let the warm water soothe her bruised bum and body. She must have soaked in there for an hour before Bess came in carrying her clean gown and her pair of diamond earrings. "Gabe wants ya ta meet him in the dining room for supper, lass."

Abby was still not about to leave her room. "Please thank him for his invitation but I am not hungry and wish to stay in my room this evening."

Bess glanced over to the tray she had brought in earlier and it had not been touched. "I donna think that was an invitation, lass. I think that was an order," Bess said hoping she would just go and meet Gabe. But Bess could not convince Abby to go down the stairs.

Bess left the room and five minutes later Gabe entered without knocking. Abby was lying on her stomach under the quilts in bed with her cut feet hanging over the side.

"I ordered ya ta meet me in the dining room for supper," he said in an angry tone. Abby did not turn over or acknowledge him. "Do I need ta drag ya down those stairs just the way ya are?"

Abby picked her head up and looked straight into Gabe's eyes. It was the first time he noticed her face since last night. He had not noticed the bruise or the scratches and today she was not looking pretty.

"Ya would not have had that if ya had not fought me, lass but I do apologize for the bruise on ya face."

"I do not want to leave my room right now. I am asking you to just let me stay here," Abby said having a hard time to talk with her swollen cheek.

"If ya donna come down, ya will not eat," Gabe said then he noticed the untouched tray of food. Abby was hurting and Gabe new it.

"Please, just let me stay here for now. I really don't think I could eat anything anyway," she asked again.

Gabe knew he best let her rest. "Let me check ya bruises and I will decide if ya should stay or not." Before Abby could protest, Gabe pulled the quilts back to expose her naked body. Abby just buried her head in the pillow to hide her embarrassment. First, Gabe checked her arms. She had his finger prints in black, blue and yellow. He then checked her backside. It was never his intention to strap her this much but he had no choice. This too was welted and covered in black and blue as well. Finally he checked her feet and then he noticed strange scratches going up the inside of her legs. Abby was right she was too bruised to go anywhere and Gabe decided to give in a little.

"Alright lass, ya may stay here tonight but not tomorrow. Donna make me come and get ya." Then Gabe had an even bigger change of heart, and said "Would ya like some tea?"

Abby shook her head and said, "No thank you." Gabe left the room without a word and Abby was alone for the rest of the night.

By morning Abby was feeling a little better physically but not emotionally. She was feeling guiltier than ever. All she could think of was how lucky they were not to have had a hand cut off and she thanked God Joseph and the men that were with him did not come upon those four murderers in the woods. She even felt bad about cutting the hair Joseph's horsetail. She had lied and caused innocent men to stand in the stocks for hours. If her grandfather was still alive he would have done what Gabe did. Her behavior was unforgivable and there was nothing she could do about it now. Or was there?

She hoped Martin had delivered the box. She needed to leave and soon but she did not need to endanger the Scots especially when they had only tried to help her even though she did not want their help. Abby was a prisoner still. By rights, she should try to escape again, but if it meant hurting someone again, she would not do it.

Running from James would have been so much easier. She did not care for him or his men and no one would have got hurt but her. Her stomach was still in knots and her mouth still hurt when she tried to talk. Abby decided to wash, dress and venture out a little. Maybe some fresh air would help.

When she limped down the stairs, she could hear Bess and Theodore talking in the kitchen so she decided to stop in and say good morning. Gabe and all his men had left for the day. He had given strict instructions to Bess not to let Abby leave the inn. As Abby limped closer to the kitchen, she could not help but over hear their conversation.

"But Bess, if I could just win once, it would mean good business for a whole year. I know ya do not like me competing but I promise I won't get mad and break something like I did last year."

"Teddy, ya always enter and ya always lose. They just donna like ya cooking and ya have ta come ta that realization."

At that point, Abby walked into the room. "Good morning," she said with a happy tone. Both Teddy and Bess where most surprised to see her out of her room and dressed. "I just wanted to say hello before I take a little walk. I won't be long. My feet will not like it." Both Teddy and Bess gave her a disapproving look. "What is the matter?" Abby asked noticing their apprehension.

"Lass," Teddy said. "Gabe has given us strict instructions not ta let ya out of the inn today." Abby lowered her head and said, "I guess I am still being punished."

"Gabe is a good man Abigail. Give him a chance and all will be fine," Bess encouraged.

Abby was just about to turn and return to her room when she said instead, "I am feeling very guilty and upset. When I feel like this the only thing that makes me feel better is to cook and cook a lot. Can I at least help you in the kitchen today?"

Both Bess and Teddy asked at the same time, "Ya can cook?"

Abby smiled and said, "Yes and very well in fact."

"Do ya know any recipes that could win a contest?" Teddy asked hopeful but not expecting the answer he received.

"Well maybe we can help each other out here," Abby said with a huge smile and a mischievous twinkle in her eye. Bess and Teddy were very interested. "What if I help you win that contest? Will you let me make a peace offering for the men this evening?"

"What is a peace offering?" Teddy asked.

Abby bowed her head and said, "Well, I am not proud of how I treated Gabe and his men and I want to do something to say that I am sorry. But saying sorry just isn't enough and I can't even face them right now without crying."

"Maybe ya feel like that because Gabe punished ya," Bess said trying to make her feel better.

"No, I was feeling like this way before he punished me. The punishment has nothing to do with the way I feel. Even if he had not hurt me at all, I would still feel this way."

"Then a peace offering is ta just say ya are sorry?" Teddy asked.

"No, it is more than that. Gabe rescued me from James and again, without knowing it, when he found me near the ocean. He didn't have to come after me. I was nothing but a pain in his backside, but he did and that is why I need to say thank you," Abby explained.

"Cooking them supper will do all of that?" Bess asked half teasing Abby.

"Probably not but I need to do something, and this is the only thing I can think of," Abby said.

"Ya are going ta have ta tell them what a peace offering is, lass." Teddy instructed.

"I can't. I can't stop crying long enough to say anything. All I am asking is…let me cook supper. I promise I won't poison anyone and we will let them believe it was you who cooked it."

"They still may be angry with ya lass," Teddy said with an encouraging effort.

"I know and I deserve it, but at least I will know that I did something to make them a little happier. Now tell me about this contest and let's get started. We will need the whole day if we are going to pull this off."

"Ya think ya can win a ribbon?" Teddy asked hopefully.

"One ribbon? I plan on winning all the ribbons now get me some parchment and something to write with. Someone needs to go to the market and fast."Abby replied with a confident smile.

Abby was very detailed in her shopping list. She wanted certain kinds of potatoes, cream not milk and ground lean beef, creamy butter, salted and unsalted, a certain kind of apples well ripened and chocolate. Bess was out the door with the list and that left Teddy and Abby to make a pie shell.

When Bess returned, Abby was teaching Teddy to make a pie crust without much luck. He could not get the consistency right and he was getting very frustrated. Abby however had made enough pies to feed the entire inn for supper.

"Bess," Abby said, "I need your help to get your husband to make a good pie crust. He needs to learn how it should feel and there is only one way, I know of that will show him."

Bess put her bundles down on the table and came over to help. Before either one of them could object, Abby took Teddy's hand and placed it on Bess' breast. Both of them turned red at the same time. "None of that now," Abby ordered. "He needs to win this and to do this he has got to make a fantastic piecrust. Now gently squeeze her breast." Teddy did as he was told and Abby watched correcting him when he squeezed the wrong way. Then she said, "Now when you mix this next crust up, remember what you just felt and make your crust feel like her soft round breast." Both Bess and Teddy were giggling but Teddy did make a perfect pie crust the very next time. Of course, he just had to squeeze Bess' breast again to see if he got the right consistency.

When the pies were all put together and ready for the oven, Teddy said, "Abigail, I really like the way ya cook. I haven't had so much fun in the kitchen in years." Then Bess spoke up with red cheeks, "Neither have I."

Abby looked at them both with a twinkle in her eye and said, "The next time you make a crust and if you are alone, try feeling her breast without her clothes on. It feels so much better." With that Abby got hit with a wet rag that Bess flung at her from across the room. The three laughed and kept working.

With the apple pies ready, Abby started on her famous sticky buns and then her chocolate morsel cookies and finally her peace offering. Teddy worked right beside Abby mimicking all her actions. As she made hers, he made his. Abby made sure he measured and put in the exact amounts. The kitchen was hopping with warm bread, apple pies, chocolate morsel cookies and shepherd's pie.

By the time Gabe and the men returned the inn was full of great mouth watering smells. The table was set and Abby was up in her room. Bess was getting ready to serve her guests and Theodore had taken his creations to the contest.

People came from all over Scotland to enter this cooking contest and it was a great honor to win it. One of the prizes was to actually cook the winning dish for the king himself also bragging rights for a year and a lot of business. Guests would be plentiful if the cook won this prestigious contest. Teddy was nervous, but Abby had taught him well and it was now time to wait for the results.

Meanwhile at the inn, Bess was getting ready for dinner. Gabe was not about to let Abby skip supper again tonight. For all he knew, she had stayed in her room all day and he was not about to let her stay there tonight. All the men were in real good moods this evening. They had a very profitable day and Gabe was well pleased.

Abby had slipped up to her room just before they came in. She wanted to take a little break before dinner plus her feet were extra sore from standing on them all day. She needed to wash and re-bandage them before Gabe called for her or she would not be able to stand up. When she tried to put her shoes back on, her feet had doubled in size. So she decided to go to supper in stocking feet.

Abby was still having trouble sitting so she lay on her stomach while she waited and closed her eyes for just a moment. "Been sleeping all day, lass?" Gabe asked standing in the doorway of her room, "time for supper."

Abby did not appreciate his remark especially after working hard all day but she was not going to fight with him. Without saying a word, she rolled out of bed and followed him down to dinner. When she reached the hall, the men were all standing around talking between themselves and the other guests. It smelled so good that the guests were remarking about it. Abby just had to smile to herself. She was always in the kitchen and rarely heard the comments before dinner.

Bess came in and asked everyone to take their seats. Abby waited until the very last minute before she sat down. Gabe insisted she sit next to him. When she finally sat, Gabe noticed her flinch a little and pinch her mouth shut to hide her pain. Bess had two serving girls to help her this evening. First they came out with the sticky buns, followed by the shepherd's pie.

Abby sat playing with her food barely touching it while she listened to the comments about her cooking. She was beaming on the inside only. She still did not want them to know that she had made the supper. Gabe noticed her playing with her food and said, "Do ya know what I do ta my children when they play with their food, Abigail?"

Abby looked up when she finally realized what she'd been doing. Truth was she had tasted her food all day and was just not hungry. When Abby did not answer him, he said, "I feed them."

"I am just not very hungry. Thank you," Abby replied politely.

"Are ya angry because I made ya stay at the inn all day?" He asked trying to get her to look at him.

"I will admit I did not like the feeling of being a prisoner, but I made the best of the day anyway," she replied.

"Ya most likely slept all day didn't ya lass. Especially now that ya are not sitting or standing comfortably," Simon teased.

Abby said, "Well I did manage to get a little nap in." And she was not kidding. It must have been a whole five minutes before Gabe came to get her.

"Need ya backside rubbed lass," Joseph teased and the other men laughed.

"No thank you," Abby said. "But you will be the first to know if I do." Then she added, "Need your horse's tail brushed?" And the men all laughed again.

They had just about finished their dinner and Abby was getting tired of their insults and teasing. When the door of the inn swung open and hit the wall with a large bang. Teddy came in bellowing at the top of his lungs, not considering his guests. "Where is she? Where the hell is she?"

Bess came running out of the kitchen to see what he wanted with her and to calm him down. "What is it Teddy? I am right here."

"Not you, my love." And he kissed her on her cheek. "Abigail!" He screamed as loud as he could. Abby's heart sank. He must have lost the contest and he was angry at her. She couldn't imagine what had gone wrong. She never lost at home. Then she saw Gabe looking at her with a "*Now what did you do*" look across his face.

Again Teddy bellowed her name. This time she stood and said, "I'm here Teddy."

Teddy walked over to her with an expression she could not read. She did not know if he was happy or angry. Puzzled, she just stood there on her sore feet waiting for the worse. She thought she was going to be reprimanded in front of the whole room and that would really ruin her peace offering.

Teddy walked over to her stamping his feet as he walked. He grabbed her by her shoulders and pulled her away from the table. Abby thought for sure he would start shaking her at any minute. She was so sore now. She didn't need to be hurt any more. In fact, there weren't many parts of her body left that could be hurt. Her back was facing the table so she could not see Gabe starting to rise as he watched Teddy or hear the silence that came over the men as Teddy talked.

"I cannot believe what ya did," Teddy said with the same expressionless face.

"I'm so sorry Teddy, really, I thought I was helping," Abby said meekly flinching from the tight grip he had on her shoulders.

"Helping?" He hollered. "Ya thought ya were helping?"

"Theodore," Bess interrupted. "Ya are hurting her. Calm down."

"I will not calm down. She is going ta hear just what she did and I am going ta tell her and everyone is going ta hear it like it or not," He replied with a raised voice.

"Theodore," boomed Gabe. "Let her go."

Abby was just about in tears at this point.

"Ya are the most," and Teddy paused then a smile stretched across his face, "wonderful, incredible, talented woman I have ever met and I am proud ta have met ya." Abby still looked puzzled trying to hold back tears. "Your wonderful peace offering….. It won…..It won," Teddy screamed at the top of his lungs. Then he put his arms around her waist and picked her up and swung her around and around, whooping and hollering at the same time.

Before he could put her down, Gabe was hollering "Teddy put her down. Abigail ya better be telling me just what ya did now."

Bess came in to help Abby. "It's the contest, Gabe. Abby helped Teddy all day. She taught him her recipes. They never stopped all day. She did nothing wrong. She is the reason we won and now we will have a great year for our inn." And she ran over with outstretched arms and gave Abby a big hug and kissed her good cheek.

Abby did not look happy. "What is wrong, lass? We won. Be happy," Bess said.

"I am but I was hoping for more. One ribbon is not too bad, I guess," Abby said disappointed.

"No lass. Ya didn't win just one ribbon," Teddy said still smiling.

"Teddy, for God sakes, will ya tell us what happened," Gabe ordered.

"Ya woman….. That wonderful special woman, worked with me all day on those cut feet, never complaining or asking for a break. She taught me her recipes and asked for nothing except ta make ya all a peace offering. She is the one that really won." Then he turned back to Abigail and finally gave her all his news. "Abigail, ya won a blue ribbon for ya peace offering and for ya sticky buns and for ya apple pie."

It was the first time that Abby had smiled in a long time and Gabe noticed it. She was beautiful especially when she smiled even with her bruised cheek. He looked at his men and they were smiling as well.

"Well, three out of four is a lot better than one," Abby said with a big smile of pride across her face.

"No lass," Teddy said. "We won the whole thing and best-in-show for your cookie."

The whole room broke out in applause and a standing ovation. Abby was thrilled. Finally, she got something right. She thanked her well wishers and started to go upstairs.

"Just where do ya think ya are going?" Gabe asked as she put her foot on the first step.

Teddy went over to her and pulled back into the room. "Ya helped me, lass. Now I am going ta help ya. Ya are going ta tell them what ya told me or I will." He left her standing in the middle of the room in front of Gabe and his men and the other guests.

When she did not say anything, Gabe spoke up. "Abigail, da ya have something ta tell us?"

"I can't," was all she would say.

So Teddy said, "Start with the story of ya grandmother, lass."

Abby nodded, cleared her throat and said, "My grandmother on my mother's side was a very little woman. She would say, 'When you get old no one wants to touch you anymore', and she loved her kisses and hugs. My grandfather was half German and half Swiss. He would never enter or leave the house without giving her three little kisses. They did not live with us but would come over to our house on Sunday and she would make us dinner. My grandmother believed a second helping was a compliment to the cook and she would say, 'If you liked my dinner you have to kiss the cook.' It was her way of getting us grandchildren to give her kisses. So when we were finished we would all line up and give her three kisses, one, two, and three. The shepherd's pie you ate tonight was her recipe with a few changes. It was my peace offering," she said lowering her head.

"What is a peace offering, Abigail?" Gabe asked carefully seeing her fidget with her hands.

"Ya are doing just fine, Abby. Keep going," Bess encouraged.

Abby took a deep breath and said, "A peace offering is a way to say "*sorry*" when saying sorry isn't enough." Her voice started shaking, but she went on fighting back tears. "I am not very proud of the way I acted. I really didn't think any of you would be harmed. It is so different here for me. Which is no excuse for my actions, but I would never forgive myself if one of you were injured because of me. I feel so guilty and it has nothing to do with being punished. I would feel this way anyway. You would think being punished would help the way I feel but it doesn't."

Then she shifted her weight to give her feet a rest and continued. "But it is more than saying *sorry*, it is also a 'thank you.' By rights, you should have left me at James, but you didn't. And if you had not found me when you did, by the ocean, the four men would have found me again and killed me like they killed that poor man in the woods. Being strapped is much more appealing than being stabbed."

"Ya saw the man die?" Gabe asked surprised with this news, trying to control his emotions.

"I saw the man beaten, stripped and stabbed to death and then his body eaten by wolves," she said slowly without hesitation while looking at the floor.

"Can ya identify the killers Abby?" Gabe asked trying not to get upset.

"I have seen them somewhere but I cannot put my finger on where."

Gabe wanted to question her further but she was having such a hard time to talk about it that he decided to go back to her peace offering but before he could say anything, she asked, "May I leave now?"

Bess carried in the hot apple pie and put it on the table in front of the men.

"Ya made dinner, Abigail?" Gabe asked.

"Yes."

"So ya are saying ya are sorry?"

"Yes."

"And ya are thanking us for saving ya?"

"YES," Abby said hoping she could leave before she started to cry again.

Gabe looked at his men and they all nodded. He rose and walked over in front of Abby.

"Your apology is accepted." Then he turned her around and gave her a swat on her sore backside. He turned her back to face him and pointed his big finger at the baffled look on her face and said, "Donna ever do it again. And ya donna have ta thank us for saving ya. It was our pleasure and I will be talking ta ya more about those men and what happened in the woods." Then he put his hands under her arms and picked her up right off the floor. Looking directly into her misty eyes, he said, "And this is for the cook." He kissed her, "One.... Two......Three." Then he whispered in her ear, "Well done."

"May I leave now?" Abigail asked quickly wiping a tear from her eye so no one would see, trying not to look at Gabe or anyone else.

"No," Joseph answered from behind her. "It is my turn." He turned her to face him and said, "Apology accepted and if ya ever cut my horse's tail again, I will shave your head." Then he turned her around and swatted her backside. When she faced him again he said, "Never, never do it again and ya donna know how relieved I was ta find ya alive. I thought ya were the one in the woods dead and this is for the cook." And he bent down and gently kissed her one....two..... three..... Again Abby tried to leave and Simon stopped her. He too accepted her apology and her thank you, he swatted her bum and then kissed her, one...two...three...

When it was Dougal's turn he said, "I just want ya ta know, the next time I need ta guard ya I will be making sure what I am guarding is ya and not a bloody horse's tail. Donna think ya will ever be getting away from me again." Then he too swatted her backside and then ended with three kisses.

Abby was approached by each of Gabe's men after Dougal and each accepted her apology and her thank you. Each swatted her bum and kissed the cook, one...two.....three.

Finally when they all had their turn, Abby was excused.

CHAPTER 12
Almost Home

Abby ran up the stairs as fast as her cut feet would let her, slammed her door shut and landed face down kiddy-corner on the bed. Her head was buried in her arms on the pillow while her injured feet dangled over the edge of the bed. Tears and more tears came. She just could not stop crying. Her peace offering went well, better than she expected, but still she cried.

Bessie entered the dining room while her guests were enjoying their apple pie and cheese, pleased with what just happened. She was carrying a large pan of warm water and a few white pieces of linen.

"What is that for Bessie?" Gabe asked as she started up the stairs.

"It is for Abby's feet, Gabe. They are really bad. I told her not ta stand so much today but she insisted on making amends and helping Teddy. I just hope she will let me tend ta them now. She is just a wee bit strong headed ya know," Bess answered with a look to come and help.

Gabe cut a large piece of pie and cheese and put them on a plate. He looked at his men and said, "Excuse me gentlemen, someone is in need of doctoring."

"Be gentle Gabe," Joseph called out as he went up the stairs with Bess.

Abigail heard a knock on her door. Bessie called, "Abby, I need ta tend ya feet and check ya bum. May I come in?

"I am fine Bess there is no need," Abby answered.

"I will not be taken no for an answer now. May I come in?" Bess asked again.

"Yes," Abby answered through sniffs and tears. Abby was still face down and crying uncontrollably when Bess and Gabe walked into the room. Gabe just stood back and watched quietly. Abby was completely unaware of his presence in the room.

"May I check your bum Abby ta see if I need ta use ointment?"Bess asked sweetly.

"That is alright but I think I am fine," Abby answered still hiding her face in her arms.

"Better let me check anyway aye?" Bess said looking at Gabe. She wanted him to see what he had done to her.

"Okay," Abby said keeping her eyes buried in the pillow.

Bess lifted Abigail's skirts high enough to let Gabe see his handy work. Gabe couldn't believe how bruised her bottom was and how she never screamed out. There was no broken skin so Bess lowered her skirts and started to work on her feet.

"Ya know, I had my backside tanned many times by my brother but I never remember him hitting me this much or marking me this badly. Whatever did ya do ta deserve this?" Then she turned and gave Gabe another most disapproving look.

"I would think," Bess said addressing Abby but mainly for Gabe's ears, "that he could have made his point without so much bruising." Then she gave him another dirty look.

"It's my own fault, Bess. Don't blame him. He warned me and I didn't listen. Wait! Did you say 'your brother'?" Abby asked still sobbing.

"Aye, I did. He is my oldest brother. I was one of the babies."

"He strapped you too? How many little McKenzies are there anyway?" Abby asked.

"Oh aye, many times, but never like this. There are nine of us, seven boys and two girls. Now, stop that crying lass before ya make yaself sick," Bess ordered.

"I can't help it. I cannot stop. I never cry. I never cried when I had my babies, but I can't stop. I feel so guilty for what I did. Gabe and his men only treated me kindly. I let my temper get the better of me.

I didn't know that they cut hands off here. If I had, I'd never done something like that. I thought they would just put them in the stocks, which would give me time to leave so they could not follow me. I am so ashamed of myself."

"They forgave you, Abby, and they still have all their hands," Bess replied.

"That's just it, I can't forgive myself. I was such a fool. And when I was out there alone for two days, I was helpless. I could have survived in the colonies but not here. I had no food or water and I couldn't stop to get any because those men and wolves were not far behind me. I really wanted Gabe to find me and hoped secretly deep down in my heart that he would."

"Tell Gabe that Abby," Bess encouraged.

"NO."

"Why?"

"I don't want him to see me cry."

Gabe just smiled lovingly at Bessie and silently motioned her to leave.

Thinking she was alone with Bess in the room, Abby said, "I don't understand why I care what he thinks of me, but I do." And she sobbed and sniffed some more.

Gabe softly washed her feet and then poured liquid on them to stop infection. He wrapped them in the linen. When he was done he said, "There, we will check them in the morning. Ya should not be wearing shoes for the next few days until ya're feet heal. Ya are not ta ever do what ya did today and stand on them all day. Ya are just asking for trouble."

Abby quickly turned over on her side surprised he was in the room and not Bess. She scooted up to the headboard, her face covered with tears still huffing. "How long have you been there?"

"Long enough," he said, and then sat down on the edge of the bed. "Ya didn't have any pie. Sit up lass."

"I'd rather not," Abby whispered.

He made a movement to adjust his belt and noticed her flinch.

"Relax, lass. I am not here ta punish ya. Do ya know how many coins ya and Teddy won?" Gabe asked with a grin.

"No and I don't want to. I just wanted to cook for all of you."

"I see…pie?" Gabe asked holding the pie he'd brought up.

"It does look pretty good, doesn't it? I am hungry."

"Ya should be. Ya ate nothing. Ya didn't try ta poison us did ya, lass?" Gabe asked teasingly.

"Not very nice, Laird," Abby said with a frown.

"I was really proud of ya tonight, Abigail."

"You were? Thank you," Abby said as she took her first bite of pie. Her bruised face was turning a deep shade of blue and yellow now but, at least the swelling had gone down.

"I came ta tell ya that we will be leaving early in the morning. Do ya want me ta wake ya or can ya get up on ya own?

"Just rap on my door to make sure I am up please," Abby answered.

He watched her eat the rest of the pie, tear stains still on her cheeks.

"Have we come ta an understanding then?"Gabe asked with lifted eyebrows.

"Yes."

"I need ya word lass," Gabe demanded.

"You have my word. I will do my best to behave," Abby said in a whisper.

"I donna want that."

"What then?"Abby asked surprised with his answer.

"I want ta be able ta trust ya not ta try ta leave ever again without asking me for permission first," Gabe said firmly. "And we will talk about what happened in the woods and ya will not lie ta me and tell me everything."

She lowered her head and said, "Okay."

"Is that an Aye or a Nay?"

"It is an Aye," she said clearly.

"Very well then," he took the dish from her and then took her hand. He pulled her out of the bed and said, "Let me help with ya laces." He loosened the laces on her gown and lifted it over her head. She stood facing him wearing her under shift.

"To bed," he barked playfully.

She squirmed into the bed. He covered her with the soft quilt and gently tucked her in. Gabe started to leave her room. She just couldn't resist. “What, no kiss goodnight? Isn’t that what you do after you tuck someone in?”

He stopped dead and turned to look at her. She gasped when she saw the look on his face and quickly covered her head with the quilt. She couldn’t help but giggle at the expression on his face. When she didn’t hear anything, she assumed he’d left the room and peaked out from under the blanket. *Surely he’d left*, she thought to herself. But when she lowered the quilt to see, his head was inches from her face. She yelped in surprise and jumped. He kissed her forehead, chuckled and said, “Now go ta sleep.”

“Gabe,” Abby said softly with misty eyes as he was leaving her room. “I really am sorry.”

“I know. Now no more tears.” And he wiped a tear from her cheek and said, “Sweet dreams.” He kissed her again and walked out of her room shutting the door as he left.

Abby smiled, turned over, closed her eyes and slept like a baby. After a restful night at the inn, they left bright and early the next morning. Gabriel was determined to reach the highlands in three days but was worried it might take longer because of Abigail.

All thirteen Scotts were ready and saddled when Abby came out of the inn. She was dressed in the green gown she had earned in the marketplace while Gabe and the others were in the stocks, but she was only wearing wool socks on her still sore feet. Teddy walked her out holding her elbow.

“I want ya ta have this,” he said holding up a gold chain with a rather large ruby pendent.

“I cannot take that. Give it to Bess,” Abby said pushing his hand away.

“No,” Teddy said. “We talked it over and she wants ya ta have it as much as I do.”

Abby looked at him doubtfully, but then Bess came out smiling wearing a large floured hand print on both breasts. “We really want ya ta have it Abigail. We could not have won without ya and it is our way of saying, thank ya.”

“Were we making pie crusts this morning?”Abby asked Bess, giggling.

"Yes, why would ya ask that?" Bess asked unaware she was wearing the evidence. Abby just pointed at her breasts and Bessie's face went beet red. She quickly turned to wipe the flour dust off her chest before her brother noticed and revealed a large floured hand print on her backside. Abby and all the men broke out in laughter. Bess threw her arms around Abby and kissed her cheek. "I'll see ya the day after Christmas," Bess whispered in her ear.

"Ya best be there the day after Christmas or I will come and get ya," Gabe said from behind Bess. He took the pendent from Teddy and put it around Abby's neck. "Time ta go lass."

Teddy came up to Abby and gave her a huge hug and then kissed her one…two…three. Gabe reached in between them and pulled Abby away. If Bess didn't know better, she would think her brother was a little jealous when it came to Abigail. "Maybe by the time we come at Christmas ya will have some good news for us Gabriel," Bess teased her brother.

Gabe gave Bess a playful look and shrugged his shoulders, but would not let Abby see what he did. He picked Abby up and gently settled her on her mare trying not to hurt her feet or bum. Then he hugged his little sister and slapped his brother-in-law on the shoulder and said goodbye. He mounted his stallion and asked "Abigail?"

"Yes Gabe, my feet are in the stirrups," she answered. He smiled and gave the order to ride toward the highlands.

Gabe really pushed everyone and he watched Abby carefully. They rode nonstop until late into the afternoon. Abigail really needed to stop. Gabe noticed her fidgeting. "Lass da ya need ta take a break?"

"Yes."

"Ya just need ta ask, lass." Gabe stopped and dismounted but Abby was off her steed and running into the woods before he could help her down.

"Well, I guess she really had ta tend ta her needs, Gabe," Joseph said teasingly.

"I guess so," Gabe answered with a smile. She came back a few minutes later limping.

"Feeling better lass?" Joseph asked.

"Yes, thank you," she said indignantly.

They didn't break long. Gabe had a stopping point he wanted to reach before dark. Abby's legs were sore and chapped. Her backside still felt like sitting on pins and needles from her punishment and she was becoming exhausted. Stopping was all she could think of. There wasn't much chatter between the men to keep her mind occupied. It seemed everyone was as determined as Gabe to reach their stopping point before dark. The countryside was breathtaking. She tried to concentrate on the landscape and not on her backside, feet or legs. Without thinking, she said out loud, "Oooooo, it is so beautiful here." She wasn't expecting an answer but Gabe said, "Yes and it only gets better lass."

About an hour later, Abby's head started bobbing. She had all she could do not to fall asleep while sitting on her mare. Gabe circled around her, grabbed her waist and pulled her onto his mount before she could refuse. Her bottom rested on his lap and her legs were dangling over his right thigh. His arm circled around her.

"Are ya cold, lass?"

"I am fine."

"Lass?"

"Well just a little bit."

He pulled his plaid off of his shoulder and wrapped her in it. He was so warm. She just wanted to curl up in his arms and put her face against his chest and fall asleep.

"Abby, I know ya are tired. Lean against me, I have ya."

She didn't answer him but snuggled in his arms. It wasn't long before she was sound asleep. Gabe woke her later.

"How long have I been asleep?" She asked still groggy.

"A few hours, lass," he answered.

A few hours seemed like five minutes. Gabe swung down then helped her to her feet. H held on until she was no longer shaky. "We will camp here lass." Abby went to tend her needs while the men unsaddled their horses. Her feet were very swollen and aching. She found a small stream where she took her socks off and dipped her feet in the cool water. Before she could get up and return back to camp, Gabe found her.

"I was just soaking my feet and I know I have not been gone that long and I won't let you hit me again," she blurted out.

"If I want ta hit ya I will and ya cannot stop me. Now relax, I came ta tend ta ya feet. Are ya going ta give me a hard time?"

Abby bowed her head and said, "No". He reached into the water and washed her feet with soap then he dried her feet and poured salve on her wounds.

Then he asked, "Do I need ta check ya bum?"

Abby was appalled. "No you don't, thank you."

"Maybe I should look anyway," he said smiling up at her with a devilish look in his eyes.

"I think, sir you have seen the last of my backside and don't even think of asking again!" Abby said lifting her chin in defiance.

Gabe could not help but tease her just a little more. "Does that mean that ya are going ta be as good as gold?"

"It means whatever you want to think," she replied with clenched teeth.

"I think it is time we return back ta camp before I check ya bum." Gabe grabbed her hand and pulled her to her feet and they walked back to camp.

"After supper we will have our talk," he said as they reached the camp. The horses had been unsaddled and brushed and the wood fetched for the fire. The man they called Cookie had a rabbit stew well underway. Gabe went and made a bed for Abby with a tented area to protect her from the wind. He had every intention of sharing her quarters from now on.

Cookie hit a pot to announce dinner. His rabbit stew was the best Abby had ever tasted. Whether it was the cold or the length of the day, the single meal seemed like a royal banquet. After they finished Abby fetched chocolate morsel cookies from her bag that Teddy had packed for her and shared them with the men.

"Cookie," Abby said. "That was a very good stew. Maybe we can exchange a recipe or two?"

Before Cookie could answer her, Joseph called out. "Gabe, do we have ta kiss the cook?"

"Donna ya even think about it," Cookie said. "Not bloody well likely."

Abby laughed. She had the sweetest laugh. It was very contagious. She also had quite a sense of humor. "I don't understand, Cookie," she teased. "You are kind of cute. Don't you like kisses?" Then she giggled more.

"Lass, ya are not being funny," Cookie answered. Abby giggled more and all the men joined in with her.

"Maybe ya need ya bed lass," Cookie teased back. "Isn't it her bed time Gabe?"

"I know when I am not wanted," she said still laughing.

Abby went to the bed Gabe had made for her, but before she could settle down, Gabe came and sat down next to her. "We need ta talk and I am not waiting any longer. What happened in the woods that night?"

Abby took a long breathe and started to tell him about the wolves and how she climbed the tree to get away from them. Then she told him about the four killing thieves who beat the man to near death. "I think the man was looking at me when he was lying on the ground. I could not make out his face but I think he knew I was there. He took his ring off and buried it in the loose leaves. He pointed at it to make sure I knew where it was. The men who beat him stripped him looking for something. I think it was the ring, but I don't really know. They saw me Gabe, those four men saw me too, but not until after they had stabbed the man. It was a strange looking knife, very long and pointed with a rounded ball like handle. I am being hunted and the longer I stay with you the more I endanger you and your men and their families. You should not take me home. That is why I buried myself under the bush. I was too tired. They had been trailing me for a day and half and I just could not go on."

"I donna think we have ta worry about just four men Abigail," Gabe said now holding her around her shoulders trying to get her to stop shaking.

"No, Gabe it is not just four men and they are not just after me, but what is in my box and what I can give them."

"What is in that box that has ya so scared, lass?" Gabe asked expecting an answer.

"My dreams, Gabe, and the dreams of my family are written down and in that stupid box."

"Abigail I want ta help ya, but I cannot if ya donna tell me everything."

"Have you ever heard of the 'dreaming family'"? She asked.

"Aye my mother use ta tells us children that story, when I was but a lad."

"What did she tell you?" Abby asked hoping he already knew what she needed to tell him.

"She said there was a gifted family who would have wonderful dreams that would predict the future. They were suppose to live in a faraway land where they were treated like royalty. Until one day when their land was attacked and they were never seen or heard from again, but the dreams that were recorded and left, all came true."

"I am one of the gifted or cursed. It depends how you look at it. In fact I am the only one still surviving. My children were born with mixed blood so they only have half of the dream power and not as valuable as I am. Until I get that box to its rightful place I am in danger and so is anyone who is with me. That is why you need to let me go. My grandfather was gifted too that is why I was only allowed short visits with him."

"Ya said ya had eight brothers and sisters."

"I said, my father would say, 'I have eight wonderful children and then I have Abigail.' I was adopted. They kept me safe from harm all those years. Old Joe taught me how to interpret the dreams and not to fear them. He also taught me how to stop them. My grandfather taught me my language and what was in the box. It was his dying wish that I return to my country and give the box a proper home. There are always going to be treasure seekers, Gabe. They think that stupid box has some wonderful value, but it is just a box with a few old documents including a deed, a key and a few rings. It carries a prediction but it is for me only. No one can benefit from it but me. My family destroyed all they could but left the last documents to give back to the people that now occupy my homeland, the Wikings. They have hunted my family for a century. Now I will return that box, and hopefully they will leave me alone."

Gabe and Abby stayed up late into the night talking. "My family was captured and imprisoned, force to dream and then predict. When the predictions or the dreams did not come true they were usually tortured and finally killed. I do believe whatever the last prediction says will free me. At least that was what my grandfather use to tell me.

Mr. Pinkerton knew very well what my box was and was just waiting for the owner to come and get it. It was useless to him in his bank. He needed me to lead him to the object that the key opens. Most people are not interested in dream people anymore, but they are in treasure."

"Is there a real treasure Abigail?" Gabe asked.

"Technically, yes, but is it of value to anyone but me. I don't know. A set bellows is valuable to a smithy but not to a merchant." Then she looked at Gabe and sighed. "Actually I do know what is supposed to be hidden and I cannot tell you what it is. The only person I am allowed to tell is my husband and I would never tell Roy anything about my family. Even my children are not allowed to know. I am taking a big risk even telling you as much as I have. My identity has always been hidden and so has that damn box. I would like it to stay that way, but my grandfather has managed to bring all this to an end which means eventually I will have to divulge everything. Maybe that is what will finally set me free."

Gabe looked at Abigail and said, "So no more talk of leaving and danger. Ya are in good hands Lass. I will protect ya. When the time comes we will both know what we have ta do."

"But I already have people hunting me," Abby replied with a trembling voice.

"Are they hunting ya because of the box or are they hunting ya because of the murder ya saw?" Gabe asked with raised eyebrows. "Now we need ta get some sleep."

Abby started to lie down on the plaid when she felt Gabe lie down next to her.

"What are you doing?" Abby asked expecting him to leave.

"I am sleeping with ya lass. What did ya think?"

"Oh, no you are not!" Abby said moving away from him.

Gabe just reached out and grabbed her around the waist and pulled her close to him. He held on tight so she could not move away and covered them both with his plaid. "We are no longer in the low country. It is still winter up here. It will get a lot colder as the night goes on and the fire goes down. Now stop wiggling and go ta sleep like a good little girl." Gabe heard Abby gasp in annoyance to his comment but she did not disobey him.

But she said, "I am not a little girl Gabriel McKenzie and I would appreciate you not treating me as one."

"OH! Is that the way ya want it. Very well, I will do my best." Then Abby felt Gabe loosen her laces and reach into her gown and cuddle one of her breasts in his big warm hand. It always amazed her how nice that felt, but she was not going to let him get away with sleeping like this all night. She tried getting his hand out of there, but Gabe said, "I hold ya breast or I will have my way with ya, your choice lass." So, Abby fell asleep warm and close to Gabe with his hand just where he had left it, gently squeezing her breast now and then.

When morning came Abby found herself alone. It was so warm under the plaid. Abby did not want to come out so she decided to just stay right there until she absolutely had to move. She covered her head with the plaid and closed her eyes.

Abby hurt so much the previous last night from the long ride. Her bruised feet and bum would be worse this morning. Then Gabe peeked into the tent, "Time ta wake up, lass." Abby laid there not moving completely ignoring him. Gabe could not believe how stubborn she was. He gave her a little poke but Abby only groaned in protest.

"Abigail, I know you are awake. Do ya need help getting out of bed?" Gabe asked a little forcefully.

"No. Just five more minutes," Abby said from under the plaid still refusing to move.

Gabe's eyebrows rose. She was defying him. He could not believe she was blatantly disobeying him. "Maybe a good soak in the loch will get ya going," Gabe teased. He reached for her.

"I'm up," she squealed. "I'm up." Abby was not out of the plaid and she could feel the coolness of the day. A good soak, as Gabe had called it, would not be pleasant at all.

"Good," he said and started to walk away. Gabe happened to look back as he was leaving, and what did he see, Abby still under his plaid and still not moving. "She's just asking for trouble and I am the one that can give it ta her," he whispered to himself. He went back in the tent and pulled the plaid off her. She gasped from the cold. He grabbed her arm and pulled her up and over his shoulder.

"No Gabe. I'm up. I'm up. I am really up," she said squirming to get free.

"That is what ya said last time. I'm just helping ya. That's all."

"No. Gabe, no," she begged.

He carried her to the edge of the loch being greeted good morning by the men as Gabe carried her by. "Are ya ready for a swim, lass?" He asked?

"No Gabe, Please."

"One…Two…Three…," Gabe counted. Abigail squealed thinking she would be soon in the loch. A second later, Gabe put her down next to the loch and not in it. He pointed his finger at her and said, "Next time lass, I will not hesitate ta throw ya in. Now get ready ta go."

Abby was wide awake now. She tended her needs, washed and tried to comb her hair with her fingers. Then returned to camp where Cookie handed her a sweet biscuit, some cheese and fresh water to drink.

"Eat up lass. We have another long day," Gabe ordered. Fifteen minutes later, Abigail was being hoisted on to her mount. Gabe checked her feet and finally let her wear her shoes which he put on while she was in the saddle. "Lass, these are boy's shoes. Why would ya buy boy's shoes?"

"They were the right price," Abby said with a proud smile.

"Goodness, ya feet are small. I donna think my youngest son could wear these and he is seven."

"Good, you will not be taking them away from me and besides they have a buckle. The cobbler insisted it made them look more like women's shoes." Gabe rolled his eyes and fixed her skirts. He readjusted her hold on the reins again and said, "Lass ya have a great seat ta ride but ya know nothing about the reins or stirrups."

"Well that's because we never used them or a saddle. I only rode the workhorses and I never needed them."

Gabe mounted his steed with his usual graceful leap and started off. The pace was slow to start with. Gabe didn't want the horses to get too tired too quickly. They still had another full day and maybe a half of another one.

"Did ya ride with ya feet tucked under ya bum when ya were a child, lass?" Gabe asked as they rode side by side.

"Yes I did in fact."

"And ya father allowed ya ta ride like that?" Gabe asked like a protective father.

"I am not a child Gabe, and I would appreciate you stop treating me like one." Then she added under her breath but loud enough to be heard. "And no it would make my father almost as angry as it makes you."

"And tell me lass. What did ya father do when ya did disobey him and rode with ya feet tucked under ya bum?"

"Well, he would just forbid me to ride for a whole week and sometimes more if he really became angry," Abby admitted guiltily.

"I like ya father. He must have been a good man. He certainly must be sainted after having a child like ya."

"I admit I did give him a hard time but I wasn't a bad child. I just never had any fear. So I was always getting into trouble," Abby confessed.

"And did the absence of a ride make ya stop?"Gabe asked.

"For a while, but then I'd forget and get caught again."

"Well if I catch ya riding like that today, ya are going ta ride on my lap. I haven't decided yet if ya will be sitting or lying face down." Then Gabe urged his horse to increase the pace but not before he saw Abby's mouth drop open and then she gave him a very dirty look.

It was beautiful in the Highlands. The hills were just coming alive again after winter. The air was crisp but clean and the smell of spring was in the air. The sun shone bright today, which was unusual for this time of year giving needed warmth to the day. Abby kept track of the animals she saw, rabbits, birds, sheep, and a few cows and of course wolves. They stopped just outside a small patch of woods near a small loch.

At the end of the day Abby was still on her own mount. Gabe had to smile a little when he dismounted. She was just like a child in many ways. This was the first day he did not have to remind her to keep her feet in the stirrups and today was the first day her feet looked better. She always surprised him with her attitude. She never whined or complained and she would join in the conversation as the men would let her.

When it came time to go to her bed area, Gabe followed her again. He made sure she was covered and said, "I will be back in a little while I need ta do something first, make sure ya save enough room for me." Abby gave him one her dirty looks and Gabe left the tent chuckling to himself.

......She was back in her crate. The rats were coming in. The more she fought the more they came. James was laughing. And then the man in the green jacket was coming at her with his hands all blood, laughing. She started screaming, get them off. Get them off. Don't hurt me, don't kill me......

"Wake up lass," Gabe said gently as he held her in his arms tying to keep her from thrashing. Abby woke with a start, tears running down her cheeks. Her breathing was hard and fast as if she'd been fighting for a long time.

"Come with me. The men need their sleep." He pulled her to her feet and then picked her up like he was holding a baby.

"I'm sorry," she whispered.

"Not ya fault lass. No one is upset with ya. But since we are not going ta get much sleep, I think ya can use a good bath." He stopped at his saddle bags and took out a bar of soap.

"Bath!" Abby said in protest, "in the middle of the night? It is freezing out here. You must be joking."

"No."

He took her away from the men and down a very steep path, which lead to the water below. It was the early morning and still dark, but the moon was bright casting enough light to see clearly. When they reached the bottom of the path, Abby could see a very small pool of water surrounded by a stone ledge on three sides. Somewhere nearby she could hear the sound of water splash on the shore which led her to believe they must be close to the loch.

"Alright," Gabe said. "In ya go."

"What?" Abigail protested. She was not about to go into that freezing water.

"Time for ya bath."

"It is freezing out here," Abby said as she started to inch her way back up the path.

"Now Abigail, ya will feel so much better and I will take one with ya. I was going ta wait for the sun ta show ya this but ya're not sleeping anyway… Jump in," Gabe encouraged.

Abby stood there trying to figure a way out of this. She really would love a bath but it was just so cold. A hot bath would be so much better. Gabe reached his hand out. "Come lass, you'll like it, I promise."

Abigail shook her head, "no."

Gabe shook his head, "yes." "Trust me lass. Take that disgusting gown off and get into the water."

Abby looked down, she was wearing her faded blue gown with the patches. "This disgusting gown, as you call it is next to all I have and believe it or not it was beautiful at one time," Abigail scolded trying to buy some more time.

"But it is not beautiful now, is it? In fact I'm going ta burn it as soon as I can get it off your back along with that green one," Gabe said.

"You will do no such thing Gabriel McKenzie." When she became angry she would always use his full two names. He decided to take the challenge.

"OH, I won't will I?"And he took a step toward her.

"Gabriel," Abby said warning him not to come to close.

"Aye."

"That is far enough."

"Ya take it off, lass and get in the water or I will rip it off and throw ya in. Your choice," he said with a smile, hoping she'd give him the chance to rip it off.

"I'm not going to get out of this am I?" Abby asked still hoping.

"No lass, ya're not."

"Very well," she said. "At least you can do is turn around. I'm not taking anything off in front of you," holding her hands on her hips and sticking her chin out in complete defiance. Gabe smiled and turned while Abby slipped her dress off and slid into the water.

He laughed when he heard her exclaim, "It is warm," sputtering in complete surprise. "Why didn't you tell me?"

"I asked ya ta trust me," he answered with his back toward her. Still wearing her shift, she changed her mind and slipped it off and threw it on the ground near her gown. She lay back in the water and enjoyed the warmth that surrounded her.

"Okay," she said when she was out of his sight in the water. "You can go now. I will be fine. Come and get me when the sun comes up."

Gabe could not believe she was giving him orders. "Lass where are ya?"

"Here," she answered splashing the water to get his attention.

"Donna go out ta far it is over ya head," Gabe ordered. But Abby was a very good swimmer, her grandfather insisted on it. She remembered being thrown off the deck of one of his ships from time to time and being made to swim back to shore because she would not do as he ordered.

"I know," she said as she splashed about moving out a little deeper.

"Can ya swim lass?"

"Is the water warm? Trust me," she teased.

The next thing she heard was a very big splash from someone or something hitting the water.

"Gabe?" Abby called with a touch of panic in her voice.

"Aye lass," he said coming up from under her in the water. She spun around to see Gabe. His hair slicked back from the water and his naked shoulders sticking out of the water.

"What are you doing?" Abby asked a little nervous with him so close and her so naked.

"Swimming," he answered.

"And what are you wearing?"

"Same as ya are," he said smiling.

Gabe noticed her apprehension. "Relax lass. It is ta dark ta see anything."

"Seeing is not what I am worried about."

"Ya can swim, right?" Gabe asked again.

"Yes. Why?"Abby answered treading water.

"The pond isn't very big but it makes for a good swim. Are ya ready?"

"Aye," Abby said mimicking Gabe's low voice.

The pair swam a foot apart. Gabe was an excellent swimmer and was surprised by how easily Abby could keep up with him. As they swam away from the shore the water started to cool down. Abby was not about to complain. It felt good, this warm water, and she wanted to stay in it as long as she could.

Her skin was white. He could see her very well through the water in the moon light. This was like heaven on earth, a warm swim on a cool night with a beautiful round, voluptuous, naked woman. He was going to make her his. Gabe could not understand the attraction he had for this woman. As much as he loved his wife, she did not hold his attraction as this woman did. He wanted her and needed her but he had to consider his family and clan. She would have to be accepted by them and vice versa. Gabe would not take no for an answer. Somehow he was going to have her. He wanted to hold her naked body against his and feel the warm water surround them, he wanted….. A few more strokes and they had made it to the other side.

It was quite a bit cooler over here and Abby was anxious to return to the warmer water. The sky was just beginning to lighten with the morning sun.

"Are you alright Gabe? You seem to be far off in thought," Abigail asked as they stopped at the other side.

"Are ya alright Abigail?" Gabe asked refusing to answer her question.

"Yes. Why?"

"Can ya make it back?" Gabe asked as he treaded water. Abigail rolled her eyes at him and said, "If you need help, just holler." She turned and started back giving him a gentle glimpse of her beautiful full bum. Gabe smiled and followed staying close to her side.

By the time they reached the other side, the sun was rising. It was so warm on this side. Abby had to ask, "Why is it so warm over here?"

"Hot springs," Gabe answered watching the water slosh against her big round breasts. He loved how her bosoms floated in the current of the waves. The water was crystal clear giving him a full view of her roundness down to her tiny feet. All he could think of was touching her, squeezing that voluptuous bottom, cupping her breasts with his large hands. She dipped under the water and then came out with her chin up smoothing her hair back with the dripping water. She was beautiful and he was handsome in the morning light.

His shoulders were thick, broad and muscular with large strong looking arms. His chest was speckled with curly black hair giving way to his rippled flat stomach. In the water, she could look down and see his manhood floating gently with the current. She felt heat come into her face with the sight of his giftedness. Abby thought her husband was large but nothing like Gabe. Gabe noticed her reaction. "Like what ya see lass?" he asked teasingly. Abby became defiant and said, "What makes you think I see anything?" she said,trying to hide her embarrassment. "Oh, maybe because I can see as much of ya as ya can see of me," Gabe answered with a grin. Abby gasped when she realized he could see her very well. She tried to cover herself as much as she could with her arms and swam to the shore. When she looked for her gown and shift it was gone. "Someone took my gown," she sputtered.

"Aye, it was I."

"Now what am I suppose to do?" she asked sitting just under the water at the shore covering her breasts.

"Wash," he said giving her a piece of soap. He was already soaped up. "Wash my back Lass?" Abby looked surprised he would ask such a thing. "I donna bite," he teased again.

Abigail drifted over to his backside and began to wash his back in circular motions. She had a wonderful touch giving him goose bumps.

"Ah lass, ya do have a way," he praised. "Now it is ya turn," he said. "Turn around or shall I wash ya front too."

Abby had had it. She was uncomfortable naked with a man. Even her own husband, did not allow nudity in front of him. The warm water had been so enticing but she started to feel a little overwhelmed.

"I can wash myself, thank you." She started to move away from him. This did not set right with Gabe. Women did as they were told by him. He was laird and no one refused him. He reached over and grabbed her shoulders, turned her around and scrubbed her back and bottom. He lifted her out of the water exposing her black and blue bum. He gave her one good swat and then set her down. She ducked down in the water and turned around appalled he did such a thing, but before she could say anything, he said, "When are ya going ta trust me lass?"

"I will trust you when you let me decide to stay or leave, in other words when you trust me." She swam to the shore and walked out of the water, giving him a good view of her voluptuous bottom, grabbed his plaid and wrapped herself in it. She sat on a boulder with her back facing the pond. Gabe came up behind her. She refused to even look at him.

"Here lass," he said holding a new gown and shift and a pair of wool socks. She took them slowly.

"Where did you get these?" she asked.

"Bess," he replied softly. "I thought ya might feel better about meeting my clan in a decent gown."

"Thank you," she whispered as Gabe started to dress.

"Gabe?"

"Aye?"

She walked over to him. "I am sorry," she said, eyes down, head bent. "Will you help me with my laces?"

"Aye lass, get dressed."

Abby moved to the side and put the shift on. It was warm and soft made of white flannel linen. She was hoping that the dress would not be too small. After slipping it on she found it to be a perfect fit, maybe a touch too big. It was a warm wool gown in her favorite color, baby blue, clean from the stench of the debtor's prison and from the memories of James.

Walking around the rock, where she had dressed she found Gabe watching her.

"Do you like it?" She asked looking pleased.

Gabe smiled. "Aye lass. I like what's in it better."

"You stop that or you're going to make me blush."

"Looks like ya already have," Gabe said chuckling. Abby didn't notice but Gabe did. She had lost a good many pounds since the first time he laid eyes on her. At this moment he found her very beautiful.

"This feels wonderful. Thank you so much," she exclaimed.

Gabe reached down and kissed her forehead. "Ya are welcomed, my sweet, now put ya socks on."

"I cannot."

"Why not?" Gabe asked surprised with her answer.

"I left my shoes at camp. I don't want to ruin them by walking on the dirt." Then she looked up at Gabe with a sheepish expression and smiled deviously. "Will you give me a piggy back ride if I do?"

"A what? I donna knows what that is but I can carry you if ya like."

Abby sat on the rock and slipped the socks on then climbed on top of the rock and wiggled her finger at Gabe for him to come here.

"Lass what are ya doing," Gabe asked a little skeptical.

"Turn around," she said. Then she added, "Trust me."

Gabe rolled his eyes and turned his back to her. "Ready?" she asked. "Aye," he answered.

She jumped up on his back wrapping her legs around his waist and her arms around her neck. He reached and grabbed her legs. "Okay," she teased. "Giddy-up," and then she giggled.

Gabe gave her legs a little squeeze and chuckled, "Aye lass."

He carried her up the path and back to camp where the men were just beginning to rise. Abby could hear the excitement in their voices, but because they were speaking Gaelic she could not understand what they were saying. Gabe noticed her reaction and said, "Today, we will be home." What he didn't tell her was all the chaffing he was receiving from the men, carrying her that way.

CHAPTER 13
Welcome Home

The men were ready and mounted much quicker than the other days. They were ready to get home and see their families. Abby sat quietly on her mount listening to the conversations even though she had no idea what they were saying. Gabe circled around to her side and asked, "So, do all your dreams come true Abby?"

"Most of them," Abby replied looking for the first glimpse of her new home.

Gabe could see how uneasy she was and tried to keep her talking to calm her down. "So tell me one dream that has not come true."

"There is only one off the top of my head, that I can think of and I really don't want to tell you that one."

"Why not?" He asked very curious.

"It is a little girl's dream, a fairytale, but it was always my favorite. I would always wake up so happy and not screaming."

"Well, I will tell ya anything ya want ta ask me if ya tell me the dream. Will that make ya tell me?"

Abby thought a minute and said, "Anything?"

Gabe nodded.

"Ok, I will tell you but remember it was my childhood dream and I don't want you to laugh at me."

"I promise I will not laugh at ya, besides ya might laugh at me later when I answer your question."

Abby took a deep breath and started to tell Gabe about her dream. She did not notice the chatter of the men stopping so they also could hear. "I would dream about going on a journey, far, far away, to a place that was very strange to me. I remember having a hard time to understand their language. The journey was very difficult. I remember getting stuck and could not get out. I had to reach my destination, but people kept keeping me from where I needed to go. I asked and asked to leave but they would not let me. I remember getting cold and crying because I was hurt, but finally I got there. I don't know how, but I made it to my very own castle." Then she smiled and said, "Now this is the part you are not to laugh. The castle was pink and had six turrets and a real draw bridge. It sat on a hillside overlooking the ocean. It had a large wall surrounding it but it was peaceful. It didn't need protection anymore. I remember being very nervous about meeting the people and there was a lot of them. But I knew I would be safe, loved and happy. The best part of my dream was I lived happily ever after with my husband and our twelve children and all the people that lived in the pink castle. Did I tell you I always wanted twelve children?"

Gabe smiled at her and so did the other men. They were all grinning at her and she was beginning to feel uncomfortable.

Finally she said, "What are you grinning at?"

Gabe pointed to the hillside. When Abby looked, she gasped and said, "It is like I am a child again."

"Well little girl, welcome home. Welcome ta Fuchsiall," Gabe said with a grin.

There on the hillside, overlooking the ocean was Abby's castle with the six turrets and the drawbridge. The men watched as Abby viewed the castle for the first time. The sun hitting the stone gave the illusion the laird was pink, but just in the later part of the day when sun started to go down. Abby was just about standing up to see the view. Gabe and the men watched as Abby smiled and clapped her hands in excitement. This just might work, Gabe thought to himself.

Abby had that warm fuzzy feeling. The one she had when she left Riverton and here it was again. She felt safe and happy. She knew everything would be alright. She only wished she could have shared this moment with her own children.

As they watched the castle the pink color seemed to heighten. The activity on the wall and the surrounding countryside also seemed to increase with excitement of the Laird's return. As they came closer Abigail became more nervous. Was her castle a home or a prison? Where would she stay, in a crate, a tower or the dungeon?

Fear started to take over her warm fuzzy feeling. There are all kinds of prisons and this may be just another one. Then Abby decided to enjoy her freedom and this wonderful moment but as much as she tried visions of a crate waiting for her in the barn seemed more realistic.

The little group of weary travelers was greeted with cheers as they rode across the drawbridge. Just over the drawbridge was a group of stone hounds carved into the entrance. Abby remembered seeing those same hounds in her dreams. They walked into a large courtyard enclosed by the stone walls, which encircled the entire castle. Although Abby called it a castle, Gabe informed her it was a laird but to her it looked like a castle. Sheets and other bedding were being pulled off the clothes lines and hurried into the laird as if to get rooms ready for the home comers. Staff was coming out of the castle to greet the men and the men from the fields came in to say their hellos.

To the right of the courtyard was a magnificent barn made from the same stone as the castle. Gabe was known for his fine horse stock and his breeding stallions. He obviously took very good care of them. Up near the castle was some kind of smokehouse and just on the other side of the horse barn was a hay barn and a chicken coop.

Abby was fascinated by the people coming out to greet Gabe and his men. The men all dressed in kilts and in the same plaid, speaking nothing but Gaelic. The women were dressed in warm woolen gowns. What pleased her more were the children. They were everywhere. All seeming to have round faces and beautiful.

Because of all the commotion, Gabe had dismounted and let the stable master take Samson. A small redheaded boy came over and took the reins from Abby's hands and started to lead her mount to the barn. Gabe had not helped her to dismount, so she just sat there and waited not knowing quite what to do. Instead she found herself being taken into the barn still seated on her horse.

Gabe's barn was nothing like James'. There was a long walk with box stalls on either side of it. Each stall had a name carved on a sign just over a sliding door. The barn was clean and well cared for. Abby could just see horse ears in some of the stalls from where she sat on her mare. Finally the little boy said, "Hey, lady is ya going ta get off? I need ta tend ya mount. The stable master will not like ya sitting on her while I tend ta her."

Abby smiled at the boy and said, "I am sorry kind sir, I did not realize I was to get off. I am grateful you told me." Then Abby got down and moved to the side of the walk. She watched the little boy take her mare to a stall at the far end of the barn. She started to look around not knowing what she was supposed to do.

"Here ya are. I was looking all over for ya," Gabe said from behind her. "What are ya doing in here lass?"

"Looking," Abby said with a nervous look.

"Looking for what Abigail?" Gabe asked concerned.

"A crate," Abby said softly.

Then Gabe realized what she was doing. Very forcefully he said, "Ya'll not be staying in the barn lass ever. Now come with me I have some people I want ya ta meet."

Abby breathed a sigh of relief. She was out of the barn, but he could still put her in the dungeon or a tower, he had six of those. He took hold of her elbow and led her out of the barn and back into the courtyard where Gabe introduced her to Martha, the woman who took care of Fuchsiall.

Abby thought Gabe would tell her what her chores were to be but instead he introduced her to Eva, the head of the kitchen and chief cook. "Take Abigail to her quarters," Gabe instructed Martha. "Ya know where I want her." Then he said to Abby, "Ya are ta stay there until dinner. Someone will come and get ya." Then he leaned down and whispered in her ear for only Abby to hear. "Do I need ta post a guard or can I trust ya?"

Abby just looked at him.

"Abigail, I need an answer," Gabe urged.

"I am all yours for now Laird. I won't be going anywhere today."

"Come lass," Martha said. "This way, I'll show ya where ya are going ta stay."

To Abby's surprise, Martha took Abby into the laird through the front door. The doorway itself was incredible, carved from thick oak which led into a foyer with a stone mosaic type floor making a picture of a group of hounds. A McKenzie coat of arms was displayed on the wall by the opposite doorway. From there, Martha led her to the marble staircase with a railing just right for sliding down.

Abby wondered if Gabe's kids were allowed to do such a thing, but she was sure going to try it with or without Gabe's permission. "To the right there," Martha said, "is the great hall. Tonight we will be holding dinner in there. That is where ya are ta go later. Two doors down is the formal dining room, which we only use for very special guests. The door in between is the Laird's study where he meets his clan and hears their complaints and suggestions. The very last door at the end there is the library. Ya must have special permission ta go in there. The Laird is very protective of his books. Ta the right and down that hall is the kitchen, the finest ya will ever see. The Laird has made it a wonderful place ta works. The next door is the ballroom."

"Ballroom? Is it used?" Abby asked surprised.

"Aye lass, the Laird loves ta entertain and have many guests. He is quite a good dancer. He just loves music of any kind that is why we have a special music room with every instrument ya can imagine. Do ya play an instrument?"Martha asked.

"I try more than play," Abby said with a smile. Truth was Abby could play more than one instrument well including the drum.

"Well, ya will play more if the Laird has a say in it."

"What is the last door on the right?" Abby asked as Martha started to lead her up the stairs.

"That is the Laird's private study. If he is in there, he is not ta be disturbed. Now and then he needs his privacy and he goes in there. Anyone that needs his help or advice just has ta wait. Now follow me. This way lass." Martha took Abby up the stairs to the second level. *Well I'm not going to be in* a *dungeon*, Abby thought to herself, *must be one of the towers*. "Maybe I will have a nice view of the ocean," she whispered while trying to encourage herself.

She was starting to get a little nervous again. Martha stopped at the second landing and pointed up the next staircase. Abby was sure she wanted her to go up there but Martha only told her what was up there and what they used that floor for. Then she started down the hall on the second floor. Abby stood not knowing if she should follow or not. Martha turned and said, “Come, lass this way,” and she raised her hand and motioned her to come along.

“The paintings on the walls are of the Laird’s family, he has a big one. There is one of him when he was just a wee lad sitting on his mother’s knee just over there.” She pointed to the wall on the left. “Those rooms on the left are used for family when they come to visit. The next room is for Gabe’s father, the old laird. He has his own house now about two hours ride north, but he comes to visit and stays when he feels like it or when Gabe needs his help. The Laird’s rooms are here on the right and that hall down there.” Martha pointed to the hall at the other side of the Laird’s quarters, “are the children’s chambers, all six of them. Did ya know the laird has six children?”

“Yes,” Abby said with a smile.

They finally came to the end of the hall where Martha opened the last door. This was it. The place Abby would be living when she was not working. Abby braced herself for the worst, but when Martha moved out of the way for her to see, Abby was a little overwhelmed. “Are you sure this is where the Laird wants me?”

“The Laird said ya would be nervous, and aye, this is the room he wanted for ya. It is his favorite and he usually saves it for special guests and family.”

“But I am neither,” Abby protested.

“Well ya must be someone special ta the laird because this is where he wants ya, close ta him,” Martha smiled. “Ya should find everything ya need but donna be bashful. I am not far if ya need something else.”

Abby tried to conceal a yawn but Martha saw her. “Ya best take a nap while ya can. Tomorrow will be a big day for ya. The laird wants ya up early and ready for him.”

Abby just had to ask. She thought Gabe would tell her tomorrow but she did not want to wait any longer. “Do you know what my duties are going to be Martha?”

Martha looked surprised at Abby’s question. “The Laird will let ya know tomorrow. I am sure.” Then she left Abigail to herself.

The room Gabe gave Abby was the most beautiful room she had ever seen. It had a huge four poster feather bed and a large walk-in fireplace. It had two huge windows on opposite walls, one overlooking the courtyard and the other overlooking the ocean. It was bright and sunny with large planked floors and a fresco of angels painted on the ceiling. A dry sink with a basin and a large pitcher sat on the right, and two overstuffed green chairs sat in front of the fire with a small table between them all resting on a large sheepskin rug.

Abby was standing at the window overlooking the ocean when a light knock sounded at the door. "Come in," Abby said unsure what to expect. The door opened and a small little girl came in carrying a bouquet of small spring flowers. "Hello," Abby greeted with a smile. The little girl was just as Gabe had described. This was definitely his little Emily. The child just stood quietly holding her bouquet. So Abby said, "You must be Emily I am guessing?" The little girl's face lit up when she mentioned her name. "Those are beautiful flowers you have."

Emily was unsure how to address Abigail. She tipped from one foot to the other trying to decide what to say. Then, "Ya talk real funny," Emily said.

Abigail giggled at her comment. "I have been told that many times since I came here." Then Gabe stepped into the room from the hall where he'd been waiting for Emily to present her flowers. "Emily are ya going ta da something with those flowers or not?" Gabe urged.

"Da, ya dinna tell me she was beautiful," Emily said trying to be brave.

"Your Da told me you were beautiful Emily," Abby said and then she smiled.

Emily liked Abby from that moment on. She ran across the room and gave the flowers to her without saying a word trying to overcome her bashfulness then she ran back to her father.

"Very nice Emi, now go back ta ya studies ya professor is waiting." Emily gave a little wave with her pudgy fingers and skipped out of the room right after she kissed her father's cheek. Abby waved back and said, "Come again."

"She is just beautiful Gabe, thank you for bringing her here."

"Ya welcome lass, but it was her idea. She wanted to meet the lady from the colonies. Do ya like ya chamber?"

"It is just a little better than the crate," she teased. "I need to know what my duties are Laird," changing the mood. "I should be in the servant's quarters not on the family floor in this beautiful room."

"Are ya telling me my job now lass?" Gabe asked with raised eyebrows.

"Gabe, please, I am anxious enough. What are your plans for me?" Abby asked like a scared rabbit.

So Gabe answered her, "I have not decided yet. For now ya will stay here until supper. Tomorrow is soon enough ta discuss your duties."

Gabe turned and left her alone. She crawled into the most wonderful bed she'd ever slept in and fell asleep. Martha woke her for dinner and escorted her down to the hall. "Go in lass. He is waiting for ya," Martha encouraged. When Abby reached the door she was shocked with the people in the hall waiting for dinner. She felt a little out of place sitting at a table when she should be serving instead.

Taking two steps into the hall, she looked around to see huge tapestries hanging down from the rafters, one large walk-in fireplace and many benches and tables with people engulfed in conversation. She stood on a small platform looking at the three stairs which led down into the hall. The floor was flat polished gray stone leading to the platform at the far end where she spotted Gabe at the head table flanked by Joseph and Simon. His six children, all present, were sitting at the table just in front of him. As Abby stood there, a woman came up to her. She was young, about twenty-five with dark red curly hair and brown eyes. Abby felt a little uncomfortable with the way she was looking at her. "So ya are what Gabe brought home. Ya are ta old ta be his mistress. I canna believe he is removing me from his bed for ya. I know what he likes and I guarantee he will get sick of ya soon and ya will be out in the barn where ya belong." The red haired woman hissed.

Abby took a step back. She was so surprised with the conversation. She did not know what to say, but she was not about to let this little vixen bully her.

"Apparently, you do not know what he wants or you would still be in his bed. Maybe you should go practice somewhere else and come back when you can keep up with the big girls." Then Abby gave her the most sickening smile she could muster. The red headed woman turned on her heels and left the hall in a huff. Abby wanted to leave too and after looking around to see if anyone would notice she left the hall. Gabe had noticed Abby talking to Gretna and then she was gone. He sent Joseph to find her and bring her back, but Abby was very good at hiding especially if she did not want to be found. Joseph went straight to her room, but she was not there. He searched the next level and the first level before he returned to let Gabe know he could not find her.

Gabe wanted to know what Gretna had said to Abby but he also wanted a pleasant evening his first night home. When Martha came in to check on the dinner she noticed Abby missing. "Martha I want ta talk ta Gretna as soon as dinner is over and see if ya can find Abby. She is missing. Let me know when she comes back ta her chamber."

Sitting on the ledge just outside her bedroom window two stories high was a small figure wearing a blue and green plaid cloak. Her knees where pulled up to her chin and she sat alone looking into the darkness. Resting her head on her knees, Abby's heart was back with her family. It made a lot of sense, what Gretna had said. Why else was she so close to his chambers and on a floor for family and close friends. Was she to be his mistress or lemon or whatever they called it over in Scotland. Abby's heart was breaking. She really cared for Gabe, but was sex all he wanted from her? Did he just want her for his toy? It was very cold out on this ledge, but Abby was not about to go in and certainly not about to go to Gabe's bed. And why now, she thought, he had ample opportunities to take her at James and all the way from England, why now?

Abby was confused and very discouraged. A *crate must be better than* a *gilded cage*, she thought. The wind started to pick up and she was having a hard time keeping her hood on. From behind her, she could hear people in her room looking for her, but she was not about to go in now or anytime soon. Then from behind her she heard Gabe and Gretna arguing loudly. He had called for her and they were quarreling but not in Gaelic, in English. Abby could understand their conversation. Was he doing this for her benefit or did he even know she was out here?

"I want ta know what ya said ta Abigail and right now! And donna lie ta me or it will be the last lie ya ever say. Your tongue has caused much problem in the past and that is why ya are not in my bed anymore and no other reason."

"I know the real reason that I am not in your bed Laird and it has nothing ta do with my tongue and I told that old hag just what I thought," Gretna snapped back.

"What did ya say, Gretna? Tell me now," Gabe demanded forcefully.

"I told her ya were replacing me with her of course."

"Ya what?" Gabe said, angrier than Abby had ever witnessed. He was furious with Gretna and was not about to let her get away with such viciousness.

"What am I going ta do with ya? It was a big mistake ta takes ya as my lemon, and for that I am sorry, but that woman has done nothing ta ya ta have been so cruel ta her. Ya are angry at me and I am the one ya should have faced not her. Ya could have just left my bed and still lived in my clan, but now I am going ta have ya thrown out. I will not tolerate cruelty toward any person I bring into the clan for no good reason. She is not the first ya have attacked but she will be the last. Ya will leave tonight."

Gretna screamed in protest but Gabe would not listen to her pleas. She had crossed him for the last time. He ordered her immediate exile and had two of his men escort her off his land and straight to his business partner James. He would be most pleased to have her especially now that Gabe had taken Abigail.

Abby waited until her room had quieted down and finally slipped in off the ledge through her window. The room was dark with just the fire throwing a small glow. Abby went to the fire and sank down into one of the overstuffed chairs. She curled up and covered herself with her cloak and fell into a deep sleep.

In the morning, when she woke, she found herself in the bed, stripped out of her dress and shift and laying naked under the quilts. The fire had been stoked and a note from Gabe was lying on the dry sink. (*Meet me in the barn after your break your fast and do not take too long.*) Abby hurried. She washed, dressed and went down the stairs looking for the place to eat. Martha came around the corner as Abby was peeking into the hall.

"Looking for something Abigail?" She asked from behind her.

Abby jumped and squealed a little. "I'm looking for the room to break my fast, I cannot find a soul anywhere."

Martha gave her a pleasant smile and said, "Come follow me. I will show ya, but ya best hurry, the Laird has been out in the barn for a while." Abby was just going to go out and miss breaking her fast, but Martha insisted she eat. "The Laird would not be happy if ya miss another meal, lass. It would not be unlike him ta feed ya himself."

Abby ate quickly and ran out to the barn. On her way she was greeted by Joseph and Simon. "Our brother was not ta happy with ya last night. Where did ya go?" Joseph asked scolding her.

"Did ya say, 'your brother'?" Abigail asked surprised.

"Aye, he is our oldest brother. Simon is the youngest and I'm two years younger than Gabe," Joseph said with a grin.

"Got to go," Abby said starting to run again. "Gabe is waiting."

"Ya never told us where ya went?"

"Bye," Abby hollered back ignoring their question.

"Simon, I think she just avoided answering my question," Joseph said shocked.

"Oh donna feel ta bad brother. I avoid ya questions most of the time too," Simon answered teasing his big brother.

When Abby entered the barn she stopped and just looked around. Part of her was still sure Gabe was going to have a crate waiting for her especially after talking to Gretna last night. Slowly she started walking in when Jake the stable master came in from outside the barn just in back of her. "It's about time," Jake said. "Gabe has been waiting for hours. If ya donna hurry ya are going ta miss it."

"Miss what?" Abby asked, but Jake just pointed down to the last stall on the left.

When Abby reached the stall Gabe was there with a mare just about ready to foal. "It is about time," Gabe said when he saw her in the stall door. "Come in. I think I am going ta need some help with this one. The foal is too big and we are going ta have ta help. Hopefully it won't kill the mare."

When the foal's feet started to exit the womb, Gabe tied one end a rope around them and then the other end to the center of a broom handle. Gabe took one end of the broom handle and Jake the other. They sat on the floor of the barn side by side holding the broom handle with the rope stretching tightly from the handle to the foal's front feet. They patiently waited for the next contraction but just as they were about to start pulling Abby said, "Wait don't pull" just at the moment the contraction started. "The foal's foot is twisted around the cord and you'll rip her."

"How the hell do ya know that?" Jake asked shocked with her statement.

"Never mind that, someone must reach in and see what is twisted," Abigail ordered. Gabe jumped up and gently worked his hand way into the womb. Abby sat on the floor taking the other end of the broom handle next to Jake. It only took Gabe a minute to find the problem and untwist the hind leg. He barely removed his hand before the next contraction started. "Pull," Jake ordered Abigail. It took Abby, Gabe and Jake pulling on the broom handle, to help the foal come into the world, a beautiful black colt with a white star on his forehead and one white stocking. Abby was thrilled with the sight of the foal's birth.

"Good job, lass," Jake said happy the prize mare made it with little tearing. "Ya most likely saved that mare's life and the babe's too."

The three left the new mother and colt about mid-morning just after they watched the wobbly foal stand for the first time. All three were in good spirits.

"Pleased to have met you Jake," Abby said as she started back to the laird.

"The pleasure is all mine lass. Sometime ya will have to tell me how ya knew about the foal," Jake answered.

Abigail was almost to the laird hoping she would get away from Gabe before he'd ask about last night, but no way.

"Come with me Abigail. I want ta talk ta about last night."

Abby's shoulders drooped as she followed Gabe into his study. This room was as grand as all the rooms she had seen so far. It was the room next to the great hall, a lot smaller, but it had the same size fireplace in it and a huge red mahogany desk with a large red leather chair behind it. Book filled shelves lined the opposite wall of the fireplace and a soft oriental carpet with gold tassels partially covered the oak plank floor. Just in front of Gabe's desk was two leather arm chairs. A cadenza just behind the desk held his liqueur supply and to the right was a large chest of drawers used for filing papers.

Gabe walked into the room and sat behind his desk waiting for Abby to join him but she just stood at the door entrance and did not come in.

"Abigail come in and shut the door," he ordered. Then he motioned for her to sit down. Reluctantly, Abby came in and sat down waiting for the next lecture.

"Ya are ta eat with me every night with no exceptions and that is it. I donna knows where ya hid last night, but ya are not ta do that again. Ya are a part of my clan now and they need ta meet ya as much as ya need ta meet them. I will severely punish anyone who does not treat ya as such." Then he gave her a warning look and said, "And if ya are not good ta my people than plan on getting severely punished as well." Abby opened her mouth to talk and Gabe said, "I know what ya are thinking and ya do belong. Ya haven't given this much of a chance yet, now have ya?" Gabe stood up and said, "I know I promised ta take ya around today, but one of the old folks is dying and I need ta pay my respects."

"Is there something I can do Gabe?" Abby asked concerned.

"No lass but thank ya for offering. This death has been long in coming and it is a blessing if he goes. Now have a good day and I will see ya at dinner. Both Gabe and Abby left the study. Gabe left the laird and Abby went down to the kitchen.

CHAPTER 14
Keeping Her Safe Is A Real Challenge

Abby walked in slowly unsure of what to do. The great hall was as full of people tonight as it was last night. She was feeling a little intimidated. At least that redheaded women Gretna was not here tonight. Abby spotted a small empty table. She walked slowly over and sat down keeping her eyes pinned to her lap.

Gabe was talking to Joseph when Abby had entered the room and did not notice her sitting in the corner by herself.

Martha entered the hall with some parchment in her hand and noticed Abby sitting by herself. Without saying anything, she walked up to the head table and whispered something in Gabe's ear after giving him the parchment. He looked at the corner, shook his head and smiled as he watched Abby sitting alone in the corner with her head lowered.

"What are ya doing way over here lass?" Gabe said from behind her.

Abby's head popped up and turned around to see Gabe. She looked at him surprised. He wanted her to sit near him. He held out his hand, "Come lass." Leading her across the room, he stopped at the head table. "Here lass. From now on this is your seat. I expect ya in it each night. If ya are not, I will find ya, carry ya in and put ya in it myself if I have ta." Then he surprised her with a quick wink.

Dinner turned out to be quite pleasant. Gabe's children bombarded her with questions about Indians and the rough life in the colonies.

Abby answered each one without hesitation. Gabe noticed Abby's coloring to be a little peeked and she was coughing just a tad. He put meat and bread in her trencher. "Ale lass?" He asked.

"No thank you. Just water will do."

She ate very little and drank all her water. Gabe kept the conversation going and watched her like a hawk.

"Still tired, lass?" Gabe asked.

"I'm fine." She yawned holding her head up with her hand that rested on the table.

"Do ya like ya chamber?"

"Oh, it is lovely, thank you."

"Come," Gabe finally said as her eyes started to close.

"Where are we going?" She asked.

"Ya are going ta bed."

"NOW?"

"Aye, now."

He walked her up to her room and went inside. She looked uncomfortable with him in her room especially after the conversation she had with Gretna the night before.

"This is my house lass. I will go in any room at any time without knocking."

Across the foot of her bed laid a fresh shift made of heavy warm linen. Gabe handed it to her and pointed to a screen in the corner. He first helped her with her laces and then told her to put the shift on. Gabe sat on her bed waiting for her to finish taking her time washing at the dry sink.

"Are ya stalling lass?" Gabe teased.

"No I'm not. Why did you ask that?" Abby asked indignantly.

"Because ya taking ya time like one of my children who doesn't want ta go ta bed. He pulled the blanket back and motioned her to get in. Reluctantly, she crawled in. He tucked her in and then he kissed her goodnight one…two…three…but did not climb in with her. She wondered if Gretna had been wrong.

"Tomorrow, I'll show ya around," he said. "But tonight ya will sleep. If ya need me, my chambers are down the hall on the right.

"Gabe?"

"Aye lass".

"Thank you for not putting me in a crate or dungeon or a tower or…" And she started drifting into sleep.

"Ya are welcomed," he whispered and closed the door.

In the morning Abby woke to the room filled with sun, but cold. She rose, stoked the fire and crawled back under the covers waiting for the fire to take off but it just kept smoldering. Again she got up and stoked the fire but it would barely stay going. Pushing the partially burnt logs over, she crawl up into the chimney to see what was wrong. The chimney was not getting enough draft and she wanted to see why. Straddling the burning embers she carefully looked up through the smoke to see a bunch of something way up at the top of the chimney. *It must be a nest of some kind, she thought to herself.*

Coming out of the fire, she tested the flue. It too seemed stuck which might also be the reason the fire would not stay lit. Abby decided to attack the bunch way up in the chimney first, but when she went to find her gown it was gone. *Martha must have taken it to be cleaned*, she thought. Wrapping a quilt over her shoulders she peeked out of her room. No one was in sight. Running down the hall she made it to the upper staircase where she was sure it would lead her to a higher window on the roof where she could get out to her chimney.

She climbed the stairs and found a dormer window leading out to the roof just as she was hoping. With one hard push, the window swung open giving Abby the outlet to the roof she needed. Wedging the quilt in the window so it would not close leaving her stranded, Abby stepped barefooted onto the slate covered roof four stories from the ground.

Meanwhile, out on the wall, a guard spotted a woman in a white garment looking down a chimney. Gabriel was in the yard, training with the men. The guard signaled Gabe's attention and motioned for him to look up. Terror went across the yard as all the men watched a round woman in white half submerged down a chimney. Her head and upper torso were completely submerged in the chimney with only her bottom sticking up. Her bare feet were swaying in the thin air, her skirts flapping in the wind exposing more leg than necessary.

Gabe went charging into the house followed by Joseph close behind. By the time they reached the roof, the dormer window had been shut and the woman gone. Frantically the two men searched the roof and the ground with their eyes. Luckily there was no sign of the woman anywhere.

After unsuccessfully retrieving the nest at the top of her chimney, Abigail returned to her chamber determined to find out why the fire would not stay going. She crawled into the hearth and straightened up, carefully straddling the smoldering embers. Abby could see the other end of the damper up in the chimney stuffed with something but just out of her reach. Finding a couple of footholds in the stone, she put her toes in and carefully climbed up into the chimney completely submerging her entire body from view except her tiny feet. The fire was smoldering still and Abby was having a hard time to breathe. Intending to spend as little time as possible in here, she tried to loosen the nest. When the nest refused to come out of the damper she started using the language she learned from the sailors on her grandfather's ships, the same ones her poor mother use to try and wash out of her mouth with a large bar of soap.

Gabe and Joseph stormed into Abby's chamber only to find it empty. They started to exit when the worse vulgar language came spiraling out of the fireplace. It was then that the two men noticed two small bare feet extending out of the chimney.

"Son of a bitch, what the hell is this F***...Damn it all to hell..."

"Abigail is that ya?" Gabe asked still disbelieving what he was seeing and hearing.

A moment of silence was all they heard coming out of the chimney and then in a tiny timid sweet voice Abby said, "Yes Gabe."

"Would ya mind telling me, what ya are doing up in the chimney?" Gabe asked trying to hold his temper.

"I almost got it. I will be out in a minute," was all Abby would say.

Joseph was trying to hold his laughter with little results. He was laughing so hard he had to sit down on the bed.

Looking at Joseph, Gabe said, "I'm glad ya find this amusing." Then there was a loud bang, a sound of something letting go and a lot of soot coming down the chimney and into the smoldering embers sending smoke and soot into the room and into Gabe's face, which was looking up the chimney.

"I got it!" Abby called excitedly.

When Gabe turned to look at Joseph, his face was covered with black soot. Joseph held his stomach and rolled on the bed laughing hysterically.

"Abigail!!" Gabe bellowed at the top of his lungs. "Ya come out of there now!"

He hollered so loud, it startled Abigail making her lose her footing causing her to fall bottom first down into the middle of the smoldering embers still holding the extremely large nest she'd rescued from the damper. With her, she brought a large amount of soot and smoke exploding everywhere into the chamber. Gabe reached in and pulled her off the hot embers before she could get too burnt. Joseph quickly scooped up the embers that had fallen out onto the floor and threw them back into the fire.

Abby stood in front of Gabe covered in black soot. Her hair was stiff with the back ash that had clung to the inside of the chimney. Every inch of her except her teeth and eyes were covered with black soot.

"Thank you," she said opening her eyes wide giving Gabe a great big smile showing her bright white teeth.

Joseph turned his face away to hide his smile but Gabe was angry and said, "What were ya thinking climbing out on the roof and then up the chimney?"

As Gabe reprimanded her, Abby began to smoke.

"Did ya ever think for one second that ya might fall and it is dangerous ta do something like that?"

"The fire wasn't working…," Abby tried to explain.

"Ya dinna think ta ask someone?" Gabe said holding on to her shoulders. The smoke started to get worse. Joseph adjusted the damper to get the smoke out of the room and then opened the window behind Abby. At that moment, Abigail's shift ignited into fire. Gabe saw what was happening even before Abby knew. He bent her over his knee and started hitting the fire out with his bare hand.

"Owe, owe, owe," Abby squeaked. "You don't have to hit me that hard Gabe."

"Actually I should hit ya harder for doing such a fool thing." Gabe got the fire out, but still kept her pinned over his knee. Abby's shift was now missing over her entire backside, exposing a black sooty bum.

Slap……. "That is for climbing out on the roof."

"Owe!"

Slap…"That is for climbing up the chimney."

"Owe!"

Slap… "And this is so ya won't ever do it again.

"OWE!"

"Do ya need more?" Gabe asked firmly.

"I didn't need those," Abby answered back.

Gabe stood her up and made her face him. "What were ya thinking?" He demanded.

"I was thinking I needed some heat."

"Ya need ta ask Abigail and someone will do that for ya."

"Why, I fixed it myself. See!" And she held up the nest in her very black sooty hands.

"Donna ever let me catch ya on that roof again," Gabe ordered shaking his finger at her.

"You could have just told me, you did not have to hit me." And she reached around to rub her backside noticing that she was fully exposed.

"Ya are lucky that I stopped when I did," Gabe sputtered.

Then, Joseph seeing the fire was out and everything was under control decided to leave and give Gabe a little privacy with Abby. "Joseph, ask Martha ta bring up a bath on ya way out and another shift."

Then turning to Abigail he said, "Ya will clean this mess up yourself and when ya and ya chamber are clean ya will come down ta my study. If I am not there than ya will wait for me." Gabe stomped out of Abby's room leaving her still holding the large soot covered nest.

It took Abby the rest of the morning and into mid-afternoon before she was done cleaning her room and taking her bath. Abby did not want to face Gabe again so she took her time cleaning her room. She finished by taking all the linens out of the room and the large heavy drapes and washing them out in the yard. She hung them up to dry and then finally went to Gabe's study.

When she entered the room, Gabe was just finishing some paperwork, but before he could address Abby a guard came in from the wall announcing that four men were coming across the meadow.

"Have Joseph and Simon join me at the bridge," Gabe ordered the guard. Abby looked scared. Although Gabe was still upset with her, he saw the look on her face. "Do ya think ya could identify the men in the woods if ya saw them again Abigail?"

Abby shook her head yes.

"Come with me. Ya will stay where I tell ya and out of sight. Ya will be able ta tell me if they are the ones before they come ta close."

Gabe grabbed Abby's hand and led her out into the courtyard and over to the bridge. Everyone in the courtyard was ordered to find safety. The guards were triple on the wall. Joseph and Simon were both at the bridge waiting. Joseph handed Gabe his claymore and then stood on his right side. Abby watched from just behind the front gate. She could look through the crack in the door to identify the men if she needed to but remained very well hidden.

The four men cantered right up to the bridge only stopping when Gabe ordered them to. Abby had a clear view from where she was hiding. Gabe heard her gasp when she saw the four men. He asked under his breath so they did not hear him "Are they the men Abby?"

"Yes," she whispered.

"Stay there and do not come out no matter what," Gabe ordered.

"Hello Gabriel. It is I, Lester McHale from the lowlands. Do ya remember me?"

"Aye," Gabe said with his arms folded still holding tight to his sword. Archers where brought in on the top of the wall.

"We have been looking for a single man that may have come on your property. I am here ta ask permission ta look for him."

"What do ya want with this man?" Gabe asked to see if they were still looking for Abby.

"He kind of stole something valuable from me," Lester said.

"How can someone '*Kind of steal'*?" Gabe asked. "He either did or didn't."

"I kind of dropped something valuable in the woods, and I think he found it and took it knowing it was mine."

"What woods would that be?" Gabe asked.

"About two days ride south of here."

"Maybe he is already dead," Gabe said, then asked Joseph. "Dinna ya tell me about finding, a half eaten man in the woods two days south of here?"

"Aye, I did brother," Joseph answered.

Then Lester asked, "We are pretty sure that was not our man and would appreciate ya cooperation on this very important matter."

"I insist on sending my men with ya while ya look and if ya find him I am ta be notified immediately," Gabe instructed.

"We do not need ya men, Laird but will be glad for the extra help," Lester said with an approving nod.

"Is there anything else McHale?" Gabe asked hoping he'd say no.

"No Laird, not unless ya can tell me the whereabouts of a woman from the colonies named Abigail Fox."

It was at that moment Abby recognized the four men from the docks in Boston on the day she was herded into the W & W Shipping Co. office. When she saw them in the woods that night, she knew she had seen them before and here they were hunting her both as a man and a woman. Abby was terrified. After the fire this morning, maybe Gabe was more than ready to get rid of her.

Gabe just had to know why they wanted Abby so he asked, "I cannot say I know this woman or her whereabouts. But if I hear of her I will let ya know. Ya wouldn't mind telling me why ya are looking for her now would ya? She isn't dangerous is she?"

"Abigail Fox is a partner in the W & W Shipping Co. I have been hired ta find her by her very unhappy partners and a man named Pinkerton. Apparently she has a very valuable box they want and will pay anything ta get. She was arrested at the docks in London and put in a debtor's prison. Someone bought her note and took her away. No one knows who purchased her. We went to talk to James, but he was no help. He didn't have her either. So far she has disappeared, but we will find her we always do."

"If I hear anything I will send word, but I canna imagine a woman coming up here. She'd have ta been beat and forced up here," Gabe said and all the men chuckled.

McHale waited in the meadow for Gabe's men to join them. Gabe gave strict instructions to his men not to turn their backs on them and above all, not to tell them about Abby. When Gabe went to get Abby from her hiding place in back of the gate, he found her sitting on the ground rolled up in a ball with her head face down on her knees shaking.

"Oh lass, none of that now ya are safe here. I will not let anything happen ta ya and neither will my clan," Gabe said bending over her whispering in her ear.

"I told you they would come and there will be more. I have put you in danger and your family. You should let me go before someone gets hurt because of me," she pleaded.

"No, and do not ever ask me again. I canna protect ya out there. Ya are safe here and here ya will stay."

Gabe grabbed Abby's arms and lifted her to her feet. As they walked to the house, Abby asked, "Why didn't James tell them you had me?"

"James can be cruel when it comes ta the prisoners and I don't condone his ways, but he would never betray my trust or friendship. He would not endanger my clan or ya. He knows those four. They are not anyone ya want ta cross. I think I am going ta talk ta my cousin."

Gabe needed to send a word to his cousin and soon. He knew how upset Abby was. As they started back across the courtyard, he noticed her bedding and curtains hanging on the clotheslines. This gave him an idea to keep her busy for a while and not suspect what he was up to. "Ya haven't finished ya room have ya?"

"I just need to take the linens and curtains back in and make the bed," she answered.

"Well I suggest ya get on with it and ya are ta stay in ya chamber until I come and get ya. That should be enough punishment for today."

Abby could not believe he was still punishing her after what had just happened at the gate. She almost wished he given her over to the McHales and got it over with. She stomped off toward the clotheslines and Gabe sent for a messenger. An hour later, Abby had pulled all the linens off the lines and taken them back to her chamber. Two men left the laird on their way with a message for Gabe's cousin, the King of Scotland.

When Abby returned with her last linens, a runaway was in her room. Little Emily was hiding under Abby's bed. She happened to look down to see two tiny feet sticking out. Abigail wanted to laugh, it was so cute. So she finished making her bed and hung the drapes and then it had been long enough for the stowaway. Abby sat on the floor with her back on the side of the bed next to the tiny feet. "Okay," Abby said, "you can come out now and tell me why you are hiding under there."

A few seconds later Emily peaked out from under the bed. "SHHHHHH," she said holding her little forefinger against her lips. "I am running away and I donna want Da ta find me."

"Are you being punished?" Abby asked her.

"Aye," Emi said with a pout.

"Me too," Abby said. "If you tell me what you did, I will tell you what I did."

"Alright," Emi said slowly a little unsure. "My Da is real mean. He sent me ta my chamber all day just because I spread glue on his desk chair. I was just trying ta make it shiny for him." Then her lower lip came out into a very sad face. "How did I know that he would sit in it before it dried and get stuck? So I am running away and I am going ta stay under ya bed until I am all grown up. That will show him." Abby almost started to laugh. The thought of Gabe stuck in his chair was priceless.

"Da said that it was a good thing uncle Joseph found him or he would have never got out."

"Uncle Joseph found him?" Abby asked holding back giggles.

"Aye, Da told Uncle Joseph not ta laugh or he'd punish him too."

Abby turned her head so Emily could not see her laugh and said, "Do you want to know what I did?"

"Alright," Emily said still a pout across her face.

"Well, first, I went on the roof, and then I climbed up the chimney and then fell in the fire that burnt a hole in the back of my new shift. My room became all smoky and sooty and your Da made me clean the whole room by myself."

"Oh my," Emily said giggling in her hands. "That was real bad. Even I would not dare ta do that."

"And," Abby added, "he made me stay in my room until he comes and gets me."

"Da is really mean," Emily said sniffing.

After Gabe sent his message, he decided to free his two prisoners. He walked up the stairs quietly to see if they were where he ordered them to be. Emily was not very good about staying in her room, and Gabe really hated paddling her. He was hoping she would still be there so he would not have to. He sneaked down the hall to catch any wrongdoing. As he reached the end of the hall he noticed Abby's door opened and he could hear talking. Slowly he crept to the doorway staying out of view where he could listen.

"I bet he is as mean as my deceased husband was to my children," Abby said trying to get Emily to change her mind. "Their father never read them a bed time story."

"My Da always reads me a story, every night," Emily said surprised.

"Too bad you will not get any more stories from him." Abby was starting to get through to her. "My children's father would never kiss them good night or tuck them in either."

"OH my," Emily said.

"Sometimes he would leave for months without leaving us food or wood for the fire. My children went to bed hungry and cold many nights."

"My Da leaves sometimes, but he always makes sure we have food and we are always warm. Ya children had a very bad Da. My Da would never do that."

"That is right he never would, but it is his job to keep you safe and teach you right from wrong. I know you are not happy with him right now, but you know very well what glue is for and it is not to make things shiny, is it?"

"No," Emily said now sitting on Abby's lap.

"You are five almost six years old now and it is time for you to act like a big girl and take your punishment because you know very well what you did was wrong. Now tell me, what's the right thing to do?" Abby asked holding Emily in her arms.

"I have ta go back ta my chamber and stay there," Emily said still pouting.

"I am very proud of you Emily. It takes a real big girl to admit she is wrong and you are definitely a big girl."

As Gabe watched and listened from the doorway just out of sight, he saw Abby give Emily a great big hug and a kiss on the cheek. Emily got up and hugged Abby. Gabe hid in the next room so Emily would not see him as she passed to go back to her chamber. Abby walked Emily to her room and then returned unaware that Gabe was watching her as usual.

When his prisoners where back in their rooms, Gabe went to talk to Emily first. He found her in her chair hugging her sock dolly. "You can come out now Emi."

"Da I did something wrong," Emi said with her head down.

"Oh, what did ya do?" Gabe asked.

"I ran away but I came back because ya aren't as mean as I thought."

"I am glad ya are back. I would be very sad if ya left me," Gabe said. "I have ta punish ya for leaving ya chamber though."

"Are ya going ta paddle me Da?" Emi asked with a very worried look on her face.

"I was going ta but since ya told me the truth I think five more minutes in ya room should be enough." Emily started to wail loudly. "I can make it longer." Gabe said. The wailing stopped as fast as it started. "Good, ya may leave in five minutes without me coming ta tell ya."

Then Gabe went to see his other prisoner, this was not going to be so easy.

CHAPTER 15
My Children Need A Mother

"Do ya need a guard?" Gabe asked Abby as he walked into her chamber without knocking.

"NO," Abby answered indigently.

"No, what? Ya went on the roof, up the chimney and didn't stay in ya chamber as I ordered."

Abby's mouth dropped open in surprise. She had only just walked Emily to her room five minutes ago. She could not believe she just got caught again.

"I went on the roof to fix the chimney. It was the right thing to do. What if someone had gone up there and fell because of me? Better me then someone else. Besides I didn't fall now did I?"

Gabe could not believe she was arguing with him.

"I went up the chimney because of that damn nest, which I loosened and removed. Your hollering caused me to fall and get soot everywhere and burned a hole in the backside of my new shift."

She was now blaming him for her behavior.

"And I left my chamber to walk your daughter to her room because you left her much too long. All day for a five year old is too long."

Gabe could not believe he was being scolded. She had turned her behavior around and blamed him.

"Is that right," Gabe said through gritted teeth.

"Yes," she said folding her arms and staring him in the face defiantly.

"I am Laird here. When I give an order or punishment it will be obeyed or there will be a price ta pay."

Abby's eyes opened wide. Her arms uncrossed and she took a step backwards.

"How I choose ta punish my children is no concern of yours. Ya will not ever interfere again. Do not tell me what I should or should not do," Gabe demanded.

"I am sorry," she said lowering her eyes and head. "I should not have interfered with Emily even though what you did was wrong."

"What am I going to do with ya lass?" Gabe said in frustration.

"Set me free," Abby answered quickly.

"That will never happen," Gabe answered as quickly. "Do ya need more time in ya chamber or your bum warmed again or maybe bed without supper?"

"I'm not a child, so stop treating me as one!" Abby protested.

"When ya stop acting foolishly like a child, than I will stop treating ya as one," Gabe answered back. Actually he loved her spirit, her defiance, and her attitude even though she infuriated and frustrated him.

"Fine," she sputtered, folding her arms again and lifting her chin, ready for whatever he had in mind. "What exactly do you want me to do, stay in my room, bend over or go to bed without supper or all three?"

Gabe did not answer but turned around and said, "Bring ya shoes and follow me."

Abby's heart sank. *What was he going to do to her now*? *Why couldn't she just keep her mouth shut*? Thoughts raced through her head as she watched his kilt sway back and forth as he walked down the corridor in front of her. His stride made two of hers and he was not slowing down. She almost had to run to keep up with him. He could hear her shoes scuffing on the floor behind him. Gabe had not given her time to lace or buckled them but she did follow him without a fight which pleased him.

He rounded the railing at the bottom to the stairs and entered his study. He held the door opened until Abby entered. He closed the door hard behind her with a loud bang.

"I need to work and ya need someone ta watch ya."

Abby just stood fidgeting with her hands waiting for the next order.

"See that corner?" He began. "Ya will go and stand there facing it until I tell ya ta turn around."

Abby's eyes and mouth opened wide. She wanted to give him a good piece of her mind but did not quite dare. She turned and stomped to the corner, folded her arms and tapped her foot on the floor. She was so angry. She was about to blow up. Abby could not see Gabe, but she could hear his quill scratching on the parchment. She even could hear the pen dipping in the ink well.

There was a knock on the door. "Enter," Gabe said not lifting his head to greet the visitor. Joseph entered and glanced over to the corner to see Abby standing there.

"I see ya are still in trouble lass," Joseph teased.

"Yes, what is new," Abby answered.

Joseph couldn't help smile at Gabe. Both men were enjoying Abigail's defiance.

"Ya wanted something brother?" Gabe asked still trying to hide a smile.

"Aye, ya wanted ta check the fence in the south pasture, remember?"

"Aye, take Dougal. I am needed here ta watch the spoiled brat." Then he nodded at Abigail. The two men watch the reaction of Abby after Gabe made the statement. She shifted from side to side, crossed her arms tighter and lifted her chin just mumbling something under her breath. Joseph and Gabe wanted to laugh out loud but did not. They were sure they would be physically attacked by the woman in the corner.

"As ya wish," Joseph answered Gabe and then left the study. "Enjoy the day lass," he said as he passed her. Abby wasn't sure but she thought she heard him laugh as he went out of the study.

Gabe continued to work spouting numbers. "twenty-three and forty-six…"

Abby answered "sixty-nine."

He ignored her and said "seventy-two and forty-one is…"

"113," Abby answered.

Gabe was surprises and impressed so he threw out some more numbers. As fast as he said two numbers, Abby added and answered him. He had a few pages to tally, so he finally called Abby away from the corner. Gabe handed her the sheets and said, "Tally these up and then ya can leave if ya promise me ya won't get into any more trouble today." He expected it to take her an hour but in less than five minutes she said, "Done. May I leave now?"

Gabe couldn't believe how fast she'd finished the additions. As he checked her work, every entry was correct and very neatly written.

"Ya are very good with numbers lass."

"Yes, I like numbers of any kind. I have a knack with them," she answered proudly.

"Now ya may leave," Gabe said. "But you are not to leave the courtyard. Ya allowed anywhere in the house except for the bed chambers that are in use. Do ya understand?"

"Yes."

"The next time ya cross me, it won't be a corner ya are sent ta. My word is law here. It doesn't have ta be right it is what I say."

"Fine," Abby sputtered still angry. "I will try to comply even if your word is not right." And with that announcement, she quickly left the study before he could punish her again.

"Be at dinner lass." She heard him call as she reached the bottom of the stairs.

Abby wanted to go and spend some time alone to work off some of her anger when she heard a man's voice scolding someone fiercely. She moved to the other side of the stairs to see what was so bad he had to talk like that. The voice was coming out of the music room. Abby peeked in to see a tall thin man with a very long nose bending over to the level of a small boy. Abby recognized the boy to be Gabe's son Colm. His head was bent as the tall man verbally reprimanded him for a very poorly played lesson. His punishment was to stay and practice until he could play the piece of music without a mistake. Then the tall man stormed out of the room leaving Colm by himself with his violin.

Abby watched as the little boy just stood there not even attempting to play. He hung his head and seemed to be crying. Abby's heart was breaking for him. She had promised not to interfere with his children's punishments, but she just had to go in and see what she could do. The music room was impressive. The acoustics were perfect. As Martha had said, every instrument imaginable was in the room lined up against the far wall. A grand piano was in the far left corner and a harpsichord in the other. Abby walked in trying not to be too conspicuous.

"Hello Colm," Abby said hoping he would answer her.

Hello Lady Abigail," Colm answered.

"Please call me Abby," she said and smiled. "So what is your violin's name?"

"Name? It is a violin. Ya don't name a violin," Colm protested.

"Oh, yes you do," Abby said. "It is your partner. You have to have a name for it or it won't work right for you. My Grandfather said, 'to play well you name your instrument. If you make mistakes it is always the instruments fault never yours'." Then Abby smiled letting Colm know she was playing with him. Little nine years old Colm just smiled. "First, is it a boy or a girl violin?" Abby asked.

"A boy of course," Colm answered highly insulted.

"Ok, we need a boy's name." Abby paused pretending to think then said, "I got it, Herkimer."

"Herkimer?" Colm said with a giggle, "absolutely not"

At that moment Abby noticed he sounded like his father. In fact he looked the most like Gabe with his dark coloring, brown cow eyes and very big feet. Abby continued to try to find a name, "Ichabod, Percy or Broomhillda." Colm started to giggle as Abby called out the worst boy names she could think of.

Finally Abby said, "Ok then, if you can do better you come up with a good name."

"I like Pete," Colm said with a smile.

"Oh what a great name for such a fine instrument," Abby agreed. She was a very good violinist but had not played much since her grandfather did. Abby was unsure she could play now but she felt so bad for Colm that she was determined to try.

"When I use to play with my grandfather, I would play one hand and he would play the other. Colm was a little skeptical but he was so discouraged after his instructor left, that he would try anything.

Abby sat in a chair and invited him to come over. Gabe watched from the hall. He had to get something out of his private study and happened to look in as he passed. There was Abby sitting in a chair directly behind Colm holding the bow to the strings while Colm fingered the neck. Then Gabe watched as they switched the positions, Colm use the bow while Abby fingered the neck. Together Colm's violin had never sounded so beautiful. Gabe did not want to leave. He was enjoying the loving view of Abby and Colm embraced in each other's arms with a violin between them.

Not only did he hear beautiful music, but he heard Abby humming the tune in Colm's ear. When they completed the music, Gabe watched the expression on Colm's face. He was so pleased with himself and the music he played.

Colm's instructor returned to see how his student was doing. When he saw Gabe watching from the hall, he said, "Your son is hopeless." The instructor said still frustrated from the earlier lesson. "I will require more pay if I am ta continuing ta teach such a difficult student." Gabe only pointed into the hall. Colm was now facing Abby with a big smile on his face while Abby played a spare violin with him. The music they played was perfect. The music Colm had been working on for the last month and could not play, Abby managed to get Colm to play in less than an hour.

The two men watched the music room light up with the excitement of the violinists. Abby jumped up and clapped her hands as they finished their private concert still unaware of the little audience that had gathered in the hallway. Not only had the music attracted Gabe and the instructor, but Martha, the servants, and even some of the cooks from the kitchen.

Abby reached down and grabbed Colm under the arms and swung him around and then finished her play with a tickle on his belly. Colm giggled uncontrollably.

"That woman has interfered with my instructions. Your son is being punished for his terrible performance today and there she is swinging him around and tickling him. She must be asked to leave the music room immediately," the instructor insisted. Gabe saw how Abby was interacting with his son and could not break them up. Colm was just five when his mother passed and never was tickled by her or swung around. Abby was acting like a mother he never had and this pleased Gabe.

Instead of discouraging their play, Gabe just shut the door without them noticing and let them be despite the objections of the inept instructor.

An hour later Abby came out of the music room and went down to the kitchens. Abby found the kitchen as grand as the rest of the laird. There was a large wood planked table in the center for working. She counted five working ovens, a sink with running water and three walk in pantries. Pots and pans hung from a rack over the table. Smells of fresh baked bread filled the air. A large kettle of soup was already simmering on the far stove.

Abby had to smile when she remembered her serving the soup to James. There was also a side kitchen door which led out to an extensive herb and vegetable garden, truly a cook's paradise.

Eva the head cook saw Abby standing in the entry way and welcomed her in. "His Laird said ya would come down. He said ya like ta cook. Is that why ya are here? I'm sorry I missed ya the other day."

Abby was thrilled she was allowed to cook and spent the rest of the day helping in the kitchen. By the time Abby left, Eva had become a good friend.

Abby left the kitchen to find another one of Gabe's sons sitting on the stairs waiting for his turn to see his father. A slate rested in his lap and a piece of chalk in his hand. Adam, ten years old, was having major problems with time tables especially the nines. Abby sat down next to him and that is where Gabe found them laughing and enjoying the numbers Abby was writing on his slate. By the time Gabe came out for Adam, Abby had solved his problem and the two of them were busy looking at the slate.

"Can I be of assistance ta ya Adam?" Gabe asked getting their attention from the slate.

"No Da, Abigail helped me, and I really understand. I can do the nines Da, just ask me." Gabe grilled his son on his nine times tables and was amazed how well he knew them. Adam was so proud of himself.

Abby still dusted with the kitchen flour; rose to go up stairs when Gabe said, "And where do ya think ya are going Abigail?"

"I was going to wash before dinner."

"Before ya go upstairs, I would like ta have a word with ya," Gabe said.

Abby's heart sank. Now what had she done. She took a deep breath and followed Gabe back into the study. He shut the door behind her and Abby braced herself for the worst.

"Shall I go to the corner Laird?" She said snippety. She was still upset with how Gabe treated her earlier and was still waiting for whatever he had in mind.

"Are ya still angry with me?" Gabe asked standing in front of her.

Abby refused to answer and turned her head.

"Well if ya think I should punish ya again, I can oblige."

Abby still said nothing but folded her arms ready for the worse.

"I saw what ya did with Colm this morning, and Eva enjoyed ya in the kitchen this afternoon, and ya certainly made Adam happy just now. So what have ya done ta need another punishment?"

Abby eyes shot up in surprise. "You are not upset with me?"

"Nay lass, on the contrary, I am very pleased. I would like ya ta keep doing the good work."

"Then why have you marched me in here if you are not going to reprimand me again?"

"Well I promised ta show ya Fuchsiall and the grounds. We have about two hours before dinner. Would ya like a personal tour of my home?" Gabe reached out and took her hand and led her out the side door of his study into the rose garden. From the windows above and the kitchen, the servants watched the couple stroll through the garden arm in arm. Hopeful expressions were on their faces. The Laird had been alone too long and it was high time he take another wife. This woman would be the perfect mother for his children and the perfect women for his bed.

CHAPTER 16
I AM NOT A WITCH

Two days later, the messenger Gabe sent to his cousin returned. Gabe's cousin, the King of Scotland was out hunting quail just a day's ride south. Dougal, the messenger, had found him quite by accident and had relayed Gabe's message. A meeting had been arranged at Edinburgh in one week. Gabe was to meet him there to discuss Lester McHale, The W & W Shipping Co. and Abigail Fox. The King insisted on secrecy, Gabe was to come and stay under the premise that this was a family visit only and stay until they could all agree on a plan of action.

The King already knew of The W & W Shipping Co. and their involvement in illegal activities with England. Now that Lester McHale was involved Scotland the King was not going to lose any precious Scottish treasures to thieves. Part of Gabe's message informed his cousin of the murder, Abigail witnessed in the woods as well.

Dougal informed Gabe that his cousin was aware of England's loss of valuable jewels and gold which they blamed on the smuggling activities of the W & W Shipping Co. The English King felt that the actual culprit was a pirate known as Black Dog. No one knew his real name but Abigail was believed to be the innocent link. Both kings wanted her protected. And now that the Scottish king knew Gabe had her at Fuchsiall, he wanted her kept there until they could get more answers. They believed Abigail was Back Dog's next target. They also believed Abigail had something or some information that the pirates wanted. Abigail would be the bait that would lure Black Dog to the shore where the Kings could catch and hang him.

Fearful for the lives of his children and his clan, Gabe ordered the guards doubled and asked his father to be acting Laird until he returned. Joseph was to stay with his father. Simon was to come with Gabe. A pirate does not act alone. Gabe knew Black Dog and his men would come for Abby as soon as he discovered where she was hiding. Until then, Gabe wanted everyone safe, especially Abigail.

Abby knew there would be more than four men after her. She thought the McHales did not come to the laird that day looking for a single man, but were actually scoping to see if she lived there. Gabe would be leaving the next day to meet with his cousin. He was determined to free Abigail from the treasure seekers, but had no intention of letting her go. He also had another purpose in mind and for that he asked his other brother, Dunkin for his help.

...She was cold. The amber liquid was swelling up around her. Her calls for help were not heard. Where were her friends that came with her? Help me..... Help me..... I am drowning. Find me...don't let me drown...Help!....

Abby woke from her nap wet from sweat. She leaped up from her bed and ran out of her chamber without putting her shoes on. Down the hall she ran, as fast as she could. She slid down the railing and out the door into the courtyard. Gabe was practicing with his men when he saw Abby run out of the house at a full run, terror across her face.

A woman came running in over the drawbridge screaming her son's name.

"Abigail, what is wrong?" Gabe asked stopping the sword fighting.

"Amber liquid, I am looking for amber colored liquid in a large vat. Where is it?" Abby screamed at a full run.

Gabe pointed to a building just south of the courtyard. The woman was screaming her son's name, tears coming down her cheeks.

"He's in the vat," Abby screamed, her skirts flailing around her legs. Without stopping, Abby plucked a rope, which was hanging off a fencepost and wrapped one end around her waist and tied it on. The two women reached the vat building at the same time followed by

Gabe and some men a few strides back. Abby climbed the ladder of the vat without stopping and dove head first into the vat of Ale after handing the other end of the rope to the boy's mother. Silence filled the room as they waited for a signal on the end of the rope. Gabe climbed the ladder to see inside the vat but foam covered the surface not allowing him to see into the amber liquid. It seemed like forever before the mother felt a tug on the rope in her hand.

"Pull!" She screamed franticly. The men grabbed the end of the rope and pulled Abby to the surface holding a little boy coughing and sputtering. Abby handed the boy up to Gabe on the ladder and then waited for him to help her. She was having a hard time seeing. The amber liquid was burning her eyes so she kept them shut. Gabe reached and grabbed the back of Abby's gown and pulled her out of the vat. She wrapped her arms around his neck and her legs around his waist. Slowly he climbed down the eight foot ladder to the stone floor below were the others were waiting. Gabe took his plaid and wiped Abby's eyes and then ordered water to rinse them. Both the boy and Abby had red puffy closed eyes and complained of burning. The other little boys who had been playing in the vat building came out from hiding to see if their friend was alright. Gabe wrapped his plaid around Abby and carried her up to the laird after ordering the boys to his study. Gabe ordered Simon to carry the wet boy and followed him up to the house.

By the time they reached the house, a tub of water was already being filled for the boy and another one for Abby. Gabe took Abby and dunked her in the water clothes and all. He pushed her head under the water and ordered her to blink. Simon did the same for the little boy. A few more dunks under the water and Abby's eyes were getting better. The little boys in the vat room, one being Ben, Gabe's youngest son, slowly walked past the panicked crowd and entered Gabe's study with their heads bent down.

As soon as Abby could see, she asked Gabe to let her up and then whispered, "Be gentle with them, they had a real bad scare."

Gabe could not believe she was telling him what to do again. So he said to her, "Abigail, I do know what I am doing, and I want ya up in ya chamber until I can talk ta ya."

Abby stood up out of the tub, her gown drenched with water and ale. Gabe wrapped a dry plaid around her shoulders and she went up to her chamber not saying another word.

The mother of the half drowned boy asked, "How did she know Laird? She saved his life?"

The other people in the room also asked the same question to Gabe hoping for an answer. Gabe knew what they were thinking. "Abigail is not a witch and she had nothing to do with that boy falling into the vat. Meet me in the hall and I will explain but first I need to speak ta the boys in my study."

By the time Gabe came into the hall, the room was full of confused people. He walked to the head of the room to answer their questions. After she changed into a dry gown Abby heard what was happening at the bottom of the stairs and to his surprise joined Gabe at the head table. "They have a right to know," Abby said to Gabe. "I should be the one to answer their questions." Gabe smiled at her and nodded.

"Are ya a witch?" a woman called out.

Abby shook her head and said, "Please, if you want me to tell you then you are going to have to listen." The crowd quieted down and let Abby explain herself. "I am not a witch and do not ever accuse me of being one. I am a dreamer. Sometimes I dream and the dreams come true. It is a type of seer that is described in the bible. I sometimes see the future through my dreams. Today I was taking a nap and I saw the boy in amber liquid. I do not dream every day and it can be years before I have another one. But I have had enough dreams to know not to ignore them. If I have frightened any of you then I am sorry. I assure you that I am not dangerous and have never harmed anyone."

"I donna care what ya are. Ya saved my son. I will be forever be grateful. I thank God the Laird brought ya here," the mother praised.

The rest of the clan in the room said, "Aye." Gabe watched as one by one his clan lowered to one knee giving Abby their pledge of loyalty and acceptance. She had won her place in his clan. Gabe was so proud of her and his clan as well.

That night after dinner Adam and Abby worked on numbers again. Gabe watched the two as they figured out problems with excitement. Adam had conquered the nine times table with pride.

"We are finished here." Gabe then added, "This matter is closed." He said to his men, with one eye on Adam and Abby.

Abigail and Adam were so involved with what they were doing that they didn't notice the Laird coming over and sitting in the chair right behind them. He just sat and listened to the two as they worked together on the slate while sitting on the floor in front of the fire.

"That is it Adam. You are so smart," Abby encouraged.

"I can do it!" Adam shouted.

"I knew you could," Abby said with a big smile. To Gabe's surprise, Adam reached out and hugged Abigail.

"Thank you," she said pleased. "We must do more homework together."

"Aye," Adam agreed.

Then Adam noticed his Da. "Is there something ya wanted Adam?" Gabe asked knowing Abigail had already helped him. Abby sensed the guys need time together so she stood and started to leave. As she walked out she called back, "Adam? Nine times seven is sixty-four right?"

Then Adam called back, "No it is sixty-three." Then he smiled at his Da proudly.

"Good job," Abby called and left the hall. Gabe sat and listened as Adam repeated every trick Abby had shown him. It seemed so good to see his son excited about his studies. Maybe I have hired the wrong teacher, Gabe thought to himself.

Gabe decided to leave in the morning instead of today. Abby was required by the Laird to join him every night for dinner. Tonight, however, Gabe had to send Joseph to fetch her.

She sat at the table next to Gabe with her hand against her cheek. Gabriel didn't notice that she was hiding something. She was very quiet and didn't eat anything. Finally Gabe confronted her, "Are ya okay lass?"

"I'm fine," she said refusing to look at him.

"Ya haven't eaten."

"I'm just not hungry," Abby replied fidgeting.

"What is it lass?" Gabe asked worried.

"Nothing," she replied, keeping her head down and her hand over her cheek. Joseph walked behind Gabe and whispered something in his ear. Abby's heart sank. She had been fingered.

Gabriel reached out and took Abby's hand down to expose a very large welt across her cheek going down her neck.

"What is this, lass?" Gabe demanded touching her cheek.

"Nothing," Abby answered pushing his hand away.

"Who hit ya?"

Her cheek was swollen with a long red welt with black and blue bruising.

"Abigail…" Gabe whispered. She would not talk.

Adam came to her rescue, "She got hit because of me Da."

"What?" Gabe asked.

"The professor thought I cheated. I didn't Da. I know my nines. He would not believe me. Abby got between the two of us. She wouldn't let him hit me, so he hit her, hard Da. She fell down. He hit her with a yardstick right in the face." Gabriel started to turn red but let Adam continue. "It was my fault, Da. Don't punish her. Punish me Da not her," he pleaded. Gabe was surprised, his son was defending her. "She didn't know she shouldn't interfere, Da!"

"Abigail," Gabe said. "Let me see."

"Please Da."

"Relax Adam. I'm not going ta punish her." He went to the sideboard, wet a clean rag and then came back and placed it on her cheek. "Cold will help lass."

Gabe motioned to Joseph. "Get me the professor," he whispered.

"Ya two can be excused seeing that ya are finished with ya dinner." Abby and Adam wasted no time leaving the hall.

"Thank you," Abby said to Adam.

"Thank ya," Adam said to Abby. "Does it hurt?"

"It is getting better every minute," Abby replied.

Meanwhile, Gabe was furious. He had all he could do to wait for Joseph to return with the professor.

Finally the professor strolled in to the hall unsuspecting Gabe's anger.

"Yes Laird, what can I do for ya?"

Gabe started right in with, "Did ya hit Abigail?"

"Yes, she interfered with my class for the last time. I caught ya son cheating. It was in my right ta punish him. Abigail would not let me."

"What makes ya think my son was cheating?"

"Simple, he handed in a slate without an error." The professor bragged. "Your son has no mind for numbers unless ya beat it into his head. It was in my right ta teach him a good lesson… the little cheat. And I would have ta if she had not got in the way."

Gabe saw red. "Are ya in the habit of hitting women?"

"I was tired of her interference. She is always interrupting making excuses ta disrupt my class. She plays outside my window with your daughters distracting my students. She needs ta be taught a valuable lesson Laird."

"I think it is time I teach ya a valuable lesson sir," Gabe growled. "Hold him. Strip him." Joseph and Simon grabbed him by the arms and ripped his shirt off. Gabe took the yard stick the professor was holding. "Now let me teach ya what this feels like." When Gabe was through, he ordered the professor to leave and never return.

There was a soft knock on Abigail's door but before she could answer, Gabe walked in carrying a tray of food. "I thought ya might be hungry lass."

"I'm sorry Gabe. I know I should not…"

Before she could finish, Gabe said, "Abigail, I am not angry with ya and I know my son did not cheat. But ya should not have dealt with the professor by ya self."

"The next time….."

"No lass. There will not be another time, the professor has been dismissed."

"Oh that is great," Abby said happily.

"Ya think so?"

"It's not?" Abby asked confused.

"Well lass, I am short a professor."

"Oh, that is too bad, but surely you have someone in mind."

"I do," Gabe said with a smile.

"Good, I am sure he will be better than that beast."

"Not him lass, her."

"Her?"
"Her…YOU."
"OH! NO!"
"OH yes. Starting tomorrow after I leave ta see my cousin. That should keep ya out of trouble until I come back. Now eat your supper and get some sleep."One…Two…Three…

CHAPTER 17
An Alliance Is Formed

Before Gabe left in the morning, he announced to his staff that there would be visitors coming at the end of the month. Gabe had made arrangements for stud services with James in exchange for Abigail. The horses Gabe owned were very valuable and proven for their speed. James had racing stock and wanted to combine his with Gabe's. The agreement had been settled two days before Gabe started home with Abigail and it was now time for the breeding. James was bringing ten mares and would stay a good month to ensure successful pregnancies.

Fuchsiall was to be made ready for their arrival. Gabe ordered the entire third level prepared. He was confident that he could leave knowing his home would be safe. The staff would have plenty to do. His children were in good hands and Abigail would not get into any trouble. So he bid everyone goodbye after Dunkin had arrived and left with his men to visit the king.

Edinburgh was a good week's ride from the laird. Dunkin was briefed about Gabe's plan and agreed to help. On arriving at Edinburgh, the King made everyone comfortable. A meeting was arranged behind closed doors. To Gabe's surprise, he and his brothers were not the only members at this meeting. James greeted Gabe as he walked into the room as well as the English King himself.

No one knew the English king was in Scotland. He had come to elicit help from Scotland in regards to the pirate, Black Dog, although the Scottish king was skeptical about his real reason for coming. English ships had been repeatedly pillaged, and good men lost their lives because of Black Dog. The English King was furious and was determined to find Black Dog and put an end this problem. Black Dog's pillaging did not stop with England. France, Germany and Italy had been in contact with England hoping for some solution.

It was Black Dog's habit to attack merchant vessels, strip them of their cargo, kill the crew and then sink the ship leaving no witnesses. The ocean was not safe as long as Black Dog was on the high seas and there had been reports of his numbers increasing. Before Black Dog could get too powerful the five countries involved needed to formulate a plan and work together until all parties involved were apprehended and severely punished.

The king of England was positive that the W&W Shipping Co. was a front for Black Dog. Mr. Webber and Mr. Washburn were not smart enough to run such an intricate operation.

When Abby was arrested in London and thrown into debtor's prison, information connecting Black Dog and the W&W Shipping Co. had not been discovered yet. Only the debt owed by the shipping company had been recorded.

The English King felt Abby was coerced into coming to England under the premise that she was a partner to the shipping company, but really it was to lead Black Dog to a valuable box she was seen with leaving the Riverton Bank. However, after interrogating his newest guest in the Tower of London, the English King determined that Black Dog did not want the box but what Abigail was hiding. The box was only a key to the whereabouts of a lost treasure which Black Dog was after.

"Mr. Pinkerton was so kind to inform us that he was part of Black Dog's operation. He seemed to dislike his new quarters in the Tower," the English king said smiling. "Because of him, we have been able to find information which connects Black Dog to ports throughout Europe and Italy. We have lookouts to help us find him but so far he has eluded us."

"Believe it or not, Gabriel, holding Abigail Fox in prison saved her life. That woman has more lives than a cat. The day after she was sold to James someone broke into the prison and killed the guards. Her cell was the only one opened. Whether they were there to kill her or free her we do not know, but until she brings them to the treasure, they need her alive. They also broke into the Tower and freed my guest, Mr. Pinkerton."

All the men in the meeting were full of questions and the English King answered as much as he knew.

"One thing we are certain of, is that Abigail Fox had no idea what she was getting into. She was not involved in any debt of the W&W Shipping Co., and she is not who she says she is."

"Who do ya think she is?" Gabe asked waiting for an answer.

The English King did not know but said, "It just seems strange that a common woman from a town no one has heard of, until now, has in her possession a box that has eluded treasure hunters for over one hundred years. James informs me that this woman is very educated and can speak more than one language fluently. He caught her speaking German to his head cook. Doesn't it seem strange that she has remained hidden all these years?"

"What is that box?" Gabe asked.

The English King smiled. "We had to be a little more encouraging with Mr. Pinkerton while we had him before he would tell us. He now has one leg permanently shorter than the other." The King stood up and brought out a map. "Many years ago, a small country existed here," and he pointed to a land north of Scotland, "It was invaded and completely destroyed. It was rumored, that the royal family escaped but the country's wealth was hidden. A small box was the only key to its existence. If there really is a treasure, Abigail Fox is the key to finding it."

Then the real reason for the English King's visit finally came out. He wanted the Scottish King to hand Abigail over. Gabe was furious but kept his emotions hidden. Both his brothers Simon and Dunkin watched as Gabe tried to stay calm. The Scottish King would not give the whereabouts of Abigail and insisted that it was more important to find Black Dog. The two kings were like two dogs fighting over one bone, Abigail, but neither had any rights to her.

Abigail had been right. There would be more treasure seekers and they would not stop. Gabriel at this moment decided to help her even if he had to take her to the treasure himself. The only way she would be free from predators was to rid her of that box and what it represented. Abigail had confided in Gabe. All she had said was now confirmed by the English king. When she talked about the box, fear came over her face. Gabe knew she had not told him everything because she was more concerned with the welfare of his children and clan than the treasure. Abby had begged him to let her go. She feared they were getting to close. Gabe felt the treasure had no value to her or she would have retrieved it by now.

The meeting went on for hours and Gabe's cousin still refused to reveal Abigail's hiding place. Even James, who knew Abigail's location kept silent. They finally agreed on an alliance which would guarantee the arrest and conviction of Black Dog. As for the treasure and Abigail, the kings could not agree and decided to act after the pirate was apprehended and not before.

When the king of England finally left for home Gabe was ordered to have a private audience with his cousin.

"I cannot by law protect her for long. She is not Scottish. If she was I would not have ta deal with the English King. I need ta know ya intentions. Did ya know about this treasure and are ya keeping her ta have it for ya personal gain?"

Gabe and the King had been like brothers. They grew up together, never mistrusting each other. Gabe was as devoted to his cousin as he was devoted to himself. Lying was never done between the two of them. Gabe was always straightforward regardless of what the Scottish King might do to him. The King trusted Gabe with his own life. So when he asked Gabe about Abigail, he knew whatever the answer was it would be the truth.

"Gabriel, I am waiting for ya answer," the King said.

"Abigail is the first woman since my wife's death that I have wanted permanently in my bed and in my life. I have every intention of having her. I do not care or know what this treasure is, but she did tell me about the box."

"Are ya telling me that ya love her or that ya want ta bed her?" The King asked.

Gabe was surprised with that question, but did not hesitate to answer. "Aye, I love her with my whole heart."

"Then ya best keep her hidden. She will never have a chance if she is discovered and neither will ya."

Gabe had a plan of his own and he wanted to share it with his cousin. Together they refined the plan and set it in motion.

First, Dunkin, who was a sea captain who sailed the ship belonging to Gabe, would leave for the colonies and bring back Abigail's children. Gabe feared they would be sought by Black Dog and held in order to force Abigail to reveal the secrets of the box. He also feared for their lives. The pirates would definitely kill them when they were no longer needed.

Dunkin was obligated to keep his shipping agreements, so it could not be a straight trip but he would make it back in a couple months. He would also keep Abby's four children safe. Gabe felt keeping business as usual would bring less attention to Abby's children and would keep them safely hidden from the pirates.

Dunkin did not want to waste any time especially if the English King knew about her family. It would be just like the English king to abduct the children and hold them for ransom. The sooner, Dunkin, left the better for everyone. The king of England would not return home for a few days and that would give Dunkin the head start he would need to rescue Abby's family and keep them out of the hands of England and Black Dog. Gabe said, "Be safe little brother and bring them home. I will expect ya in a couple months." The two men hugged and then Dunkin was off.

Gabe stayed at Edinburgh for a few more days. The cousins needed to catch up on family gossip and it would disguise the real reason for the visit. The King, however, loved the stories Gabe told about Abigail, from the soup at James' manor to the serenade at the chapel, the roof and chimney and even the drum. The two men laughed at the stories. Gabe even told him how she had single handedly put him and his two brothers in the stockades. The King wanted to meet her and had every intention of doing so.

The cousins spent time hunting together and discussing horseracing and breeding. All in all it was a very good visit. Gabe agreed to return and he would bring Abigail.

At the end of the week Gabe and his men headed back home two days early.

CHAPTER 18
Welcome Back Laird

The staff ran for safety in the hall before the war began. Any member of the staff who was caught in the war zone, which was the entire laird except the hall, would be fair game.

Each night after dinner the hall would be full of servants. Abby felt they needed time to just sit and enjoy each other without working all the time. She also wanted to play with the children. Gabe's children were always in lessons. In the morning, it was lessons with her and in the afternoon they would have music, defense, or art. They would have a few hours before dinner which included some reading and study and a little play. So Abigail was determined to roughhouse and let them be children.

Abigail would prepare treats ahead for the staff as they waited until the coast was clear to leave the hall. She would cook special foods for them and would have games set up like chess which was usually played in the study. But the staff loved watching the children running through the laird and they especially loved Abigail, she was ruthless. They were also grateful that Abigail thought to give them time off and cook for just them as well. Such treatment would be discouraged as soon as Gabe came home, but for now it was great to be waited on.

Gabe's father loved Abigail and allowed her to do whatever she wanted. He described her as a breath of fresh air. Even Joseph loved to watch the war and sometimes would deliberately get to the hall late. This would result in a direct hit or two which he always took like a man with loud wailing sounds.

When the war started, each child and Abby were armed with five wet sponges, the wetter the better. Points were given for each direct hit and double points were awarded when Abigail was hit. Extra points were given for unarmed staff running into the hall. Martha and Eva kept the score. The war lasted one hour and sometimes two. The staff insisted that the hall doors be left open so they could have a good view of the fighting. The staircase was the best place to get points because the scorekeepers could see better, so most of the war was fought up and down the stairs. Any sponge on the floor became the ammunition of the finder. Buckets of water where strategically placed here and there for necessary reloads. Gabe's father would whistle loudly signaling the beginning of the game. A second whistle meant the end of the game and time to clean up before bed. Usually the warriors would protest the second whistle and sometimes he would grant five extra minutes. But too much protesting would result in suspension of one night, so the children were very respectful.

Gabe and his men had entered the courtyard ending their long journey just after dinner time. They were greeted by the guards stationed on the walls. Gabe gave the order to close the drawbridge at night from now on and called a mandatory meeting of his men first thing in the morning. The horses were bedded down and then Gabe and Simon walked to the laird. As they came close Gabe noticed the laird lit up more than usual. As they came closer, they could hear the screams and laughter of his children.

"What the hell are they doing in there?" Gabe said to Simon not expecting an answer but Simon and Gabe answered the question at the same time. "Abigail!"

The two men bounded up the stairs and slammed into the laird only to be bombarded by wet sponges flying everywhere.

"Quick Laird, Simon, come in here," the butler called waving his hand in the air. Gabe and Simon ran into the hall to be greeted by the entire staff huddled safely in the room, playing table games and eating fancy finger foods.

Gabe was not use to seeing his staff sitting around and was not sure he liked it but they were happy and having a good time. "What the hell is going on here?" Gabe asked a little too loudly dripping from the water left by the direct hits.

Martha called him over and said, "Watch Laird. It is the sponge war."

Then Gabe's father strolled over and said, "Relax son, ya won't get hit if ya are in the hall. It is the safety zone."

"Here they come again," the butler called enjoying the view from where he was standing. Gabe and Simon ran to the hall doorway where they could get a good view. Down the stairs, running at full speed, screaming as they went were Gabe's six children wet and dirty, followed by the mad sponge thrower herself, Abigail, just as wet and dirty. She had her skirts jacked up to give her ease in running and she was armed with at least a dozen wet sponges. As she reached the top of the stairs, she began to fire. Her aim was deadly. Gabe watched. She never missed. When the hit was made the child would dive for the sponge and then run to the bucket to reload. Abby, now out of ammunition ran up the stairs to get out of arm range. She definitely had a longer reach but there were six of them and one of her, but this seemed to be a perfect match.

Gabe was about to stop this at once, but Martha said, "Wait Laird, ya have got ta see this." Gabe settled down to watch the next battle. He could hear the children hollering threats at Abby and he could hear her laughter as she ran from them. Then Gabe watched in amazement as Abby darted out from the upper level and jumped onto the railing and slid down it on her bottom at full speed exposing her legs up to her knees. Gabe gasped as he watched her come to the end of the railing expecting her to fall and crack her head on the floor, but she leaped off with the grace of a deer and landed square on her bare feet not wavering a bit.

Sponges were flying in the air from the top of the stairs. Gabe watched as she darted away from them and reloaded, hurling them back up the stairs at his laughing, wet, dirty children. Martha and Eva were having a hard time keeping score, but Abby was definitely in the lead. The two scorekeepers were giggling as much as the children were and the butler was calling plays from the doorway. Now and then Gabe's father would compliment a good hit and the servants would cheer them on. As usual, Joseph came in late, which meant fair game. The target turned from Abby to Joseph and before he could reach the hall he was hit at least ten times making funny sounds that always increased the children's giggles. There was water everywhere. Sponge prints stained the walls and the floor. The children and Abigail were drenched from head to foot.

The buckets of ammunition were winding down and Gabe's father gave the signal to stop. Gabe and Simon stood back out of the view of the little soldiers to see just how this war game ended. Martha announced the score and tonight Abby just barely won. The children cheered with excitement from the near win. This was the first night they had even come close to beating her. They were getting better. Each night the children came closer to winning and tonight they just about had her.

Abby gave the order to clean up and the boys ran to get the mops. They each had an area they needed to clean and in less than twenty minutes, the stairs railing, walls and upper level hall were cleaned from sponge marks. The buckets were gathered and the sponges put in them for the next war tomorrow night. Gabe was impressed on how quickly they cleaned the mess without complaining, and they laughed and teased Abby and each other as they finished the clean up. Together the seven walked up the stairs to get ready for bed.

Gabe had no idea what to do about this. Abigail had his servants imprisoned in the hall while the seven of them ransacked his house. Gabriel had very precious paintings and tapestries on the walls. It would not take much to ruin them and even though they cleaned everything up his children knew better to treat his house with such disrespect. This kind of play belonged outside not in the house. The worst part of this was his father. He had allowed his grandchildren to act like hooligans. Something Gabe would have never done when he was growing up. As he looked at his servants, they were comfortable with having to stay in the hall. They were playing games and relaxing. His children were happy and Abby was playing with them which made him happy, but he could not let this behavior continue. He did not have the heart to stop it or punish them.

"Da what the hell do I do about this?" Gabe asked baffled.

"I know just how ya feel lad. I have never seen anything like this and I don't know if I want ta throw my arms around them and play ta or put them over my knee," Gabe's father said.

"Oh, they're just having fun Gabe," Joseph added.

"We like watching them play especially with Abby," Martha said.

"Please donna punish them. They've done no harm," Eva pleaded.

"I cannot let them destroy my home," Gabe said still rubbing his chin in disbelief.

"Welcome home Laird and Simon," the butler greeted trying to calm things down.

"They have no idea ya are home lad. Ya can just pretend ya didn't see any of this," the older Laird encouraged. "Take time ta think this over Son, ya donna want ta make a mistake and regret it later. Besides, they always clean up and they do a really good job."

"I have servants for cleaning. My children do not mop floors."

Gabe did not notice the servants slowly leaving the hall one by one, their mood deflated. Joseph too left the hall, but not quietly as the servants. He threw his trencher across the room and stomped out.

"Has everyone gone mad?" Gabe asked as he watched his servants leave silently.

"No Laird," Martha said sharply, but most professionally and left the hall.

The butler resumed his stiff stance and said, "Welcome home sir."

Eva politely, but with a cold air about her, asked if he was hungry and resumed her servant demeanor.

Gabe took his father's advice and said nothing that night, but in the morning he called Abigail into his study. Abby was thrilled he was home. She hurried to his study and entered with a big smile on her face unaware of his anger.

"I'm so glad you are back, I have so much to tell you. When did you get home?" Abby asked excited to see him.

But he did not even look up at her or return her smile. "I got home last night," he said sourly.

Abby was beginning to suspect something. Her smile left her face and she asked, "When?"

"During the sponge war, I was privileged ta see my children acting like hooligans and my house being destroyed," Gabe said now looking straight at her with a disgusted expression. Abby was dumbfounded. She just stood there, her heart racing and let him finish what he wanted to say.

"So, tell me Abigail, were ya brought up in a barn?"

Abby was hurt. The last thing she met to do was to anger him. She just wanted his children to have fun and his servants to have some well deserved free time. She could not see any harm done by the sponges especially after the clean up. So she said with a snippety attitude.

"I was not brought up in a barn but pretty damn close and from now on that is just where you will find me, you pompous ass." And she turned and stomped out of his study before he could stop her. By the time she reached the bottom of the staircase, she was at a dead run. Gabe followed her out of the study, but was too late to stop her. He opened the door to the laird to see her run across the yard and into the barn ignoring the greetings from the clan in the courtyard.

Gabe decided to let her alone for now and he would talk to her again after he talked to his children. A stern warning was all he would give them and he had no intention of punishing anyone. To his surprise, the children acted much the same way as Abigail and the servants.

When it was time for dinner, Gabe noticed a quiet murmur of talking in the hall. No one laughed or spoke louder than a soft voice. His children sat down quietly, not talking to each other or anyone else. Abigail's seat was empty. Gabe had to send Joseph out to the barn to retrieve her. She was not about to come in on her own ever again. She was a prisoner and it was high time she acted like one.

"He is not going ta like that Abby," Joseph said when he saw what she was wearing.

"I don't seem to do anything but anger him. So what difference is my green gown going to make and I have no intention of coming in without a fight," Abby said as she sat on a bunch of hay she had made into a bed for herself.

Joseph did not know what to do. He was sent to get her and he had to obey his orders. "I donna wish ta fight with ya lass." Joseph then looked around the hay loft. Abby had moved what little possessions she owned out to the barn and she was planning on staying there. "If I ask ya nicely, will ya come in for me?" he asked. "The children and servants are as miserable as ya are."

"Misery does like company, doesn't it?" Abby sputtered.

"I'm asking ya please. If ya want ta fight me tomorrow, I will let ya. But tonight those people need ta see ya in that hall walking in with ya head held high," Joseph said hoping she would do as he asked. Abby turned without saying a word and climbed down the ladder of the loft and walked across the courtyard and into the laird followed by Joseph.

"They will damn well see me, Joseph, but they will not hear me. I intend to be silent."

Gabe couldn't believe she still had that ugly green gown she earned with her drawings. He hated that gown. It did not fit her and it was damn ugly. Abby walked into the hall and said nothing to anyone not even the servants. She plopped herself down in her assigned seat and waited for her chance to leave.

Gabe tried to make conversation with his children, but received no more than a yes or no or a shrug of a shoulder. They were as quiet as the rest of the clan. Martha walked in as usual and handed him her parchment for the day. "Thank ya Martha," he said as usual. But Martha did not say a word. She just walked out of the hall. Abby sat with her hands in her lap refusing to say a word or eat. Gabe reached out and put some meat in her dish along with a piece of bread with butter. He turned his head to talk to Joseph and when he turned back around, he found the meat and bread back in his trencher untouched, and Abby walking out of the hall. He started to rise when Adam asked to be excused before dessert. Gabe told him he could leave and all six children got up and left.

Abby marched back to the barn to get ready for a very a cold night. She propped hay all around her and laid a plaid on it. Under her green gown, she had wrapped four plaids. They kept her warm especially in her room with the chimney still not working. It had worked to keep her warm in her room, but she in the barn was feeling the cold already and the worse part of the night was yet to come. Abby had found two more plaids in the barn. She was planning to borrow them. She hoped whomever owned them would not come and get them until morning.

She heard the sound of the door opening in the barn and then footsteps were coming up the ladder. Abby watched fearfully hoping it was friend and not foe. She had little to defend herself with. As the footsteps climbed closer, Abby pushed further into the hay. The loft was dark and Abby was depending on the dark to hide her. Then Joseph's head popped up over the ladder.

"Are ya ok lass?" He asked. "Gabe sent me out to make sure ya were warm enough."

"I am fine. Thank you."

"Are ya sure ya want ta sleep in the barn?" Joseph asked.

"It seems like the best place right now until Gabe lets me leave." And she pushed some more hay around her. "He thinks I am an animal and animals belong in the barn."

"He will not let ya go lass and ya know that."

"I cannot please him and I am tired of trying. Just ask him to leave a list of things he wants me to do and hopefully I can stay out of his way," Abby said trying not to let him see her cry.

Joseph sighed and said, "Ya are as stubborn as he is and ya both deserve each other." Then he climbed down the ladder and Abby heard the door of the barn shut.

In the morning, Abby had every intention of suggesting that she stay at Gabe's father's house, but for tonight she would concentrate on staying warm.

Gabe returned to his chambers after reading his children a story which was poorly received. They had been polite and respectful to a fault not even complaining when he announced bedtime. He started to think about their behavior. It was too perfect, those rascals were up to something and suddenly he had the urge to go back and check on them again. When he opened the door to their rooms, his suspicions were correct. They were gone, every one of them.

Frantically he started searching the second level. He had left them just a few minutes ago so they could not have gone too far. As he was running down the hall, Joseph came up the stairs. He saw Gabe panicked expression and knew exactly what was wrong. Together they combed the house looking for the runaways. They were making so much noise opening and closing doors that soon the whole house was up searching.

Gabe started to become quite concerned when not a trace of the children had been found. The next place to look was in the yard. So they all headed out to the courtyard where they resumed their search. The guards on the walls had been watching the outside of the walls not the inside so they had not seen anything either. Two hours of searching still did not uncover their whereabouts. Some of the staff went back inside and traced their steps in hopes they were still hiding in the house. The guards confirmed the absence of movement outside the walls so Gabe knew they were still somewhere inside.

Then Jake came out of the barn calling out to Gabe the good news. Running down to the barn, Gabe and Joseph followed Jake to the very spot where he had found them. Gabe was ready to punish them all until he saw where they were. Jake pointed up the ladder to the loft. Joseph knew just what those children had done.

"Gabe," he said. "Go up quietly." Gabe climbed the ladder followed by Joseph holding a lantern.

On reaching the top the two men just stopped, holding the light so the whole loft was lit. There in the corner lay six small bundles all snuggled up together around the unsuspecting sleeping Abigail. "Have ya ever seen anything so sweet in ya life Gabe?" Joseph asked with a grin on his face. "I think they thought she might be getting cold? Look they all brought a blanket." Abby was sound asleep and never felt one of the children. She had been crying, a tear was still puddling on her nose near her eye.

Gabe looked around and saw Abby's things placed around as if she was planning to stay here a long time. Gabe's heart melted to see his children so close to Abigail. He had so wanted them to bond and now they had. His children were keeping her warm and protecting her. At that very moment Gabe realized that she had passed all the tests except one. He wanted her love. Abigail had earned the love of his clan and his children. In return she had given them her love but now he wanted her love as well. From the first moment he'd seen her dancing with that mop at James' manor, he had wanted to make her his and now there was only one more obstacle in the way, Abigail herself. And right now she was so angry with him he did not know if she would ever talk to him again.

"What do ya want ta do about this?" Joseph asked. "Do ya want ta bring them back inta the laird. It is so cold out here?"

Then from a deep sleep, Abby woke and sat up to see the lantern shinning in her face but she could not see who was holding it. She jumped, but surprisingly did not scream. “It is ok lass. It is just I and Joseph. We came ta get the children.”

“I do not have the children Gabe,” she said defensively.

“I tend ta differ with ya lass,” Gabe said smiling but she could not see his face from behind the lantern.

Abby started looking around and counted as she searched. “They are all here,” Abby said in complete amazement. Then she felt she should defend herself. “I had no idea Gabe. Really I didn’t.”

“Aye lass, I know. Now come in and they won’t come back out here.”

“NO,” she said defiantly, laying back down and covering herself up with her plaid.

“Well, if that is the way ya want it,” Gabe said looking at Joseph, “Fetch me some more blankets. They are all going ta need them.” Joseph disappeared down the ladder leaving Gabe holding the lantern. “Abby, we need ta talk.”

Abby did not move but stayed buried under her plaid freezing. Gabe thought he heard a little sniff. “Very well, I will talk and ya can pretend not ta listen.”

“I am not coming in. I am staying out here with the animals. You think I was raised by animals I might as well live with them. Now leave. I do not want to hear anything you have to say. I am sick of fighting with you,” then Abby rolled a little further away.

“Fine, do not listen then, but I am going ta talk.”

But before he could say a word Abigail said, “I am sorry you think I was destroying your house. I should have asked permission first and that was my mistake. I realize you have precious things and I should have been more respectful. And the staff was not imprisoned in the hall, as you thought. I was giving them time to have some fun. They are always working and so aren’t the children. They need time to relax and your children need to be children and have fun.”

“Are ya done or do I need more lecturing?” Gabe said now standing as close as he could without stepping on one of his sound asleep children with his arms crossed over his chest.

Abby was not done and he needed more lecturing. "You could have met us halfway. Maybe given us a new place to play that needed a good cleaning, but would not be in danger of damaging. Have you ever played hard with your children other than a tickle or a story?" Before Gabe could get another word in Abby went on. "I didn't think so. A sponge war cannot be played outside. It is too cold and the sponges will get all mud that could get in their eyes."

Then Adam who was lying at Gabe's feet rolled over giving him a direct route to Abigail. Gabe realized she was not about to stop his lecture. She was not going to forgive him and she was not going to come in. So he reached down and pulled the plaid off from her. He grabbed the front of her ugly green gown, which she was still wearing and lifted her up to her feet. He looked into her eyes which were filled with tears and pressed his lips over hers.

He wrapped his arms around her and squeezed her close to him. She smelled of fresh hay and baked bread. Gently he pushed his tongue into her mouth tempting her and loving her. Her tenseness softened into his arms and she returned his kiss. He opened his mouth gently entering hers a little more, rubbing his tongue against her tongue, tasting the sweetness of her mouth. She wanted the kiss to last forever. He wanted to take her and make her his for all eternity.

Then the sound of Joseph climbing the ladder broke the moment. Gabe pulled away from Abby leaving her standing in the middle of his sleeping children. He went to fetch the blankets from Joseph. He had brought enough to cover every one of them twice. "Do ya need help brother?" Joseph asked as he watched Gabe cover each one of his children with two more blankets.

"Nay. Thank ya. Ya can find me here if ya need me. I am staying in the barn tonight with the rest of my animals. Have Martha bring some food up in the morning. We will be staying here until we are all in agreement." Before Abby could protest, he gently took her shoulders and pushed her down. He lay beside her and covered her and himself with two more plaids and pulled her close to him. He loosened her laces and slipped his hand down into Abby's gown and cupped one of her naked breast in his hand. He gently fondled her breast and whispered "That is for wearing this ugly gown. Now go ta sleep," and he kissed her on the top of her head, one…two…three….

CHAPTER 19
The Compromise

In the morning the children awoke to find their father sleeping amongst them. One by one they started to get up quietly tried to leave the loft before their father woke and had a talk with them. But just as Adam and the other children reached the ladder to go down, they heard, "Where do ya think ya are going? Get back here and face me." The six children slowly walked back to face their father. Abigail was still lying under the blanket with Gabe's hand cupping her breast. She did not dare move. "Sit down children," Gabe said. "We need ta talk." Then he squeezed Abby's breast under the blanket and said. "I know ya are up lass. Time ta rise and take what is coming ta ya." Abby felt his warm hand leave her gown and she did rose to a sitting position, still buried under a blanket waiting for Gabe to have his say.

No one said anything until Gabe asked, "What are ya doing out here without permission? Did ya know the whole house was looking for ya and how worried ya made everyone?"

All six children started to speak at once. Gabe just put his hand up and said, "One at a time." Abby watched as Gabe listened to each one of his children. He was very good at being a laird and a father. After listening to each one of them he said, "Abigail it is your turn. I listened ta ya last night but do ya have anything else ya would like ta say?" Abby just shook her head waiting for Gabe to past judgment, but he surprised her yet again.

"I understand why ya were out here, ta keep Abigail warm, and I understand why ya are upset with me. But running away has never solved a thing and I am speaking ta all of ya that includes ya, Abigail. I would not be a very good father or Laird if my own children or my clan could not come and talk ta me. I am not perfect and if ya feel I have not dealt with something properly than I want ya ta come and talk ta me and not run away from me. If ya have done something wrong than it is my duty as ya father and laird ta help ya know right from wrong.

All of ya know how I feel about destroying my home. Roughhousing is not allowed. Abigail did not know this but all my children know. I am still not happy with ya behavior, any of ya, but I did like the sponge war game and I myself would love ta play it. Throwing a good wet sponge at all of ya would make me happy right now. So I have decided ta let ya play ya game." The children began to clap and cheer. "But," Gabe said slowly, "We will need a few new rules. First ya will play where I tell ya and nowhere else. And second, I insist that ya let me play or anyone else that wants ta join in."

The seven sat on the hay and listened to Gabe talk to them. Then he said, "Ya have done wrong and ya know it. I need ta know what ya think would be a fair punishment."

Abigail just sat in the hay and waited for her turn. Gabe let each one of them give their opinion and then he said, "Abigail it is ya turn. What punishment do ya feel is fair?"

She sat there not knowing what to say, and then said, "I do not know."

"Ya will accept what I think is fair than?" Gabe asked.

Abby just sighed and agreed.

"Very well this is what I want. First, I want all of ya ta promise me ya will never run away again. Second, I want ya ta give me ya words that ya will come and talk ta me no matter how angry ya are at me or I am at ya. Third, ya will find a place ta play other than the stairway at the entrance. I want a list from each one of ya and then I will decide the best place ta play. There will be no arguments or there will be no place at all.

Last, Abigail because ya would not tell me what a fair punishment is, ya are ta take that gown off when ya return ta ya room TODAY and bring it ta me ta burn." Abby opened her mouth, but Gabe was ready for her this time. "There will be no argument or there will be no sponge war." She could not believe what he had just done. Abigail would have to return to the laird or the children would not get to play and she would have to give him her gown she knew he hated. He had won again.

Martha called from the bottom of the ladder with their morning feast just as they finished their discussion. They all sat in the hay and ate together. All had been forgiven.

Gabe had one more injustice to deal with. That afternoon when Abigail was out in the courtyard being kept busy by his two brothers, Gabe called the entire staff together and heard their complaints. By the end of the meeting, the staff walked out happy with the compromise. Eva would be given one day off a week for needed time with her family and the others would get to take time as well but not all at once. Gabe thanked them for their hard work and apologized for not showing his appreciation more.

Before Gabe could leave the hall, Simon came in frantic. "It is Abigail, come quick." Gabe jumped up and ran out with Simon. He led Gabe across the courtyard and in back of the barn to Goliath's paddock. Goliath, a Belgian work stallion was considered very dangerous. Unlike most Belgians, Goliath was vicious. He kicked and snorted whenever anyone came near him and bit constantly. Gabe was seriously thinking of destroying him. He was such a beautiful stallion but his temperament was dangerous and Gabe did not want a dangerous stallion around especially when breeding. Because of his beauty and his makeup Gabe had put off making his decision but he could not wait much longer.

Simon brought him to Goliath's paddock. There Gabe found Jake, Joseph and, a small group of his guards watching helplessly. Gabe's heart skipped a beat when he saw what they were looking at.

There was Goliath standing still not moving a muscle holding his chin way up in the air while Abigail knelt on her hands and knees on his back focused on a spot just in front of his hind quarters sputtering words that only the roughest sailor would say.

Gabe knew enough not to holler. He was sure Abigail would be thrown or would fall and get trampled by the angry stallion.

"Abigail," he said quietly but firmly. "Ya get down from there this instant. He is very dangerous."

Without looking up and between cursing she said, "Gabe, stop ordering me around and get your ass over here and help me. I cannot push it in. My hands are not strong enough." Carefully Gabe entered the paddock careful not to startle or provoke the stallion.

"I need your help and you cannot help me down there."

Gabe without hesitation leaped up onto Goliath's hindquarters. "Here," she said. "Can you feel this?" Abby took his hands and guided his thumbs down the huge stallion's backbone. "There," she said. "Can you feel it?"

Gabe moved his thumbs along the back bone until he felt a slipped disc.

"When I tell you, push it down and in as hard as you can." Then she looked up and saw Jake the stable-master looking on. "Jake, when I tell you, see if you can get this stud to take a step forward and Goliath if you give us a hard time I swear I will eat your ears right off your head. Now Gabe, push as hard as you can. It has been out so long I am not sure we can get it to slip back in." Abby placed her hand on top of his and together they pushed. "Now Jake, get him to step forward." The massive beast move one hoof forward and the disc slid into place with a loud pop. Gabe looked up in surprise as Abby cheered.

Quickly Gabe dismounted and reached his hands up to help Abigail down, but she just turned on top of Goliath's back, still on her hands and knees and crawled up to his withers. She plopped herself down, straddling him ready to take him for a ride. "Abby get down from there now," Gabe ordered not expecting her to refuse him.

"Not now, I need to take him for a run. I'll be back in a few minutes. I need to see if the disc will stay into place. Open the gate Jake," she ordered. Jake could not believe what she just asked him but he went and opened it anyway.

Gabe was beside himself. There Abigail sat on one of the meanest stallions he had ever known without a halter, bridle, or saddle. She curled her feet under her bottom and grabbed a lock of his mane and ordered Goliath to go. The stallion lunged forward into a full gallop with Abigail in complete control without any tack.

The men watched as the magnificent stallion galloped out of sight behind a grassy knoll. The men waited silently unable to say a word while watching for a glimpse of Abigail and Goliath to return. Gabe ordered his stallion, Samson saddled. He was going after her. He and the others were sure Goliath had thrown her and she was laying hurt or dead somewhere.

Then they heard the pounding of very large hoofs and then Goliath appeared running straight out with Abigail kneeling on his back leaning forward to give his back room to move. They could hear her talk to him as he ran flipping his head as if he was a new born colt. It was the most beautiful sight. That massive stallion and Abigail perched on his back, her blonde hair flying in the wind and that ugly green gown flapping over her legs.

She ran him straight into the paddock and then announced. "I'm not done yet, he still wants to go. I'll take him out in the meadow. Are you coming, Gabe, I am not suppose to ride alone?" Then she giggled and without waiting for permission, road him out into the courtyard and out through the drawbridge careful not to run anyone over. Jake was just bringing Samson out of the barn. Gabe wasted no time mounting him and catching up with Abby. The men on the wall gathered to watch the two stallions gallop across the meadow with Gabe and Abby on their backs. Gabe could hear Abby urging the stead on hoping to keep Gabe and Samson behind them. Still amazed with what just happened he would not let Abby get too far in front of him. Samson was a racing stallion and Goliath was a work stallion.

Gabe had little problem catching them. He wanted to get beside her and pull her off that horse and take her back to the laird to give her a good tongue lashing, but she was in perfect control of the stallion. Even without tack, she was guiding Goliath where ever she wanted him to go by just talking to him. They rounded the woods towards the ocean and Abby finally slowed Goliath down to a well needed walk. Samson was not tired but Goliath was not use to running.

"Abigail," Gabe said coming up beside her carefully so that the two stallions would not fight. "Ya are going ta tell me what ya just did and yare explanation better keep me from taking ya over my knee."

Abby looked surprised at Gabe. She did not see a dangerous horse but a horse that was acting mean because he was in pain. So she said, "When I grew up, real close to the barn," she could not help but putting in a reminder of the day before, "my family did not have much wealth. My father could only afford horses that were old and not much good. One day he was at an auction and a large Belgian mare, we named Dolly, was going to be put down because of her temperament. No one could do a thing with her.

They thought she was crazy. My father saw something in her. She wasn't very old, maybe three of four and she was a beauty. We only had workhorses. My father could not justify the expense of a riding horse. There were too many mouths to feed. It took four men to help my father bring her home. My mother was furious with him for bringing such a dangerous animal to the house. She feared for the safety of us children. Mother was so angry with my father that we were not allowed anywhere near the barn until he went to get Old Joe.

Old Joe was a horse whisperer and an Indian shaman. He had a real gift with animals. I think I told you about him. He would say they would talk to him through their thoughts. It always amazed me. Old Joe would just show up when we needed him. Dolly told Old Joe about the pain in her back. The rest was easy. Now and then my father would have to push the disc back in, but he found the more we worked her the less problems we had with her back. My job was to run her every day.

Dad finally gave up trying to get me to ride with my feet down. Dolly was so gentle. We never had to worry about her hurting me. She would even let me stand on her back when we use to pick apples. Dolly was better than a ladder."

Gabe listened to her and could not take his eyes off of her. At this minute she looked like a little girl again. She was just beautiful. As she told the story she would smile and giggle. All he wanted to do was take her in his arms and kiss her. She, without knowing it, had just saved Goliath's life.

The two rode for hours and then finally decided to return to the laird. They cantered across the meadow unaware of the caravan that had stopped at the edge of the meadow to watch the two stallions run.

James stepped out from his carriage to watch the two magnificent stallions canter across the field. "Do you think that is the stallion we will be breeding with?" A woman asked standing near James.

"I certainly hope so," James answered. "Gabe would not hide such a beautiful stallion from me. He was not exaggerating when he told me about him. It will be a very good match for some of my mares." When the two stallions and riders disappeared into the laird, James gave the order to proceed. They had finally reached their destination.

Gabe and Abby rode into the courtyard. Abby rode Goliath into his paddock while Gabe dismounted and gave Samson's reins to Jake. He then met Abby in the paddock, helped her down and pulled her out of the paddock before she could object.

"I thought we had a compromise," Gabe said, still a little upset with her.

Then he pinched some fabric of her green gown and said, "Take it off or I have a mind ta rip it off ya."

Before Abby could say anything, a guard announced the sight of a caravan just rounding the field and soon to be entering the laird.

"Come lass, James and his people have finally arrived. We can wait for them on the steps of the laird."

The last person Abby ever wanted to see again was James. He had been so cruel to her, but Gabe would not let her arm go and forced her to walk with him across the courtyard to the steps of the laird.

James' carriage crossed the drawbridge first followed by a fancy carriage Abby recognized to be the one owned by Lady Jennifer, the biggest bitch she'd ever met, a woman who had her sights on Gabriel for a potential husband. As James exited his carriage he reached in and gently pulled out Gretna, Gabe's old mistress now obviously James'. Gabe did not like seeing the extra women that James brought but he was not surprised either.

James always brought what and whom he wanted. Gabe raised his arm to greet his guests dropping his hold on Abby's arm. "Come lass, let us greet our guests," he said to Abby but when he looked down for her she was nowhere to be found.

CHAPTER 20
James Has Arrived

James had come with a large group of grooms, footmen, personal servants and his own mistress, Gretna. Gabe, as always, was the perfect host. The animals were taken to their new quarters and the others were settled in. James and his mistress were given two rooms on the third level and Lady Jennifer was given the two rooms next to him. By the time Gabe and James had come back in from the barn Gretna and Jennifer had the whole house in an uproar. Jennifer wanted the room at the end of the hall on the second floor which was now occupied by Abigail and Gretna felt that James should have the entire floor not just two rooms. Abigail was nowhere to be found. Eva was frantic with all the menu changes Lady Jennifer made and Martha had gone to the town to pick up some new supplies.

Gabe gave one strong look at James and then went to his study. Gretna went up to the two rooms at the third level and Lady Jennifer went to her two rooms on the third level as well. When James was finished with his misbehaving females, he joined Gabe in his study until dinner.

When Abby felt the coast was clear, she sneaked down the backstairs to the kitchens and helped Eva with dinner. The three women had all they could do to keep up with Lady Jennifer's constant demands and prepare dinner as well. The servants were running from one level to the other and still Lady Jennifer was not waited on fast enough.

Finally it was dinner time. The children had been fed first, so Gabriel could have the dinner alone with his guests. Gabe sat at the head table with Joseph and Simon. James, Gretna and Jennifer were sitting in the children's places and Abigail's place was empty. James noticed the empty seat and asked who was missing. "Abigail," Gabe said with a slight grin. "She is feeling a little under the weather tonight, but I assure ya she will be here tomorrow evening."

"I would have thought," James said, "that you would have killed her by now or at least kept her in irons."

"Neither," Gabe said, thinking of the lecture he was going to give Abby when he finally found her. "I promise she will be joining us tomorrow evening and maybe during the first breeding with Goliath."

Gabe saw James begin to open his mouth and before he could ask, Gabe said, "My bed and who I do or do not have in it is none of your concern and I will ask your respect in that matter."

Then James looked at Gretna and then back to Gabe and said, "Have I thanked you for sending me my newest whore? She is a delight and will be a wonderful addition to my working ladies as soon as I am finished with her."

Gretna face became hard. She knew very well that her body was the only way she could survive out of the laird without a husband. Her tongue and deceitfulness had discouraged any clansman from marrying her. She had sealed her fate and now she had only one option. Gabe had sent her to James knowing this was her only answer. Gretna knew that even though this was a fate almost worse than death, death was the only alternative.

Abigail and Eva managed to lay out a fabulous banquet with sweet honey nut bread, baked pheasant, and fillet of scrod with asparagus, Cornish hens, sweet potatoes and turnips with butter. Dinner was capped with Abigail's blueberry pie and Brandy in the study with a good game of Chess for the men and visiting at the hearth for the women.

Abigail stayed as far from the guests as she could, sneaking up the backstairs when the kitchen work was completed well after 10p.m. She slipped in her chamber, shut the door behind her, leaned against it and let out a great big sigh of relief.

"Good dinner tonight lass," Gabe said from the stuffed chair in front of the hearth. Abby gasped. "Laird?

What are you doing in here? Do you want something?" She asked refusing to move away from the door.

"This is ya home, lass. Ya will not hide from anyone including my guests."

Abigail was startled to find Gabe waiting for her. "I'm glad you liked dinner." She glanced down at her gown and noticed she still was wearing the ugly green gown that she had promised Gabe she'd give him to burn.

He noticed her expression and then said, "Yes, I want that gown before I leave this room. I have every intention of getting it even if I need ta take it off myself." For a moment, Abby thought her gown was the reason why Gabe had been waiting for her, but she soon found out she was very wrong.

"I am not very happy with ya Abigail and I think ya know why," Gabe said waiting for a response.

"I will take this dress off right now and then I will go to sleep," Abby stated hoping that this was all she would have to discuss. Gabe would not even acknowledge her answer.

"Alright," Abby said knowing he was in a very foul mood. "I was in the kitchen cooking your dinner. I cannot be in two places at once and I thought it would be better for everyone if I stayed in the kitchen and acted like the prisoner I am."

Gabe walked over to her and put his hands on her shoulders. "Let me make this clear one more time because ya donna seem ta listen or want ta remember. This is ya home now and ya donna need ta be frightened."

Abby would not let him finish. "I was in the kitchen working. That is all."

"Have it ya way, but tomorrow your backside will be in the chair ta my right acting as the hostess. Am I clear about this?" Gabe demanded.

"It depends Laird," Abby answered. Gabe's eyebrow shot up. Then she asked, "Are you asking me to join you or are you ordering your investment prisoner to come to dinner?"

"I would hope it is an invitation," Gabe answered not quite understanding where she was going with this conversation.

"Then I will be honored Laird," she said with a devious smile.

"What if I had ordered ya?" Gabe asked skeptically.

"Then I would have come and sat, waiting to be excused. A guest can come and go as they please." Gabe now knew what she was up to. She was planning to come to dinner, but she would leave as soon as she could.

"I hope ya will honor me all night," he said gritting his teeth.

"I will do my best," Abby said relieved he had unintentionally given her permission to leave the hall whenever she wanted.

"The gown?" He ordered. Gabe had lost one fight but there was one he had no intention of losing the war.

Without saying a word, Abby walked behind the privacy screen in the corner. She slipped the gown off and put a big uglier yellow robe on. Gabe took one look at her and said, "Tomorrow ya are going ta have some new clothes and I will not take no for an answer." Then he took her green gown and was about to throw it into the fire when he noticed it went out again. "What is wrong with this chimney? Didn't someone clean it for ya?" Abby gave him a very guilty look. "Abigail, what have ya done?"

"Nothing," she said like a child caught with her hand in the cookie jar.

"Do ya know what I do ta my children when they lie ta me?" He asked starting to come toward her.

Abby stepped back and said. "It is still plugged."

"What? I sent someone up ta take care of it weeks ago."

"And I sent him away." Abby said not fearing what he would do to her next.

Gabe could not believe how defiant she was being. He was trying to keep his temper from flaring but she had pushed him all day with her negative behavior and she was doing it again.

"Well, I wasn't about to let someone climb up on the roof or up the chimney. What if they fell because of me? It would not be right. I would rather live with cold then being responsible for someone getting hurt or dying because of me," Abby explained.

"So ya would have cleaned the chimney so no one else would get hurt?" Gabe asked.

"Better me than someone here. No one knows or cares about me, but everyone knows the members of this clan. What if he had a family to take care of and he would have a mother. I will not be held responsible if he died or got hurt."

"Abigail, I will give ya a choice. I will not have ya cold and getting sick. It is damn cold in this chamber. Ya can have this room with a clean chimney or ya will sleep in my chamber with me."

Abigail's mouth dropped open. "Fine then." she said. "You win. I won't get in the way of someone coming up tomorrow to clean it."

Then Gabe understood her meaning. The operative word was "tomorrow". She would have tonight to fix it herself. He could not believe how clever she was. Even though she had promised not to go up there again, she would break her word rather than see someone get hurt and Gabe had just figured that out.

"So we are in agreement?" He asked hoping she'd say yes. She had tricked him about the hall tomorrow night, but he was just about to pay her back.

"Yes," Abby said hoping he would leave soon so she could climb up the chimney and unplug it.

"Good… After ya," he said holding his hand out.

Abby gave him a surprised look. Then he said, "Abigail, ya just agreed not ta sleep in this room until it is cleaned 'TOMORROW'," and he really emphasized the word tomorrow. "So tonight ya have agreed ta sleep with me."

Abby's mouth was opened and her hands were on her hips but she could not say a single word. He had tricked her. She would have to go with him she had given herself no other choice and he knew it.

"Shall I carry ya?" Gabe asked trying not to laugh at her helpless expression. He had been so upset with her all day and at this moment it had all been worth it. This would be the start of many nights in his bed at the laird. She had so cleverly weaseled her way out of her duties in the hall today and tomorrow night but he had matched her move. With a big smile on his face he said, "Checkmate, my sweet." He took hold of her elbow and guided her out of the cold chamber and across the hall to his rooms still holding her ugly green gown in his left hand.

As she walked into his chamber he gave her a playful swat on her backside but instead of feeling her bottom all he felt was thick fabric as if she was wrapped up like a mummy. Without saying a word, she walked to the bed and started to climb in.

"That is my side lass," he said from behind her.

She twirled around and said, "Fine but I just want you to know this is what I am sleeping in and I am not taking anything off."

She flounced around the bed to the other side and kicked her shoes off and climbed in, mumbling all the time. Gabe came and sat down next to her on the bed.

"You are on my side sir," she said huffily.

Gabe was having such a good time watching her that he decided to help her. He wanted to bed her. There was no doubt of that, but he wanted her to come to him willingly. Even when he had taken a woman or two from his clan, he had never forced himself on any of them. Even though he had that right, he was not about to start now especially with Abby.

Abigail lay on the bed with her eyes closed holding onto the quilt waiting. "Abigail what are ya doing?" He could hardly believe the answer she gave him.

"I am waiting for you to get ready, so you can plant your seed in me," she said as the color drained out of her hands from the tight grip she had on the quilt.

"Abigail, what am I supposed ta do ta get ready?" he asked most surprised.

Still with her eyes shut, she said, "You are supposed to stroke yourself with your hand until the right moment comes. Then you get on me and slide yourself in as hard as you can."

Gabe was appalled to hear her say such a thing. "And what are you suppose ta do while I do that?" he asked.

"I am to lay here with my eyes closed and I must be very careful not to touch you in any way with my hands," she replied.

"Is that how ya husband bedded ya?" he asked absolutely shocked.

"Yes," she said in a whisper. Gabe noticed her hands turning whiter with the tight grip she held on the quilt, as if to hold on for dear life and a small tear in one eye.

"Did he hurt ya?" he asked hoping she would say no.

"Yes, sometimes it would be days before I would stop hurting." Then she added, "My husband was a mean son of a bitch. I wanted children so badly and he didn't. So he would make it so awful for me that I would stop asking for them." She lay quietly not moving or opening her eyes, but waiting.

"Abigail, I told ya before I would not force ya and I meant it."

"But I agreed to sleep with you," she said opening her eyes and looking at him.

"Ya agreed ta sleep with me and that is all."

Abigail gave a huge sigh of relief. Gabe picked her up and pulled her onto his lap. He hugged her as if she was a small child. In her ear he asked, "Why in earth did ya husband ever marry ya?"

"It was for the inheritance. I told you he received a piece of property from his aunt. But there was a very sizable inheritance, if he was married and lived there. So he would take long business trips and make sure he did his duty when he came home, as he called it, just so he could have a life of pleasures and not share it with us."

Gabe was becoming sick just thinking of the cruelty he must have put her through. "Bedding a woman does not have ta hurt Abby," Gabe said softly. "Most women really like it if done right. Maybe someday ya will let me show ya."

Then he asked, "Abby ya said he died broke."

Abby lifted her head which was resting on his chest and looked him in the eye and gave him the most sinister smile. "He finally crossed the line."

Gabe looked at her and asked, "What did ya do lass?" He knew that Roy must have done something unspeakable.

"I could take almost anything except for one thing and Roy knew it. The day he beat my son breaking his nose and putting him in bed for a week was the last time I would let him come home."

"How did ya manage that?" Gabe asked.

"Let's just say, we came to a valuable understanding. I told him the next time he showed up I would kill him. Roy could not come home, so he lost whatever he had left of his aunt's inheritance. Her will stated, he had to spend so many days in the house and I made sure he did not."

Gabe had to ask, "And would ya have killed him lass?"

"I had every intention of following through with my threat," Abby whispered.

Gabe was in love with this woman. It angered him so to hear what she said about her dead husband. Abigail Fox might not be going by her real name, but she could not hide who she was inside and she was the one he wanted.

He pulled the quilt back and lifted her off his lap and laid her in his bed. As he started to cover her, he noticed at least two different colored plaids under that ugly yellow robe. Gabe started to wonder if she was deliberately making herself look larger than she was to keep any interested prospects away. Tomorrow he would get to the bottom of this, but for now he would cuddle her in his bed. As usual he climbed in behind her and pulled her close to him. He loosened the robe and reached inside to find her wonderfully large soft breasts. Cupping her breast he said. "Ya have the most incredible breasts I have ever had the privilege ta touch. And if tomorrow ya do not come for dinner and stay, ya will sleep with me again and tomorrow I will be feeling that wonderful large bum all night. Now go ta sleep.1…2…3."

Abigail woke to the drapes being pushed back by Gabe's personal servant and Gabe in the other chamber getting ready for the day. He had ordered his dress clothes ready for tonight and Abby out of bed. Embarrassed to see another man in the room, Abby darted under the quilt.

"Out of bed sleepyhead, I have a lot ta do today and ya will have a new gown by tonight. My cousin should be here by then and the dinner will be formal."

"Formal?" Abby said sitting up in bed, "but I have nothing formal."

"Ya best have by tonight or ya will be going naked," he teased.

"How come I did not know you were having a formal dinner until today?" Abby asked.

"I just received a note from my cousin an hour ago. Now ya best break ya fast and get on with the day." Then Gabe pulled the quilt off her and left her sitting on the feather bed in her ugly yellow robe. Abby jumped up and ran for her room. When she reached the door she met a huge man covered with suit carrying a large nest he recovered from the top her chimney.

"Alright there lass, all is well. Ya chimney will work now. I got a fire going for ya in the hearth already."

"Thank you sir and I'm relieved you did not get hurt," Abby answered.

"Hurt?" the man said. "I have been doing this my whole life and I have yet ta break a single fingernail. Have a nice day lass." And he left chuckling to himself about the thought of him getting hurt.

Abby's room felt wonderfully warm. She dressed and went down to break her fast. When she walked into the hall Martha greeted her with the news that the children were taken to the town with some of Gabe's men to do some well needed shopping. Martha told her she would be back to do a fitting in a little while.

Jennifer was already in the hall talking to Gretna. Abby was going to leave when Gabe entered from behind her. He noticed her hesitation toward Jennifer so he grabbed her arm and led her over to the dry sink where the food was laid out. When Jennifer came toward Gabe, Abby went the other way. Gabe noticed how uncomfortable Abby was with Jennifer. So he decided to talk to Abby in private.

"Ya do not like Jennifer?" He asked trying to be gentle with her.

"She is not my favorite person," Abby answered.

"I need ya ta be nice ta her while she is visiting."

"She is cruel to the servants and I don't trust her with your children," she said.

"Abigail, ya are not listening ta me," Gabe said giving her a threatening look.

"The woman is interested in you Laird. That is obvious and I am in the way. I shall make myself scarce so you can get to know her better," she said in a huffy voice. "That is about all the niceness I can give her. I am sure you two will make a wonderful couple."

Gabriel's eye brows raised, he tilted his head and glared at Abigail and said, "If I didn't know better, I would say ya are jealous."

Abigail looked totally shocked, but would not give him an honest answer. "Well?" Gabe continued waiting for her to speak.

"Think whatever you wish Gabriel McKenzie. I do not need to like the woman, you do," she answered with her hands on her hips. "If she is your choice, you don't need my approval."

"What makes ya think she is my choice?" Gabe asked trying to hold his temper.

"The way you act when you are around her, of course," Abby answered.

"And how do I act?" He asked with a slight touch of anger in his voice.

"I am done with this subject Laird," Abby glared back. "I am leaving."

"No ya are not," Gabe bellowed getting the attention of Jennifer and Gretna. "You and I are not finished yet."

Abigail turned to leave, but Gabriel caught her hand. She tried to pull it away but Gabriel only strengthened his grip.

"We cannot talk here," he muttered and pulled Abigail into his study and slammed the door leaving Jennifer and Gretna smiling at the sight. He whirled her around in front of him. "Sit down."

"No!"

"Sit down or I will sit ya down and tie ya in the chair until I am finished speaking ta ya," Gabe ordered.

Abigail just turned her head, crossed her arms and stood there.

"Ya are the most stubborn woman I have ever met," he muttered.

He grabbed her by the waist and pushed her in the chair. "Sit!"

She began to rise. He pushed her back again this time causing the chair to wobble backwards. "Next time, I will tie ya."

"Very well, I shall sit but not because your forcing me, but because I want to."

Gabe pulled a chair over from across the room and placed it right in front of Abby. When he sat down, his knees were on either side of hers holding her in place. There was a moment of silence. He purposely waited for her to look at him before he would begin. How he loved this woman. She was acting jealous. Could there be a chance with her? He had wanted her for so long and now this was the first indication that she had feelings for him. This new side of her was puzzling and pleasing.

Finally she looked at him with her eyebrows lowered and a small pout across her face. She looked like a spoiled child waiting for a lecture that she didn't believe she deserved. At that moment he didn't know if he should throttle her, lecture her or both.

"Are ya ready?" Gabe asked in a very stern voice.

"I am." She mumbled, "You may proceed," as if giving him a real order.

Gabe took a deep breath and let out a long hard sigh. "Enough with this attitude, ya have no right ta interfere with my life. Who I choose for my wife and my bed in not your concern, I donna need your approval or disapproval."

"Fine," she muttered trying to conceal her hurt feelings.

"Ya will join me for dinner," Gabe ordered. "There will be no more discussion on it. Ya will dress appropriately for a formal dinner and ya will sit at my side. There will be no complaining. Do I need ta send ya ta ya room for the rest of the day?" Gabe asked sarcastically. "Or can I depend on ya ta carry out my wishes?"

More like orders, Abby thought to herself. "Stop treating me as a child," Abigail ordered.

"I will treat ya as I see fit. Act like a child, I will treat ya as a child. Have a temper tantrum tonight and ya won't sit comfortably for the rest of the week." Gabe waited for her return, but there was none. Abby just pressed her lips together and turned her head, giving him a very haughty expression.

"I see we have come ta an agreement." With that Gabe rose and stormed out of the room. A minute later Martha came into the room holding a gown under one arm along with pins, needles and thread in the other.

"Come with me Abigail, I have my orders." So Abby stood up and stomped off after Martha. They ended up in her chamber.

CHAPTER 21
The Laird's Dinner Party

"We need ta make this gown fit by tonight. Hopefully we have enough fabric ta let out. Take ya gown off so we can get started," Martha said with a smile.

Abby just stood there still upset with the conversation she had just had with Gabe. Martha noticed Abby's quietness.

"The Laird did say, if I should need help I could call on him personally," she teased with a smile.

"That woman," meaning Lady Jennifer, "should be tarred and feathered. The thought of spending dinner and the rest of the evening in the same room with that rude, self-centered, obnoxious excuse of a woman is unthinkable." Then she turned and started to disrobe. To Martha's surprise she had a plaid wrapped around her waist under her gown. "What is that?" Martha asked.

"I was cold in my chamber with the chimney plugged. I use the plaid for warmth," Abby admitted with a guilty expression, still mumbling about Jennifer at the same time.

"Well ya will have ta remove that too," Martha said.

"I will be cold," Abby complained.

"This gown is wool, ya will be fine." So Abby removed the plaid.

Martha's eyes opened twice the size when she saw another plaid under that one. "That one too," Martha ordered. Again, Abby had another plaid wrapped under that one.

"How many plaids are ya wearing?" Martha asked with her hands on her hips.

"Just four," Abby said. Each plaid was eight feet long and each one she removed was like taking twenty pounds off. By the time she removed the last one she was less than half her size.

Martha was dumbfounded. She could not believe how Abby had dressed. She was thin.

"Do ya have anything under that shift Abby?"

"Yes"

"There is more?"

"Just two more shifts," Abby whispered.

"TAKE THEM OFF", Martha shouted. Abby stood by the fire stark naked. She did not have an ounce of fat anywhere and she was absolutely gorgeous.

"Did this gown use to fit without the plaids?" Martha asked.

"Yes and rather tightly," Abby said rubbing her bottom that was being overly warmed by the fire.

"We are going ta throw this out and any other one that ya have that does not fit."

"No," Abigail said in protest.

There was a soft knock on the door. "Do ya need help Martha?" The Laird asked from the hall. Abby grabbed a discarded plaid and dove behind the chair.

"What I need is Glenna, Maggie and Sarah, now. Please!" Without asking other questions, the Laird's footsteps could be heard banging down the second level hall and down the stairs. Five minutes later, Abby was standing in front of four women all with disbelief etched across their faces.

"What are we going ta do?" Glenna asked.

"We must work very fast," Martha ordered and the four women charged at Abby. When the Laird passed by the door the next time all he could hear was "Oooooo….. Ouch….stop that….absolutely not…..too much….. That is too revealing." Gabe did not know what they were doing in there but he thought better of interfering.

Gabe's cousin would arrive soon and he had a sneaking suspicion that his cousin was coming just to meet Abigail. The King did not usually make social calls unless he had another motive. Gabriel suspected his cousin might know Abigail Fox's identity and was coming to confirm his own suspicions. The King would have to be careful with James here. England must not ever know her true identity. Abigail Fox was a mystery and both Gabriel and his cousin would discover out her secrets, but her secrets would be kept safe in Scotland.

It seemed to Gabriel that the women were taking an awfully long time in Abigail's chamber. He suspected the alterations were more than a few seams let out. It would be just like Abigail to find some good excuse, to stay in her room and avoid his guests just to spite him.

Gabriel came in from the barn after conducting a successful breeding session with Samson to work in his study for a while before getting ready for dinner. Tonight would be a very formal affair. Gabe liked to have dinners like this now and then especially when he had important guests like his cousin, the King of Scotland. As he worked in his study he could see all the commotion of servants up and down the stairs. He started to become curious. Jennifer was keeping her staff and half of his running as usual, but it was Martha, Glenna, Maggie and Sarah that he was more interested in. Finally he caught a glimpse of Martha running down the stairs, "Martha is all fine with the alterations? I want her ta have more gowns but they do not have ta be done today."

Martha stopped on the third stair from the bottom and said, "Laird we are only working on the gown for this evening. Ya have no idea what we have discovered and it is taking a little longer than we planned."

"Is everything alright?" Gabe asked fearing the worst. Martha just smiled and nodded. He noticed the whole house was buzzing. The servants had a secret but no one was telling.

Gabriel finally finished his work. He went to his chamber for a well needed soak in the tub and then to get ready for the banquet. His personal servant, Hamilton was whistling and grinning. He too knew some secret.

"Is there something I should know Hamilton?" Gabe asked.

"No Laird." Then Hamilton smiled and said, "ya will find out soon enough and this is better left a surprise."

"It is not bad is it?" Gabe inquired trying to stay calm.

"No Laird, it is not bad. I am very sure ya will be quite pleased," Hamilton said. Then he went on with his work, setting out Gabe's finest apparel, making sure every detail was tended to, whistling while he worked.

The Laird finished his bath and shave when a very light knock sounded on his door.

"Yes, come in." Gabe opened the door to see his youngest daughter, Emily standing there looking up at him.

"Yes Emi. What is it?"

"I just wanted ta tell ya ta be good ta her," she said with her eyebrows lowered and her little hands on her hips acting very seriously.

"Who, Emi?" Gabe asked trying not to smile at her.

"Abigail."

"I think I am Emily."

"No Da ya are not. Ya make her cry sometimes. We all like her and we decided ta keep her for ourselves, especially now."

"Abigail is not a pet ya cannot just decide ta keep her without her permission. And is that any way ta speak ta ya father?" Gabe said firmly.

"Well, ya are keeping her without her permission. We just thought we could as well. If ya decided not ta keep her than we would really like her."

Gabe could not believe what she was saying but it was exactly what he was doing. He was keeping her against her will.

"Emily, I thank ya for discussing this with me, but ya are not ta talk ta me ever again like that. Abigail is working off a debt that is all and when she has paid it off she can go or come as she wishes. But thank ya for bring it to my attention. I shall try."

"Good," Emily said and turned and walked away. What was that all about, Gabe wondered? "Tomorrow, I think I may have another talk with Abigail," he said out loud to himself.

The Laird walked into the hall dressed in his finest. He had his best kilt on, knee high socks adorned with gold thread, black well shined boots, and a white linen shirt with his plaid draped across his shoulder fastened with a large golden broach in the shape of a fox and hounds. His hair was combed back and his face neatly shaven.

He was greeted by his cousin and James. Jennifer joined the men a few minutes later. She was dressed in an almost obscenely low cut gown, made especially to draw attention. Lavender in color, it fit her like a glove not leaving much to any man's imagination. Gabe could understand why Abby did not like this woman. She would always single him out and hang on his arm the entire time she was talking. Her voice was loud and she liked to be the center of attention especially in a crowded room. Tonight she was in her glory, showing off her exposed chest and flirting with every eligible man in the room including the king himself.

The servants were also dressed formally and carried around trays of finger foods while the final dinner preparations were being completed. Martha came out of the kitchens to ask if the Laird wanted to start serving the dinner. Abigail was nowhere to be found. "Martha is Abigail ready?" Martha looked surprised, she had left her over an hour ago and she thought she was almost ready then.

"Joseph, Abigail needs an escort, would ya be so kind." Joseph just nodded and left the hall and ran up the stairs.

"We are done," Glenna said. "Oh Abigail ya are just beautiful." Glenna and Sarah had stayed and worked on Abby's hair, threading tinny ribbons and beads through it.

"Thank you," Abby said having no idea what she looked like. The four women had deliberately removed all mirrors from her chamber.

Martha burst into the room just in front of Joseph to see what was keeping her. "Oh Abigail," Martha squealed, "Jennifer doesn't stand a chance." And Martha laughed out loud and clapped her hands. "Well done Glenna and Sarah."

A knock sounded on the chamber door. "It's Joseph, Abigail. Gabe sent me up ta fetch ya. Now are ya coming peacefully or I am going…….." At that moment Sarah opened the door to reveal Abigail standing in front of the fire. Joseph stopped his speech in mid sentence and just looked at her. "What have they done ta ya lass? Ya are the most beautiful woman I have ever seen."

Abby was taken aback at his reaction. She smiled at him and said, "I will come peacefully. I promise."

"Wait ta the Laird sees ya," Joseph said now giving her the once over look.

"Joseph give us a minute ta get ta the hall we want ta be there when he sees her for the first time." And the women scurried out of the room laughing with excitement.

"I cannot be all that different," Abby said looking down at her gown.

"Have ya not seen ya self yet?" Joseph asked grinning and shaking his head in disbelief.

"No they took the mirrors away so I would not give them a hard time. Do you think this dress? Is cut to low?" Abby asked nervously.

"Not compared ta Jennifer's it isn't." He grabbed her hand and led her down to his chamber where he pushed her to a full length mirror. Joseph watched as Abigail saw herself for the first time. Her gown and hair were exquisite. She just stood there with the same expression as Joseph had had in her chamber moments before.

"There now, that is the proof. Are ya ready ta go and shock the rest of the clan as ya shocked me?" Joseph then noticed her hesitation. "What is it, lass?" he asked pulling her gently out of his room and down the hall to the staircase.

"This is my very first formal dinner and…I am not quite sure what I am supposed to do."

Joseph smiled at her and said. "Ya can start by holding my arm and walking tall. Ya have nothing ta be ashamed of. Ya are not going ta disappoint anyone tonight."

"I'm sure that I will do something stupid, just give me a chance. And I don't know why but Jennifer drives me crazy and James is there as well," Abby confessed. "Plus I am to meet the king himself. This could be a disaster waiting to happen."

Joseph and Abigail reached the hall doorway. The servants had all come in to witness her entrance. Joseph had every intention of holding her on the top of the platform leading down into the hall to give Gabe and the other guests a good chance to see her. He pulled her into the hall and stopped. He turned her just right so he could see the expression on his big brother's face.

"Now ya listen ta me," Joseph said watching Gabe out of the corner of his eye, "Ya are beautiful and any man in this room would be a fool not ta want ta have ya as his own and that includes me. Now ya hold ya head up high and be the beauty I know ya ta be on the inside and ya will be fine."

"Joseph," Abby said. "Do not be afraid to come and rescue me with a dance."

"Can ya dance lass?" Joseph asked watching the entire room go silent and getting Gabe's attention.

"I can dance the dances in the colonies but I have never seen a Scottish dance. I am a bit nervous," and she took a deep breath.

Gabe stood near the hearth with his other brother Simon, James, Jennifer and the King of Scotland. Like Joseph, Simon stopped talking in mid sentence when he eyed Joseph on the platform with a gorgeous woman. "Who is that beautiful creature?" he asked nodding in the direction of the hall door.

The room grew quiet and all heads were turning to see the stranger Joseph had brought. Gabe turned to look at the couple on the landing and it took him a brief second to actually recognize who Joseph had with him. "I sent him ta get Abigail and he brings that beautiful creature in here instead….." Then he paused realizing it was Abby he was looking at. His mouth dropped open and he broke the grip Jennifer had on his arm and was now walking across the hall in Abby's direction.

The entire room had gone completely silent but Abby was listening to Joseph and was not aware of it. "Any man would be proud ta have ya as his guest this evening. I only wish it was me."

"Thank you Joseph," Abby replied blushing.

Abby still was oblivious to the occupants in the hall. Joseph purposely kept her attention so he could show her off to the room without her knowledge.

"Are ya ready, lass?" Joseph asked.

"No but now is as good a time as any."

Joseph smiled at her and when she smiled back she could have lit up the entire room. The ladies had made an entire gown in an afternoon. Abby was stunning in the powder blue gown with long fitted sleeves and a scooped neckline. The gown draped over her curves revealing her slender waist and generous bosoms. The neckline gently ended exposing a small tasteful glimpse of her cleavage. She adorned her neck with the ruby pendent necklace that Teddy and Bess has given her. The ladies had pulled her hair back and skillfully woven ribbons and beads through it letting loose curls rest on her shoulders. The gown itself was plain only adding elegance to her natural beauty.

"Abigail!"

She turned to see Gabriel standing at the bottom of the stairs looking up at her. "Let me be the first ta welcome ya," and he stretched out his hand to her. Joseph took Abby's hand and placed it into Gabe's. Abby looked up just in time to see the angry expression on Jennifer's face as Gabe took her hand which made her giggled to herself.

"What is so funny Abby?' Gabe asked watching her glow.

"Nothing, Laird," then she gave him a tiny wink. That is when she saw Gabe for the first time. He was gorgeous in his red plaid McKenzie colored kilt and his black polished boots with the gold on his white socks. His hair was combed back with a slight off side part. The white linen shirt only accentuated his freshly shaven face and the plaid draped over his shoulder with the gold broach finished his perfection. Never had she seen such a view. Her knees started shaking. She squeezed his hand hoping it would keep her from falling.

The Laird could not stop looking at her. Where did she go? She was so small. What happened to his voluptuous beauty from this morning? She was still there just better. He wanted a glimpse of all of her.

"Would ya be so kind as ta turn around for me and let me see what is left of ya?" Gabe asked. Joseph stood just behind her laughing quietly at Gabe's expressions and reaction.

"What?" Abby asked not sure she should do such a thing.

"Turn please."

Abby took a big breath and turned slowly around. At that moment the entire room broke out in cheers and applause.

At first Abby did not understand why the room was applauding. Then she looked into the room and saw every guest looking straight at her. She was blushing. The Laird smiled, "Very very nice lass. Well done."

"You like it?" Abby asked with bright red cheeks.

"No, I love it. Come Lass. Ya stay with me. There is someone who is anxious ta meet ya and donna even think of leaving my side tonight."

Gabe brought her over to meet his cousin. He was amazed how she addressed him and curtsied in front of him. She was elegant and proper in her speech as if she was royal herself. The King enjoyed her from the moment he met her. He had a suspicion about who she was and her behavior just confirmed it.

He tested her on protocol, history, music, numbers, science and even the art of defense. Abigail did not disappoint him in any way. She was who he believed her to be without a single doubt. But her secret would be safe with him. She had managed to stay alive all these years by keeping her identity secret and he was going to respect that. The King would not even let her know he knew. Some day when she was comfortable revealing her identity Abby would be the one to do it not him. Tonight she would be Gabe's guest but the King had every intention of sharing a dance or two with her.

A bell sounded signaling the beginning of the banquet. Gabe took her elbow and escorted her to her seat himself although she had many offers from the other gentlemen in the room including James. Gabe's father had come over from his house and was pleased to see Abigail. "Been throwing sponges lately?" he asked with a wink.

"No, but I did get a new place to play and your son to join in," Abby answered. "Maybe you should give it a try." Then she smiled at him. The old Laird was hoping his son would not let this woman go. It had been to long since he had taken a woman and he was going to have a talk with him as soon as the king left.

James sat across from her refusing to look away. Abby knew what he was thinking and she hoped he would not say it. He had always wanted to take her to his bed but he always thought her to be too old for a whore. She knew he wanted her for himself and not just a business arrangement. He had mentioned his house in London and how she would make a welcomed addition in it. James had mentioned many times that he wished he had never let her go and even offered to buy her back.

Gabe watched as man after man address her at dinner. Each man she gave her undivided attention and kept their interest. Jennifer was her usual loud self trying to get all the attention but Abigail took over the whole room with just her smile.

When the music started, Jennifer took this opportunity to give Gabe a bird's-eye view of her chest. She wore a very distasteful gown cut way too revealing and enjoyed giving anyone who would look a view down her cleavage including Gabriel. Joseph noticed Abby becoming a little uneasy with Jennifer's chest in Gabe's face so he came to her rescue as she had asked.

"Abigail, my sweet," Joseph said. "Would ya do me the honor of having this first dance?" Before Gabe could say yes or no, Abby was up and out on the floor. Joseph turned out to be a very graceful dancer. He swept Abby around the floor and smiled at her expressions. "Ya are doing just fine lass," Joseph whispered as he twirled her around. Abby was enjoying herself. She giggled at her mistakes and was ready to try the next new dance. As the music ended, the old Laird, Philip was out on the dance floor with Abby. He too enjoyed her and smiled as they twirled around the room. Simon was next and then the king himself. The musicians knew the king's favorite dance was clogging. So when he took to the floor with Abby the music changed to his liking. Abby stood watching him stomp his feet in intricate patterns. Then to his surprise she tried it herself. The King roared with laughter as she kept right up with him. Soon they were the only two on the floor. Gabe watched intensively not taking his eyes off from her. Even Jennifer could not get him to look away from her with her half bared chest.

Gabe's father finally leaned over and said, "If ya wait much longer son, someone may snatch her up and it might as well be me." Gabe gave his father a surprised look and then looked at Abigail. James had asked her to dance. As much as she hated James she danced with elegance. "You are a rare beauty," he whispered in her ear.

"Thank you, but you of all people should not be nice to me now," Abby said.

"Why is that Abigail?" James asked surprised at her comment.

"I do so much enjoy hating you and I would not want you to spoil it," Abby said with the most sickening smile. James let out a very loud laugh just as the music ended. He bowed low to her and then gave her hand to the next dance partner, Gabriel himself. "Do ya need a rest, lass or can I have this next dance?"

Abby smiled, "I thought you would never ask." The music changed to a waltz, Gabe's favorite and he wrapped his right hand behind her waist and took her right hand in his left and gently pulled her in tighter to him. He started to the waltz, moving her as if her feet were not on the floor. She floated gracefully following his every move.

For a moment she felt all alone with him. Her gaze was directly at Gabe's face and his gaze at her. The two made the perfect couple, oblivious to anyone else in the hall. Slowly, one by one the other couples moved off the dance floor leaving Abby and Gabe to dance alone. All watched as the love between them became stronger.

Gabe's father smiled to see his son so happy. Everyone was enchanted by the couple except Jennifer. When the waltz ended, Abby was disappointed. She had wanted it to last forever. Abby curtsied toward Gabe and thanked him for the dance. The room applauded. Gabe looked around to see that they had been the only ones on the floor. Then he looked down at Abby. She was blushing but waved to her fans. Gabe offered his arm and escorted her out of the ballroom and through his study and out to the rose garden for a moment of privacy. The garden was lit by lanterns giving a feeling of enchantment. They walked along the path holding hands. Then Gabe stopped and turned Abby to face him. "You are just lovely," he said with a smile. "If ya are cold in the future, I will get ya a sweater or a wool gown. You don't need to wear four plaids and two shifts."

Abby blushed. "They told you?"

"Not until after I saw you. I had ta find out how one gown could make ya half your size. There is no way a person who eats so little and weighs a little more than a child, could possibly be that round."

"I was not trying to deceive you Laird. It was just so cold in my chamber. I thought the plaids were a good idea."

"Ya should have told me lass."

"I didn't want you to find out I refused to let anyone clean my chimney," Abby answered, looking a little guilty. She was so beautiful in the light cast by the lanterns that he reached down and gently pressed his lips against hers feeling the warmth of her mouth. His tongue encouraged her to open and explored that sweet taste he craved of hers. Reaching around her, he pulled her closer enclosing her in his embrace. His thumbs messaged her back as his tongue messaged her mouth. She let out a soft moan in the back of her throat. His hands lowered until they were resting on her bottom, kneading each side of her gently with his big hands.

Squeezing and rubbing, pulling her closer to him, letting her feel his hard self. Then he picked her up still squeezing and rubbing her bum. She wrapped her legs around his waist. Gabe reached down and pulled her skirt up and then reached under to hold her naked bum in his experienced hands. Still kissing her, teasing her mouth with his tongue, she could feel his hardness touching her bottom with only his kilt between them.

He gently pushed himself up letting her feel him, letting her know he was ready if she'd let him. He slowly kissed her cheeks then kissed a path down her neck, tasting every sweet part of her. Abby put her head back to give him an easier path. Holding her in one hand he reached around and grabbed her breast. Gently squeezing making her squirm with rippling sensations all through her body. He then slid his hand under her neckline cupping her warm soft breast in his hand. Gabe groaned with pleasure. He wanted her, she wanted him. She felt so good in his hands warm, smooth, soft and beautiful. He felt so hard, strong, muscular and inviting.

"Ya are going ta be mine lass," he whispered. Abby just moaned. She was letting her senses take her into a wonderful place of complete exquisite emotions. She was allowing him to take her there with uninhibited feelings.

"Laird where are you? "Yoo-hoo," Laird, you're needed in the hall. You promised me a dance." The loud squeaky voice of Jennifer emanated down from up the path. Abby opened her eyes, letting the special moment pass away between them.

Gabe lowered her to her feet removing his wonderful hold on her bum and pulling his hand out from under her neckline releasing her breast, finally pulling his kiss away. Abby licked her lips and straightened her skirts and her neckline. Patted her hair and gave Gabe a disappointed look.

He grabbed her hand and started leading her back up the path toward Jennifer's high pitched annoying voice. He gently squeezed her hand letting her feel his approval as well as his disappointment.

They returned to the hall and Abby did enjoy herself for the rest of the night. It was uneventful and even Jennifer could not ruin her moment she had with Gabe.

Gabe gave Abby another whirl around the floor. He loved to waltz and she loved to waltz with him. After the song ended, Gabe leaned down and said, “I should have taken you tonight lass. Ya were only moments away.”

“You can do that sort of thing standing?” she asked seriously.

“Aye lass and I almost did.” Gabe answered.

When Abby finally retired for the evening, she was still smiling.

CHAPTER 22
Abby Takes Charge

A messenger arrived first thing in the morning. Gabe brought him into his study and shut the door. It was from his brother Dunkin who had left to get Abby's children from the colonies without her knowledge. The message read, *Mission* a *success. Have all four chicks in my coop, working my way home. If all goes well we will be there in* a *few months....*

The king and Gabe took a long ride. The men wanted to talk about Abigail without the danger of someone overhearing them. Gabe was curious to know who his cousin believed Abby to be, but the king refused to tell him.

"I am sure I know who Abby really is. Her whole life had been a secret and it is not for me ta tell ya. She will have ta do that herself when she feels she can trust ya. Know this, Gabriel she is a treasure all in her own. What she has is more valuable than any of us will ever know. There are secrets she may take ta her grave but it is those secrets that have kept her alive. Many have sought her but so far no one has found her.

"Black Dog is on her trail and Abigail knows it. I feel she also knows the identity of the man who she saw murdered. But for some reason she wishes ta keep his identity secret for now. She will never hurt ya or ya children or ya clan. She doesn't have it in her. So keep her safe until our plan can come about. Abigail will be very vulnerable if she does not have a country of her own. I may not be able ta help her if she is not a Scot. So hear me and hear me well. If ya love her then do what ya need ta do before I am forced ta hand her ta England, France, or Italy."

"And what about that box she is supposed ta have hidden?" Gabe asked.

"That box is the key that has kept her alive. If need be ya will take her where she needs ta go and free her from its hold. If I am correct this will be the last thing the box requires of her. She could be a free woman and she will not fail, I assure ya. Be very careful not ta let England know that I know who she is. She must be kept hidden a wee bit little longer."

The two men returned late in the afternoon to find Jennifer waiting in Gabe's study… furious.

***

Oversleeping was Abby's first mistake of the day. By the time she washed, dressed and tended her needs, the whole house would be stirring.

Abigail peeked out of her chamber. All was clear. No one was in sight. Hopefully she could make a mad dash, get out of the laird, and out to safety. Abby wanted to get as far from the laird as she could today. Last night had been the most wonderful night in her life but today was another story. Abigail was sure that if she did not stay away, she would surely attack someone and she was sure Jennifer would be on the top of her list. Staying away was her answer to keep herself calm.

Abby had planned one whole day at the ocean where she would stay until dinner. She would fulfill her obligation to Gabe and then retire early for the evening in the safety of her now warm chamber where she would read a safe book.

Well, of course that was not going to happen. Abby made it to the top of the stairs when out of Jennifer's chamber came the most foul, obnoxious, cruel complaining. Every part of Abby's body said leave but then she saw Martha coming down from the upper level, she could not leave Martha to deal with that awful woman alone. "Give me that tray of food," Abby demanded.

But Martha hesitated, "Abby ya donna need ta help. I can take care of it."

"How many times has she refused the tray this morning?" Abby asked her temper starting to flare.

"Three," Martha answered.

Abby took the tray without Martha offering it. She set it on the stairs and rearranged the food on the tray. Then without saying a word, she picked it up and marched up the stairs to Jennifer's chamber. Without knocking, Abby barged in and said, "I have brought you your morning meal and I will not leave until I know that you are well satisfied."

Jennifer was most surprised that Abby delivered the food. After what had happened at the dinner last night, Jennifer knew Gabe was interested in her. She did not want to upset Gabe especially when she still thought she might have a chance with him. So Jennifer took the tray and sat down and ate it while Abby waited. When she had had her fill Abby took the tray and left her chamber. "Have a nice day," Abby said on her way out. On the way down the stairs Abby decided to go back to her room to get a shawl in case it was cold at the ocean side. This was her second mistake.

Meanwhile, little Emily was sitting at the bottom of the stairs on the first level, playing with her dolly, named Martha. Emi was singing at the top of her lungs a song that Abby had taught her. Abby reached the top of the stairs after she collected her shawl just in time to see Jennifer sail down the steps in front of her in a fury and slap Emily across the face.

Abby could not believe what she had just witnessed. She was furious with Jennifer for striking that child. If Jennifer had been upset with Emily, she could have just asked Emily to play outside. Jennifer did not need to hit a child. Abby saw red. Emily was wailing. No one hits a child like that, no one. Abigail was at the bottom of the stairs faster than Jennifer had. She scooped up Emily in her arms and kissed her. She patted her back and comforted her. When Emi was in some control of herself, Abby told her to go play outside with her dolly. Martha wanted to play with her. Emi wiped the tears off her cheeks and went outside excited to play with Martha.

After Emily left, Abby confronted Jennifer. "You will never hit his Laird's children ever again. Do you hear me? I see you touch a single hair on any of their heads and I swear I will personally rip ever hair out of your head. Do we have an understanding?"

"No one talks to me that way," Jennifer sputtered. "I am of royal blood and I do as I please."

"Well so am I," Abby said with her face one inch from Jennifer's.

"The Laird will hear how one of his servants, you, has treated me."

"Good and when I am done telling him of all the cruel ways you have been with his children and his people, I am sure he will throw you out himself."

Then Abby stormed out of the laird and into her next hornet's nest. There in the yard was the professor that Gabe had dismissed. His belt was off and he had Adam in his sights. Abby could hear the professor accusing Adam of cheating. She was going to stay out of it until she heard something about the "9x's table again."

This matter had already been resolved and here he was again. "What do you think you are doing?" Abby hollered from the doorway of the laird.

"Stay out of this woman. You have no right to interfere," the professor said determined to beat Adam.

"Oh yes I do. The Laird asked you to leave. You are wrong, sir. Adam did not do what you are accusing him of. Now put your belt down and walk away," Abby said on a dead run to reach Adam.

"There is no way this boy knows anything. He never studies. He needs a good beating ta get it in his head. I am a very good teacher and I will prove I am right."

Abby lost her temper again. "You are an arrogant, pompous ass hole. You should not be teaching children. I would not trust you with a pig. He knows his "NINES's". Why don't you just ask him?" Abby demanded. "I worked with him, ask him."

The professor said, "He is too stupid. He cannot do it."

"Ask him or I'll rip you apart limb by limb," Abby demanded. Some of the men were training near the courtyard and they heard the commotion between the professor and Abigail. They started over to see if they could help when they heard, "9x7….9x4…..9x3…"

Over and over the professor asked Adam, and he answered each problem with the correct answer without one mistake, but still the professor was not convinced and he was sure that Adam was cheating.

"I am going to clear my name and beat this child until he admits that he is cheating and then the laird will give me back my job."

Then the professor raised the strap and swung, as hard as he could, striking Abby on the back as she darted between Adam and the professor. By this time Abby was like a mama bear protecting her cub. That was the last blow the professor got in. Abby lunged at the professor knocking him down to the ground onto his backside. Then with one hard swing of her foot, she kicked him square in the face, knocking him down the rest of the way.

By now the men had reached the fight and took hold of the professor who was just about to retaliate. The men took the professor away.

Abigail turned to Adam, "I knew you could do it. I am so very proud of you. Good job." And then she hugged him and kissed his cheek in front of all the other children and spectators. Abby looked at her class and said, "Class dismissed. No lessons for today. Go have some fun."

The children cheered and ran off in all directions. Abby started towards the ocean cliffs, but as soon as she reached the pasture to cross, she heard squealing coming from the back of the barn. *Goliath*, Abby thought. She ran to see what could possible make him cry out in pain like that. As she rounded the barn she saw James' men with a long horse whip and a mare in heat. They were trying to get Goliath to breed one of their mares without Gabe or James being present.

Abby could not stay out of it. She hollered to Goliath to come. The big stallion heard her voice and reared pulling the restraints from the men's hands. Goliath came charging at Abby but stopped just in front of her to let her mount. Abby climbed up on the wagon which was nearby and with one big leap mounted the large steed and held on for dear life. At a dead run Goliath and Abby rounded the side of the barn and jumped the fence heading toward the ocean disappearing out of sight as they went around the grassy knoll.

***

When Gabe and the king returned and found Jennifer waiting in his office, all hell broke loose. As Gabe entered his study he was followed by his servants, the children, James' men, his men, Jake and the professor Gabe dismissed. The servants were all talking at the same time. Jennifer was trying to talk as well along with all six of his children, the other children of the laird, his men, and Jake and James' men.

There was only one common denominator with each story he was hearing and that was Abigail. Finally Gabe had to put a stop to all this commotion. "Silence," he ordered. "Where is Abigail? I want her found and found now. I will hear each and everyone of ya but first, I want her found."

The servants and children combed the house. The men looked in the barn and the grounds. Within an hour all had been thoroughly searched with no trace of Abigail. Finally, one of James' men admitted seeing her take Goliath. Gabe became a little suspicious of the man. Why did he know she took Goliath? Then James confronted his own man and the truth came out.

Gabe was furious that at discovering these men had tried to breed his stallion without permission. Retribution would be paid, but not until Gabe found Abby. He needed to find her and fast. A storm was coming in and it would not be safe if she was out in that dangerous weather. Jake went to saddle Samson. Gabe mounted and took off in a full gallop followed by Joseph on his honey colored horse just as the rain began. Both men were sure she had not tried to escape again and Gabe was pretty sure he knew where she'd gone. It was beginning to get dark and if she was still with Goliath they would be easy to spot.

As the two men rounded the grassy knoll Gabe spotted Goliath. They galloped as close as they could not to spook the big stallion. From Samson, Gabe could see Abigail all curled up sitting on a ledge overlooking the ocean. She was soaked with her hair plastered with rain against her head shivering violently.

"Abigail, come ta me lass," Gabe called but Abby would not move or acknowledge him.

He called again and this time she said, "No. I'm not going back."

"Abby ya're wet and I can see ya shivering from here. Ya'll catch ya death. I promise we will talk about this tomorrow."

"I'm not going back," she repeated.

Gabe dismounted and tried to walk closer to her but Goliath was acting like a guard dog. The huge stallion was not about to let anyone near her. That was when Gabe thought of a different approach.

"Abigail, Goliath needs medical attention. I donna think he will let us take him from ya. Ya need ta help us get him back ta be tended ta and then ya can come back if ya like." Abby turned to see Goliath lunge at Gabe.

It worked. Abby stood and came off of the ledge. Gabe was an expert horseman and he could have easily herded Goliath back to the barn but this was the perfect excuse to get her back as well.

Gabe went to touch Abby to help her to mount but Goliath would have no part of it. Gabe wondered what James' men did to him to make him so devoted to Abby.

"Goliath down," Abby ordered pointing her finger to the wet ground. Gabe and Joseph watched as the massive stallion lay down on the ground to let Abby mount. She kicked her shoes off and with a running start, ran up his hind leg and sat by the withers holding a clump of mane in both of her hands.

Immediately Goliath rose. "Take me home," she commanded the beast and they were off in a full gallop. Gabe and Joseph rode on either side of her encouraging her to hold on. She was to tired, cold and wet. She slumped forward on Goliath's neck. The big stallion slowed when he felt her collapse and walked the rest of the way.

When they reached the barn Jake met them at the doorway. Goliath still would not let anyone near her. He dropped to his front knees and let her get off. Abby smiled at the possessive horse and said, "Come my boy, time to put you to bed." Without a halter or lead line, Abby walked Goliath into the barn and into his stall by just holding her hand on his massive neck. Goliath was finally safe. All three men were amazed with how she handled the dangerous stallion so when she ordered the strawberry roan filly brought in and put in the stall next to the stallion's, no one questioned it.

Gabe however needed to get Abby in the house, a hot bath, dry clothes, hot food and to bed in that order. So he tried Abby's tactic, "Come Abigail it is time ta put ya ta bed." He was pleasantly surprised she just followed him without a fight. This was a lot easier than putting her over his shoulder kicking and screaming.

When they reached the laird, Abby was shivering so that Gabe scooped her up in his arms and carried her up to her chamber. He opened the door just as the men finished filling a tub with hot water. Martha was also in the room waiting for her orders. She was so happy Abigail was alive and not harmed. "Welcome home Abby. We were so worried about ya."

"Get her something hot ta eat and a dry shift Martha. I will take it from here."

Martha scurried out of the chamber happy Abby was home. A little knock sounded on the door, "Da is she alright? Is she hurt? Can we help?" Gabe went to the door and opened it. Six children stood at the doorway trying to get a glimpse of Abby. "See she is fine, but she needs her rest. I thank ya for ya offer but for now there is nothing ya can do. Tomorrow, I promise ya will have ya chance ta tell ya side of the story, but now Abby needs my help." He kissed each one on the top of their heads and bid them good night.

Abby's gown was so wet that Gabe had to cut the laces to get it off. The gown fell off her with a splat on the floor. Gabe picked the naked Abigail up in his arms and set her in the tub under her severe protest.

"Quiet lass," Gabe ordered. "I'll not have ya getting sick with fever. Ya be lucky if ya did not catch ya death."

"Then why don't you just shoot me and get it over with then," Abby sputtered in return still frustrated with the events of the day.

"No lass, that would be the easy way out and I will not do that. Instead I am going ta wash ya."

"Oh! No you're not," Abigail protested indigently trying to hide herself with her arms.

"Oh, but I am." Gabe answered raising his eyebrows and giving her the look she knew too well, the one that said "don't even try to stop me."

Abby was horrified but Gabe did wash her, every single inch of her from her head to her toes. She was pleasantly surprised how gentle he was. He washed her with such expertise that she just had to ask, "Done this before?" Gabe gave her another look and said, "I have six children, they all needed a good bath from time ta time. Now up ya go," holding a large piece of linen to wipe her with. "I can do that much," Abby protested again but Gabe was not about to let her do a thing including wiping her own backside. He just reached down and pulled her from the tub and to her feet. He dried her, wrapped her in a dry cloth and picked her up under her arms and set her down in front of the fire.

Martha had perfect timing. At that moment she entered with a soft clean shift, and a tray of food which included hot soup, meat and bread. Without waiting for Martha to leave Gabe pulled the cloth off Abby leaving her standing naked in front of the fire. a moment later, Gabe threw the shift over Abby's head and pulled it down. Martha left the room smiling to herself.

"Now, time ta eat lass."

"I'm not hungry," Abby said protesting again. So Gabe picked her up and tossed her in bed. She flew through the air and landed in the middle of the bed with a squeak. He tossed the covers over her and taking the tray of food, sat down on the side of her bed next to her.

"I told you, I am not hungry," Abby mumbled through clenched teeth.

"If ya are not going ta eat ya self then I am going ta feed ya."

"Oh fine then, give me the tray," Abby ordered in a huff.

"NO"

"No?"

"Ya had your chance, now open wide."

Abby's mouth dropped open in surprise and Gabe wasted no time shoveling warm soup into her mouth. Abby almost choked. "Ya are going ta eat this lass and I am going ta feed it ta ya like it or not. Ready for bite number two?"

To Abigail's dismay that was exactly what he did. He fed her bite for bite until he was satisfied she'd had enough without spilling a drop. "Now lie down and get some rest. Tomorrow is another day and hopefully ya will not come down with the fever. And just ta make sure ya donna, ya will not leave this bed tomorrow except ta tend ya needs."

"I will not…," she began to say but it was cut off with, "Oh aye, ya will or I will tie ya in that bed." Abby knew she'd been completely defeated. She slid down into the feather bed all warm and soft. Gabe covered her with another quilt and Abby finally surrendered to the day and fell asleep while Gabe watched her in silence. Then he kissed her lightly 1…2…3… and left.

The next morning was worse than last night. Gabe had a line of people waiting to tell their side of the story. Each story that he heard, Abigail was involved. It became clear exactly what happened yesterday and who was at fault. All James' men and Jennifer were against Abigail. Gabe's entire clan, servants and children defended her, even little Emily.

"Ya will not punisher her will ya Da?" Emily asked.

"Does she need punishing Emi?" Gabe asked his little girl. Having a conversation with a five and a half year old took some skill and Gabe could do it with ease. He knew of all people Emi would not lie to him.

"Abby was real angry at Lady Jennifer. She told me Lady Jennifer was bad. She'd done a bad thing and I am ta stay away from her. I will Da I promise. I donna want her ta hit me ever again."

"She hit ya Emi?" Gabe asked trying to not show his anger.

"Aye!"

"Where?"

"At the bottom of the stairs, I had ta keep my dolly safe. She might hit her too."

"What did Abby do?" Gabe asked.

"Oh Da she is so nice. I like her, this much," and she put her arms up and out as wide as she could stretch them. Then she smiled and put her little hand to her mouth, "Want ta know a secret Da?"

"Aye Emi, I do."

"Abby kissed me," then she giggled.

"Did she now and where did she kiss ya?"

"On my cheek, right where Jennifer hit me," Emily answered.

Gabe saw red. Emily did not deserve that kind of treatment.

"I think Abby likes me Da."

"I'm sure she does lass," Gabe answered with a smile.

Emily looked like her mother. She had big green eyes and red hair and two deep dimpled cheeks which always melted Gabriel's heart.

"Ya do as Abby says Emi, ya hear?" Gabe ordered.

"Aye Da, I will. I donna want Lady Jennifer ta hit me or my dolly again." Then she smiled devilishly, "I do like Abby's kisses!" and then she giggled.

Next on the list were the children in Abby's class. Gabe was very serious about education, even the girls needed to read and write. He was very pleased with Abby's teaching. The children seemed to be happier there was less complaining. Everyone of the children waited in the vestibule for their chance to tell their side. They stood on one side and the professor stood on the other with two guards. Gabe called the children in first. They all entered his study. Gabe had to calm them down more than once but finally he got the story out. More stories surfaced that had nothing to do with Abby, but the same ending always resulted. Abby had been very vocal about hitting children. She hated it. Now Gabe understood why.

Next he called in the guards. They told about the fight and how Abby had kicked the professor to the ground. The men were very impressed with her technique. They also felt Abby was defending his son which pleased Gabe.

The professor was next. "Ya know my feelings on discipline Laird. I will not spoil any child in my class. I have proven that every day and will again if ya will give me my job back."

"Every day?" Gabe asked somewhat surprised at how proud he was about this statement.

Then Gabe remembered what Abby had said. She argued that children learned faster and better if they were not afraid of being hit.

"When is ya class fun?" Gabe asked the professor while he loosened his belt.

"Fun? Learning is not fun," the professor said.

"I feel ya are not what my children need and it is high time ya learn your own lesson well this time." Gabe took a step forward and the professor took a step back. "It is not much fun being afraid. Is it professor?" Gabe said through gritted teeth. "When I am done teaching ya your second lesson I want ya ta leave my land and not come back."

There was still a group in the entry waiting to be heard. They stood in silence while they listened to the professor scream and cry. The laird was also loud. When the professor left the study he had definitely had learned his lesson for good.

James and his men entered next. Gabe sat behind his desk quietly while James' men told of the breeding session with Goliath. James sat quietly not interfering. When they had finished Gabe said, "Gentlemen there is time ta try breeding again but if ya take a whip ta one of my horses again I guarantee I will use it on ya." James and his men left the study quickly.

Next Jake came in and reported Goliath's health which, thanks to Abigail was alright. By the time Gabe listened to the servants he had had enough. He fully understood what Abby had gone through yesterday. He found himself surprised by her actions but also very proud of her.

Finally there was only one person he needed to talk with, Abigail and he would do that as soon as he talked to his cousin the king. While Gabe had been dealing with his people today, the king had received a message that he wished to share with Gabe. The king's men had found Abby's ship, The Lady Fox, abandoned in a lagoon covered with tree branches. It had been searched thoroughly and blood stains remained on the deck. The king felt someone had attacked the vessel and killed the crew but for some reason did not want to destroy the ship. Gabe was pleased his cousin was bringing it up to Scotland where he could watch it.

After the king left Gabe ordered a tray of food for himself and Abby. Gabe had sent James' physician to examine Abby and as suspected that did not go well, no surprise. Gabe usually ate with his clan and children but tonight he would dine with Abigail alone in her chamber.

When he entered her chamber, he actually found her in bed and asleep. She always slept on her stomach with her arms curled around her head. She had kicked the quilt down just below her bum and her shift had risen just above giving Gabe a beautiful view of her naked round backside. How he loved her bottom. He wanted to reach out and touch it, rub it, make love to it and her. Carefully, he lifted the quilt to cover her and then nudged her awake so she would not know she had just given him the best sight of the day.

"Time ta have dinner or aren't ya hungry again?"

Abby didn't dare say she wasn't hungry or she'd be fed again. Once was bad enough for a lifetime.

Abby could feel Gabe's mood. He was going to speak to her and she wished he would just do it and get it over with. Gabe laid the trays out on a small table by the fire and then motioned for her to come and sit down. Abby fidgeted all during dinner. She ate next to nothing and said about the same. Finally Gabe asked, "Not hungry again lass?"

"Oh I ate," she said as convincingly as possible.

"Have ya?"

"Well yes…Not really. Maybe we should just get this over with and dish out my punishment so I can go back to bed." Abby could feel herself getting warmer. She was getting feverish and she knew it. That feather bed was all she wanted right now and the sooner the better.

"Aye lass, it is time ta get this over with." He pulled a piece of parchment from his shirt.

"You made a list of my crimes?" Abby asked beginning to panic. Surely this would be a strapping punishment. The way she was feeling at the moment he could have run over her with a wagon and she wouldn't care.

"One," Gabe started, Abby's heart started sinking. "I have need for a permanent teacher. I hired ya until I could replace the professor but after talking ta the children and all their parents, I have decided on ya.

"Me?"

"Aye, Ya." His eyebrows raised and that "*better not argue*" look came over his face. "And no more class dismissed at nine in the morning."

"No," Abby said pouting.

"No what? No argument or no and ya need some friendly persuasion?"

"No argument," she mumbled.

Gabe could see she was feverish and he knew she would not give him much trouble.

"Two, Ya seem ta want ta protect my children. I've watched ya with them and I like what I see. As far as I am concerned the look for a new nanny is over."

"Me? You're asking me?"

"No, my children asked if ya would be their nanny."

Abby said nothing but he could see this really pleased her.

"So I take it that is settled?" Gabe asked but again Abby said nothing.

"Abigail I need ya answer now," Gabe demanded.

"Yes."

"Good. Three, Ya seem ta help the servants even though I have asked ya ta let them do their own work. And my men think they should get one of ya peace offerings for helping ya with the professor and Eva has been asking ta have one day off for needed time with her family. So ta please them all, ya will be the official cook on Wednesdays and only help the servants if they ask ya on the other days."

"Understood," Abby said almost grinning.

"Four, Jake cannot do anything with Goliath now. We still need his services for a few more mares and then James will be leaving and taking Jennifer. We are both in agreement that ya have a calming effect on the big stud. So ya are ta be present at the rest of the sessions. Understood?"

"Gabe I know nothing about breeding horses," Abby protested but Gabe would not take no for an answer.

"Understood?" he asked again with a little more force.

"Understood," Abby answered with her head down.

"Five and six."

"There is more?" Abby asked.

"Five, ya will be nice ta Jennifer until she leaves, as a favor ta me." Abby only nodded. "I did not like how she treated my daughter or my staff and have given her a severe warning but James does not deserve an early dismissal because of her," Gabe explained.

"Six and last, Your punishment." Abby looked up at Gabe with a slight pout. She was so beautiful but at this minute, she reminded him of Emily.

"Ya will spend one whole day and I mean one whole day…" Then he paused waiting to see what she would do.

"One whole day doing what?" Abby said almost afraid to ask.

"With me and me alone, understood?"

Abby stayed speechless and her mouth dropped open.

"Agreed?" Gabe said waiting for her answer.

Finally she asked, "What will you do with me?"

"That depends on ya. It could be a very nice day or a very bad day. It will be your choice. I personally would prefer a good day. Now answer me please."

"Agreed and understood." She said through gritted teeth.

"Good now go ta bed."

Abby did not have to be told twice. She was out of her chair and crawling in bed before Gabe could rise. She pulled the quilt up and was asleep in less than five minutes. Gabe gave her a kiss on her very hot forehead and then went to talk to Martha.

Abby had a fever for two more days. The children would take turns to read to her when she was awake. Gabe also made his visits often. He was very happy when the fever finally broke.

CHAPTER 23
I Want One Day

"How are ya feeling?" Gabe asked Abby as she sat up in her bed first thing in the morning.

"With my fingers," she replied with a little grin on her face.

"Anyone who can make a joke and a very bad joke, I might add, must be feeling fine. So get up, it is time ta have ya one day of punishment."

In his hand he had a new gown and shift in her favorite color—pale blue. "Martha made this for ya. Wear this today. We are going on an errand and I donna want ya ta get cold." Abby sat in bed not moving. "Do I need ta help?" Gabe asked. Abby pulled the covers over her head and said, "No and as soon as you leave I will get dressed."

"I will meet ya out in the barn and ya have five minutes." Gabe chuckled and left after hearing her growl from under the quilt. As soon as she heard the door shut she jumped out of bed and dressed as fast as she could. Abby was hoping she could sneak out of the laird without seeing anyone, but then she decided to go down the back stairs to the kitchen and get something to take to eat. She had barely eaten anything for two days and her stomach was complaining loudly.

Eva was already packing food for their day when Abby reached the kitchen. "Is that for the Laird?" Abby asked as she walked into the kitchen. "Aye lass and ya can bring it with ya. Glad ta see ya feeling better," Eva said giving her a great big smile.

So Abby grabbed the basket and asked, "Am I supposed to look in this?"

"Absolutely not lass and ya behave ya self today if ya know what is good for ya," Eva said teasing her.

Abby smiled back at her, grabbed the basket and said, "I'm going to look, so there." Teasing her back, but Abby did not see Gabe come in the side door. "No ya won't," he said and he took the basket right out of her hand and gave her a playful swat on her bottom.

Abby whirled around holding her backside and said, "I did not deserve that."

"No, I should have spanked ya harder." Then he laughed as he watched her mouth drop open. "Now come along 'brat'. We have got a long day and I am not wasting a single minute." He took her hand and pulled her out of the kitchen winking at Eva as he left.

Finding only Samson saddled when they reached the barn, Abby began to think she'd be walking. Gabe knew what she was thinking. So he grabbed her around the waist and settled her on his horse before she could object. Then he mounted behind her lifted her up and sat her on his lap snaking his hand around her waist. He gently urged Samson on and headed out of the courtyard toward the ocean.

"Am I allowed to ask where we are going?" she asked as he playfully lifted her breast with his thumb. She pushed his hand down on her waist but he put it back under her breast and used his thumb to bounce it again.

"I have a surprise for ya, but ya have ta promise me ya will only use it today," Gabe said.

Abby agreed not understanding what he had in mind.

"And when I tell ya it is time ta go, ya will not give me one complaint."

Abby agreed again just as she saw what he was talking about. As they rounded the cliffs, there in the water sat her ship. Abby was so surprised. She couldn't believe what she was seeing. She was so excited that Gabe had to give her a tight squeeze to settle her down before she made both of them fall off.

Gabe came to a stop and dismounted. He lifted Abby down. Before he could stop her she ran down the path to the ocean. Gabe had a man waiting on the shore with a skiff to take both of them to the ship. He had other men on the cliffs watching for danger, out of view. It was dangerous to let Abby out of the laird unattended. Black Dog had been seen near France and the McHales were still searching for her in Scotland. But today was for her. She had protected his children, fought for them, helped his servants and saved his horse from a beating. Today was not a punishment but a reward.

Gabe joined her at the shore and helped her get into the skiff. He started to row her out to her ship. "Abigail we need ta talk before we board ya ship." Abby twisted her hands and waited for him to continue. "We have been looking for ya ship since I took ya from James," he said watching her expressions.

"Who is '*We*' Gabriel?" Abby asked most curious.

"The king and I," he answered. "When we found it, it had been deserted and searched thoroughly. But from what we can see, nothing has been removed. I must tell ya that there was a nasty struggle and the deck was covered with blood. The King feels that ya crew has been killed or taken. England has been looking for ya ship as well. It is lucky that we found it when we did. No one knows we have it and the King wants ta keep it hidden until ya are ready ta use it again."

Abby gave Gabe a surprised look. "What makes you think I am going to use it again? Are you going to set me free?"

"Abby, the King suspects," was all Gabe would say. He was hoping she would tell him her secret.

"Suspects what?" she asked trying to look innocent.

"I canna help ya if ya won't confide in me," Gabe said rowing a little slower.

"I never asked for your help and in fact I asked you not to interfere. What I have to do and where I need to go is very dangerous. I will not ask you or anyone else to risk their lives for me. It is not your problem."

"Well, the King and I feel that whatever ya have ta do involves this ship, which by the way I now own. If ya are planning on using it then ya are going ta have ta take me."

"Did you hear what I just said, Gabe? It is dangerous. I will not be responsible for taking a father away from six children. They have already lost one parent. They do not need to lose another. You have your hands full with Fuchsiall, the clan, and your children. You do not need my problems as well."

"Abigail after today the ship will be brought ta safety where no one will find it including ya. Ya will have ta accept help sometime. When ya are ready ta talk about it, will ya at least come ta me?"

"Gabe, I have been taught to trust no one. For all I know you and your cousin are like all the other treasure seekers. Befriending me is a way of getting close to that box and what it contains. If the King '*suspects'*, as you say he does, then he must also know about the box and who I am."

"He has pledged ta keep ya secret and has asked nothing of ya in return. I donna know what he suspects. He refuses to tell me or anyone else. Ya are the only one that can reveal ya secret. I only ask that when it is time, ya will trust in me enough ta let me help ya," Gabe said and dropped the handle of one ore and put his hand on her knee.

"I cannot do anything until early spring at the earliest. So there is no need to talk about this now, but I will consider your proposal," Abby said looking into his big brown eyes and placing her hand over his.

The skiff bumped into the hull of her ship where a rope ladder was hanging down. Abby watched Gabe climb the ladder. "Ya are not looking up under my kilt are ya lass?" he said when he was half way up.

Abby's face turned beet red and she said, "NO." Then she smiled and said, "But the thought did cross my mind once or twice." Gabe let out a booming laugh and then helped Abby aboard.

"Well Laird let me give you the grand tour of your vessel." Abby reached out and slipped her arm under his and guided him to the bow. Abby showed him inch by inch of her grandfather's ship, explaining all the wonders the ship was capable of. They ended up at the helm. "See here," Abby pointed, "this is my grandfather's mark. He always marked a ship if he built it. And see here right under his," then she smiled proudly. "This is my mark."

"Ya helped build this ship?" Gabe asked surprised.

"Yes I did, from stem to stern and even took her on her first voyage out to sea," she said proudly.

"Abigail, aren't ya going ta show me my quarters?" Gabe asked knowing she had deliberately excluded the two cabins in the belly of the ship.

"Well the room on the left is mine and the other one is for the captain, but I don't know what condition it is in."

"Abby what is wrong?" Gabe asked seeing her mood change very quickly.

"It was Marty's cabin, my captain." Then she bowed her head and wept in her hands.

"Abby what is it? Tell me lass. I did not bring ya ship here ta make ya sad. It was supposed ta make ya happy."

"I love that you brought the ship for me. It has made me very happy except…" and she cried some more. Gabe took her in his arms. He could not stand to see her cry like this.

"Abigail, please talk ta me. Donna be like this, ya donna have ta do all of this on ya own," Gabe whispered in her ear.

Abby looked up at him and knew she must tell him what she had been keeping from him. "The man I saw murdered and eaten by wolves was my best friend, Marty. I did not know it when it was happening but he pointed to the ground and buried his ring for me to find. I watched and could not do a thing. There was too many of them. He knew it and that is why he would not tell them where I was. He died because of me and that is why I cannot let you take me. I don't want to watch someone I care …" and then she could not go on. Her tears were coming down so fast that Gabe's shirt was soaked.

"Are ya sure it was Martin?" Gabe asked.

"I could not see his face and his clothes were different but it was his ring. When I went to check the next morning, I could not find the body.

"Maybe it was not him. Would ya like me ta see if I can find him for ya?"

"You would do that for me?" Abby asked trying to stop crying.

"Aye I would." Then Abby said something that made Gabe angry. She said, "But I cannot pay you and it is not fair you use your funds to help me when I already owe you so much."

Gabe took her hand and opened Martin's door and went in pulling Abby behind him. He found a chair and sat down. He pulled her over his knee and said, “Do ya want me ta help ya or are ya going ta insult me again with that business about pay. If so I have every intention of tanning your backside.”

“I want your help. I want your help. Please let me up,” she said squirming to get up.

“I will let ya up as soon as ya apologize for hurting my feelings,” Gabe said half teasing her but still serious.

“Please Gabe, I’m sorry I did not mean to hurt or insult you.”

Gabe stood her up and let her face him. “Alright then, let’s look around his cabin, maybe we can find something that will help us locate him.

Abby reached out and flung her arms around his neck and kissed him. “Thank you,” she whispered.

Gabe was surprised by her show of affection. “Ya’re welcome lass. Now let’s look.” What he wanted to do was take her in his arms and use the cabin the way he wanted. Somehow he was going to make her his and then he would use this vessel to show just how much he loved her, but for now he would be happy that she had kissed him on her own.

After they searched Martin’s cabin, Gabe wanted to see hers. Abby was a little reluctant to show her cabin to him. Finally she opened the door. She peeked in the cabin first to make sure there was nothing out she that did not want him to see. To her surprise her cabin was untouched. Everything had been left exactly the way she’d left it the day she was arrested in England. How strange she thought. “Why was my room left and unsearched?” she said out loud, but to herself.

“This is the way ya left it? It is a mess. They most likely thought someone had already rummaged through it.”

It was a mess. Abby had left in such a hurry that day. She did not have time to tidy it up. If her grandfather had seen her quarters like this, he would have made her swab decks for a week. She had tried on at least five gowns and then decided against them. She had dishes left from the dinner the night before and she had maps and charts opened on her table and some on the floor. Her bed was unmade and her shoes were everywhere. Even her pillow was thrown on the floor. Her trunk was opened and the contents in disarray.

Abby looked around the room and was a little embarrassed to let Gabe see it like this. "Well I was in a real hurry that day. It was my first time in England," Abby tried to explain.

"Admit it, ya are bad lass and ya know it."

Abby blushed and said, "My cabin speaks for itself I do not have to admit anything."

Gabe laughed and pulled her into his arms. "Donna ever change lass. Ya are a breath of fresh air." Then he kissed her gently and gave her a big hug lifting her off her feet. "Is there anything ya want from ya cabin taken ta Fuchsiall?" he asked.

Abby looked around and said, "My shoes and some of my charts." So Gabe sat on her bed watching her while she packed the things she wanted. Then she packed one gown. "Are ya sure ya want ta take that? It will not fit ya anymore lass."

"I know but it will make a dress for each of your girls and with any luck I will have enough left to make a dress for Emily's dolly. Gabe smiled at her.

"We need ta leave now that tide is going out and we have another stop ta make before ya punishment is done."

"I almost forgot I was being punished," Abby said. "Maybe we should get the worst of this over with and then I can settle down."

"Are ya asking me ta give ya what ya deserve?" Gabe asked.

Abby lowered her head and said, "I guess that is what I am asking. I am sorry Gabe. I know I should have not interfered with Jennifer but when she hit Emily, I wanted to throw her out on her backside and then the professor. He would not believe Adam. He was going to hit him until he confessed to cheating. And poor Goliath, how can any horse breed with someone whipping him? I don't know what they were thinking. Maybe it would be a good idea if I go stay with your father until your guests go home. I am afraid I am really going to hurt someone especially Jennifer."

"Come here. I will give ya what ya deserve right now," Gabe said with a serious expression. Abby walked over to him. He put his hands on her shoulders. Abby closed her eyes and waited for whatever he was planning to do. Gabe pulled her into his arms and kissed her on her forehead. Abby opened her eyes surprised at what he gave her.

"Ya want something else or do ya not think that was enough?"

"That is it? You're not going to do anything else but hug and kiss me?"

"Well, I would like ta put ya in ya bunk and bed ya, but ya have made it very clear ya will not be my mistress. Did ya change ya mind?"

"I am not going to let you have me like that and don't ask again," she said insulted he would even bring it up.

"Relax lass. I was just teasing. Now come we have one more stop before we go back," Gabe said smiling.

"Gabe, would you lower me into the skiff first?" Abby asked with a devilish expression.

"Why?" Gabe asked knowing she was up to something.

"So I can look up under your kilt," Abby teased waiting to see his expression.

"What?"

"Relax laddy. I was just teasing," and she gave him a little wink.

Gabe rowed them back to shore where one of Gabe's men was waiting. Samson was ready to go. They road about two hours away from the ocean arriving at a lovely little cottage that looked like something out of a fairytale. It was a hipped straw roofed stone cottage with a small black iron fence surrounding it. Gabe helped her down and tied Samson. The cottage had flower boxes under each window and flowers lining a stone walk leading to the front door. Abby looked around and smiled. Gabe was pleased with her reaction.

A very small man came out of the door after he heard Gabe call to him. The little man was white haired, mostly bald with a big thick mustache. He had a big round belly and very pink skin. Smoke swirled around his head like a white halo from his hand carved pipe. An even smaller white haired woman came out wiping her hands on a white apron waving to Gabe as she walked toward him. She was a gift of loveliness with a very warm smile.

"Is this her Gabe?" The woman asked looking at Abigail. After he nodded she extended her hand out and welcomed Abby to their home. "Are ya staying for dinner Laird? It would be our pleasure ta have ya. I have it all ready."

Gabe and the little man walked around the side of the house and disappeared, leaving Abby with Wilma. The woman was so sweet.

She pulled Abby into the cottage for some tea while they waited for the men to return from the barn. Abigail heard Gabe call for her. When Abby came outside she found Gabe leading the sweetest pony she'd ever seen. The little mare was dark brown with a black bushy mane and tail, and a white star on her forehead. She was all saddled and ready to go. "Do ya like her Abby?" Gabe asked smiling. "She is for Emily's birthday."

Gabe and Abby left shortly after dinner. Another storm was coming and Gabe wanted to get home before it hit. "Can ya ride her Abby?" Before she could answer Gabe put her on the little mare. She was so tiny compared to Gabe's huge stallion but the little mare liked Samson and stayed right behind him. As soon as Gabe started Abby started giggling, the little pony had a very tiny gait and was trotting so fast Abby could not sit to it. Finally she dropped the stirrups and curled her feet under her and let the little mare run.

When they reached the barn Abby jumped off the mare without help. As Gabe led Samson to his stall and the pony to her new stall he happened to glance back at Abby. She was standing in the doorway of the barn rubbing her bum. Gabe let out a loud roar of laughter. If he had really wanted to punish her, this would have been a good way to do it. "Abigail do ya want some help rubbing ya back side?" Gabe asked from Samson's stall but Abby only growled. "Wait for me," he ordered. "I'll walk ya ta the house. Your day ends when I bring ya back ta ya chamber."

Abby stopped at her door to her chamber. She wanted to say something but hesitated. Gabe noticed her apprehension and asked. "Abby, what is it?"

"I just wanted to thank you. I had a wonderful day even though my backside is hurting." Then she said, "When it is time, I will tell you my secret and if you are still willing to help me after you know it, then I will not prevent you from coming. But if you choose not to help me, I will understand." Then she stood on her tip toes and kissed his cheek. "Good night Gabe."

CHAPTER 24
Jennifer Is In Control

Abby was awakened by Martha first thing in the morning. She had news that she knew Abby would not like.

"I wanted ta tell ya right away so ya would know what that woman is doing now." Martha said in a very huffy manner. "She is planning a dinner party to make up for her behavior. She is trying to get on the Laird's best side. Poor Eva is frantic with the menu that she has ordered and was wondering if ya would come and help her? I feel this is a trap so watch ya back. I think she is planning revenge and ya are her target. Ya best be careful she wants restitution tonight."

"Maybe I can talk Gabe into letting me out of this dinner," Abby said sitting up in her featherbed.

"No lass. Ya can't. He will not hear of it. His father is coming and the king will be here. Ya must pay ya respect ta the king. What really makes me angry is it is little Emily's birthday and Jennifer knows this. She is still having her dinner tonight anyway. The Laird has taken Emily ta the barn ta give her his present. He plans on spending the whole day with her. We will have a little celebration with the children in the small dining room off the kitchen. Hopefully ya can eat two dinners tonight. Ya best be getting up and fast. We have a lot ta do and little time ta gets it done."

This could be a nightmare just waiting to happen. Abby wasted no time getting down to the kitchen to help Eva. Jennifer had a large complicated menu for the evening and it took both women and three others to get it ready. Plus Abigail wanted to make Emily's dinner special as well.

Gabe brought Emily back to the laird late afternoon. All the children and Abby had to go outside and watch as Emily demonstrated her skill with her new pony she named Candy. That was followed by a celebration in the small dining room. Abby had prepared Emily's favorites and then the children gave out their gifts. Abby had quickly stitched a dress for her dolly from the fabric of the gown she had brought back from her ship but it was nowhere near done. Emily was very gracious and expected it done tomorrow. Then Gabe took the children up to the special room for a quick sponge war while Abby returned to the kitchen to help with Jennifer's dinner.

One hour before dinner, Gabe showed up in the kitchens. "Abby ya have an hour before dinner and I have come ta make sure ya are getting ready." Before she could say, "just one minute", he grabbed her elbow and pulled her up the back stairs to her chamber.

A tub of hot water was waiting for her and Gabe gave her fair warning. "Ya are ta get ready for dinner and ya will be there on time and ya will not be arguing with me. This is the last night. James and Jennifer will be leaving in the morning as will the King. Ya can behave for just one night." He gently pinched her floured chin and smiled at her worried looking face. "Ya will do just fine. Now stop worrying and wear my favorite gown." She did not say a word but did nod and then Gabe left. A hot tub was just what she needed. Sinking into the well perfumed warm water, Abigail soon drifted off to a restful sleep.

She was awakened by Martha rapping on the door. "Abby it is getting late are ya ready. Abby woke with a start and jumped out of her tub. "No Martha, I fell asleep in the tub. I still have to get dressed."

"Want some help?" she asked.

"Yes, I did not mean to fall asleep and I do not need to start this evening with Gabe upset with me. All I need is for Joseph to come up and carry me into the hall over his shoulder. Jennifer would be in seventh heaven to see that." Abby sputtered.

The two ladies worked together. Martha helped Abby tie her laces and pulled her wet hair on top of her head. She put a ring of fresh holly leaves around the bun disguising the wet hair. Abby had such a short little neck. She looked beautiful with her hair up like that. Martha was sure Gabe would not object.

Gabe was just about to give Joseph the order to fetch Abby when she entered the hall. As usual, her beauty always attracted Gabe's undivided attention. He met her at the door and escorted her to the head table where her usual seat had been changed. Gabe put her on his right side between him and his father. The King was on his left and James and Jennifer were directly in front of them.

Jennifer was wearing the most vulgar gown yet. Her gown was cut so low that some of her nipples were exposed. It was way too long which gave her the excuse to raised her hem a little too high as she walked. Abby wondered what was keeping the rest of her breast in the dress. She was getting disgusted with the amount of leg Jennifer was showing when she lifted her hem to walk. As usual the men came for their bird's eye view, which only fueled Jennifer's obnoxious behavior. Jennifer was loud and in charge of the events to come including the dreaded parlor games which were all the rage in England. But Abby absolutely hated these games. She had witnessed many of them when she was at James' manor. They were good for a laugh at the expense of one of the guest's humiliation. Abby had every intention of leaving before Jennifer started her games.

Jennifer, like James, treated the staff very disrespectfully. Through the dinner she managed to find fault with everyone of the servers especially, Sarah. Each insult she passed on to the servants made Abby's anger rise a little more. She tried to focus on the conversation but Jennifer was too hard to ignore.

When dinner was finished the musicians prepared to play but Jennifer had to play her parlor games first. Each game she played was humiliating and Abby saw no humor in them at all. Jennifer noticed Abby's sour expression and the fight was on. "You do not like my games Abigail?" Jennifer said stopping the play.

"I am not very good with games and I would rather not play, thank you, but I will be happy to watch," Abby said politely.

"Nonsense, I have seen you play chess and backgammon and those silly games in the yard with the children," Jennifer said making an insulting gesture toward Abby.

"There are some games I prefer and yours are not my forte but thank you for asking me," Abby said with grace. Jennifer was not going to let her off the hook. She insisted she play and recruited Gabe and the King to help persuade heAbby. Gabe knew Abby was having a hard time and wanted to leave, so he put his hand on her knee under the table to calm her down.

Sarah came in with hot cider as Jennifer was standing waving her hands in the air trying to get the rest of the guests to involve Abby. She was not paying attention even after Sarah warned her about the hot liquid. Angry with Sara's interruption Jennifer raised her hand again, deliberately hitting the pitcher of cider, spilling it down the front of Sarah's gown and apron.

Abby jump up and ran behind Sarah and loosened her ties and pulled the hot apron away from her before she could get burnt. Sarah was most appreciative and thanked Abby over and over but Jennifer did not apologize or admit it was her fault but coldly asked Sarah to leave the hall. Abby had enough. When Jennifer started on her again, Abby took her up on her offer. Before Sarah could leave the room, Abby whispered for her to stick around to enjoy watching the new game.

"Surely there must be a game you played in the primitive colonies that we could play that you would participate in," Jennifer teased.

"Well, now that you've mentioned it. There is a game we played but I will not play it if I do not have a volunteer," Abby said waiting for Jennifer to take her bait. Gabe was sure Abby was up to something, but he also had his fill of Jennifer as well and decided not to interfere with Abby's antics. Jennifer deserved what she was about to receive and Gabe would enjoy watching it. Jennifer had met her match and Abby was her name.

Abby stood up and addressed the room. "Do I have a volunteer to help me with the easiest of tasks? But before anyone volunteers, I will need a coin. Do I have some kind soul that will allow me to borrow a coin for a short time? I promise I will return it unharmed as soon as the game is over." Gabe's father threw one on the table. "Will this do Abby?" Abby gave him a devilish smile and said, "Yes sir thank you. Now I need a volunteer but before anyone decides to help me, I will tell you exactly what I will ask you to do with this coin. All you have to do is pick it up off the floor. It will be placed directly in front of your toe and in plain sight. There will be no obstacle in the way and no one will be near you to push or hit you to prevent you from picking it up. Nor will it be stuck to the floor. It will be the task of the other guests to decide if my volunteer will be successful or not. In the colonies bets are accepted at this point but not required. I will place my bet after everyone has cast theirs, so not to influence anyone. Now it is time to ask for a volunteer. Do I have a taker in this easiest of tasks?"

As expected, Jennifer jumped right in saying, "It is my dinner and I will not be accused of not wanting to participate as did Abigail. I will be a good sport unlike Abigail and volunteer." Abby was so pleased. She smiled at her and said, "Very well, I will accept you as the volunteer. Do I have any objections?" She asked hoping no one would want to take her place. "I hear no objections to Lady Jennifer as my volunteer." Abby was really thinking, *My victim not my volunteer*.

"Let us begin." Abby walked over to the wall near the hearth. She instructed Jennifer to stand with her heels touching the wall. Abby very tactfully made sure her victim was standing on the back hem of her overly long gown without her knowing it. "Are you comfortable Lady Jennifer?" Jennifer, as always was playing to the crowd paying little attention to Abby, making obscene comments on how cold the wall was on her bum. "Now I need someone to come and place this coin in front of her toe on the floor." James, to Abby's surprise, jumped up and placed the coin in the appropriate place. "Thank you James. A fine job if I ever did see one," Abby teased. "Now time to place your bets everyone. Who amongst you will place the first bet?" James again stepped forward, "I know that she will pick up the coin."

"We have one for Jennifer. Put your coin on the table sir." Abby said watching from the corner of her eye, the musicians who were betting amongst themselves as were the servants who were watching from the hallway door. Soon there were more coins falling on the table. All the bets were for Jennifer so far. "Surely there must be one of you that feel she will fail at this task?" Abby said hoping one person would get her point.

Gabe and his father Philip took Abby's lead as did the King. When all the bets had been cast and no one was changing their minds. Abby said, "All bets are in and the betting is closed except for mine and I choose nay. She will not be able to accomplish the simplest task of picking up a coin off the floor.

Philip said, "Abby I will put a coin in for ya." And before she could object he tossed a coin into the pot. Jennifer was fuming after hearing Abby accuse her of not being able to perform the simple task of picking a coin off the floor and was determined to prove her wrong.

"It is time, Jennifer," Abby instructed. "You are to pick up the coin but remember if any part of your hand or hands hit the floor, I win and all these people lose their coins."

Jennifer was playing to the crowd again, waving her hands, picking up the front of her skirts a little too high, rubbing her bum on the cold wall and laughing at Abby for such a stupid game. Abby however just watched waiting for the Jennifer to fall head first into her trap and with any luck two little "*somethings*" would be falling out as well.

Jennifer adjusted her obscene neck line, pulling it down just a little lower which made the men cheer. Then she lifted her arm above her head and bent over to get the coin. Abby watched with a smile. Jennifer hit the wall with her bottom which thrust her forward making her land hard on her two hands with her heels still pinned to the wall stepping on her gown and her bottom up in a most unladylike position. She hit the floor so hard with her hands that her very exposed breasts came bouncing out of her low cut gown without her knowledge. Her feet where tangled in the hem of her skirts and she was more focused on getting out of this embarrassing position then discovering that her entire breasts where hanging out of her gown. It did not help her undignified position that the entire room, including the servants, the musicians, the guests and the King himself were hysterical laughing at her.

Jennifer finally kicked her hem away enough to stand up. In full blown glory Jennifer stood up thinking all was well to a room that wailed louder with laughter. She stood with her hands to her side and her breast fully exposed unable to understand what they were pointing at. Then Abby made a gesture for her to look down. Jennifer screamed in shock. She whirled around facing the wall trying to shove her big chest back in the skimpy gown with no success. She covered herself with her arms calling for a plaid to cover her, but no one except Abby would come to her aid.

Abby stood in the middle of the hall straight faced. She was the only one except Jennifer that wasn't still laughing, holding a plaid. "Bring it here," Jennifer ordered.

"You want it come out here and get it and say please," Abby said refusing to move an inch. Jennifer lunged for Abby reaching for the plaid. Abigail did not try to pull it away but just held it out for her to take. "Not much fun being humiliated is it?" Abby said when Jennifer took the plaid.

"You did this on purpose. You planned on making me look like the fool in front of everyone and I will see you pay for this dearly," Jennifer screamed at the top of her lungs. Abby watched as Jennifer ran from the room covering her exposed breasts with the plaid.

Remembering Philip's coin, Abby went and picked it up and brought it over to him. "That was the funniest thing I have ever seen," he said. "Well done lass, but she will make ya pay for that dearly. She is a royal person and there are laws against disgracing royalty in public. But it was great ta watch, I'm glad someone put that obnoxious bitch in her place."

Abby looked at Gabe who was now in some control from laughing. He decided Abby should leave before anything else happened. He motioned the musicians to play and then escorted her out of the hall and up to her chamber. Abby waited until he left and went up to the tower where she could get on the roof. That is where Gabe finally found her four hours later cold and wet.

"Abigail, come in," Gabe ordered.

"No."

"Lass, please come in."

"How did you find me?" Abby asked holding back tears.

"Abby donna makes me come out there and get ya."

"Leave me be," She demanded.

Gabe stepped out on the roof, grabbed Abby's wrist before she could stop him and yanked her inside. He turned her around to face him holding her by her shoulders.

"How did you find me?" Abby asked with misty eyes.

"I asked Emi," Gabriel replied. "To find a child ask a child."

"Are you angry with me?" Abby asked with a worried look across her face.

"No lass."

"I am so sorry Gabe. I don't know what came over me. I just hate to see how mean she is to the staff. She should spend a little time in James' crate. Sarah could have suffered severe burns. Jennifer did not even care and it was her fault. She is lucky I didn't dump hot cider over her head."

Gabriel wiped a tear from her cheek and wrapped his arms around her holding her tightly.

"What are you going to do with me?" Abby asked and sniffed.

"This," he answered and he took Abby's face in his hands and lowered his mouth to hers. His lips were warm and his kiss tender. He split her lips with his tongue gently driving it into her sweet mouth enjoying her soft lips and her taste. His tongue roamed in her mouth tasting and teasing until Abby returned his kiss edging her tongue to his. He pulled her closer deepening his kiss making love to her with his tongue, causing Abby to make a soft groan in the back of her throat. Then as gentle as his kiss began, it ended.

Abby looked up at Gabe unknowing what was next. "Come lass," he said, "It is time ta get ya out of those wet clothes and ta bed." He walked her down to her chamber, opened the door and escorted her in.

"I'm so sorry Gabe," Abby said again.

"I know," he answered then said. "We will talk in the morning."

"Maybe I should go and talk to Jennifer. I doubt it would do any good, but I should at least try," Abby said.

"Abigail, ya are not ta get anywhere near her. I donna want ta pull the two of ya apart and right now I am sure she will want ta kill ya. Now let me help ya with your laces." He gently loosened the ties of her gown and let it drop on the floor around her ankles. Abby stood there in just her shift shivering. She slipped a dry shift on after he helped her remove the wet one then slid his hand under her knees and picked her up like a baby. Walking over to her bed he said in her ear, "We will have a talk in the morning." He gently laid her in the featherbed then covered her sweetly with three quilts. He bent down and kissed her forehead 1…2…3…. "Get some sleep," he urged. "It will be a very long day tomorrow." With that he blew out the candle and left her chamber.

Abigail was exhausted but she lay awake for hours. Finally the exhaustion took over and sent her into a deep sleep.

…She was sailing on the most beautiful aqua colored water with her hair blowing in the warm wind, her husband standing to her side but she could not see his face because the sun was in her eyes. A sense of freedom filled her body and a great happiness came over her…

CHAPTER 25
Take Your Pick

Abby woke feeling extremely happy and peaceful. She then noticed her door opening and servants carrying a bath in for her. Martha came in with a tray of food to break her fast and laid it on the foot of her bed. "The Laird has instructed you to eat in your chamber this morning Abby." Martha smiled at her but left the chamber before Abby could ask why. Actually Gabe was trying to avoid another confrontation with Jennifer.

As usual Jennifer was barking orders left and right. She was leaving as soon as possible. James was getting his mares ready to leave and his men were helping.

Gabe had been in his study all morning trying to come to some compromise. He had meetings with Jennifer alone, then the King and Jennifer and then just the King. Jennifer wanted blood and she would not bend. She was English royalty and humiliating a royal person would result in a public flogging. She was leaving and going straight to the English king who would definitely summon Abigail to appear in front of him. And because Abby was not Scottish, Gabe's cousin could not protect her. Gabe would be obliged to turn her over to England something he had feared. Then England would know that Scotland was hiding Abigail. England would most likely keep Abby for the secret the box held.

It would also put her in another kind of danger. She would be publicly punished and those people who have been a threat to her earlier could very likely find her—especially without Gabe's protection.

Gabe watched as Jennifer followed by her servants and James prepared to leave with his staff. James was leaving pleased. All his mares were successfully bred. He had already made plans to return for more breeding. He promised Gabe he would leave Jennifer home. As he was saying goodbye to Gabe, the two men broke out in laughter remembering the night before. "I am still sorry I let Abigail go. I had every intention of making her a permanent addition to my London home. If you ever change your mind, do let me know. She is never dull," James said as he shook Gabe's hand.

"I will never let her go. She is mine and that is the way of it. Be safe," Gabe said as James mounted and left.

Gabe waited until his guests were out of sight and returned with the King to his study where their next move would be discussed.

After her bath, Abby found another gown laid out on her bed with shoes to match. She dressed and decided to go check on the children, but when she opened the door, Joseph was standing there and would not let her leave her chamber. "The Laird feels it would be better if you stay in your chamber this morning lass," he said with a little smile.

"Just this morning?" Abby asked panicking.

"Well I am not sure lass. It is best for right now," Joseph said hoping she would not give him any trouble.

"So I am being guarded. I really am the prisoner I always felt I was?" Abby asked, her stomach churning.

"Lass donna make this harder than it is. Gabe is doing all he can for ya now. Let's just wait and see, alright?" Joseph said trying to be encouraging.

Abigail knew she had gone too far this time. There was something really wrong if Gabe would not let her leave her quarters and having Joseph guard her made her feel worse than before. When lunch and dinner came, she refused it and spent the entire day pacing her chamber like a caged animal. Finally as it turned dark she grabbed a quilt and went and sat on the floor in the far corner of her room. She wrapped the quilt around her and pulled her knees up and rested her head on her knees.

Abby did not tend her fire or light a candle, but sat in the dark terrified. Where was her warm fuzzy feeling now? She had awakened this morning from a beautiful dream. She had been so happy and now a few hours later she was back to being a prisoner trembling in a corner waiting for the worst.

Finally the door opened and Gabe walked in carrying a tray of food in one hand and a lit candle in the other. He was surprised to see the fire was out and there was no light in the room. Gabe glanced around the dark room to see her bed unused. His eyes finally rested on a small figure sitting on the floor alone in the shadows at the far corner. Gabe's heart went out to her.

"Lass?"

"I'm here."

"Come, we need ta talk," and he motioned for her to sit in the chair in front of the fire.

Abby rose with the quilt still slung around her shoulders and sat down slowly.

"Eat lass," Gabe urged.

But Abby did not move or even try to eat. "Let's get this over with. Are you sending me to England?"

The Laird sat down in front of her so he could look at her when he spoke. He sighed and then began, "What ya did last night was very clever and well deserved, but that is not our way. We are Scottish. It is not allowed ta humiliate the royalty, no matter what they have done. We have pledged our oath ta respect them no matter what, even if they donna deserve it. I know it is different in your country, but here we must follow our laws. Because ya are not familiar with our laws, the King is taking it easy on ya despite what Jennifer has ordered."

"What are you going to do with me?" Abby asked half buried in the quilt.

"That depends on ya lass. Believe it or not ya have a choice and I will respect ya wishes. Jennifer has left ta petition the King of England. She has every intention of having ya publicly whipped and that is her right. If ya go ya will stand in front of the King and state ya case. He will decide how many strikes ya are ta have. Ya will be beat, how much is up ta the King." Gabe took another breath and said, "It is uncommon ta flog a woman, but Jennifer is asking for the worst punishment for her humiliation and a public apology. Once the sentence has been passed down then ya will be led ta the whipping post. They will strip ya down ta the waist and the punishment will be carried out. It will leave marks but it shouldn't rip ya flesh if it is just a strapping."

Gabe waited for Abigail to say something but she just lowered her head.

"Abigail, I need ta tell ya what is in store for ya. Do ya want ta hear ya other option?" Gabe asked.

"Not really," Abby said. "Why don't you just let me go?"

"Ya know better than I what is waiting out there for ya. Black Dog has been sighted near France and the McHales were just up north talking ta my neighbors." Gabe moved in front of Abby and put his hand on hers. "Abby there is another way."

"Is it better than the last two we just talked about?" Abby asked expecting that it wasn't.

"My cousin will offer ya safety and a pardon if ya do just one thing," Gabe said hoping she would ask what.

"What is it I am supposed to do?" Abby asked.

"Ya must marry," Gabe said.

"Marry? Who?"

"A Scot, in less than one month the king will take ya with him and hand ya over ta England or he will leave ya with a Scottish husband," Gabe explained.

"And who am I suppose to marry?" Abby asked with anger in her eyes.

"That is up ta me ta decide," he said slowly.

"Out of the frying pan and into the fire, I will have to think this one over," and she turned her head away again.

"I need your answer tonight before he leaves and he leaves first thing in the morning. If it helps, I will do my best for ya lass. Is there anyone ya might consider for a husband that I may talk to?"

With that Abby broke out in tears and asked Gabe to leave her chamber. She ran over to her bed and jumped face down onto the mattress.

"I will give ya one hour and then I will be back ta get your answer. One or the other and I will not let ya go," Gabe stated and left Abby alone.

Abigail just wailed.

One hour later there was a knock on the door. Abby refused to answer. Gabe walked in. "I want an answer now….. a beating or a marriage? Donna take the flogging lass there is a good chance ya will not survive."

"Marriage." was all she would say and she would not even look at him.

Gabe noticed her reluctance and said. "Abby this must be a true marriage. It must be consummated."

"Is the King going to watch?" Abby asked sarcastically.

"Abigail."

"I have agreed to a marriage and I damn well know what it entails and I don't have to like it." Then she asked, "What is next?"

"I will let ya know," and he walked out of her chamber.

...She was standing on the deck with the sun beating down and the wind blowing in her face. Waves splashed over the bow and the cliffs were near. Her husband was standing near her waiting to see what she did not want him to know. He knew her secret and he did not care. He loved her and she loved him. Happiness filled her body. But then the pirate ship was sighted...

When Abby awoke in the morning her chamber was warm and toasty. The fire had been tended and extra wood had been left near the hearth. A larger copper tub, fancier than she had ever seen was placed near the fire. Rose water was laid on the table to sweeten the water. Soft folded linens were laid on the edge of the tub. A warm woolen robe laid at the foot of her bed and a tray of sweet pastries and cheese. A barrette carved from bone was on her nightstand next to a hand carved mirror and hair brush. A pair of slippers rested on the floor next to the bed and another gown lay on the stuffed chair next to the fire. A pretty little teapot with a cup and saucer was on the dry sink.

How could she have slept through all of this and why was it here. As she scanned the room she found more gifts, a pair of riding boots, a pair of shoes as if made to order, two bone carved hair combs and many other things. She sat up in her bed confused. I am being punished but I have been given all these gifts. Maybe all is forgotten; maybe something happened…… she could not seem to figure it out. She rose and walked over to the door. "There was only one way to find out," she muttered to herself. "If all is right than I will be able to leave and if not I will have a guard." She flung opened the door, hoping with all she had that there would not be a guard, only to be disappointed. Joseph was still there.

Anger and disappointment crept over her. "You can take all these gifts back to the Laird. They won't make me feel any better. A prison is a prison even if it is in a gilded cage."

"They are not from the Laird, lass." Joseph said now standing at the door so she could not leave.

"There not, then from who and why?" she asked feeling her temper defuse.

"They are all from the servants and the clan lass. Ya defended them even though it met ya have ta suffer. They are just trying ta make your stay the best it can be. They are showing ya their appreciation and their gratitude."

"Can I have visitors?' Abby asked getting upset.

"Aye."

"Then I wish to see no one and I don't want these gifts. I don't want any of this," she said and stepped back away from the door.

Joseph gave her a look of surprise. "These gifts were not ta upset ya lass."

"I know. I just cannot take any more. Good or bad. Please make them stop," Abby pleaded.

Abby shut the door then she picked all the gifts up and put them outside her door in the hall. Joseph tried to talk to her, but she shut her door and then put a chair in front of it so no one could come in without some difficulty. From the inside of the door she said, "Tell them thank you, but ask them to stop."

It was early afternoon when Abby began to hear voices in the hall, doors slammed and people kept coming up and down the hall. She looked outside her window to see people coming in and out of the laird. *What was going on now*? She thought. They were carrying things in and leaving empty handed. Little Emily came riding her pony, Candy, under her window and she waved to Abby.

A few days ago she was asked to be the children's nanny and now she was stuck in her room a prisoner again.

Curiosity was too much, she had to open her door and find out what was going on. Joseph was still there but not alone, he was surrounded by more gifts. They were everywhere from her door down the hall to the top of the stairs and people were still coming.

Abby could hear angry male voices coming up from Gabe's study. She could hear Gabe's voice over the others and he sounded angrier than all. *Must be no one wants to marry me.* She thought and started to shut her door. "It is not what ya think Abigail," Joseph said seeing the expression on her face. But Abby was so upset he could not talk to her.

Gabe came up to talk to Joseph a little while later. Abby could hear him out there but he did not come in. "How is she doing?" Gabe asked Joseph. "And what is all this stuff?"

"She is not doing well at all and she hasn't eaten a single thing since I have been in front of her door. I am really worried about her. She thinks no one wants ta marry her but look at the gifts she has been receiving. Instead of making her happy they seem ta be making her more upset. Is all decided yet?"

"Not yet," Gabe said with a growl. Then he went back down the stairs to end all this confusion.

Just before dinner, Gabe knocked on her door. "Abigail, open this door now."

"I would rather not. It is ok if no one wants to marry me. I can take the beating. Tell them it is alright and thank them for the gifts but they need to take them back."

"Abigail if ya donna open this door in one minute I will break it down."

Abby decided to let him. She was sick to her stomach to think no one wanted to marry her. Gabe did not wait until she opened the door all the way. He reached around the door and grabbed her wrist and said, "Ya are coming with me. Ya got me into this mess and ya are going ta get me out of it right now."

He pulled her out of her chamber and dragged her down the hall. She had all she could do to stay up with him and not step on all the gifts. "They must come and get their gifts. I don't want them. It is not that I don't appreciate them but there is no need for this," Abby said as she stumbled behind Gabe.

He stopped dead in his tracks. "Ya just donna understand do ya?" he said. "Ya fought for them and they want ta help. I know ya donna want their help but they have pledge their devotion ta ya and this is how they are showing it. Ya fought for this and they have a right ta reciprocate and this is how they are doing it." Then he turned and pulled her down the stairs behind him and then into the hall. He stopped when he reached the center of the room. Abby looked around and saw a large group of men surrounding her, some older, some younger and some her age, but all looking directly at Abby. They were craftsmen, farmers, guards and members of the clan. Abby's heart began to sink. *What now?* She feared. *What have* I *done now*?

The Laird was furious. He glared down at her. Abigail just stood there completely confused with his anger or why these men were in the hall surrounding her.

"Abigail," Gabe said, "Do ya know who these men are?"

"Yes," she said softly.

"No I donna think ya do." Abby gave him a puzzled look. She was so confused and her stomach was growling loudly.

"These men have all come forward ta volunteer ta be ya husband. These are the ones I let stay. There was a lot more." Abby looked around the room at the men Gabe had chosen for her.

"Decide," Gabe ordered. "Ya may have any man in this room. Who will it be? Any man in this room will make a suitable husband for ya. I will let ya decide."

Abby was a little overwhelmed. Two minutes ago she thought no one was interested and now there were at least twenty men to choose from, but the only one she really wanted had made it very clear that he was not shopping for a wife.

Her heart was breaking. How could she possible live here loving him and his children and married to another man. This was too much for her and she started to step back but Gabe grabbed her arm and pulled her back into the center of the room. "Look them over and decide," Gabe ordered, "any man in this room."

"Now?" Abby asked panicking.

"Now," Gabriel ordered, "any man in this room."

At this moment, Abby felt like a brood mare picking her stud. She was shaking inside and out. Think she kept saying to herself, think.

Then she whispered, “Someone help me. How can I get out of this?” Then she got an idea.

“Alright,” she said and she began. “Gentlemen, I am so honored and pleased that you would consider me as your wife. But before I give you my decision there are a few things I want from a husband. First, my first husband married me because it was his duty. If you are here because you feel it is your duty then I am asking you to leave. I do not want to marry because of duty ever again.

Second, my husband did not love me. He spent most of our marriage with another woman in another town. You need to have feelings for me. I want you at least to like me and as you can see I tend to get into trouble a lot.

There are young men here. I am older. I do not know if I can bear any more children. It is not fair to you to give up your chance to be a father. It may be alright this moment but some day you will regret it and me because of it.

I will not share my husband with another woman again. It is too painful. So if you are planning to marry me and have another lover than please leave now.

I see amongst you older men as well. The King has made it very clear that this marriage is to be consummated and if that is a problem for you than you must leave as well.

I have a family, three boys and a girl. I want to see them. They are part of this deal. I will not deviate from this demand. I will not be kept from them. You must accept them as you accept me and their families when they have them.

Finally, I am not Scot yet and where I come from the majority rules. I cannot decide. I do not know any of you that well. So I am doing what we do in the colonies. You will make the decision for me. You know each other better than I, so please choose for me and choose well. Who amongst you will love me, accept my family, and take me to his bed and home willingly and most important, let me love him.

The last thing I ask is that you do not tell me the man’s name you choose. Just tell me where and when I am to marry and I will be there. I will not object to whomever you choose. Again I thank you for all your offers. I really did not think anyone would step forward. I feel very honored."

Then she pushed through the center of the men and walked out of the hall and up to her chamber never looking back to see who left behind her.

Gabriel said after she left, "Well ya heard her. Is there anyone who wished ta withdraw his name?" A few younger men and a few older men exited the hall.

"Close the doors." Gabe ordered and lock them. Donna brings food or water. We stay in this room until a decision is made that we all can agree on. This may be a long night. May the best man win."

When Abby returned to her room, she was still shaking. Her chamber had more gifts. By now they were everywhere, socks, shoes, plaids, hats, mittens, jewelry, perfume, bath water and more. This should have pleased her, but it did not.

"Lass," Joseph said from the door way. "Gabe wants ya ta eat something before ya make ya self sick," and he brought in some hot soup. "Do ya want me ta stay with ya for a while? Ya look like ya could use a friend right now."

"I really did not think anyone wanted to marry me," Abby whispered. "Did you know all those men volunteered to be my husband?"

"Aye, and there were many more. Gabe had ta argue with a lot of them to leave. The arguing ya heard was Gabe refusing any unqualified suitors. I know because I was one of them. My brother would not allow me near ya."

"Why?" Abby asked surprised.

"Gabe knows what he wants for ya and the right man has finally come forward."

"Do you like him Joseph?" Abby asked in a whisper.

"Aye lass, he is the only man I would step aside for. I donna know if the hall will choose him but I know he is the best one for ya. He loves ya with his whole heart. I know ya donna want ta know his name so donna even ask me."

"I am sick to my stomach right now," Abby said. "I really need to be alone but I thank you for your offer. Maybe later. Alright?"

Joseph smiled at her and touched her cheek. Then he left the room and shut her door.

Abigail was watching the sun drop below the horizon when a knock finally sounded on her door. Before she could say enter, Gabe came into her chamber. She turned from the window where she was standing to look into his face. As usual she could not tell if he was happy with the decision or not.

"It is done," he announced. "Tomorrow ya will leave with Joseph ta stay at my father's house. No one will tell ya his name. It is better ya stay there until the wedding. It is ta late now. I can no longer help ya. Ya will marry on Saturday when my cousin, the King returns with the monk from the Abby. The choice has been made. Ya will not be allowed ta say no and there will be no arguments.

Abby didn't respond but lowered her head and nodded. Then she asked with her voice shaking, "Do you like him Gabe?"

"Aye, very much and just remember Abby, he loves ya with all his whole heart. Give him a chance. All I ask is that ya be good ta him."

Abby broke into tears and turned her back on him. He did not help her to bed or kiss her good night. He just left the room without a word.

CHAPTER 26
HANDFASTED FOREVER

Abigail did not sleep that night. She never even laid in her bed. Instead she straightened her room, sorted all her gifts and carefully stacked them in the corner. She wanted to leave her room useable for someone else and she did not want the servants to clean up after her. So she scrubbed the floor and cleaned until way after midnight. Then she packed a small satchel and opened her door. Joseph was still standing there wide awake as well. "I'm ready if you would like to leave now," she said.

"It will be light in an hour. If I order the horses ready it will be close enough ta daylight ta leave lass," Joseph answered.

In thirty minutes she was mounted on the little mare that had brought her here in the first place. Joseph was in the front, she had a man on each side of her, and one in the back. Gabe was still nervous about her leaving Fuchsiall and he wanted her to be safe. The McHales were too close not to take precautions.

They left just before sunup. There was no one to say goodbye and no sign of Gabe but as always he was watching her without her noticing it. Standing in the window of his chamber, he watched the men and Abigail leave Fuchsiall. He had set the marriage contract, the date, and it would be one more week before he would see her again. He only hoped that she would be happy with her new husband.

They road slowly, never stopping until they arrived at Gabe's father's house just before noon that. Philip was waiting for her as they arrived. Abby was quiet all the way over to the old Laird's home. Philip had been excited to have her in his home for a week. He really like Abigail and was very happy with the husband that had been chosen for her.

Philip was smiling when Abby entered his home, but when he saw the look on her face his heart went out to her. He opened his arms in a fatherly gesture and Abby walked into them and wept. Philip hugged her and kissed the top of her head. "Now lass it will be fine. It is not all that bad. Ya wait and see all will be fine." Gabe's father said holding her tightly but Abby was inconsolable. Joseph had followed her into the house and watched helpless as she wept in his father's arms. "It will be alright lass. Ya must trust Gabe. He won't let ya down. I promise ya," Philip encouraged.

"That is just it, he already has," Abby said with her head resting on Philip's chest.

Philip pulled her away and looked into her teary eyes. "Ya love my son. Don't ya?"

"Joseph or Simon or Gabe?" Abby asked trying to act like she did not know what he was asking.

"Donna ever lie ta me lass. I donna like it one bit and pretending like ya donna know what I am talking about is the same as lying," Philip barked pointing his finger at her.

Abby blushed and said, "How did you know? I never told anyone."

"I am an old man lass. I dinna get ta this age without learning a thing or two on the way. I have seen the way ya look at him and the way ya allow him ta treat ya. It is about time that ya admit it," He said.

"I do love Gabe with my whole heart, but he does not return my love," Abby said through sniffs.

Joseph stood behind his father and Abby listening to their conversation. He smiled at his father from behind Abby's back where she could not see him. Philip smiled back at him and gave him the nod to leave. Without saying goodbye, Joseph left leaving the other men behind to help guard the old laird's home and returned to Fuchsiall to help with the wedding.

"Abigail, tell me, if ya love him so much, why did ya not choose him when he asked?" Phillip asked waiting for an honest answer.

"Gabe made it perfectly clear that he was not shopping for a wife and his bed was his concern and not mine and I was never to interfere again. I will not force anyone to marry me. I know what it feels like to be married to someone who you don't love. It is too painful. I would not put him through that," Abby explained.

"Ya would have learned ta love each other, lass."

"My husband never learned to love me and I cannot go through that again. I will be alright," she said and cried some more.

"Then why do ya cry lass?"Philip asked moved by her tears.

"I don't know. I just can't seem to stop," Abby whispered.

"Come with me lass and play a game of chess. It will keep ya mind busy. Gabe tells me ya are pretty good. We shall see." And he grabbed her elbow and led her to his study.

Philip did his job well. He kept Abigail busy every minute of every day. He would not allow her to think about the wedding. His house was beautiful and full of wonderful things that made Abby happy, like his library and his kitchen. Abby loved to read and Philip was impressed with the number of books she had read. They had long discussions over their favorite books and she showed him how to make an apple pie. He spoke in Gaelic and she tried to answer.

One day he brought her in a poem that was written in Gaelic. He insisted that she learn it. Two or three times a day he would have her repeat after him. Patiently he corrected her accent and encouraged her to learn the poem well.

Abigail learned it because he asked her to, but she had no idea the real reason he wanted her to memorize it. Abby mastered the entire poem except the last word. Philip would laugh at loud as she would say the last word. "No, no lass not that way," and then he would repeat it again.

"What am I saying?" Abby asked when Philip rolled with laughter.

"In English it means man's penis," Philip said still laughing. Abby tried to get the word but the harder she tried the more Philip chuckled. Finally Philip figured it out. Abby was pulling his leg and he loved it.

The week went faster than Abigail wanted. Her visit with Gabe's father was wonderful. She found herself laughing and forgetting her troubles, but reality showed up again and it was now Friday night, the day before her wedding.

Philip knocked on her door to her chamber. "It is time ta go lass. The horses are ready and if we leave now we will arrive just after dark about ten o'clock."

On the way Philip asked Abby to recite the poem over and over. Abby thought it was to keep her mind busy and each time she would stop at the last word. Philip would give her a fair warning and then she would say it correctly. It was a game they played and it always made the two of them smile.

When they arrived, Philip took Abby in the back way and up the backstairs to her old chamber. He gave her a gentle kiss goodnight and pushed her in. The room was just as she'd left it except hanging on the screen in the corner was a wedding gown. It was beautiful. Someone had worked very hard on this gown. The details were incredible. It was Abby's favorite color a very soft pale blue almost a white. It was trimmed with lace and ribbon with small beads sewn tastefully in the scooped neckline.

The sleeves were long and covered with lace and there were satin shoes similar to the ones she had from the colonies. There were loose ribbons and beads in a basket waiting to adorn her hair and the fancy copper tub was still in the same spot she'd left it. Her gifts were still in the corner and she could swear the piles had grown.

Abby lay on her bed not getting into her night shift….*She was standing on the deck looking down at the two big hands out stretched in front of her beckoning her to come. He was safe and made her happy. The sea was calm and the wind warm in her face, but the sun would not allow her to see his face. But she was happy……*

Abby woke and sat up in her bed. She had fallen asleep. It was now daybreak still and she was still wearing the gown she came in. Goliath would be out in his pasture and if she was careful she could take him for a short ride. Abby opened the door to her room and peeked out. Seeing no one guarding her chamber, she tipped toed down the hall to the front staircase and slid down the banister, landing lightly at the bottom on her feet. She slowly opened the door and then once outside ran to the pasture before anyone could catch her.

She had just awoke from a wonderful dream and she was so happy. She wanted to get on Goliath and run him to the ocean. Abby climbed the fence and when she reached the top Goliath was standing there waiting for her. "OK boy lets go have some fun." Goliath started slow and little by little broke into a canter and then into a full gallop. Abby held tight to his mane as he took her at full speed across his pasture to the cliffs of the ocean.

As they reached the cliffs the sun came rising over the ocean sending a spectacular array of color over the water and into the sky. Abby sat on Goliath and watched peacefully as the sky was lit by the morning sun. Then from behind her she heard. "What do ya think ya are doing out here this early in the morning with no chaperone on ya wedding day?" Abby turned around to see Philip, Simon, Joseph and Jake on horseback right behind her. "Ya best be marching that bum of yours back ta the house and into ya chamber before I decide ta tan it," Philip ordered angrily. Abigail looked surprised that the men had come after her but she did not dare argue with them. The looks on the four men's faces meant business and they were not fooling around with her.

Abby turned Goliath back toward the barn and then with a devilish look in her eyes urged him into a full gallop keeping him in front of the four men. She rode nonestop loving the feeling of this powerful animal under her and the wind blowing in her face. Joseph came up beside her and reached out and took her off Goliath and onto his saddle. "Ya are very naughty Abigail Fox and I am taking ya back ta ya chamber before anyone sees what ya are doing. Ya are going ta stay there until the wedding," He ordered firmly. Joseph was always easygoing. Abby was surprised at his display of anger toward her.

"Let me go Joseph, I am just riding. I am not doing anything wrong," Abby snapped back at him. Joseph did not say another word but stopped his horse at the fence and handed her down to Simon while he dismounted. Joseph took one arm and Simon took the other and they walked her around back and up the backstairs up to her chamber where the ladies were frantically waiting for her. Joseph pushed the door of her chamber open and said, "We found the runaway riding Goliath."

"I did not run away. I was just going for a morning ride," Abby protested.

Joseph and Simon pushed her into her room, and managed to give her a good swat on her bum before they left. Martha, Glenna, Maggie and Sarah took over before she had a chance rub her backside. The door was shut tight and locked. Abby was stripped and sitting in her tub being playfully scolded by the four women. "What time is my wedding?" Abby asked not really wanting to know.

"Three o'clock and that doesn't give us much time. We need ta fit the dress on ya and do ya hair. Ya must be perfect today." The next thing Abby knew she was being dunked down under the water. The women were acting like foolish school girls picking on Abby and asking her stupid questions.

"Do ya know what a penis is, Abigail?" Maggie asked trying not to smile.

"Do ya know what ta do with it?" Glenna asked and then laughed.

"Do ya need us ta talk about the wedding night?" Sarah asked.

It felt good to laugh. These women were her friends and they were really happy today and happy Abby was going to marry and become family. Abigail did not share their enthusiasm. She had no idea who she would be in bed with tonight and if she would be happy about it. Roy had always limited the sex to his satisfaction only and Abby wasn't looking forward to a night like that.

Many times she would listen to the ladies in the kitchen at James' manor describing the pleasure they received from their lovers and it wasn't just five minutes like Roy wanted. The women talked about hours of pleasure. They talked about how the men enjoyed touching them and watching them climax.

Roy was a very selfish lover, pleasing himself, rushing for his fulfillment then leaving her in pain and unloved. He never cared how she felt or if she was satisfied too. He always made her feel he was having sex because his body demanded it like a duty but not an expression of love. The thought of having to marry another man like Roy was frightening.

Abby really needed her friends today. They made her laugh and forget her fears. They approved of her marriage, hopefully Abby would too.

At two o'clock the women said their goodbyes. They had worked their magic one more time and left the room pleased with their creation.

Abby walked over to her window that overlooked the courtyard and watched as carriages pulled up and people started gathering. She saw the Monk come in and also the King, James was here as well as Bess and Teddy.

There were so many people. She was beginning to wonder just who she was marrying. She noticed other clans coming in with their brightly colored plaids and adornments. She counted at least ten different plaids and their families. Coming up from the hall Abby could hear the sounds of voices indicating a lot of guests. There were so many carriages that they had to be parked in the courtyard. The last person she saw coming in was a large man carrying bagpipes. Abby loved the pipes and was so hoping he would be playing sometime this evening.

Then there was a knock on her door. It was time. The moment she had been dreading for a whole week. She turned from the window and said, “Come in.”

Joseph entered wearing his finest kilt and plaid. His hair was combed back and his face freshly shaven. He stopped at the sight of her standing in the sunlight and said nothing.

“I take it that you are not going to be my new husband,” Abby said teasingly to break the ice.

“Abigail ya are the most beautiful woman I have ever seen. I only wish it had been me but if not me than I am happy with the man they chose,” he answered grinning.

“You do like him?” Abby asked trying to keep her voice from shaking with little success.

“Aye lass, I love the man more than life itself and there is nothing I wouldn’t do for him. I know ya are scared but remember what I am saying, he loves ya with his whole heart.” Then Joseph stretched out his elbow and said, “Would ya do me the honors of letting me escort ya ta ya ta meet your new husband?” Abby nodded reluctantly and slid her hand under his elbow. She curled her hand around his bicep and held on. With his opposite hand he covered hers and said, “Ya won’t be disappointed. I promise.”

When they reached the top of the stairs and looked down she was surprised with the number of guest at the laird. The hall was spilling over with people from servants to farmers to royalty all here for one reason. Abby stopped and asked, "Just who am I marrying, the pope?"

"Nay lass, but someone as good and even more loved by all these people," Joseph answered.

Abby refused to take another step. She started to tremble. She was not going down there. "Joseph, I cannot do this. Tell them I decided to take the beating," and she tried to take her hand from his arm and run back to her chamber. Joseph just held on tight. "Nay lass, ya cannot do that now. It is ta late. Ya made ya choice and now ya are going ta go through with it."

Abby still stood there refusing to move watching the crowd at the bottom of the stairs. "One step at a time Abby," Joseph whispered. Then with a gentle tug from Joseph, Abby stepped down on the first stair then the next and the next. As she stepped on the next stair she trembled more. Joseph tightened his grip. He was not going to let her go. "Easy lass, we are almost there. Ya will be just fine."

Standing at the bottom of the stairs were Mary from James' manor, the Scottish woman who had given Abby her plaid, also Olga the cook and Abraham the footman that had been so kind to her. "What are you three doing here? I am so happy to see you. Are you alright?" Abby asked not stopping long enough to let them answer a single question. Finally it was Mary who said, "Abby it was my plaid. Gabe brought it to my father and he came for me. My Father also needed a new cook so Olga came and so did Abraham."

A man wearing the same plaid as Mary had given Abigail stepped forward and said, "It is my pleasures ta meet ya Abigail Fox. Gabe tells me that it was ya who insisted I get her plaid. I have been looking for my Mary for years and now she is home thanks ta ya. I am forever in ya debt. I am Mary's father, Laird Murray."

"Thank you for coming. I am so happy you are all here and happy to meet you sir," Abby replied with a smile.

Then from the hall door the pipes began to play. "Abby it is time to go in," Joseph whispered.

"In the hall?" Abby asked shaking again.

"Aye, it was the only room big enough."

Joseph tried to lead her but her knees were knocking so badly she could hardly stand. "Baby steps lass, take baby steps." Joseph whispered. Maggie handed her a large bouquet of freshly picked pink roses and gave her a hug and kissed her cheek.

"Joseph, I can't," Abby whispered.

"Do I need ta put ya over my shoulder and carry ya in?"

"You wouldn't?" Abby asked shocked.

"Aye, I would, now move," and he gave her a quick pull and she started off. Abby for once did as she was told. She knew Joseph would carry her if he had to.

The hall had been transformed to look like a church. The tables were removed and benches lined each side of a center isle left for her to walk down. Rose peddles were spread on the isle for her to walk on and flowers adorned the hall in huge baskets against the walls. Banners portraying the McKenzie crest hung from the rafters along with the Scottish flag.

Abby started to look around and noticed some of the men who had volunteered to marry her spread throughout the hall. She started to count them off in her head but could not figure out who was missing. Who was she about to marry? Finally the pressure got to her and she decided not to look. She lowered her head and watched the floor. Maybe if she did not see him she would not turn and run. The hall seemed endless as she kept walking.

The Monk was waiting on the platform where the head table usually stood. An arbor adorned with flowers was placed in the center of the platform for the bride and groom to stand under. The piper played beautifully and Abby tried to concentrate on the music one step at a time. Everyone was standing. She could not see if she wanted to. Abby kept her eyes looking down. Maybe if she concentrated on the floor she would make it. Her heart was pounding so hard she thought everyone in the entire hall could hear it.

When she reached the end of the isle she stopped dead. Joseph whispered, "Remember he loves ya." then he escorted her into the arbor and left her side.

"Come forward," the Monk ordered. Abby would not look up. A pair of large black boots came to stand with her under the arbor at her right side. She could also see the hem of his kilt. A gentle smell of his cologne filled the air.

"Let us begin." the Monk started. "You may face each other and hold hands." Abby turned to face her new husband but would not look up to see who it was. Two very large opened hands came into her view. Someone reached around her and took her flowers. Her hands were cold, clammy and trembling. She placed them into the large warm hands still refusing to looking up. She kept focusing on Joseph's words, "Remember he loves ya very much."

His hands gently closed over hers and he gave her a little squeeze. She was shaking so she quivered a little. "Easy lass," her soon to be husband whispered. Abby then realized she knew that voice. *No it couldn't be*, she thought.

The Monk began, "Dearly beloved we are gathered together to join …" Abby's mind was racing. Then those words came, the words she was dreading, "Do you…… Gabriel Alexander Patrick McKenzie take Abigail Fox to be your…" Abby's head flew up and looked into the eyes of Gabe. He was looking directly at her, smiling with such love in his eyes. Before he could answer the Monk's question Abby whispered, "Are you sure?"

Gabe said loudly. "I do."

"And do you Abigail Fox take Gabriel Alexander Patrick McKenzie to be your husband?" There was complete silence in the hall as they waited for her answer. Abby had all she could do to breathe never mind talk. Her mouth was bone dry and her lips could not form the words. Then came her warm fuzzy feeling the one that let her know everything would be alright. She whispered, "I do."

Then a switch in the ceremony, something else she was not expecting. "Before I can pronounce you man and wife, there is something else you must agree to." Abby's heart sank, this could not be happening.

The Monk stepped back and let all six of Gabe's children line up in front of her. "Please turn and face the children," the Monk directed. "Do you children take this woman to be your mother, to have and to hold…" There in front of Abby stood all six children, dressed in their best clothes waiting for their question. "We do," they all said in unison. Then it was Abby's turn. The Monk began, "And do you Abigail take these children"… But she interrupted the Monk. She dropped Gabe's hands and walked over in front of Gabe's oldest son. "I Abigail take you Ian Patrick Bennett," then she moved to the next child, "and you Bethany Ann Helen," and the next child, "and you Adam Nicholaus Joseph," and continued, "you Colm Simon Brian, and you Benjamin Nathan Alexander and you Emily Rebecca Clara to be my children from this day forth for better, for worse in sickness and in health so help me God." The faces on the children were priceless. Each smiling as she said their full name like only a true mother would know. Abby was filled with such love she could barely make it through her vows for the children.

"Turn and face Gabriel," the Monk instructed. Then Philip stepped forward and tied Gabe's hand and Abigail's hand together with a leather strap. Gabe noticed the expression on Abby's face and said, "It is all right Abby, it is our way."

This couple is now hand fasted as is the Scottish custom but it is the McKenzie custom that the un-Scot must speak a few words of Gaelic. *OH no,* thought Abigail. Her head was spinning. All she could remember was what Ian use to say to Adam, roughly translated it meant, "I am going to kick your ass." The whole hall broke out in laughter. Abby's face turned red and Gabe gave his son a dirty look.

Then Abby remembered the poem that Philip had taught her. She cleared her voice and started to recite it. The old laird looked on with such pride as Abby recited the poem word for word, a poem that was like the McKenzie coat of arms. The hall listened as Abby made it through and then stopped at the next to the last word. She playfully looked at the old laird and smiled. He shook his finger at her and shook his head. Finally she did say the last word pronounced perfectly. Philip breathed a sigh of relief and then bent down and whispered to Abigail, "Ya will pay for that one lass.,." with a teasing look in his eyes. The old laird was satisfied and so was the clan.

"Ya will repeat after me," the Monk instructed. Then the Monk recited the wedding vows in Gaelic which Gabe said first. Then it was Abby's turn, he went very slow and exaggerated every syllable. Abby almost laughed at herself but made it through it. Gabe then recited them again but this time in English so she would understand.

Philip now stood directly in front of the couple. It was tradition in the McKenzie family that if the father of the groom approved of the bride and the marriage was made from love and not the betterment of the clan, a gift was bestowed to the bride. It was a tradition seldom seen. Most marriages were performed for the clans benefit as was Gabe's first marriage. Philip did not bestow a gift for Gabe's first wife even though they grew to love each other in time. It was Abigail that held Gabe's heart and made him laugh. Gabe had chosen her but so didn't his children and his entire clan.

Philip had requested Abigail spend a week with him. He wanted to get to know her better and teach her the poem so she would recite it at the wedding, again a tradition that went with the gift. Gabe stood waiting, wondering if his father would pass on the gift or would he just lay his hands on the leather ties and accept the marriage.

Abigail had no idea what was happening and why there was silence in the room. She had successfully said the poem/prayer. She had recited the vows in Gaelic. She had accepted his children and the clan. It was such an honor to receive his gift. Gabe didn't know if Abigail would understand the true meaning.

Philip put his hands over Gabe and Abby. He began speaking in Gaelic. Abby did not understand what he was saying, but the clan and Gabe did. Philip was going to offer Abby the talisman, a symbol of the McKenzie strength. It was believed that the talisman protected the clan. It kept the families together through war and bad times. It brought prosperity and fertility. But in order for the talisman to work, it had to be bestowed to a couple in love. Abigail had to take it on her own he could not place it in her hand. She had to accept it, not understanding what it meant.

The talisman was a gold staff, sixteen inches long with a large red crystal ball held by a golden claw. A set of fox and hounds were etched in the handle of the talisman.

Philip looked down at Abby. He held it out in his hand but did not hand it to her. She had to take it on her own. The room waited to see what she was going to do. Somehow Abby sensed it was important. Something inside her wanted to take it. That warm fuzzy feeling came again. Without hesitation she reached up and put her hand around the staff just over Philip's and under the glass ball. When Gabe did not reach to hold it, Abby began to think she did something wrong.

Then Philip let go of it allowing Abigail to hold it by herself. The entire room broke out in cheers. The Monk said, "I now pronounce you man and wife. You may kiss your bride, your children and your clan." Gabe and Abby's hands were still tied and Abby was holding the talisman in her left hand but Gabe reached down and gave her the most loving kiss she had ever felt. She looked up at him and smiled and he smiled at her. Then they were surrounded by the children and the clan pulling them into the hall where they were congratulated with hugs and kisses.

The benches were replaced with the tables brought in and dinner served. Gabe and Abby were still tied together all through dinner. Finally Abby leaned over and asked Gabe, "How long are to be tied together?"

"Forever," Gabe teased. "They will let us go to our chamber soon. Then we can take it off before I bed ya." Abby blushed. "lass," Gabe whispered "Ya do know how much your new husband loves ya?"

Abigail smiled and blushed again. "Aye," she said. "Gabe?"

"Aye?"

"You do know how much your new wife loves you?"

"I do now," Gabe said smiling. He could not believe what he was hearing. This was more than he had hoped for. She was so special, so beautiful. He loved her ways, her spirit, her determination andeven her temper. She was gentle and strong, wise and naive. She was his dream, his hope and now she was his. Tonight they would seal the contract.

The pipes began to play and the crowd moved into the ballroom where they danced and celebrated some more. Finally the clan decided the bride and groom had stayed long enough. Gabe and Abby were picked up with their hands still joined and carried them up the stairs and into Gabe's chamber. The door was shut and the two were left alone in the room.

Abby stood there while Gabe loosened their ties and released the hold of the leather strap on their hands. He tended the fire and then went to his bed and pulled the quilt down. Abby stood by the door not moving, not knowing what she should do.

CHAPTER 26
You Are Finally Mine

Abby stood by the door overlooking his bed chamber. The servants had laid a new white quilt on his enormous four poster mahogany bed. They placed fresh fruit on the dry sink by the wall facing the courtyard. The fire box was filled to the brim with wood and kindling and the walk in fireplace had been cleaned and polished. The full length curtains that hung on either side of his two bay windows had been changed from green to blue and a fresh sheep's skin was placed on the wood planked floor in front of the fire. Her fancy four clawed copper tub had been brought in and now stood to the right of the fire just off the sheep's skin.

Some of her things had also been laid out. Her night shift with the pretty pink lace and her sheep skin lined slippers. A hairbrush with the two hand carved combs were placed on the nightstand and a bottle of rose water for her bath was resting on the hearth near her tub. Abby looked around at this beautiful room once very mannish and now made a little softer for her.

Although Gabe had slept next to her before, this was different. She was now supposed to allow him to take her willingly. He had fondled her breast and messaged her bottom, but he had never pushed himself on her. Abby had mixed emotions. She loved Gabe and wanted nothing more to let him do as he pleased, but she had done that very thing with Roy who continually hurt her cruelly. Gabe in many ways was larger than Roy and it had been over twenty years since she had taken a man to her bed. She stood by the door as if keeping a way out if she needed it.

Then Gabe turned around and looked at her after he tended the fire. He noticed her uneasiness. She always fumbled with her hands when she was scared or nervous. Gabe slipped his jacket off and laid it on the chair then he loosened his ties and he walked over to her.

Abby was looking at the floor. Without looking up she said softly, "I was so hoping it was you."

"Then why dinna ya choose me when I asked ya? It would have saved a lot of time fighting for ya," Gabe asked.

"You said you were not shopping for a wife and that who you had in your bed was not my concern. I thought you did not want to marry me and I was not going to force you," she answered softly.

Gabe chuckled. "Lass, never change. I never know what is coming out of that head of yours. I was not shopping for a wife because I had already found her and ya will never be concerned about who I have in my bed because it will be ya and only ya."

Abby blushed. "It was a beautiful wedding. Thank you." And she stood on her tip toes and gently kissed his cheek.

"It is my pleasure, lass." Gabe watched Abby play with her hands then her gown and anything else she could pick up and set down.

"Nervous, my dear?" Gabe asked smiling at her.

"No… Yes… I have a confession to admit too."

"Aye?"

"I have only been with my first husband and no other man."

"Aye, I know."

"I am afraid that I will not please you. I am not very good at this," she said still looking at the floor.

Gabriel put his finger under her chin and guided her face to look at him. Smiling, he said, "I will make ya happy and give ya what ya should have had all ya life, my sweet, and I am about ta show ya just how much I love ya."

"Be gentle," Abby whispered.

"First ya must be comfortable with me," he said with a smile.

He loosed her laces and pushed her dress down over her shoulders and let it slip down to the floor. He did the same with her shift. She stood in front of him naked. She started to get embarrassed and tried to cover herself but he pushed her hand away and said, "Never be ashamed or uncomfortable around me lass." He lifted her up under her arms and carried her out in front of him to the stuffed chair in front of the fire. Gabe then sat her down in the chair and removed her shoes and socks leaving her completely naked in front of him. He pulled her to her feet and stood her in the middle of the sheep's skin in front of the fire. Then he sat in the chair and crossed his legs. "Damn lass, ya are beautiful and I just want ta look at ya. Now would ya turn around so I can finally see that wonderful full ass of yours?"

Abby's mouth dropped open. He laughed at the expression on her face. She wanted to fidget with her hands. She could not believe that she was standing naked in front of him and yet it wasn't bad or scary. She actually liked the look on his face when he looked at her. He really made her feel beautiful. Reluctantly she turned around slowly and stood facing the fire. She heard the thud of his boot as it fell to the floor behind her and the other one shortly after. "Alright lass, ya can turn back around." He was sitting in the chair with his boots and socks off and his shirt opened up, un-tucked from his kilt. "Come here lass," he asked gently not to scare her. She slowly came to his chair. He reached out and pulled her onto his lap. Abby sat naked on him, his warmth surrounding her. She could feel his hardness increasing from under his kilt.

"I am going ta make love ta ya and I want ya ta tell me if ya like it or if I hurt ya." She was so scared that Gabe wanted to go slowly with her. Roy had been a monster toward her and he was not going to make this another bad experience. It was there first time together and he wanted it to last and for her to have complete joy in every way. In many ways Gabe felt she was a virgin. She had never experienced a release. She had never touched an adult male penis with her hand. He wanted her to be comfortable with him as well as him with her. So he decided to give her a chance to explore his body. "Lass, I will not hurt ya ever, at least not on purpose. I want ya ta touch me anytime ya want and where ever ya want. And we can start here." He took her hand and slid it into his shirt where she could feel his hard chest covered with soft curly black hair. She smiled at him as she rubbed her hand through his chest hair stopping at a nipple hard from the sensation her hand was giving him.

She mimicked his actions encircling his nipple with her thumb. Her mouth watered with the thought of tasting him. He smelled so good. She lay her head on his shoulder putting her nose in his neck and breathed in his wonderful scent still rubbing his chest. Gabe was pleased with her reactions to him so far, but there was a long way to go. "Ready ta go on?" he asked when he felt her getting comfortable. She sat up and looked at him wondering what he wanted next. He lifted his shirt off and then picked her up and had her straddle him like a horse in the chair. He reached around her and gently started messaging her bum, squeezing, lifting, and holding her lovingly in his large strong hands. As he played with her bottom she played with his chest rubbing, feeling and then with her tongue reached out and licked the tip of his nipple. She gave him a look of surprise when he did not stop her. "Ya are doing just fine lass. Donna stop, it is alright ta taste me." He gritted his teeth when she returned her tongue to his breast and then twirled it around it in circles first one and then the other.

He lifted her up in his hands bringing her mouth to his and he kissed her, but he did not want to go too quickly so he broke his kiss and then rose from the chair still holding her bottom. He stood her on the sheep's skin and then said, "Touch me." Abby watched her fingers glide over his hard flat stomach and then walked around him exploring every inch of him. She glided her hands over his biceps and then over his shoulders. He experienced goose bumps when she slid her hands down his back in circling motions, using her finger nails to gently scratch him. When she got to his kilt she stopped. "What are ya waiting for? Ya know ya have wanted ta see what is under my kilt," He teased. "Take it off." Abby hesitated but then walked back around to face him. His hardness was very prominent now from under his kilt. Gabe saw her face. He grabbed her hand and placed in on the man sex with just the kilt between her hand and him. "I will not harm ya lass. It is alright donna be afraid."

She unbuckled his belt and let it drop to the floor and then his kilt. Looking up at him she said, "I would like to start in the back please and work my way around." Without looking at his maleness, she walked behind him. He was beautiful with his hard muscles coming down his back and his bottom so warm and hard. She gently touched his backside so softly at first she tickled him and he chuckled. "Ah you like that," she teased.

"Aye, I admit it, I do." Then she finished with rubbing him and squeezing him the way he had touched her bottom. Finally she got enough nerve to come to his manhood. First she just looked. She became embarrassed and blushed when she saw him looking at him. "Ya have something ya want ta say?" He asked with a smile.

"You are certainly gifted aren't you," she answered.

Then he saw the look on her face. "Relax lass it will fit I promise ya."

Abby took a deep breath and reached out and finally touched him for the first time. "Oh you are so hard and velvety feeling at the same time. Are all men like this?" then she blushed again.

"Aye lass, just different sizes that's all." Abby rubbed her hand over him. He gritted his teeth with the sensations that were rippling through his body. "Easy lass, ya donna want this ta be ta quick." The last place she explored was just under his stiffness. "Oh," was all she said and she gently raised and lowered him in her hand.

The fire was just right. Gabe was ready and so was Abby. He gently laid her on the sheep's skin in front of the fire, which gave off warmth making their bodies glow in the light. "Ya are so beautiful and I love ya with all my heart and now I will show ya just how much. Trust me lass," He whispered. Gabe lowered his lips to hers slipping his tongue into her mouth. Sliding his tongue in and out he made love to her with his kiss, tasting her and letting her taste him. He cupped her breast as he enticed her mouth gently kneading her.

Then he broke away from her mouth and kissed her cheeks and down her neck, kissing licking and tasting her until he ended at her breast where he took her nipple in his mouth and kissed it with his tongue still holding the other one in his hand. She moaned with the pleasure he was stirring in her. When he had his fill he started kissing her flat stomach and she giggled when he put his tongue in her belly button. He then continued down to the soft blonde curls at the junction of her legs. Gabe felt her tense. "Lass, do ya love me?"

"Yes with all my heart."

"Do ya trust me?"

"Okay," she said shaky.

"Lass?

"Yes, just be gentle please," she pleaded.

He kissed her little blonde curls then parted the soft folds separating, stroking arousing, waking her body up from a long sleep, letting her feel the rippling sensations of what her body was meant for. She moaned and arched her back letting him tease and excite her. He started to kiss her folds "Are you…..?" She asked wide eyes with what he was about to do.

"Aye lass, trust me." He smiled at her and then pushed his tongue in between the folds finding her most sensitive nub and messaging it with his tongue, until she exploded into the height of her sensation shaking from the pure pleasure she was receiving.

He then slid his big finger deep inside of her. Starting the sensations he was about to give her with his hardness. Stroking her slowly with his finger getting her ready to receive him, feeling the moisture surround his finger, he gently slid in another, opening her more to accept his size. She moaned from the pleasure he was giving her. "Don't stop," she whispered. He smiled to see her relax and let him take over. When he felt she was ready he slid his body between her legs. He saw her grab the sheep skin with her fist panicking a little. Gabe reached up and kissed her. Pushing his tongue into her mouth stroking her breast with his hand, letting her feel his hardness resting at the entrance of her womanhood.

He felt her touch him, curl her arms around him and give him a gentle hug, her way of letting him know it was time and she would not fight or fear him. Gabe lifted her hips and with one gentle motion entered her body. She moaned as he settled inside her letting her get use to him. He then pulled out and entered her again this time pushing in a little deeper. She instinctively curled her legs around him and arched her back to accept him deeper. She moaned as he started to glide in and out slowly allowing her to feel him.

He enjoyed the tightness of her and the moisture that surrounded him as he pushed deeper inside her. She was giving him sensations he had never felt before with anyone else. He was having a hard time waiting until she found her release, but he would not let himself reach fulfillment until she had reached hers. "Gabe you need to stop I cannot take any more," she moaned. "No lass, let it come donna fight it." He thrust himself in harder and sent her into complete fulfillment. She found her first release. She moaned as she enjoyed the ride he was giving her. He began to thrust faster and harder until he himself reached his release and spilled his seed deep inside her.

Gabe lay on her letting his body relax his heart beating hard, his breathing fast. He was so warm, so hard and she loved the feeling of him on top of her. Abby reached around him and gave him a loving hug.

Her hands wondered lower to his bottom and gave him a little squeeze. Then that little devilish feeling came over her. Abby waited until he looked at her face still rubbing his bottom and she smiled up at him with that impish look and…slapped his ass.

"Lass?"

"Yes."

He held on to her and rolled over taking her with him. One second she was under him and the next she was on top of him with his hands on her bum.

"Gabriel?"

"Aye."

"No."

Slap… "Oooooo," she squealed. Then giggled and leaned down and kissed him, deep, hard and long until he moaned with pleasure. He stood, picked her up, and carried her like a little child to his bed. Gabe lay back on the bed still keeping her on top of him.

She rolled off him, pulled the covers up and turned away.

"Just where do ya think you are going?" He reached out and pulled her back to his side.

She looked at him with surprise on her face. "You still want me?" She asked innocently.

"Always," he answered. His arm snaked behind her pulling her close. She rested her head on his shoulder and fell asleep in warmth, love and with that warm fuzzy feeling that everything would be alright.

When she woke the next morning she was warm and still snuggled in his arms. She was resting on her side with his arm around her holding her naked breast. His breath was tickling the hair on the top of her head. She tried to wiggle out of his grip so not to wake him but the grip on her breast tightened, "Where do ya think ya are going?" Abby gave him an approving groan and said, "Good morning husband."

Gabe chuckled, "I like the sound of that wife."

They continued to cuddle together. Familiar hard warmth became quite evident against Abby's bum. "Oooooo," she whispered. "Oooooo is right lass." A moment later he slipped himself into her most warm part entering from behind.

Two hours later they strolled down to the hall to break their fast.

The hall was not empty however; six little people were waiting to greet their father and their new mother. They enjoyed a wonderful meal of sweet rolls, cheese, eggs and sausage. Afterward Gabriel announced that he would be leaving for a few days. The children were given strict instructions about their behavior while he was away. Abigail just looked disappointed. "What is that sad look for?" He asked her.

"Well, I was hoping we would have a little more time together," she whispered.

"OH, ya liked last night and this morning then?" He asked.

Abby face went red and Gabe laughed out loud. His laugh was so infectious. He was not inhibited at all and boomed his laugh not caring who heard him. Abby just smiled.

"Well pack a few things, lass. Ya're coming with me."

"I am?"

"Aye, I have ta pick up a new mare and my Da has offered his house ta us for a few days of privacy. Meet me in the barn in ten minutes. When Gabe left the room she quickly kissed and hugged each one of her new children and thanked them for adopting her and confessed how happy she was to be their new mother.

"What do we call ya? Mother?" Ian asked.

"What did you call you mother?" she asked.

"We called her Ma," Adam said.

"Well I do not want to be called Ma. That was her name and I am not here to replace her. She will always have that special spot in your lives. My children in the colonies call me Mom. I would really like that if that is alright with all of you. I know it is not Scottish but I would still like it."

The six children spoke amongst themselves and all agreed. Abby would be called Mom.

Then she said goodbye to all of them and went off to get ready for Gabe.

He was waiting for her in the courtyard with Joseph and Simon. "Have a good night?" Joseph asked teasing her.

"You should have told me and I would not have given you such a hard time," she scolded.

"Ya seem much happier this morning than when I found ya in your room before the wedding." Joseph said hoping she would spill a bedroom secret.

"If I look happy it's because I don't have to look at you today guarding my room," Abigail teased back not letting him get away with his goading.

Both Gabe and Simon broke out into laughter.

"She is only been in the family for twelve hours and she is already insulting me. Ya are going ta have ta control ya wife Gabe," Joseph said smiling.

Gabe swung onto Samson and then Joseph handed Abby up to him after tying her bag to the saddle.

"Donna be gone too long. Ya hear," Simon ordered.

"Keep the laird safe. Da will be staying here for a few days. If any trouble comes about, send word and I will return immediately," Gabe ordered. Then for his brothers eyes he reached up and grabbed Abigail's breast. She squeaked in surprise and Joseph and Simon rolled with laughter.

Gabe left with Abby but also took six men in case of any trouble from the McHale's. When they were out of sight of the laird Abby asked. "Will there be any more trouble from Jennifer now that I am married?"

"She will demand that the King turn ya over to England but now that ya a married ta his cousin, he will protect ya. If there is a problem still, he will let me know but he is confident that the incident will be forgotten, especially now that ya are as royal as she is and had every right ta protect ya family and home."

"You didn't marry me just to make me royal, did you?" Abby asked as she realized what he had just said.

"Ask me that question again and I swear I will tan ya hide. Donna ever doubt my love or the reason I married ya. Do ya hear me?" Then he gave her a tight squeeze to let her know he was serious.

"I'm sorry Gabe. I just had to ask," she said looking over her shoulder at him.

"Ya will not be asking that again."

They rode for a few more minutes and then Gabe said. "My whole family is coming ta the laird the day after Christmas. It is a tradition we honor each year. I am sure ya will not be playing any of your parlor games while they are here."

"You just had to bring that up. You could not just let it go," she teased. "Tell me is there a good set of stockades in this town we are going to?"

Gabe laughed and understood her meaning to well. "Are ya telling me ta behave or else?"

"Yes and don't forget it," she said smiling at him.

"Do you think they will like me?" she asked hoping he would make her feel a little more secure about them coming.

"No," was all he said.

"NO?" Abby said looking back at him.

"No they will love ya. Now turn around and behave."

They reached the town about two hours later. Gabe stabled his stallion and then took Abby for a walk through the market place.

"Why are we here?" Abby asked looking at the wares as they passed.

"There is something I need ta buy."

"Obviously," Abby said sarcastically. "What?"

"Ya will see," and he took her hand in his and kept walking. They rounded a corner and stopped at a goldsmith. Gabe walked right in dropping Abby's hand. He thought she was just behind him but when he turned to ask her a question she was gone. Panic set in and he quickly looked outside the door. He was relieved to see her just standing outside the goldsmith's waiting for him to come out.

She was busy watching the crowd and not paying any attention that she was alone. He was going to have to give her a little lecture later about this but for now he didn't want to spoil their day. His hand came out of the door, grabbed Abby's forearm and said "Ya too." And pulled her into the shop. When they came out Abigail was wearing a gold ring with the McKenzie fox and hounds carved in it. "It is so beautiful Gabe," she said humbly.

"Ya like it then?" he asked with a smile knowing very well she did.

"Do you know I never had a ring that I could call my own? This is my very first one. Thank you."

"Ya welcome lass," and he hugged her and kissed her 1…2…3… "One more stop and then we will go ta my father's home."

They strolled back to the stable where Gabe had left his horse and the men. Gabe walked into the barn to get his next surprise. When he turned around, she was not there again. He was going to have to really talk to her about her going off on her own. Gabe came back with the little mare to find Abigail standing at the fence watching the street entertainers. Gabe was thankful for his men who had spread out surrounding her in case of danger.

"Abigail," Gabe called getting her attention. She turned around with a start thinking something was wrong. There standing in front of her was Gabe leading the most precious mare Abby had ever seen. She was about fifteen hands high with a thick black mane and tail, chestnut in color with four black stockings and one white sock and a sweet white star on her forehead. Abby put her hands to her mouth and said to the mare, "Aren't you the most beautiful little thing I have ever seen." Then she reached out and stroked her velvet nose.

"Ya like her Abby?" Gabe asked still holding the reins.

"Oh yes, she is so sweet."

"Good, she is ya wedding present," Gabe said with a big smile.

Abby dropped her chin and did not smile. "What is it Abby? She is ta make ya happy not sad." But Abby and already started to look misty eyed. "I thought ya just said ya liked her."

"I do," Abby whispered trying not to let a tear fall.

"Than what is it lass? Talk ta me?"

"I have nothing for you," she cried.

"OH! lass," Gabe chuckled and pulled her into his arms and hugged her. His heart was melting and kissed her 1…2…3….as his men looked on with smiles.

"Ya are all that I ever wanted and will want or need," He said lovingly. "Now I donna want ta see those tears. I want ya happy. Are ya ready ta try her out?" Before she knew it, he had lifted her onto her new horse and plunked her in the saddle. He walked around and adjusted her stirrups giving her fair warning that this was where her feet belonged. After giving her the reins, he mounted his steed with the other men and started off to his father's house before anyone could identify them.

It took two hours to reach the old laird's house. Abby rode her new mare with ease. She was so comfortable to ride. Her gates were smooth and soft. That is when Abigail decided to name her Comfort Ann.

Gabe rode in the lead and Abby was surrounded by four men. One either each side and two in the rear. Gabe kept looking over his shoulder to see if Abby's feet were in the stirrups or under her backside. He was pleasantly surprised to see how she enjoyed her new horse and how easily she sat to her gates.

As they approached Gabe's father's house, one of the men spotted two riders coming up behind them. It was the McHales. Abby started to panic. "Relax lass, there is two of them and seven of us and ya. Just stay quiet. If they think we are hiding something we will get another visit later. Best ta put ya out in the open."

Lester road up to the group as if he were a long lost friend expecting to be asked for supper. "Hello Laird," Lester greeted. "I just was hoping ya would allow me ta look on ya land again for Abigail Fox?"

"Still looking for her?" Gabe said acting surprised. "Didn't I hear she was arrested and being sent to England or was that another Abigail?" He asked one of his men.

"I had not heard that Laird," Lester said as he was noticing Abigail sitting on her horse surrounded by guards. Gabe saw him look at her.

"Have ya met my wife, Lady McKenzie?" He asked hoping Abby would not give herself away with her accent. But as always Abby surprised him, "Please ta meet ya sir. I have only known one other person by that name and he was my uncle and homely as they come," she said in a perfect Scottish accent. Then Lester said something in Gaelic hoping to trip her up but Abby surprised herself. She actually understood what he asked and answered him in English. Both Gabe and the men were thrilled with her performance. "We must be going Lester. Ya have my permission ta scout the land one more time, but I will be having guests and they will not like a stranger on the grounds. Ya can look for two more days and then I'm afraid I will ask ya not ta look again."

"Two days will have ta do and I thank ya for ya hospitality." Then he said goodbye and again addressed Abigail in Gaelic. Abby this time answered him back in French.

When the McHales were long gone, Gabe said, "Abigail, ya just had ta do it. Ya couldn't resist and when did ya start speaking Gaelic and French?"

"Abby blushed and said. "This might be a shock to you but I have heard Gaelic every day since I came into Scotland. You would have to be a blooming idiot not to know "good morning and I like your horse."

"Well I guess ya are not a blooming idiot because that is exactly what he said, but if ya ever do that again I will deal with ya afterwards. There is no need ta take chances like that. What if he asked ya something else ya did not know? Ya were lucky this time but I guarantee if he finds us again he will be more selective with his questions," Gabe warned.

"Then I best be learning more Gaelic," Abby said with a little huff. Gabe knew he had upset her so he said. "Abigail McKenzie are ya not trusting that I might know what I am talking about." Then Abby realized she had been a little sharp with him. "I did not mean to endanger anyone I am sorry."

"Abby, we are only protecting ya. Donna be so defensive. No harm done."

"This time," Abby said under her breath.

They reached Philip's house just before dark. Gabe dismounted and helped Abby down then he surprised her with a swat on her bum. "What was that for?" she asked holding her backside. "That is for the comment under ya breathe, donna ya think I did not hear it."

Abby blushed and gave him just a little innocent smile. Then he shook his finger at her as he led the horses into the barn. The six men Gabe brought with them spread out around the walls with the other men. Gabe was not taking any chances. She was too valuable to him to lose her now but he planned to give her a short lecture when they were alone.

"Where are the servants?" Abby asked when no one opened the door for them.

"We have the house ta ourselves for three days and I plan on taking advantage of every square inch of it. But right now I am hungry." They went down to the kitchen to find a stew simmering on the stove and fresh bread. A pot had already been sent out to the men leaving Abby and Gabe privacy for dinner. "Take off ya clothes," he ordered.

"What?"

"Ya heard me. Take off ya clothes."

"Here and now in the kitchen?" Abby asked surprised he would ask such a thing.

"We seem ta have a trust issue ta overcome and this is how I intend ta get ya ta trust me. Now take off ya clothes." He ordered.

He watched as she did as he asked. When she was completely naked she went to stand by the fire. "Are going to take off all of your clothes?"

""NO"

"Why not? She asked indignantly.

"Ya are going ta learn ta trusts me. Plus I want ta see ya in the kitchen with nothing but an apron on and ya can plan on me fondling ya the whole time," he said with a devilish grin.

"I do trust you," Abby insisted.

"Really, did ya not stay with me all day and never let yourself be alone?"

"I was right outside the barn and smithies almost in your sight," Abby protested.

"And the little stunt ya pulled with the McHales, do ya wish ta explain that one?" Gabe said keeping the lecture he wanted to give her at minimum. "I know ya are independent and that is one of the things I love about ya, but until I know all the secrets in that head of yours I need ta make sure ya are safe. I donna know what ya are afraid of but I know I best be on my toes when it comes ta helping ya. Ya told me once that ya couldn't tell me things because they were only for ya husband, but if ya donna trust me ya will not tell me, husband or not. I am not Roy and ya are not my first wife, but we will be together a long time and hopefully we will do better the second time around. What do ya say?"

Abby stood with her backside warming by the fire naked from her head to her toes. "You are asking a lot of me but I know you are right. Just remember trust works two ways. And if I am expected to trust you then you are expected to trust me. Now take off your clothes and I plan on fondling you as well."

Gabe had been beat at his own game. He slipped his clothes off as she watched and dished out the stew. Then they sat at the kitchen table naked and ate their supper answering each other's questions. Then he chased her upstairs threatening her with a good ass slap when he caught her.

The night was spent with the same loving passion as the night before. Abby always went to sleep thoroughly exhausted and well satisfied as did Gabe.

CHAPTER 28
They Have Come

When morning came, Gabe was walking around the room undressed. Abby lay in bed while he tended the fire and then prepared the bath. She lay in bed warm and contented until she noticed, lying on the floor, near the bath were three sponges.

"Are you sure we are alone?" Abby asked devilishly.

"Aye, lass, the servants have been asked ta stay away while we are here."

"Are you sure?"

"Aye."

That was all it took, the sponges were too much of a temptation. Slowly she slipped out of the bed so not to arouse attention from her soon to be victim.

Silently she dressed into her shift and tiptoed over to the tub. Slowly she dipped each sponge into the warm water and waited until she had the perfect target. Her victim was not paying any attention to her and started to bend over to pick up his kilt. SPLAT….. A wet sponge hit her target, Gabe's backside. "OH lass! Ya shouldn…….." SPLAT in the face, then SPLAT she got him again straight to the chest leaving him dripping with water on both sides.

Abigail giggled then ran for dear life, out of their room and down the hall toward the stairs giggling the whole time. She squealed when she turned to look over her shoulder to see a huge nude man charging down the hall after her.

She slid down the railing listening to the pounding of Gabe's feet as he descended down the staircase after his assailant. Abby leaped off the banister and landed on her feet and turned left to the kitchen where she would find more ammunition. She could just see the doorway to the kitchen when he caught her. "Ya should not have done that Lass now ya will pay for ya're crime." He teased. Abby let out a loud shrill when he lifted her up and threw her over his shoulder. She reached down and playfully paddled his naked bum.

"OH Lass, ya should not have done that either." It was then that Abby realized that the hem of her shift was hanging over her head leaving her backside completely exposed. SLAP… "Ooooo" she said as he spanked her bum teasingly. "And that is not all ya are going ta get."Gabe threatened. He carried her back to the front door almost reaching the staircase when his father walked into the house to see his naked son carrying his new daughter-in-law over his shoulder with her backside all exposed.

"Hello Da," Gabe said not acting at all embarrassed or surprised to see him. "Staying long?"

"No son. Like ya, I came ta pick something up. I'll be leaving right after I enjoy the view." Philip said smiling as Gabe and Abby passed by.

"That's good Da," Gabe said nonchalantly continuing to walk without slowing his stride. Abigail was trying to cover her backside with her hands but Gabe kept pushing them away. "Gabriel Alexander Patrick McKenzie," Abby scolded.

"Excuse me Da, I need ta take care of a very naughty wife," Gabe said chuckling.

The old laird began to laugh hysterically and Gabe joined in as he carried her up the stairs. Philip could not resist embarrassing her just a little more, "Ya are looking very pretty this morning Abigail."

"I'm glad you think so," Abby said covering her face with her hands to hide her embarrassment. "Close the door on your way out won't you? Thank you." And with that Gabe rounded the top of the stairs disappearing out of the old laird's view. Philip left his house still chuckling at what he'd just saw. It seemed so good to see his son laugh again. Abby had made his son happy.

"Am I going ta have ta make ya stand in the corner?" Gabe said to his wife as he returned her to the bed chamber. "And I donna believe I gave ya permission ta put ya clothes back on, now did I?" He said dropping her to her feet. "Now take it off," he commanded still playing her game. Abby did as she was told and stood in front of him with that devilish look on her face she had earlier. He wasn't sure what she was up to but so far he was enjoying her antics.

"If I kiss you, will I have to stand in the corner?" She asked with a sheepish smile.

"I will think about it," Gabe said waiting for her next move.

"How about here?" She asked and then kissed him on his nipple. "Or how about here?" And she kissed his other side. "Or here?" And she started to work down his chest. "I have always wondered what it would feel like to kiss you… here." And Gabe gritted his teeth as she made sensations run through his body.

"The ladies at James' manor talked about this," and she heard him groan in the back of his throat.

"Lass if ya keep doing that I will not ever put ya in a corner again," Gabe said weak in the knees.

"Am I forgiven then?" She asked a little while later.

"Maybe we should play that sponge game again some time," Gabe said with a smile.

The next few days were wonderful. They enjoyed each other often. Abby cooked for Gabe as he watched her in the kitchen, usually undressed. Gabe was getting very good at throwing wet sponges. Their three days were going much too fast.

On the last day, Gabe was getting the horses ready when Joseph and Cookie came storming into the yard. Gabe was needed back at the laird. A large group of heavily armed, very strangely dressed men showed up in the field in front of the laird threatening to attack. When Joseph left to get Gabe, the strange men were making camp out in the field despite warning shots from the guards on the walls. The woman and children were all safe inside Fuchsiall and the walls were well armed with men and the drawbridge was in the up position. Joseph thought nothing would happen until Gabe came back but they would have to ride very hard.

When Abby came out of the house she heard Joseph's voice but could not quite understand what they were saying. "We need to go back now and fast," was all Gabe would say. Before she could ask any questions she was plopped on her new horse and they were headed in a dead run toward Gabe's house. Abby's new mare had little trouble keeping up with Gabe's stallion and as usual Abby was surrounded by the guards. Joseph kept a watchful eye on Abby from behind her in case she tired. Gabe did not want to slow down and he was not letting her stay behind. Comfort Ann had such smooth gates that Abby rode her with ease tiring less quickly.

Abigail's head was full of thoughts to what was wrong. She was almost sure it had something to do with the children. Hopefully one was not hurt.

Along the way home the men spoke Gaelic as if to keep her from finding out what the problem was. Although she was trying to be understanding, she found it very rude not to speak English. She hated being left out. They road fast and never stopped. What usually took two hours to get from one house to the other, Gabe managed to make it in half the time.

As they were about to come in view of the laird, Abby's heart sank to a new low. About fifty well armed men, wearing animal skins speaking in a strange tongue surrounded them on all sides. They were large men all towering over six feet. Gabe and his seven men, equal to their size were out numbered and he could not call on any help from his laird, they were too far away. This ambush was well planned and these men were skilled worriors. They had purposely shown themselves at the laird to draw Abby into the open and it had succeeded.

The head man drew his sword and said, "Dismount please." Gabe and the others had no choice but to follow the order. "And you too Empress."

Gabe looked at Abby and did not say a word.

"Bind and gag them all and make sure the leathers are tight."

"We have been looking for you for a long time Empress Abigailia and your box and now we have you both. It is such a pleasure to finally meet the last blood empress and survivor of Mania," the headman said with a sinister smile.

"I sent you that damn box delivered by my captain when I was imprisoned in England. You do not need me as well and I am not an Empress. I do not have a country anymore because you destroyed it and all the occupants," Abby sputtered. "You have what you wanted now be gone with all of you."

"You are mistaken Empress. We do so need you to translate the gibberish you call language. I hope for your sake that your grandfather taught you your native tongue. It is a dead language and so is your country and so will you be if you fail," the headman said standing inches away from her face.

"And if I do not fail, what then will I be free to go?" Abby asked knowing what the answer was but she wanted Gabe to understand what she was up against.

"Then we will kill you. Either way once we have the treasure. Your life will be worthless to us unless my father chooses to use you for enjoyment purposes."

Then he took an interest in Gabriel and his men. "Who are these men you ride with?" the headman asked.

"He is my owner," Abby answered.

"You are his slave? Have you risen from an Empress to a lowly slave? How perfect," the headman sneered.

"Yes, I owe him a great debt and for that he has my life in his hands," Abby answered hiding the fact that Gabe was her husband.

"Kill them all," the headman ordered.

"You best think twice before you do that sir," Abby said quickly.

"Why? Does he have a large enough army to defeat my whole country in revenge?" The headman asked and then laughed.

"It is your law, if I am not mistaken, not to steal a slave from another man. A crime I believe that is punishable by death and your law does not have boundaries. Kill these men and I will testify to your father that you stole me from them and he will not disappoint me. You would not be the first son your father has put to death for such a crime," Abby said with an air only a true Empress could conduct.

"How do you know about our laws and my brother?"

"My grandfather taught me well. He always said knowledge is the best weapon of all," Abby answered.

"I could still kill them and no one would be the wary," the headman said smugly.

"You have fifty or so witnesses. Aren't your people known for their blackmail skills? Just think what they could ask of you to keep their tongues from wagging," Abby said with the same sinister smile he had just shown her.

The man knew she was correct and he did not want to take that chance of someone betraying him for his position or his life.

"Very well Empress, I will give them their lives as payment for you. Surely you are worth eight men's lives although I highly doubt it."

Gabe knew what she was doing. Abigail was selling herself to save him and his men. He stood bound and gagged not able to help her. All he could do was watch as they took her from him.

"Just how far south is your country? I have never been there and I would like to prepare myself for the journey." Abby asked hoping he would give Gabe the direction of his island.

"I guess your grandfather did not teach you as well as you think, you stupid witch. My island is north not south and it will take about one week," he snickered.

"One week?" Abby asked hoping to give Gabe more information. "Aren't we going through the pass? It will cut off at least three days? The ships my grandfather built always sailed through the pass using fourteen foot poles to keep them in the middle providing safe passage."

"We do not have a ship your grandfather built. My ship is much too large to mess with that damn pass," the headman said again unknowingly giving Gabe insight to how he could cut him off before he reached his island. Abby was giving him the way to go and how to catch him.

"That is too bad," Abby said again trying to get him to divulge more information. "I take it than that you do not need cannons either?"

"I have six cannons on either side, unlike your grandfather's ships who could only house four on a side. I always thought it strange that he would keep them in the bottom of the ship instead of on the deck where they could be used."

"He used their weight to stabilize the ship. It sailed better through the water." Abby answered again giving Gabe knowledge to where the cannons where hidden and how to get the most sail out of her ship.

"Enough of this stupid conversation," the headman ordered angrily. "You are only biding time in hopes that someone will see you and rescue you. It will not work Empress. You have been captured and will sail with us now before the tide prevents us safe passage."

The man gagged her so she could not give Gabe anymore information. Her hands were tied behind her back and her feet were bound together. One large Wik hoisted her over his shoulder allowing the moment she needed to look into Gabe's eyes. In that second Abby could see the anger Gabe was concealing and the determination that he would come for her. Then the men disappeared into the trees just as the McHales left their hiding place. Both Gabe and Joseph saw the McHales leave on their horses at a full gallop heading south toward England. Abigail was in deep trouble from both the Wikings and now Black Dog.

It wasn't long before Gabe and his men were rescued by his clansmen. Samson had been let go and he had returned to Fuchsiall alerting the clan of danger.

Abigail's ship was safely tucked in a cove two days away, ready to sail at a moment's notice. Once Gabe had informed his father of his plans, he headed out to find Abby's ship. He needed his brother Dunkin.

Dunkin was the sailor in the family. Gabe had sent him to the colonies to bring back Abby children to Scotland. He was due back any time, but Gabe could not waste precious time to wait for him. Sailing the vessel was going to be a challenge, but no one could talk him out of it. Gabe was hoping he would pick up a captain on his way to the ship but he was not counting on it. Abby had little time and he was not wasting a second. Gabe had sailed with Dunkin from time to time and could sail, but he did not have the experience of a running a ship all on his own. This would not deter him from departing.

The Wikings carried Abby to their ship, which was well hidden in a cove just south of Gabe's land. Abby had never seen a ship as the Wiking's. The vessel itself was quite large with only two sails, one large red and white striped and a smaller sail at the bow. Abby counted at least twenty oars protruding from the side of the ship. This ship was heavy and sat flat in the water making it slow moving giving Gabe a chance to catch her.

Abby was so hoping that Gabe understood all the information she had inconspicuously given him and would come and rescue her soon. She had also seen the McHales and was sure she would be pursued by the pirates as well. Her hope was that Gabe had seen them too. Abby also feared that Gabe might end up between the pirates and the Wikings. Either way Abby knew she was in trouble even worse than before and Gabe was her only hope.

She started counting the many ways her life had been in danger the last few months: one, my first husband died, two, pirates, three, prison, four, James, five, Gabriel, six, Wikings and seven, the pirates again. Each time she thought it could not get any worse she was proven wrong.

The only good thing that she could agree upon was marring Gabe, but at first Gabe was as bad as James. That thought gave her some hope that maybe this too would turn out alright as well.

All these years, Abby believed that the box was her answer. She thought that giving it to her enemies would free her from the constant pursuit. Tired of hiding and protecting a treasure she was not sure even existed, Abby was willing to give it all away for a chance for freedom.

Her grandfather had been right. As long as she had the box she would be safe. Now she was on her way tied and gagged to a certain death. Safe was not what she wanted anymore. She wanted the freedom from the constant predators. Abby wanted her childhood dream of a pink castle nestled on a hillside next to the ocean with her loving husband and twelve children.

The large Wik Abby was riding on carried her onto the strange vessel and then down to the underbelly of the ship, which was dark and smelling of old water, and dead rotting fish. He turned left and entered a very small cabin just large enough for a bunk and chamber pot. He dumped her down on the bunk with a hard thump. He did not loosen her restraints or allow her to tend her needs but shut the door and locked it leaving her in total darkness listening to the waves hit the side of the ship.

It wasn't long before Abby could feel the vessel rock with the ocean waves, letting her know they were underway. She had nothing else to do but listen and think. Abby could hear the squeak of the oars as they rocked back and forth propelling the ship into uncharted waters, kept in unison by the constant beating of a large drum. All she could think of was the primitive men that had taken her. These were the ones that had conquered her native country chasing her royal ancestors into hiding and destroying ever inch of her homeland, Mania.

These men had not changed in hundreds of years. Somehow time had stopped for them. The Wikings spoke a dead language and never progressed into the nineteenth century but the headman could speak English very well. Their weapons were as primitive as they were, using knives and swords much shorter than the highlanders. Skilled as they were in battle, the Wikings would be no match for modern weapons.

Abby had a hard time staying in the bunk now which meant they were way out to sea. Her leather restraints were cutting into her wrists and ankles each time she bounced back and forth in her bunk. She was frightened, alone and helpless, unable to defend herself and completely at the mercy of her captures. Abby laid thinking of Gabriel, her children, his children and Scotland. She tried to keep her hopes up, but finally the tears puddled in her eyes causing her to cry uncontrollably. Eventuallt she drifted off into sleep.

It seemed like hours later that the door finally opened and a lantern with someone carrying it, entered. Abby's eyes had a hard time adjusting to the light and could not see who had entered the cabin. She could feel her leg restraints loosening and then a male voice said, "Tend your needs so I can leave." It was the headman. A large chamber pot was placed on the floor in front of her. It was a challenge with her hands still tied but she managed it anyway. When she was finished, she was pushed back into her bunk with her feet tied to the opposite bed posts. She was given some water, but no food. Her mouth was gagged again before she could ask any questions.

Abby laid there for hours in the darkness, drifting in and out of sleep not knowing what time of day it was. Each time she dosed off she would have the same dream...

She was standing on the deck with the wind blowing in her hair looking into the sun, but someone was whispering .... ' The answer was in back of you not in front of you...'

Back in Scotland, Gabe was racing on Samson with his men on his heels toward Abigail's ship. He had found some of her charts in her things, all mapped out leading him toward the Wiking's island. Hoping for some McKenzie luck to come his way, Gabe turned the corner to find Dunkin coming up the road with Abby's four children and his crew.

There was a quick introduction and an explanation. Hannah, Abby's daughter was sent back to the laird with a small escort of men. Abby's sons joined the search for their mother. Abigail's twins were very good sailors and Gabe was happy to have them aboard plus it gave them a chance to get to know each other. This was not the way he wanted to do it, but it would have to do for now.

Dunkin had left his ship just south of Abigail's, but it was in need of supplies which delayed the departure one day. Gabe took advantage of this day to make sure his ship was loaded with the poles Abby spoke of and to look over her charts with Dunkin. Abby loved to sail and was very meticulous with her details and charts. Her charts were clear and well documented making them easy to follow. Dunkin was sure they could catch them without any trouble, but he felt his ship was too large for the pass and would need to go around like the Wikings.

As they were waiting for the ships to get ready, Gabe received word that the pirate Black Dog was sighted heading in the direction of Wik. It would now be a race for time.

Early the next morning Gabe set sail in The Lady Fox and Dunkin was on his ship just behind him. Abigail's twin sons, Stephan and Daniel were onboard with Gabe while Ellery, her eldest rode with Dunkin. The wind was definitely in their favor and pushed them in good time north to the pass. Abigail's twins turned out to be full of piss and vinegar. Gabe found himself the blunt of one of their jokes from time to time. However Gabe was able to retaliate, which really surprised the twins.

When the ships were in sight of the cliffs, Dunkin turned to go around while Gabe took Abby's ship through. The pass was carved in a set of very high cliffs not visible from the sea. A ship had to know where it was from a chart or they would not be able to find it. When the water was calm the cliffs allowed passage through the landmass cutting off days of sea travel. In Abigail's charts, Gabe found exact coordinances leading to the opening of the passage. Abigail had told Gabe to use fourteen poles to keep the ship in the center of the crevasse.

As The Lady Fox came closer to the cliffs it looked like Abby was wrong. No one could see any opening but they could see the wave's splash against the rocks with great force. The men were concerned that the ship would surely perish if they did not turn and go around with Dunkin.

Gabe gave the order to drop sails and then the crew carefully rowed closer to the treacherous cliffs. The water swirled pushing the ship into a current that they could not break out of. Once they started there was no turning back. The water was black and said to be near bottomless. Echoes of the waves hitting the sides bounced through the walls making sounds like the sea was singing to the sailors.

Then just as Gabe was about to change his mind and try to go back, Joseph sighted a small black opening. The men held the poles out, pushing the ship to the center of a small cave. The passage was so small that Gabe wondered if the ship could fit. Gabe sent Joseph up in the crow's nest to watch for jetting rocks from the ceiling while seven poles on each side of the ship kept it safe from hitting the sharp jagged rock which claimed many a vessel in the past. Remnants of past failures lined the passage with debris. Slowly, they inched through the pass in silence, listening to the echoes and watching for dangerous rock formations.

The pass itself was over two miles long, but it was the only chance Gabe had to catch up with Abby and worth the risk. Gabe kept his men focused on their task, even through the water which fell from the highest parts of the cliffs drenching everyone and everything.

It seemed like hours before the Lady Fox had made it through the cliffs. Gabe had a new respect for Abby's grandfather. The ship was made perfectly to stay in the center of the pass and the masts were just short enough to miss the rocks which jetted out at the top of the cliffs. Her grandfather must have taken measurements to design his ships special so they could use this pass.

Abby had mentioned he was a great sailor and this was definitely one of the areas he sailed and sailed often. She never knew if there really was a treasure but after sailing through this pass, Gabe decided that the treasure was the only thing that would have encouraged her grandfather to build ships that could fit in here. He had a good reason for sailing through this pass and the treasure must be the reason. Even the cannons in the belly of the ship were strategically placed to keep the ship more stable and easier to maneuver in such a tight place.

Finally there was the end in sight. Rays of sun streamed through the end opening encouraging the men to push harder on the poles to escape their tight quarters. As the Lady Fox exited the cavern, wave surrounded them causing the ship to sway violently. From the spy glass, Gabe could see the Wiking ship off in front of them. He gave the order to raise the sails and the chase was on.

The waves were high and it was difficult for the ship to escape from the land but Abby had left strict instructions to set full sails which would do the trick. Then from the crow's nest, Joseph sighted another ship and it was not Dunkin. A black flag with skull and crossbones flew from her mast. Gabe gave the order to raise the cannons from the belly and set them to be ready to fire but he was too far away to catch either ship at this point.

CHAPTER 29
I Will Never Let You Go

Gabe watched helpless as Black Dog gained on the Wiking's slow moving vessel. It was a ship of the past, way out dated and the design never used anymore because of its inability for speed and maneuverability. Even with the Wiking's cannons, it was no match for the larger faster pirate ship.

The pirate ship used its speed to gain on the Wiking ship and would reach her way before Gabe could help. Helplessly, The Lady Fox watched from afar as the pirate ship came up on the Wikings vessel. Cannons were fired causing great damage to the Wiking's ship and then the Black Dog was close enough to board. Gabe could see the pirates fighting with the Wikings as their rowing ship started to sink into the sea.

The Wikings with their six cannons on a side and their primitive weapons inflicted little damage to the Black Dog. The pirates were experienced in overtaking a ship and had managed to stay clear of cannon fire. But the Wikings were not so skilled. Their ship was slowly submerging into the icy water.

Gabe watched to see if he could see Abigail. He knew that they were after her, and that box, and they were both on that ship. One was not much good without the other so Gabe was pretty sure they would take Abby on board and he was right. Two men came out of the hull carrying a box and then two more were leading Abby. Gabe almost laughed to see two grown men having such a hard time to get Abigail on their ship. She was giving them quite a fight.

When Black Dog had Abby on board, they hoisted their sails, leaving their victims to be claimed by the sea and came about, leading the Lady Fox to another chase. Abby's ship was just as fast as the pirate ship but they could not gain any ground. Gabe would just have to follow them at the same distance. Dunkin would be in sight in a day or two and then maybe they could sandwich her in. Gabe's brother was very familiar with the pirate ship having had a conflict with it from time to time. He had been lucky. Never had he been boarded and always managed to out run Black Dog. Gabe was hoping that his brother's ship would be fast enough to come up on her now.

As the Lady Fox passed the sinking Wiking ship not a single person was alive in the water. The pirates had left no witnesses. Gabe was hoping the Wikings would believe that Abby and the box too went into the sea and she would finally be free of the constant hunt for her treasure from the men that conquered her country.

***

When Abby boarded the pirate ship, she was brought to a cabin in the aft of the vessel. The door was locked behind her, but first they untied her from her leather restraints. She sat on the bunk looking out of a small porthole just big enough to see her ship coming up from behind. Tears streamed down her face to see Gabe coming after her. She was amazed to see how skilled the ship was being sailed. If she did not know any better, she would guess it was being sailed by one of her own twins. They sailed just like her. But they were safe in the colonies so there was no chance of that. Gabe must be a very good seaman and did not tell her.

Abby stayed in the cabin until dinnertime when a knock sounded on her door. She heard the key enter the lock and the door swung open. A large round sailor with a gold earring in one ear and a black and white striped shirt was standing in the doorway. "The Captain wishes you to come and eat dinner in the Captain's cabin," the seaman said.

"And if I refuse?" Abigail asked.

"You will not refuse lady. You do not have a choice. Come with me and do not give me any trouble." He reached out and grabbed

Abby's arm and pulled her out of her cabin and then led her to the Captain's quarters. He knocked on the door. Abby was surprised to hear a woman's voice answer. Abby had always suspected who Black Dog really was and now she knew her suspicions were correct before the door even opened. "Come in Abigail," the woman said.

"Elizabeth Shaw," Abby greeted, "how nice to see you again."

"Have a seat Abby. We have a lot to catch up on," Elizabeth greeted.

Without saying a word, Abby walked to the table in the center of the cabin and sat down. Looking around, Abby was amazed how ornate the cabin was decorated. Elizabeth had very expensive items, stolen no doubt. There was an oriental rug on the floor and the large oak bed on the far wall. The table was hand carved with a thick wooden top polished so that you could use it like a mirror. An ornate marble chess set sat on a small table near the door and an armoire full of gowns rested in the corner.

Elizabeth wanted for nothing even the wine she served was expensive. The two women sat facing each other as the porter carried in two trays of food consisting of roast duck, mashed potatoes and green beans. Abby was so hungry. The Wikings did not feed her and it had been three days since she had had a bite to eat. She really did not want to eat but she needed to keep up her strength.

"Are you surprised to see me in the Captain's cabin and not Niles?" Elizabeth asked starting a conversation with Abigail.

"No," was all Abby would say and continued to eat.

"Aren't you curious?" Elizabeth asked again.

"Not really," Abby said after she swallowed. "I figured out that you were the one making the business deals not Niles when I rode with you to Boston and my captain and I discussed the events of our journey many times on our voyage to England." Then Abby looked up from her dinner and asked, "Would you like me to go on?"

Elizabeth raised her wine glass and nodded her head. So Abby continued, "I found it most interesting that you were waiting so conveniently outside the bank to offer me a ride all the way to Boston. The very place I wanted to go. Oh I must say you were quite convincing using the Christian persona but I was brought up to trust no one and certainly not a gift horse like you.

Mr. Pinkerton was most knowledgeable about my box and was waiting for the day someone would claim it. When I opened the box in the bank, some of my papers were not put back the way I left them, which led me to believe he had been looking in it or someone else like you and the key had been duplicated. Some clay was still on the handle. Too bad you did not know what the key opened."

"I'm impressed," Elizabeth said toasting Abby with her wine glass.

"I found it so unusual," Abby continued, "that you never asked me about the box. Anyone who ever saw it would inquire about the carvings if nothing else. But you seemed to be bored with it as if you had seen it many times and were more interested in me. The truth is that I really liked you as a friend. I had a hard time convincing myself that you were Black Dog but when you spend time in prison as I did you have a lot of time to think. There was no other answer I could think of. It made me laugh to hear England was looking for a man. I really wanted to set them straight but I was a little upset they put me in prison so I held my tongue."

"I am curious to hear more of your deductions, please continue," Elizabeth ordered still enjoying her roast duck.

"Why was it that you could not accompany me the first day we arrived in Boston?" Abby asked Elizabeth but did not wait for her to answer. "The answer was easy. You could not be connected with me at the docks. Those four men that trailed me that day were working for you weren't they?" Abby asked.

"Very good Abby, please go on."

"They could have over taken me at any time but instead they herded me like a sheep going to slaughter into the only business opened on the entire side of the docks. They waited for me to come out and did not even attempt to attack me. That was when I realized that Mr. Webber and Mr. Washburn had something to do with those men as well. I happened to see Mr. Webber nod their way when we came out of the office.

The next time you stage an office the least you can do is make it more believable. The couch was dusty and no one had sat on it in a very long time. The charts were out dated and the actors in the office were less than convincing. Mr. Washburn was sweating so badly that his white hanky he used to wipe his head was completely drenched and any company in that much financial trouble would never leave a potential customer waiting for that length of time."

"Why did you go along with the charade if you new?" Elizabeth asked curiously.

"At first I really did not put two and two together and when I saw my grandfather's ship I was willing to over look all the warning signs. It was more important to me to have that particular ship and you knew that too didn't you?" Elizabeth nodded and smiled deviously.

"What you were not planning on was me hiring my own Captain and firing yours or filling my ship with cargo. Did you ever find out what I filled it with?" Abby asked.

"Actually I tried but you left no trail," Elizabeth admitted.

"Martin was my friend and you killed him didn't you?" Abby asked changing the subject all of a sudden.

Elizabeth was taken aback with surprise that Abby knew she had her captain killed but she was not going to lie to her. She still needed Abigail to cooperate and was trying to get her on her side.

"Martin was the one who saw us coming out of the Debtor's prison that day. We were so close to capturing you from the prison, but James got to you first. James is a very dangerous man and always was discrete with his purchases in case he needed to destroy them, so the guards were not about to get on his bad side. The jailers would not divulge your owner to us even when I tried to bribe them and threatened bodily harm. Unfortunately we had to kill a few guards but they still would not talk. All sales were confidential and that made finding you very difficult." Elizabeth took another sip of her wine and then continued.

"Martin managed to elude us that day and sailed out of England, but he hovered around London waiting for any word about you. My men finally caught up with him as he was trailing you in Scotland. They were unable to get information from him about you and finally had to eliminate him. We were the ones, however who anchored your ship and searched it extensively but could not find the box. I hope we did not leave it to messy for you," Elizabeth said with a smile showing no remorse for killing Martin and the prison guards. "Tell me Abigail how did you know that I was responsible for Martin's death?"

Abby's stomach was beginning to turn. Martin was her friend and he had died to save her. He was coming to get her and warn her about Elizabeth. Abby watched him from high up in that tree. He was brutally beaten, killed then fed to wolves, all under her tree and in full view. "I was the one in the tree your men thought to be a man. I saw everything." Abby finally said staring directly into Elizabeth's eyes with such hate that Elizabeth had to glance away.

"You are the luckiest person I have ever met," Elizabeth said turning back to look at Abby again. "You have avoided capture at every step of my plan. I was not planning on England making you responsible for the W & W Shipping Companies' misgivings. That prison saved your life and so did your purchase by James, but the best one was that McKenzie. He kept us from you best of all. He messed up with the Wikings. Finally our luck had changed. McKenzie was very suspicious of the McHales and would not let them on his land without an escort of his men. We could not get anywhere near you. I do hope he treated you well. He even recruited his neighbors to help him. They are very dedicated to him and gave us a hard time as well."

"So now what are you after from me?" Abby asked trying to hide her disgust and anger.

"It is simple my dear. I want what everyone wants from you, your treasure and I will have it. I know it is real and I will stop at nothing to get it. I am a little distracted right now with that bastard McKenzie. I am afraid that I am going to have to sink that ship and I really do not want to do that. I still think that ship has something to do with the treasure but I cannot let him catch me now can I?"

Then Elizabeth went on, "Now that those stupid Wikings are no longer a threat, I will have to take care of that thorn in my side McKenzie. Do you know that he was the one that informed England, France, and Germany of my whereabouts, but he did not share your knowledge of Black Dog's true captain? They were always looking for a man making it easy for me to go into those countries and retrieve information of valuable shipments. But they increased their watch for me, which made it harder to overtake the ships all because of McKenzie." Elizabeth saw Abby yawn and said, "I see that you are ready to return to your cabin. Let me make you understand something. I have given you a private cabin and no one will attack you, but do not cross me or I will not hesitate to let my men have their way with you." Elizabeth raised her wine glass toasting Abigail.

Abby was not about to let her attack the Scots especially her husband. "Let me make you understand something as well, Elizabeth. I will give you one piece of information which will help you get closer to the treasure you so desperately want," Abby said and lifted her own wine glass. "It is impossible to retrieve the treasure without that ship. So do remember that when you are shooting at her and the Wikings will send another ship as soon as they figure out that one is missing. Hopefully they will think I went down with the ship along with my box, but this is unlikely, as they have not stopped in one hundred years. What makes you so sure they will stop now?" Then Abby rose and a man escorted her back to her cabin where she wept for Martin.

The next day Abby rose and looked out of her porthole. She wanted to see if Gabe was still behind her, but she could not see him anywhere. Where did he go she thought, maybe he is on the other side of the ship where she could not see him. Frantically she tried to look through the porthole but could not get a glimpse of him anywhere. "He is not out there," Elizabeth said from behind her. Abby turned around to see her old friend standing with the door opened holding her box. "It is time you go to work."

Elizabeth handed Abby her box and watched as she opened it. It was a magnificently carved box adorned with carvings that kept the box safe from unwanted predators. However, Mr. Pinkerton found a way to open the box and Abigail was certain that Elizabeth knew as well. Abby slowly lifted the contents out and carefully laid them down on her bunk. Elizabeth watched as Abby unfolded charts and maps and a scroll handwritten in Abigail's native tongue. "I will need a quill, ink and parchment," Abby ordered refusing to look up at Elizabeth, "and a table to write on. Don't think it will be done today either. It will take me a while to translate all these documents."

"You do not know what they say already?" Elizabeth asked surprised.

"Unlike you, I have only seen the contents of this box once before when I received it after my grandfather died. I had no need or wish to translate this until now but without that ship the information is worthless." Abby sputtered trying to find out what she did to Gabe if anything.

"You mustn't worry so about the McKenzie. I have not harmed him as yet. I do realize I will need that ship so I have just disappeared from his view until you are finished with your task. When I am ready I will take the ship and kill them all and you and I will go find my treasure," Elizabeth hissed as she laughed.

"Do not underestimate Gabriel McKenzie," Abby sputtered back. "He is not to be trifled with. You have met your match madam and then some. I will enjoy watching him vest you." Then Abby decided to let another piece of information come out. "Is Niles joining you in his ship soon? You will certainly need two ships to hall the treasure." Abby watched the expression on Elizabeth's face change from cunning to surprise.

"How did you know I had two ships?" Elizabeth asked through her clenched teeth.

Abby really did not know if there was enough treasure for two ships or if there was a treasure at all, but she loved to get a rise out of Elizabeth and this was working. Rarely had Elizabeth been seen with her other ship by her side but Martin had informed Abby that there was more than one ship, which is why the authorities could never charge her with anything. Elizabeth had been very clever but Abby was watching her as she divulged her secrets. "I am not the only one that has secrets am I Elizabeth? Too bad yours are out in the open."

Elizabeth was not sure if Abby was baiting her or not, but she had to know what Abby was talking about. "Do not play this game with me. You will not win. If you really did know something else, surely you would tell me."

"Where is Niles right now?" Abby asked trying to change the subject, but Elizabeth took it the wrong way. "Nile has been captured?" Elizabeth asked.

"I am not saying anything like that, you misunderstand. Now if you want me to continue with this box you must find me a table, quill, ink and parchment," Abby said giving Elizabeth the feeling she did not want to tell her anything else. As Elizabeth was leaving Abby said, "I do so hope Niles will be here soon. We are going to need that ship."

Elizabeth was no fool and she knew Abigail wasn't either. Abby had figured out things about Elizabeth that no one new including the slaying of Martin her captain. Now Abby would have to die. She knew too much about Black Dog and could very well lead her enemies to her.

Black Dog was spending too much time in the north and Elizabeth was getting nervous. She feared her enemies would be coming upon her. Abigail was making progress but had not finished her translations. A storm was moving into the area which would cause longer delays. She had managed to stay out of Gabe's sight, but she knew he was in the vicinity and soon he would find her. Elizabeth needed the Lady Fox but not quite yet and she needed to leave this area soon to avoid capture.

***

When Gabriel woke the next morning the sea was calm and the pirate ship had vanished. He had dropped sails for the night but the pirates had kept going and turned direction. Almost certain that the pirates would be returning for Abby's ship, Gabe dropped anchor and waited for Dunkin to catch up with him instead of pursuing the pirates on a wild goose chase. After sailing through the pass yesterday, Gabe felt that the Lady Fox was vital for retrieving that bloody treasure as well as navigating the pass itself.

Within hours Dunkin arrived, and both ships posted lookouts while they waited anchored for the return of Black Dog. As Gabe suspected a ship was sighted just after noon. But this ship, although similar in size and shape was not the Black Dog. It had a peculiar way about her. It acted as if Gabe was an ally but then hesitated. Caution spread throughout the ship as the suspicious vessel tacked closer.

From the crow's nest of the Lady Fox, the sailor posted, started to wave his arms at the incoming ship as if to warn her. Hollering down from the nest the sailor said, "I knows that ship captin' there be nothing to fear from her. She be an ally for sure. I'd stake me life on it."

Before Gabe could acknowledge the sailor Stephan came up from the lower deck. He spoke to the sailor under his breath so only Gabe could hear. "I bet you do know who that ship is," he hissed. When Gabe turned to look at Stephan he realized what he was talking about. Clenched tightly in Stephan's hands was a black flag with the skull and crossbones on it. "Looks like we have an enemy or two in our midst Captain, what say you?" Stephan said with a low voice.

Gabe nodded and signaled to Joseph, "How many new sailors did we take on back at port?" Gabe asked.

Joseph was quick to answer, "ten," without taking his eye off the oncoming vessel.

"Bring them all ta me and be quick about it," Gabe ordered.

Within five minutes, Gabe's men surrounded the ten and pushed them into the center of the deck, including the man in the crow's nest. A skirmish broke out, but the ten were not armed and the Scots quickly overpowered them in both strength and number.

"Put them in chains and get them out of my sight except those two. They may still be of use ta us yet. We will deal with the rest of them later," Gabe ordered pointing to the man who was in the crow's nest earlier and the man to his right. The ten all started to shout to the incoming ship but they were still out of ears range. Before they could warn the strange ship, Gabe's men forcefully escorted them right off the deck leaving the other two to face Gabe. Holding the black flag in his hand he asked slowly. "Seen this before?" Both men denied it at once so Gabe asked Stephan. "Who's bunk did ya find this under?" Without hesitation Stephan pointed to the man in front of Gabe. "Care ta change ya story or loose ya tongue for lying?" Gabe asked through gritted teeth.

The man hissed back saying, "It is too late for ya. Ya be no match for that ship. She is going to blow ya out of the water and that other ship as well. The Black Dog leaves no witnesses."

"That is not the Black Dog," Gabe returned. "Who is she?"

"There be more than one Black Dog, Captain Gabe. Why do you thinks we are so successful?" the pirate spit out through missing front teeth.

"We will use these men to get close to the other ship." Gabe said. "Stephan, run the jolly roger up the mast. We've just turned pirates, men." Gabe watched as his men smiled and nodded. They understood what Gabe was up to and were ready for the challenge. Each Scot went one by one off the deck not to arouse suspicion from the other ship in case they were watching them. They came back with more weapons concealed some way, ready to be taken out at the proper moment. Gabe kept one of the captured pirates at the helm with a knife at his back while Joseph had another one at knife point at the bow waving to the other ship.

Gabe slowly walked up to his men, a few at a time, and gave his orders quietly while the Jolly Roger took flight above the bow. Surprise must stay on their side and he did not want anyone to act in haste. The strange ship was watching the Lady Fox with all eyes and Gabe did not want them to become suspicious too soon. The sea was also on Gabe's side. Stephan and Daniel were expert sailors and had little trouble maneuvering the Lady Fox upside of the pirate ship. Abby's twins were also given strict orders to stay and man the Lady Fox while the McKenzie men seized the unsuspecting pirate ship. Although the twins were expert sailors, Gabe was not comfortable with their fighting skills.

The waves were minimal which allowed Gabe to give the order to tie on to the unsuspecting ship. Without opposition, the Pirate Captain allowed the Lady Fox tie on believing her to be friend not foe. "Good job mates," the pirate captain said to the man still held at knife point by Joseph. "I see ya took the Scoty bastards and left not a bit of damage to the bloody ship. Well done. Black Dog will be surely rewarding you for a fine job."

At that point, Gabe gave the signal to attack. Swords were drawn and the McKenzie men leaped forward and attacked the pirates with such skill and expertise that the fight was not long at all. The pirates were not prepared to draw their weapons and many were thrown overboard into the icy water before they had a chance to fight.

Dunkin stayed back and waited until he saw Gabe tie on and gave his order to give Gabe reinforcements. The battle went on for a few hours before the pirates finally conceded leaving only the captain and a few men. The rest were slain or tossed overboard to their deaths. The few pirates that were left were rounded up to face Gabriel who was ready to kill them all. But when he found out who he had in his hands he changed his mind for the moment.

Three cowards were found hiding in the belly of the pirate ship as Gabe started to question the pirate captain. One man had a leg shorter than the other was hobbling as he tried to keep his balance. By the look of pain on his face his injury was not an old one. All three men were expressing their gratitude for their liberation by the Scots but Gabe was not buying their act. "Gentlemen," Gabe said to get them to stop talking. "May I ask just who you are?"

The first man with the shorter leg limped forward and said, "I am Mr. Howard Pinkerton from the First Riverton bank in the colonies. I was abducted by these pirates and kept below for months."

The second man said, "I sir, am George Webber of the W & W Shipping Co. from Boston and I too have been a prisoner of these pirates."

Finally the last man stepped forward wiping the sweat off his bald head with a dirty white handkerchief. He cleared his throat and said, "I too sir, am from the W & W Shipping Co. My name is Jon Washburn. We have been treated abominably. I demand that you slay these scoundrels and let us go free."

Gabe could not believe his ears. These were the ones that had tricked Abigail. They were her so called partners and the banker. Abby had felt they were all part of the charade and now here they were in front of him. The Pirate aptain was swearing at these men nonstop threatening them with all that was holy. "You turncoats, when Black Dog gets a hold of you your tongues will be cut out and thrown to the fish of the sea. You will be roasted alive to a stake after I personally rip the flesh off your bones."

Gabe was impressed with the animosity the Pirate Captain showed toward these men.

Ignoring the three men for the moment, Gabe turned and faced the Pirate Captain and demanded loudly, "Identify yourself Captain so that I may address you properly." Gabe ordered in a loud voice.

"I am Niles Shaw the Captain of this vessel and I demand that you set us free. You fly the skull and crossbones not us."

Gabe broke into laughter at the ridiculous accusation of Niles Shaw. Gabe motioned to Joseph to bring up one of the ten pirates they had captured earlier so Captain Niles could see him. "Recognize this man by any chance?" Gabe asked Niles.

Immediately Niles denied ever seeing the man, but not before Gabe noticed the look of surprise on Nile's face, when he first laid eyes on him. Joseph had to finally silence the prisoner who now was cursing intensely at Niles accusing him of pirating on the high seas as well as many other crimes.

Gabe had finally had enough. It was more than apparent that he had captured Black Dogs' accomplices. "Niles Shaw, do ya by any chance know Abigail Fox?" Gabe asked enjoying the expressions on the faces of these four men. They all just stood looking at Gabe not quite sure what was coming.

"I take it that ya are all familiar with her?" Gabe asked.

The men would not acknowledge Gabe's question. "I do believe that I will save ya for her, and let her decide what she wants me ta do with ya. But until she has the chance ta speak with ya herself, I think it will be appropriate ta keep ya all in irons, hand and foot like they kept her in the Debtor's prison." Then Gabe gave the order for them to be taken away and kept in the belly of the ship with the other animals they had collected. "Make sure they are chained ta the wall and keep a guard on them at all times."

Gabe praised his men, thanked Dunkin for his help as well, and then said, "It is time for our next plan."

CHAPTER 30
What Goes Around Comes Around

Gabe now owned three ships. He was sure that Black Dog would be back soon, especially when her partner-ship was already here. So Stephan sailed the pirate ship to the passage by the cliffs with a few men from both Gabe's and Dunkin's ships. Gabe felt that the pass was a key to the treasure and that Black Dog would be returning there.

He needed to lure Black Dog into his trap. Abby was on board that ship and it would be just like a pirate to hold her for ransom. Like Niles, Gabe planned to draw Black Dog close and then attack her quickly.

Niles' ship would be the answer. Gabe would hide on the Nile's ship with his men and wait for Black Dog to come to him, but first he needed to hide his two other ships. The Lady Fox could be anchored in the passage. It was the perfect place for her. From the ocean the passage was undetectable. Dunkin would have to anchor his ship on the backside of the landmass and come out to assist Gabe when the fighting began just as they fought Niles before. The valuable prisoners were kept on Dunkin's ship. Gabe did not want to take any chances with the possibility that they might escape.

Gabe anchored the pirate ship and then sailed the Lady Fox into the passage. Coming from this direction, it sailed in much easier. The current seemed to draw them in, but not as violently as the other entrance. As they entered the pass, Gabe saw a space just big enough for the ship to tie into. It was as if the rock had been carved away special for just this ship to sit in. There on the wall were rocks placed perfectly to moor off from. The more Gabe was in this passage the more it looked like this was used for something more than just a passage. Someone had carved away rock to make this passage the right size and Abby's Grandfather had built the perfect ship for this cavern. Gabe was sure this was no coincidence.

Even the height of the mast was the right size. It came almost to the caverns roof but did not ever hit anything. Before Gabe entered the cavern the first time, he was concerned with the over sized crow's nest. Most vessels had a nest just big enough for one man, but this one was over built and could hold at least three men. Gabe could not figure out why Abby's grandfather had built a nest like this. The mast was oversized as well to accommodate the extra size of the crow's nest. If Gabe did not know better he would think Abby's Grandfather hauled something in that nest other than a lookout man. Because Abby was always surrounded by secrets, Gabe figured this was just another one for her collection.

After the ship was tied off and safe, Gabe and his men left the Lady Fox abandoned in the passage with plans to pick her up later. They rowed out to the Nile's ship where they waited for the next trap to be sprung.

Gabe became overly precautious. He had lookouts on each side of the ship. He was not sure which way the Black Dog would come from and he wanted to be notified at first sight of her. On his right was the land with towering cliffs at least twenty stories high. These were so high and jagged it made scaling them impossible. The current was so strong that any ship that got too close to the cliffs, other than the passageway, would be hurled into the rocks and surely sink. There was a small cove about two miles down where the water wasn't as rough and a ship could nestle unseen in unseen, but Gabe and Dunkin did not want to ambush Black Dog from there. It would be too dangerous and Gabe was fearful for Abby's life.

While Gabe was mooring the Lady Fox, Dunkin went back around the far end of the plateau where he stayed just out of sight waiting to hear Gabe's signal. Like Gabe, Dunkin feared the pirates coming from behind, so he stationed lookouts as well on his ship. Now the trap was set and they just needed the unsuspecting mouse, Black Dog.

It was just before dusk when one of Gabe's men sighted a ship rounding the corner of the plateau. From where Gabe was he could see that this was definitely Black Dog. Her sails were at full wind and she was not at all hesitant to come in closer to Nile's ship. Gabe's plan was working.

As Elizabeth's ship came closer to Nile's a large boom sounded from the cove they had just passed. A loud whistle sound came across the sky and a cannon ball hit the side of her ship dead on. As Gabe watched a huge English vessel drifted out of the cove and blindsided her. Before the Black Dog could react, another cannon ball hit her in the aft and she started to take on water.

"Where the hell did that bloody ship come from?" Gabe bellowed from the deck of Niles' ship. "She will kill Abigail."

The English ship was relentless. It was determined to sink Black Dog and the way it was firing on her she was not about to leave survivors. Gabe could see someone standing at the helm dressed in a black shirt and britches not moving as if he was planning to go down with his ship. Gabe guessed this was the captain no doubt and a small boat with four men and a woman who looked like Abigail. The woman was carrying a large box. Gabe was sure it was Abigail. He pulled up anchor and headed toward the small rowboat. Another boom sounded and the English vessel hit Black Dog again at the helm where the captain was standing. It knocked a hole into the helm causing the man dressed in black to fall below. Smoke started to fill the sky making it impossible to see all that was happening.

Gabe could do nothing for the pirate ship. She was finished and sinking fast. The English soldiers were firing at survivors in the water with muskets. They planned to make sure there were no survivors. The English had suffered greatly at the hands of this pirate and although it would be good to see him hang, the English would not waste time to bring him back to trial. Within minutes of the last cannon balls hitting the ship, it sank out of sight leaving nothing but debris in the water. Gabe could see the English drifting around the spot where Black Dog sank still firing into the sea.

The little rowboat was being tossed violently in the waves. As Gabe started to come closer another ship came into view. The Wikings were back. This time they had a smaller ship but with the same slow design and oars out of the sides. Gabe could hear the sound of their drum over the musket shots from the English vessel. Their rowing was done with such precision that it reached Abigail way before Gabe could get to her. The Wikings took her aboard with the four men.

Gabe could see the Wiking hitting Abigail and arguing with her. He watched as one by one the Wiking speared the pirates through their bellies and then dumped them into the ocean. Gabe could see the box opened and nothing was coming out of it when the Wiking turned it over. Abigail's box was empty.

Then a Wiking grabbed Abigail by her hair and pulled her head back. He raised his knife and raped it across Abigail's throat. Blood spurted out from her neck as she grabbed her throat. Gabe helplessly watched as she clasped onto the deck lifeless. Then as the Wikings had discarded the four pirates, Abigail's lifeless body was thrown into the sea along with her empty box.

Gabe screamed as if someone had put a sword through his own heart. He collapsed to the deck on his knees with his hands covering his face.

The English ship now had its sights on the Wikings and was firing on them. Gabe gave the order to come about and return to the passage where Dunkin was waiting. The English were going to sink that ship as they had Black Dog. Gabe wanted to kill each and every one of the Wikings but the English vessel was beating him to it.

He could not take the chance that the English would mistake him as an enemy especially now that he was on the other pirate ship. He still had his men, brothers and Abby's sons to think of. He could not help Abby, and because of that a piece of him died as well.

Gabe waited with Dunkin as the English vessel returned to the pass after sinking the Wikings as well. The English held out a white flag letting Gabe know they wanted to talk. Gabe's heart was breaking but he showed no emotion when the English captain asked to board.

The English Captain informed Gabe that someone had spotted Black Dog coming up the coast and had alerted the English and informed them that Gabriel was also in the area.

The English captain was thrilled when Gabe brought out his prisoners. "You have done very well McKenzie. I will let my king know that it was you who helped in the destruction of Black Dog. I am sorry for your loss," the English Captain said after he heard the whole story about Gabe's wife.

Gabe was polite and that was about all. It sickened him to see the men who had tricked her in the first place. She was so innocent in all their scheming and had paid the ultimate price with her life.

After the English Captain returned to his ship, Gabe went back to the Lady Fox. At first he thought of just leaving it in the passage but then he thought better of it and decided to give it to one of Abby's twins.

Daniel agreed to sail the pirate ship back to Scotland and Stephan agreed to sail the Lady Fox with Gabe.

Gabe had no intention of going through that pass again and decided to sail along side of Dunkin and Daniel. When all the ships were seaworthy, the three ships sailed for home empty handed.

***

Elizabeth came into Abby's cabin just before they rounded the plateau to the passage. "Take off your gown and put these on. I will need to be the bait to lure McKenzie to me. He will think he is after you when it will really be me. When he realizes it is not you, it will be too late. We will board the Lady Fox and kill all of them." Then Elizabeth laughed and handed Abby a pair of black britches and a black silk shirt. When Elizabeth saw Abby hesitate she asked, "Do you need help? I am sure I can find a few men who will be more than willing to undress you."

Abby did not say a word but slipped her gown down and climbed out of it. She threw it in Elizabeth's face and said, "You will not make it to Gabe or his ship."

"Is that a prediction from the dreamer lady or is that a threat coming from my prisoner? It really doesn't matter because I will see you die today after I watch you watch McKenzie die."

"Do not be so sure of yourself, Elizabeth," Abby said as she slipped the britches on and then the black silk shirt.

"Take her and tie her to the helm. I want her to see all that is going to happen today. Make sure she wears a wool cap to cover her hair." Elizabeth ordered her first mate. Then she said, "You are of no use to me now Abigail. I have the information to where the treasure is and how to get it. But I will do the Christian thing and keep you alive just long enough so you can see what a pirate does for a living. It was nice to know you." Then she left and Abby was dragged to the helm where she was tied standing overlooking the deck.

Elizabeth spotted Niles' ship alone in the water just waiting for her to join him anchored by the pass. "There is Niles," she shouted to her crew. "Full sail, it is safe sea to sail."

Just as Elizabeth shouted those words a loud boom sounded from just behind them. Then there was a loud whistle as a cannon ball struck Black Dog putting a hole through her midsection. There was another blast hitting her aft causing her to take on water.

The pirates scrambled for their lives. They could not fight back. Their ship was hit too badly and slowly being claimed by the frigid sea. A third boom sounded launching the next cannon ball directly at Abigail as she stood tied to the helm unable to do a thing except watch.

The ball hit the deck causing Abby to collapse through the hole, landing on Elizabeth's large oak bed with one of her hand still tied to a timber from the helm. With her free hand and her teeth, Abby managed to loosen the knots holding her. She could hear gun fire on the portside and water coming in. The only chance she had was to swim in the icy water. That English ship would never believe that she was not a pirate especially the way she was dressed, but these britches were much more suited for swimming than skirts.

Looking around she noticed the large, hand carved door to Elizabeth's cabin was blown right off its hinges. She ran to her cabin and emptied her box and concealed all the contents under her blanket of her bunk, but put the key and the rings in her pocket for safekeeping. Elizabeth would most likely get her treasure, but Abby was going to make it as hard as possible for her. Then she returned to Elizabeth's cabin. Pushing the unhinged door up the stairs with all the strength she had left, she reached the deck just as the ship started on fire. Smoke billowed out everywhere making it hard for the English ship to see any survivors to shoot.

Without hesitating she pushed the door into the icy water from the side of the ship farthest from the English and waited to see if it would float. She was thrilled when it did not sink, but rested high in the water. Taking one large step she jumped into the sea as close to the door as she could. Abby had been studying her charts and was sure she just needed to get to the warmer current which would get her to the passage. In this icy water she would not be able to swim long. She gasped from the shock of the cold water and climbed onto the door, which stayed afloat. She used her feet to kick her way to the warm current and away from the battle while resting her belly on the door to keep her afloat. Abby could feel herself losing heat fast as well as energy, and just as she thought she could kick no longer she felt the warmth of the current she needed to get to the passage.

The current was very swift and Abby had all she could do to hold onto the door and not fall into the sea. She managed to look back just as the rest of the pirate ship slipped into the ocean, and Elizabeth, still dressed in her gown holding her box get into a small row boat with the four McHales and escape.

Abby could hear more gun shots coming from the English ship. She could not believe they were shooting everyone in the water. She was praying that she had drifted far enough that she could get to the passage and out of their sight.

Abby kept kicking as hard as she could. Cold was getting to her, but she could feel in her heart that she would make it. Gabe would not abandon her. He would find her one way or the another.

The current pushed her into the passage and then started to violently swirl her around. The scroll her grandfather had written said this would happen. Terrified, Abby said a little prayer to her grandfather. “Help me grandpa. Don’t let me die this way.” Then the current slammed her against a rock wall. She could feel the water rush under it. This was it, the entrance of the treasure chamber. Abby had found the entrance just where the scroll said it would be. She quickly took a deep breath, released her hold on the door and dipped down under the wall. The current kept pushing her deep inside until she was just about out of air. Then the water started to become brighter.

She gasped for air as she ascended out of the water into a hidden chamber. Over on the far wall was a flat rock, which jetted out into the cave. Abby swam with all she could, managing to pull her freezing body on to it and lay panting for breath, trying to regain some strength. As she lay on her back she started to look around. The water had brought her into an inside cave. Someone had bore holes through the rock walls allowing natural light to pass through, which lit up the entire cave.

Abby was sure she did not have much time. Elizabeth would be coming. Then she smiled to herself. Elizabeth would be coming with an empty box and no idea how to retrieve the treasure… if there was one.

Forcing herself to sit up, she looked around some more. She had to find a stairway which would lead to some hidden chamber above the cave. The scroll described a stairway all carved out of stone, which Abby believed to be one of her grandfather's tricks to keep the treasure seekers looking. But just behind her, as her grandfather had written was the stone staircase leading up and out of this cave.

With shaky legs, Abby managed to stand despite her shivering. She made herself climb the stairs one at a time. It became warmer as she climbed, which encouraged her to continue. Step by step she climbed this seemingly endless staircase. When she finally reached the top, she collapsed onto her hands and knees trying to catch her breath.

When she finally stood up, she was in a huge chamber all carved out of the stone ledge. In the far corner of the room were three large boxes much too large and heavy for her to pick up and on the top of the box was one last letter from her grandfather. Like the cave below, someone had bore holes through the rock letting the natural light shine through illuminating the entire chamber. Abby noticed a rug rolled up and leaning against one of the large boxes. She sat down on it, still shivering and with tears in her eye began to read the very last thing she had of her grandfather's.

"My Dearest Daughter,

All of your life, I have wanted to call you that. Your life has been the only thing that has kept me going all these years. If you are reading this letter then you have found the last remaining treasure of our country. It is yours to do as you wish. Do not hide it or leave it here. Do some good with it. It has caused nothing but hardship for all these years and it is time to use it for some good.

You have always made me proud, daughter, and I will love you always. My only regret was that I could never hear you call me father. The constant harassment of the Wikings and other treasure seekers prevented me from becoming the father I wanted to be. Forgive me, but I thought it best that we spend only short times together for safety reasons. You have always been my pride and joy. I did what I needed to, to keep you safe. I pray with all my heart that you have found the love you so rightly deserve. Think kindly of this foolish father of yours. Remember I will always love you.

Your Loving Father,

DAD

Abby finished the letter with tears in her eyes. All this time he was her real father and she had no idea. She had loved him as no other and she was not about to let him down now. With new strength she read the last page of the letter which instructed her on how to remove the treasure from the chamber.

The note said to look for a hatch door on the floor of the chamber. The letter described the latch and how to open it safely, but when Abby read the last line her heart sank.

"*If you have brought my ship, moor it in the space carved out for it in the passageway. When the hatch is opened the crow's nest will sit just below the trap door. Fill the bucket with treasure and then empty it into the crow's nest. It was built special to hold such weight. Leave the boxes. Do not go back down the stairs for you will not be able to leave as you entered the current is way too strong. Use the rope to lower yourself into the crow's nest. Use the rug to cover the treasure from unsuspecting eyes.*"

Abby did not have her ship, Gabe did and he was nowhere to be found. She was stranded unable to leave. She decided to open the trap door anyway to look down into the cavern. Imagine her surprise when she opened the hatch and found the crow's nest in position. Gabe had come, he was here. He would find her soon. Abby called down for someone to help her but the ship was abandoned.

Walking back to the three large boxes, Abby took the key out of her pocket and slipped it into each padlock. She was amazed the key opened all of the locks. As she opened each cover, she was not disappointed. The lost treasure which she doubted ever existed was spectacular. The first box was filled with gold coins stamped with her country's emblem. The second box was filled to the brim with precious gems from rubies to diamonds and all in between. But it was the last box that made tears fall from her eyes again. As she opened the last box she discovered yet another gift from her father. Resting on the top of more treasure was a small velvet sack drawn together with a string with a note reading, *TO MY TWELVE GRANDCHILDREN*. With very shaky hands Abby opened the sack and looked inside. There were twelve ruby rings with her country coat of arms engraved in each one of them. There was another white sack with her name on it. Again she opened it carefully to find her crown jewels.

So Abby decided to load the treasure while she waited for Gabe. She kept expecting him at any moment, but she had completely filled the crow's nest and there was not a coin or jewel left in any of the boxes and still he was not back.

Remembering to leave through the hatch she threw the rug in and then looked for the rope but there was none. She was trapped. Grandfather had forgotten to leave her a rope to climb down. Abby had only one choice and that was to jump. She could not wait for Gabe. Because of the height of the passage roof to the ship's deck, no one would be able to hear her even if she called.

The crow's nest swayed with the waves as they hit her hull. She had managed to throw the entire treasure into it but she was not sure she could jump at the right moment and hit the center of the nest from this height. Estimating the jump would be at least a twenty foot drop, she called on all the courage. Abby watched the nest sway back and forth and then at the right moment she jumped. At the same moment another large boom sounded. The noise surprised her causing her to lose her footing at the exact moment she jumped. Missing her target, Abby's foot caught the top edge of the nest hurling her, head first into the other side. She hit her head so hard it made her dizzy. Abby managed to cover herself with the rug just before she passed out.

CHAPTER 31
Welcome Aboard

The three ships sailed side by side allowing the wind to take them home to Scotland. The feeling on the ships was a somber one. Ellery, Stephan and Daniel had just lost their mother and Gabe had lost his wife who he loved more than life itself. As quiet as Abby's boys were, Gabe was worse. For three days he stayed in his cabin only coming out in the dark of night. He ate little and slept less. In two more days they would be home and he would have to tell his children and Abby's daughter that they had lost their mother.

He felt like he had let her down. The sorrow he suffered was far worse than any he had ever experienced. If it wasn't for his children and clan, Gabe would not be going home.

On the end of the third day Gabe finally came out of his cabin to spend some time with his men. When he came up to the deck he found the men encouraging Cookie to climb the rigging to the crow's nest. It seemed that Cookie had lost a bet and for his payment he had to climb up to the nest. Each member of the crew knew how Cookie hated heights. So it was almost painful watching him try to climb up to the top but the men would not let him welsh on his bet. No one had climbed to the nest since before they had reached the passage so it was a total surprise what Cookie found.

"Cookie, I can see up ya kilt," Joseph teased.

"I hope ya like what ya see," Cookie called back.

"Ya climb like a little girl," Dunkin called from his ship along side of the Lady Fox.

"I climb the way I want, so I donna bloody fall into the bloody sea," Cookie answered.

Cookie reached the crow's nest after constant prodding from the Scots and looked inside. It seemed so good to hear the men laugh at the spectacle that Cookie was making of himself. Even Gabe had to chuckle.

Then in Gaelic, Cookie started screaming at the top of his lungs. All he could say was Holy Mother Mary of God, Sweet Jesus Christ as he looked directly into the crow's nest. He hung on the side of the nest not climbing in to it. The men on the deck could not get him to tell them what he saw. They all believed he was pulling their legs to get them to climb up and look into an empty nest. When Cookie would not stop his swearing, Stephan finally took the bait and climbed the rigging to see what Cookie was screaming about.

When Stephan looked inside the nest he too started screaming.

"Gabe, get your ass up here right now," Stephan hollered. Without stopping, Gabe climbed the rigging to look inside followed by Joseph and half the other men. There was such commotion coming from the Lady Fox that the other two ships were alerted. Thinking that they were in some kind of danger they prepared their weapons.

"Holy Mother of Jesus," was all Gabe could say.

There laying on a ton of treasure under a tapestry spun with gold thread dressed in black, laid Abigail still out cold from hitting her head three days ago.

She was the most beautiful sight Gabe had ever seen.

"Is she still alive, Gabe?" Cookie asked still standing on the rigging holding the edge of the crow's nest.

Gabe smiled as he watched her breathe as peacefully as an angel. "Aye. She is alive."

"How the hell did she get all this booty in the nest?" Stephan asked not really expecting an answer.

Gabe reached in and gently touched Abby on her cheek. "Time ta wake Abby my sweet," he said softly. "God be praised."

Abby turned her head as if to swat away a fly. "Just five more minutes Gabe, I don't want to get up yet," Abby muttered with her eyes still shut.

“Abby it is time. Wake up lass,” he asked again with such love in his voice that she had to open her eyes.

She looked up at him and gave him a sweet smile, as if nothing had happened. Then she saw Cookie and said, “Cookie I am so hungry for some reason, would you have anything to eat?”

The men who were now all around the nest looking inside smiled. Abby being hungry was a very good sign. She tried to rise but her head would not let her sit up. Reaching up, she grabbed her head and laid back down. “Oh my head,” she said with pain in her voice.

“Ya best not move yet lass. Ya took a nasty bump on ya head,” Gabe cautioned.

The men started to climb down the rigging. “Drop the sails and get me a hammock,” Gabe ordered. “We will lower her down from here in the hammock.” The men on the deck began to cheer loudly. To have found Abigail alive and in their midst was a miracle.

Dunkin had sailed upside the Lady Fox to find out what was going on and Daniel came up on the other side. When they heard the good news they too began to cheer.

Gabe climbed into the nest with Abigail stepping on the treasure and gently kept her from moving her head. He looked over the edge and called down, “Make my cabin ready for her. We will need some warm water and some strips of cloth for her head. Dunkin,” he yelled across the water to his brother. “Get the physician on board now.”

The men on the deck and on the other ships dropped sails and scrambled to make Abby’s homecoming as best as they could. All wanted to see her to make sure she was alive and was not just a figment of their imagination. The ocean was known to play tricks on grieving sailors and the men wanted to make sure this was not one of them.

All Abby could do was watch Gabe. He was such a sight for sore eyes, but she could not understand what all the fuss was about. “Gabe, I think I can climb down, I just need to lie here a little longer,” Abby said as she skeptically watched a hammock come over the side of the nest. The thought of her being lowered over the edge of the crow’s nest in that hammock was not to appealing. “I really think I ca…,” was all Gabe would let her say.

"Abigail, ya are in no condition ta climb anywhere and I will not lose ya again. Ya have returned from the dead and I will not be letting ya go back."

"What are you talking about?" Abby asked to hear such a statement. "I have been right here waiting for you."

Gabe reached under her carefully holding her head and slipped the hammock beneath her. Her head had dried blood from the cut she sustained when she hit the side of the nest. Abby kept protesting but Gabe was not listening. Stephan jumped into the nest to help Gabe. That was when she realized her son was here. "What are you doing here? I left you safe in the colonies."

"Hello Mom, I am so happy to see you too." Then he looked at Gabe with a huge smile on his face and said, "She is going to be alright. For once I will enjoy getting a good tongue lashing from her." Then Stephan smiled at Gabe and helped him tie ropes to each end of the hammock.

"I really don't want to go over the edge in a hammock," Abby protested again.

Before Abigail could say another word the two men hoisted her up and started lowering her down with ropes. Abby let out a loud scream and covered her eyes so she wouldn't look as her hammock swayed in the wind.

On deck, the crew was waiting to catch her. Some of the men had stretched a plaid out wide as a safety net in case she got away from Stephan and Gabe.

Abby could not look, she clapped her hands over her face and tried to stay calm. When she reached the deck, at least a dozen sets of hands grabbed her. Dunkin, Ellery, Daniel and the other men watched from their vessels along side of the Lady Fox.

Gaelic was being spoken in all directions. The men kept asking her questions in Gaelic forgetting she could not understand them. Finally Gabe barged through the cluster of men and took Abby in his arms. "I'll take her from here. Ya best be getting on with ya work. I'll answer all ya questions as soon as I know myself." Then he whispered, "Thank God she is alive. It is a miracle."

Gabe gently carried her down to the captain's quarters and softly placed her in his bed followed by all the men. "I need ta strip her.

Everyone get out for a moment. I'll let ya know when ya can come back in." Stephan started to protest. "It will only be a moment Stephan. Ya'll not wait long." Gabe gently pushed the men out of his cabin and started removing Abigail's britches and then the silk shirt. She looked so thin to him. Her body was full of bruises from her fall. He gave her one of his shirts which went all the way down to her knees. He rolled up the cuffs of the shirt so her hands were free and covered her with a quilt. Once she was tucked in, he kissed her lightly on her cheek 1…2…3…. Then he called for the men to enter.

"Please don't be throwing those britches out. They were great to swim in. I was so happy I had them on. They gave me some warmth against the freezing water," Abby said as she watched him fold them. "Ya and I have ta talk but right now I need ta get ya warm and that head of yours looked at. Dunkin brought the physician on board," Gabe said.

There was so much commotion in front of the cabin door that the physician had a hard time to get through. He was followed by Ellery, Daniel, Joseph, Cookie and Dunkin.

All three ships had lowered their sails and boarded the Lady Fox. Despite Gabe's orders, the men were not going anywhere until they knew what had happened to Abby and if she'd be alright. They kept a constant vigil outside the captain's quarters while the physician was inside with the other captains and Abby's sons.

Ignoring Abigail's protest to be examined, the physician checked her head and every other part of her to make sure she was fine. While the physician examined Abby, Gabe and the other men's backs were turned. Gabe would not leave the room for any reason and neither would her sons or Dunkin or Joseph.

When the physician was finished, he stitched the cut on the side of her head and then wrapped her head in linen strips. "Ya are one very lucky lass," the physician said to Abby as he finished. "By rights, a hit on the head like this should have killed ya. Now ya will do as I say and I will have no arguments, or I will give an order ta have ya tied in bed. Ya have a bad bump on that head of yours. Ya may have cracked ya skull. I want ya ta stay down and not get up for any reason for the next day and then we will decide what to do next. Ya should be having a whopping good headache and I will leave Gabe some powder for it. " The physician turned toward Gabe and said, "just put it in some water and have her drink it Gabe."

"I'm so hungry," Abby said hoping Cookie was coming with some food.

"Broth is all ya are going ta eat, I doubt ya will even be able ta keep that down. But being hungry is a really good sign. If ya can keep the broth down we will see about some porridge tomorrow." Gabe had to chuckle, when he saw Abby make a face at the thought of eating porridge. She hated porridge and would not eat that if she was starving.

The physician left and Cookie came in with some broth as ordered. Abby took it and drank it down as fast as she could. She was so hungry. She did not care about being ladylike. When she was done she said, "Bring me anymore of that crap and you will wear it out of here. Now please go get me some food. If I can't keep it down, then I will stick to broth."

Cookie smiled, "Ya not be giving us a hard time now. Ya are not so hurt that Gabe here canna put ya over his knee," then he touched her on her cheek. "Let's take it nice and slow, aye?" Abby sighed, she knew he was right.

"I'm sorry. I am just so hungry for some strange reason. I ate yesterday before Black Dog was attacked. I should not be this hungry. I don't understand and I don't know why I am so grumpy," Abby whispered so not to make her head hurt more than it already did.

"Lass ya have not been up there for just one day," Joseph said.

"How long have we been out to sea?" Abby asked.

"Three days," Gabe answered. Abby looked up from her bed and saw Gabe staring down at her. Her head had hurt so much that she was keeping her eyes shut. He looked so worried and relieved all at the same time.

Ellery popped his head around so his mom could see him.

"ELLERY" Abby screeched. Then Daniel did the same. "DANIEL." "What are all of you doing here?"

"Gabe sent Dunkin to fetch us Mom," Ellery said with a smile. Abby was angry and happy all at the same time. She really did not want them to be a part of this, but now that they were all here she was so happy to see them.

"You best be giving me a hug and a kiss if you know what is good for you," she sputtered trying to act upset, but she could not keep up the pretense and broke into tears of joy to see her sons. "I am so happy you are here. Thank you for coming to help me." Then she heard Gabe clear his throat and she got the message loud and clear. "And thank you for fetching them for me Dunkin," she said knowing that was not exactly what Gabe was hinting for. Abby saw Dunkin smile at Gabe. "Ya are welcome lass." Dunkin said. "Ya have fine sailors, all of them. They can sail with me anytime."

Dunkin was just about Ellery's age and the men had become very good friends.

"Is Hannah alright?" Abby asked her sons, but Dunkin answered. "Hannah is at the laird waiting for our return." Then he smiled. Abby's three sons made a teasing sound like "Oooooo" and Dunkin blushed.

Abby just looked at Gabe and he shrugged his shoulders. "Is Hannah anything like ya Abigail?" Gabe asked trying to keep the teasing down between the young men.

All three brothers at the same time answered, "WORSE."

Finally Abby said, "Thank you Gabe. You have made me so happy." Then she asked with the sweetest smile, "Please, I need something to eat other than broth and certainly not porridge." Gabe broke down and gave Cookie the nod to get something else for her. She was hurting and he could see it, but he wanted nothing more than to make her happy.

After she had finished Cookies' fish chowder, she closed her eyes with everyone still in her cabin and went to sleep. Gabe watched over her all night. He did not get in bed with her, but sat next to her all night. Abby woke in the morning, to find Gabe hunched over still in the chair with his head resting on her belly. She reached up and touched his hair and stroked it. He stirred and lifted his head to look at her. "I did not get married to sleep alone husband," Abby said with a sweet smile.

"Donna ever leave me again. I thought ya were dead. I saw a Wiking slit ya throat and dump ya in the ocean. I was going ta kill them all when that bloody English ship beat me to it. It felt like someone had ripped ma heart out of ma chest," Gabe said looking into her eyes which were all black and blue.

Before Abby could say a word, a knock sounded on the cabin door and then all three of her sons came bounding into the cabin uninvited along with Cookie, Dunkin, Joseph and half the men on the ship.

"What is this?" Gabe barked sitting up surprised.

"We cannot wait any longer. Is she ready to answer our questions? Is she alright? How did she get all that treasure up in the nest?" Dunkin asked.

Abby smiled and answered before Gabe could stop her. "I will answer all questions only if I am allowed to sit on the deck in the sun."

Gabe gave her a dirty look. "Lass, ya know what the physician ordered."

"Well I can sit in here or I can sit up there in the warm sun with the wind in my face making me feel so much better. I promise I will not do anything but sit or lie down which ever you choose."

"Are ya hungry lass?" Cookie asked.

"Starving," Abby answered with a smile.

"Can she come out and play Da?" Dunkin teased Gabe. "Please."

"She can, but only, if she lets me carry her and only if the physician gives his permission." Then he looked at her, "ya will not be walking on the deck and fall in the sea with ya dizzy head."

Gabe scooped her up with a plaid wrapped around her and carried her gently up to the deck after the doctor examined her again. He sat her on the seat by the center mast where she could still recline. All the men gathered around to hear what she had to say.

Both the other ships had dropped their sails and most of the sailors were now on the Lady Fox sitting or standing on the deck in front of her. Gabe started with a quick overview of what they all had witnessed. When he finished his account of what happened he asked,"What I want know is who was that woman the Wiking killed?" Gabe asked first.

"Black Dog herself," Abby said with a smile.

"Black Dog was a woman? Who was she?" Gabe asked in disbelief.

"Elizabeth Shaw." Abby answered. Then she continued before they could ask any more questions. "When I was in the colonies, I rode with Elizabeth and Niles Shaw to Boston. They were more interested with me and not my box. Elizabeth gave more orders then Niles. By the time I was at sea I had figured out her secret. When I was in England, I almost alerted the English, but they really made me angry putting me in the debtor's prison. So I decided not to tell the English they were looking for a woman and not a man and that was the reason they never could catch Black Dog.

Elizabeth wanted to draw the Lady Fox to her by making you think it was me. When you came close enough, she was going to board you and take the ship. Her plan did not include survivors. When we were attacked by the hidden English ship, there was no time. She had tied me to the helm already so I could watch her work as the pirate she was. But luck was with me when a cannon ball hit the helm and put a hole through the deck causing me to fall into Elizabeth's cabin. I landed on her bed which broke my fall and allowed me to get free from my bindings. I had just enough time to go to my cabin next door and empty my box. I put all the contents except the key and the rings under my blanket on my bunk and left the box closed.

When she came down for the box, she did not take the time to see what was in it. I only wish I could have seen her expression when the Wikings opened an empty box.

Elizabeth's cabin door had been blown off its hinges. I was able to push it up the stairs and off the backside of the pirate ship while Elizabeth was retrieving my box. By the time I was in the water the ship was on fire and smoking heavily. The smoke kept me safe from the musket fire coming from the English ship. No one was looking for someone who was swimming out to sea. Most survivors were trying to get to land and into the musket fire.

That water was so cold I almost did not make it. But I knew if I could reach the warm current it would pull me into the passage and to safety. That door kept me afloat and the britches kept me alive.

Elizabeth saw something on Niles' ship which scared her. It made her run to the Wiking's with the McHales. She knew the Wikings had never seen me. She felt the box was her ticket to get free of the English but the box was empty. Elizabeth sealed her own fate. She did not realize that the Wikings wanted to kill me after they had the documents in my box. When they found it empty they killed Elizabeth on the spot thinking it was me. The Wikings, like Elizabeth only needed me to translate the scroll. Once that was finished they were planning on killing me as well."

"How did ya get all that gold into the crow's nest alone?" Gabe asked.

Abby smiled and teased, "I am stronger than you give me credit for I guess."

"MOM, tell us and stop giving us a hard time," Ellery scolded.

"Alright, my grandfather was my real father, which I did not know until three days ago. When I found the treasure I discovered the greatest treasure of all, a letter from him admitting he was my real father. He was so clever. That passage was carved by my people hundreds years ago, but my father made some modifications. Did you notice how perfect the Lady Fox fit into that spot you moored her? My father had opened the cavern to accommodate his ship to rest conveniently under the treasure chamber.

I could have never dragged all that gold onto the ship and up the rigging into the crow's nest, but I could throw it down into the crow's nest from above. There was only one way in to the chamber and the current would not allow me to exit. I needed to lower myself down to the crow's nest after I emptied the three remaining treasure boxes, but there wasn't any rope. So I jumped, but I lost my footing just as a wave hit the boat at the wrong time. I caught my foot and t I hit my head. You now know all I do."

When Abby finished her explanation, Gabe and the men told her about their conquest of Niles' ship and their plans. Abby finally understood why they were so surprised to find her. They had watched Elizabeth die and thought it was her.

Gabe did not allow Abby to stay too long on the deck. As soon as she started to tire, he carried her back to his cabin and made her promise she would not get out of bed on her own and rest.

Cookie kept her well fed. He had always been a little cold towards her, but now he could not seem to stop waiting on her. He was not the only one who was acting differently towards her. It seemed like everyone on the entire three ships were happy she was alive and alright. Gabe especially checked on her about once every hour and could not stop smiling. Abby even caught him whistling a very happy tune.

It took the three ships another two days to return home just because they wanted to give Abigail time to recover. They were not willing to move her too quickly over the land.

Abby slept and ate for the next two days. By the time they made it to port, Abby was doing pretty well, except for the constant hunger and a dizzy and nauseous spell from time to time.

CHAPTER 32
You Are To Come

When the three ships finally reached Scotland, Gabe sent a messenger to his cousin, the King, informing him of Abby's successful rescue, the defeat of Black Dog, and his plans to return to Fuchsiall. Gabe still expected trouble with Jennifer and he wanted his cousin on his side. Abigail was still showing signs of lightheadedness and Gabe did not want to alarm her with his concerns until something definite came about. Now that Abby was considered a Scot, Gabe was confident that the King would protect her, but Gabe was still taking every precaution necessary.

Abby did humiliate a royal official in his house and there would be definite ramifications from it. England and Scotland were having trouble getting along and this could be a tool to start something unpleasant between the two countries. Diplomacy was needed and although Gabe had acted as the Scottish King's diplomat from time to time with England, he doubted the English King would give him any special consideration.

For now, however, it was more important to get Abigail home and safe. She would no longer have trouble from the Wiking's now that they thought they killed her. During the battle between the English and the Wikings a smaller Wiking vessel had came about and headed back to their island just after they witness the slaying of Elizabeth. When the English captain came aboard Niles' ship, now Gabes', he informed Gabe that the first Wiking ship was sunk, but not until after the smaller ship had escaped.

The English captain was willing to chase the smaller Wiking ship down, but Gabe wanted the Wiking's to return home with the information that Abby was dead. He did not want them to keep coming to Scotland attacking his people looking for her. Of course, Gabe made this decision before he knew that Abby was still alive. Now she would be free from their harassment forever along with all the treasure seekers. His cousin would keep her treasure safe in Scotland.

Gabe rode with Abby on his lap all the way home despite her insistence that she could ride her own horse. With one hand around her waist he would playfully grab her breast when he thought the coast was clear. She would playfully swat his hand away and scold him under her breath so the other men did not hear her.

Abby's three sons watched how Gabe acted toward their mother and they were pleased. They had originally came to retrieve her and bring her back to the colonies but after spending a month and a half out to sea with Gabe and watching the two of them together they all decided she was happy and this would be the best place for her. Gabe now owned two more ships and the twins were hopeful that they might be considered to captain them. It would be a good business venture for both the twins, Dunkin and Gabe if all agreed.

While Gabe was playing with their mother, the twins were running their ideas by Dunkin. They wanted to run a shipping company between Scotland and the colonies and Ellery could man the office in the colonies. They could see their mother on occasion when docking here and Gabe would benefit from the trade. All in all a sound plan and one they would present together to Gabe when they reached Fuchsiall.

When they finally arrived, they were greeted by very happy clansmen. Abby was warmly welcomed. A big banquet was ordered for the evening by Gabe.

Hannah ran from the house followed by all six of Gabe's children. She had resumed her mother's duties of teaching the children while she waited for Gabe and her brothers to bring Abigail home. It had passed the long days waiting to hear some news and gave Hannah a chance to get to know her new brothers and sisters. Not until she reached Fuchsiall did she find out that her mother had married Gabe.

The children described every detail about the wonderful wedding, which they were all part of and all the facts leading up to the marriage. Hannah was not surprised to hear how her mother had defended the children. She found the Jennifer story hilarious, but worried that her mother might be in trouble with the English King.

She had heard people shouting in Gaelic and was not sure why everyone was so excited until she reached the door to the laird and looked out to see her mother riding in on Gabe's lap. Hannah ran as fast as she could, and did not stop until she was in her own mother's loving arms. She kissed Abby with tears streaming down her face. Of course, her brothers had to pick on her right away which made Gabe laugh. All three of Abby's sons were no match for their little sister. She gave it back as fast as they dished it out. Finally Hannah was being hugged and kissed, one at a time by all three older brothers.

Dunkin was very happy to see Hannah as well. He went to greet her, but Hannah's brothers purposely physically interfered which made Hannah frown. Both Gabe and Abby noticed the strong attraction Dunkin and Hannah had for each other. This was the first time Abby had seen her daughter interested in any man and the first time that her sons let a man near her.

Gabe's children reached their father just after Hannah reached Abigail. He was greeted with big hugs. Abby loved to watch him with his children. The young ones were always tossed into the air and his older ones had their hair mussed and a huge hug.

Abby watched as her own children watched Gabe with his children. They never had a real father like Gabe was. Their father never would claim them as his own, but accused Abby of bearing someone else's children. Because of that, Roy would not give Abby help to support them. All her children received from their own father were constant beatings.

Feeling a little woozy, Abby put her hand to her head. Gabe was there in a moment and took her inside to rest. Despite all her protests, Gabe carried her to bed and threatened to not let her attended the banquet if he caught her out of bed before then. Abby was thankful to him even though she did not want him to know it. She was exhausted and was asleep before he left the room, only waking when he came to get her for dinner.

The hall had been decorated with fresh wild flowers in Abby's honor. The tables were set to accommodate Abby's four children. They had been accepted in Gabriel's family and now sat with them. Gabe's father was here along with his three brothers, Joseph, Simon and the baby brother Dunkin. All the McKenzie men resembled their father. All carried the dark hair and eyes with bronze complexion, but Gabe was definitely the best looking at least in Abby opinion.

It was a fine dinner with lots of stories and constant teasing. It wasn't long before Abby's sons, who were about seven years older than Gabe's oldest son were teasing them as if they were their real brothers and sisters. Abby had to laugh when little Emily had to sit on Stephan's lap and he welcomed her.

Dunkin kept waiting for Hannah to turn her head and then he'd throw a pea at her. Dinner went on as if they had all been there a lifetime. The clan had accepted Abby as Gabe's chosen wife and her family became part of the clan that very night.

Music was ordered and the table pushed aside to accommodate the Scottish dances. Dunkin grabbed Hannah and escorted her to the dance floor. He would not let her sit down for the rest of the night until Ellery said, "It is high time that we from the colonies take a moment and repay your generous hospitality and entertain you." The room went quiet as Abby's four children went after an instrument. Gabe and the others watched as they returned to the center of the hall ready to play.

Stephan was the instigator of the group. "Wait a minute," he said looking at his mother, "We seem to missing our violin and drum section." Abby shook her head trying to get out of this but he would not let her. "What shall it be, drum or violin?" Abby sat there still shaking her head no. That was when two of her sons, Ellery and Daniel came around her backside and lifted her right off her seat by grabbing her under her arms. They did not put her down until she was standing in the middle of the room with them. "I just want everyone here to know that our mother has taught us all we know when it comes to playing music so if we sound bad you can blame her." The McKenzie audience broke out into laughter. With that comment, the hall expected a simple arrangement of music, but that was not what happened.

Ellery put the violin in Abby's hand and then they were off with a foot stomping tune which made people rise to their feet to clog or clap their hands. Gabe could not believe how good they were and not one of them had a sheet of music. They played like professional musicians and switched instruments when they wanted.

The night was wonderful and Abby did not want it to end. She stood in the center of the hall, with her violin when Gabe rose and joined her in the middle of the room. "May I have this dance my darling?" he asked bowing to Abigail and taking her hand. "A waltz please," he ordered and all the musicians including Abby's children joined in to play a beautiful waltz just for Abby and Gabe.

Not one person joined in the dance however. They all stepped aside and let Abby and Gabe have the dance floor to themselves. Gabe twirled Abby around as if in a fairytale and the entire hall watched with a smile. They had such love in their eyes that no one wanted to interrupt them.

One of the guards came into the hall just as the waltz was finishing looking for Gabe. A messenger had just arrived in the dark with an important message from his cousin the King of Scotland that could not wait.

Gabe took the messenger into his office and the mood of the entire hall changed. When he came out he was not in a very good mood. He called his father and brothers into his study. Finally he called in Abigail.

"Abby ya need ta listen ta me and I donna want ya ta interrupt me until I have told ya everything." Gabe sat down in front of her and held her hand. "Ya have been summoned by the English King ta appear in court in two months. My cousin has no choice but ta hand ya over ta him. But he has vouched for ya character and expressed his anger in this situation. He has asked for leniency and will send his lawyer with ya ta speak for ya. The English King is angry that one of his family was humiliated especially in ma house… me being a cousin of the King of Scotland. He wants ta make an example of ya." Gabe watched as Abby's face went from pink to white. She said nothing and did not ask a single question, but lowered her eyes. "The kings are angry with each other and are looking ta make examples ta prove their strength. Ya will not go alone. I will go with ya, but I don't know if I can help ya. I donna know if the English King will let me take ya punishment if he finds ya guilty."

Finally she asked one question. "Will they kill me?"

Gabe answered with a little smile, "No lass, but it will not be pleasant. My Da thinks ya may end up with a beating maybe a flogging but he cannot be sure." Abby was still not feeling completely healthy and she was now feeling a bit queasy. "I want to leave please," she said to Gabe not wanting to talk any longer twisting her hands together. Gabe just nodded and let her leave. Abby did not return to the music in the hall, but went up to the roof where Gabe found her a few hours later. "Abby ya need ta come in," Gabe said softly.

"I am so sorry Gabe. I don't know what came over me. I just could not let her treat any of you like she did. If anyone needs punishing, it's her. She treated all of you, the children and the staff, so badly. Now she has turned on me," Abby said refusing to look at him.

"Abby it is not ya that she is after. It is me. She is angry that I chose ya for my wife and not her. Jennifer had James speak ta me about the match but I was not interested at all. That was why he brought her ta the house in the first place. So she is taking it out on ya ta get back at me."

Abby reached up and hugged Gabe around his neck and kissed him. "Thanks for trying to make me believe it is your fault, but we both know better. I got myself into this mess and I will get myself out even if it means I need to take the punishment. But I will tell you one thing, Jennifer is going to have a fight on her hands. I will not take this laying down."

"That is what I wanted to hear Abigail." Then he pulled her off the roof and walked her to their chamber.

***

"Mom is so sad Da," Emily said the next day. "Is there something we can do to cheer her up? Maybe we can kiss her like she kisses her own children."

That was when Gabe realized that Abby did treat his children different from hers. Abby always touched her own children and they always touched her. They had a bond that Gabe wanted for his own children, but it was still so new. They never knew a mother like Abby and he wanted her to feel free to treat them as she treated her own. Abby claimed his children, but was not comfortable touching them as she did her own yet.

Later that day, Gabe was sitting at the head table as Abby walked into the hall. She was so beautiful to watch. Emi was right, she was sad. The last thing Abby had ever wanted was to be an Empress or cause any trouble for Gabe and his clan.

Gabe watched as she came up behind each one of her children. She hugged and kissed their cheeks, but when she came to the younger children she just tapped them on their heads or tickled them. When she reached Gabe, she just greeted him with a smile and sat in her seat without touching him at all. He was going to put a stop to this starting tomorrow.

Abby sat picking at her food. She barely ate completely engulfed in thought. When she asked to be excused early to return to her chamber, Gabe allowed it. He waited until she left the hall and ordered his first family meeting with all ten children. After dinner they all followed Gabe to his study.

"I have noticed ya mother's behavior," he said addressing all the children. "She has a lot on her mind and I plan on cheering her up. Now it has been brought ta my attention that she treats the older children," then he gave them a quick wink so they knew he was up to something, "different than the younger ones."

"Yes, we have noticed the same thing," Ellery said. "And we do not think it is fair that we have to put up with her kisses and hugs while you all get away with a little tap on your heads." Then he gave Gabe a little wink back. Ellery had understood what Gabe was up to. The twins and Hannah also started to join in complaining that their mother treated them differently and they too, thought it was unfair. The meeting lasted another half hour and when they all left the study, they were all wearing smiles.

The next day Abby was in the Gabe's private study working on some house accounts when she heard a knock on the door. "I have come ta escort ya ta court in the hall ta answer ta charges against ya by no less than ten people. Ya have been accused of unfair treatment ta members of ya clan," Joseph said trying not to smile.

Abby face light up with disbelief. "Who would think such a thing about me?" she asked shaking her head. "I have enough to deal with without this too."

"Are ya coming peacefully or am I ta take ya by force?" Joseph asked enjoying Abby's reaction.

Abby stomped out of the office and into the hall ready to give the accusers a piece of her mind. How dare they do such a thing and accuse of her of such an act. When she entered the hall Philip, the old laird, was tending court not Gabe. Simon and Dunkin sat on either side of him. Joseph put his hand in the small of her back and pushed her gently to the center of the room in front of the head table where she could hear her charges.

"It has been brought ta this court's attention that ya, Abigail McKenzie have been treating members of my family unfairly. How do ya plea, guilty or not guilty?" Philip asked.

"I wish to delay my answer until I see the people who have placed these charges against me. I need to hear their complaints before I can give a correct plea, Laird," Abby said trying to control her temper. Then the side door opened and eleven people walked out starting with Gabe and ending with Emily. They all stood in front of her with their arms folded over their chests ready to declare their charges. Abby's mouth dropped open to have her entire family confronting her. She did not understand why they were so upset with her.

"Ya may start Emi," Philip ordered.

"I want ta know why ya only kiss and hug them," and she pointed to Ellery, Stephan, Daniel and Hannah. "And not me unless ya are putting me ta bed. I want ta be kissed and hug like them," Emily said with a large nod with her head.

"How do ya plea Abigail?" Philip asked.

Abby started to realize what her family was up to. She shook her head and said, "Guilty as charged."

Each one of the young ones said the same thing and each time Abby pleaded guilty. When it was Hannah's turn she said, "I charge my mother with showing me favoritism when she should be kissing all of us and not just me." Then she smiled ever so slightly. Hannah never could keep a straight face.

When it was Ellery's turn he said, "I am sick and tired of always having to take your kisses. I was so thrilled when we inherited six brothers and sisters because I thought I would finally get a break." He too was having a hard time to keep a straight faced. Again Abby had pleaded guilty.

Gabe was the last to speak. Abby was interested to see what charges he held against her. "I charge my wife with neglect in public. I want her to feel like she can hug me or kiss me when she wants even if I am training and in front of ma men." Gabe knew the story of her first husband and how he would refuse her love in anyway especially her touches.

"How do ya plea?" Philip asked for the last time.

"You really want me to show you affection in public?" Abby asked Gabe before she'd answer his father.

"Aye lass, I do," Gabe said with a small grin.

"Guilty on all charges Laird and I promise the court that from now on I will treat them all the same. What I have a mind to do is to never kiss or hug any of you ever again. You could have told me this without drawing me to court," she scolded her whole family.

"Ya should have realized this on your own," Philip said drawing her attention to the head table again from behind Gabe. "Now step forward for your punishment."

"You are going to punish me?" Abby said appalled.

"Aye I am and a well deserved punishment it will be," Philip said now standing with his arms folded as a father ready to punish his child.

"From this moment on and until I deem punished enough, ya will do the following," Philip said. Abby could not believe this. Her eyes were wide open as well as her mouth.

"When a family member is in the same room as ya, ya will hug them and give them three kiss on their cheek. Failure to comply with the court's wishes will result in a more severe punishment of which I personally will carry out," and he shook his finger at her letting her know he was not fooling around. "Ya may begin starting right now," he ordered.

Abby gave him a surprise look. He was serious and not kidding in the least. So Abby started to go to Emily first and Philip said, "Ya are starting right here." He pointed to his own cheek.

"I am to kiss you?" Abby asked surprised with this whole moment.

"Did I not make myself clear? Am I not a member of ya family?" Philip asked. "Are ya treating me different than them?" and he pointed to the older children mimicking Emi's gesture she had made earlier.

Abby just walked up to him and wrapped her arms around his waist and hugged him. He bent down and offered her his left cheek where Abby kissed him 1…2…3. She started to turn when she heard someone clear his throat. She turned to find Joseph waiting his turn and then Simon and then Dunkin. Abby did as she was ordered and by the time she got to Emily, she was giggling so hard that she had all she could do to kiss her. So she tickled her and then kissed her.

Gabe's idea had worked. It seemed so good to see Abby smile and it seemed so good to see his children relate to their new mother in such a loving manner. He also knew Abigail too well and he had a sneaking suspicion that he may regret telling her that she could kiss him in front of his men. For now, however, he would enjoy her public show of affection.

Gabe's brothers and father were going to make Abby kiss them as often as they could. Joseph would walk in and out of the same room five times before he would sit down getting Abby to kiss and hug him each time. Philip, would announce where Abby was so the family could all go into that room. Abby would no more sit down and someone would come in announcing that she need to give more kisses and hugs. Even the servants were helping by letting the family know where she was. Abby could not be alone for a moment and could not find a single hiding place.

But there was one thing she could do and that was get back at her husband who started this in the first place. She looked for him outside and found him training with his men. He was beautiful when he fought. His movements were graceful and he had an air of confidence that his men admired. So Abigail, in the most sickening voice she could make called his name, over and over and over again until he had to stop and acknowledge her. He was sweating and panting from his workout.

Abby spread out her arms and gave him a great big hug while he still held his Claymore. Then she gave him the loudest squeaky kiss she could make.

The men began to snicker and pick on Gabe a little. Gabe looked down at Abby with that sweet innocent looking face. She knew exactly what she was doing and was not stopping there. Again she hugged him and kissed him loudly. She was purposely ruining his training session and he was not about to let her get away with it.

When Abby turned to finally leave the training area, Gabe slapped her backside with his Claymore. She was so surprised. She was not expecting him to retaliate. "Low blow, McKenzie to strike an unarmed woman with your Claymore when she is required by law to kiss and hug you in public," she crossed her arms and lifted her chin.

Gabe's training session was now over. He would not be able to get his men back in the seriousness needed to train. "Ya over there," he said calling to a young trainee. "Give me ya training sword." A very young man about twelve came forward and handed Gabe his sword who in turn handed it to Abigail. "Ya are in my training field and anyone in the field has ta fight. Now get ready. Hold ya sword up and fight."

Abby couldn't believe that Gabe was making her fight. She had not held a sword since her father had trained her when she was a little girl. Abby did not know if she would even remember what he had taught her nevermind being able to have enough strength to swing this smaller version of a fifteen pound Claymore. Her father had always made her train wearing britches so Abby reached down between her legs and grabbed her back hem and pulled it forward between her legs and tucked it into the front of her belt giving her more mobility with her legs. She took her stance and waited for Gabe to start. "I am impressed lass. Has someone trained ya before?" Abby did not answer but just raised her eyebrows and grinned.

The men formed a circle around them and watched as Abby fought Gabe. He was taking it easy on her, but she did know what she was doing. She just did not have much strength. Some of the men started calling out moves to her. Abby started to laugh. Gabe was enjoying her. When she was too tired to swing the sword another time Gabe let her stop. He was not winded in the least. "DO ya concede?" Gabe asked smiling at her.

"AYE," she said. "I have had enough training for today." Abby started to turn to leave when she heard Gabe clear his throat. "Winner gets a kiss donna ya think?"Abby giggled and walked into his opened arms. He hugged her and kissed the top of her head. "Now go before I have a mind to really hit ya with my Claymore." He patted her bottom and sent her off.

Abby did not want to go back into the house so she went to see Goliath and took a ride across the pasture toward the ocean.

CHAPTER 33
Coming Out

Abby was feeling much better except for the bout of seasickness from time to time, but her headaches were finally gone.

Gabe felt they should be leaving for London but first he needed to stop at his cousins'. The Scottish King requested a special audience with Abigail. Gabe had not mentioned his cousin to Abby yet, but he was about to.

"Abigail," Gabe said finding her in their chamber in the middle of the day. "Are ya alright lass?"

Abby was curled up in their bed covered with a quilt. She woke when she heard her name. She sat up quickly. "I cannot believe I fell asleep. First I was putting clothes away and then I was lying down fast asleep. I'm sorry," she said, looking at Gabe with guilt all over her face. Abby did not take naps in the middle of the day and she was embarrassed to be caught taking one. Why she was so tired all the time? She could not understand.

"Abigail there is no need ta be sorry. Ya took a nasty hit on that head of yours and it will take time ta heel. Donna apologize, I am not upset with ya," Gabe said as he sat down on the bed beside her. "I just came ta tell ya we will be leaving tomorrow for London, but first we need ta stop and see my cousin. He too has asked for an audience with ya." Gabe saw the look on her face and added. "Now donna look at me like that. He is not going ta bite ya head off. He likes ya remember." Abby just gave him such a sorry expression. His heart went out to her.

"Ya best be packing some things and do not take anything ya wear in the kitchen. Ya pack the gowns fit for the empress ya are and ya know what I mean."

"Don't call me that. I hate it," Abby said with a pout.

"Ya are an empress and there is nothing ya can do about it. Besides I love the fact that ya are my empress and I donna have ta share ya with a whole country." Then he smiled at her and raised his eyebrows, which made her giggle. "Have I told ya today how much I love ya?" he asked after he saw her smile.

"No you haven't and an Empress like myself requires hearing such words at least ten times a day from her husband who she loves and adores," Abby said in a haughty voice teasingly.

Gabe reached over and kissed her lovingly, deep, long and passionately that led to more and then more and when they finally came out of the camber, it was just before dinner.

Gabe did not trust Abby's packing. It would be just like her to pack simple working gowns and not the fancy ones that she needed and rarely wore. Gabe liked to give formal dinners from time to time and he had many gowns fashioned for her, but she would always protest adamantly saying that she had enough. She now needed these gowns and he was not going to let he get away from Fuchsiall without them.

So he asked Martha to assist Abby in the packing with strict instructions not to forget anything. When Martha finished with the packing, she had a full size trunk filled to the top. But before she could close it, Abby tucked something wrapped in white linen about the size of a large handbag in then closed the lid herself.

Gabe decided to take a carriage from the King's castle, but they would ride from Fuchsiall to his cousins. The threat from the McHales and the pirates was over, but the road was still dangerous especially going into London. Abby's trunk was sent on ahead with men to inform the English King that she was on her way. Gabe was not sure why his King or the English King wanted to have an audience with Abigail, but he would protect her in all cause.

When Gabe announced he was leaving for London, his men started to volunteer to come along. Gabe was impressed with the support shown by his fellow clansmen including Abby's three sons. Gabe allowed Abby's sons to come as far as the Scottish line, but would not let them come into England. Gabe wanted both Joseph and Simon to come with him. Gabe suspected foul play and he wanted expert swordsmen to accompany him and Abigail. He had been training Abby's sons unknowing to her, but did not feel comfortable in allowing them to come along yet. Cookie, Colm and Dougal were also allowed to come. By the time they were ready to depart, Gabe had assembled a true arsenal of men to join him.

Abby left six very unhappy children all lined up at the top of the stairs to the laird not wanting her to leave yet again. She had to promise them she would return and bring them all a present form London. Hannah and Dunkin stood there side by side. Abby gave Dunkin a "*Don't you dare look*" and kissed them all goodbye. She was still under punishment from her father-in-law and he had refused to let her get away from kissing all her family when they were near her.

Comfort Ann was all saddled and waiting for her, but before she could mount, Gabe was up talking to all his children and Hannah. He pointed his finger at all of them and said, "I expect all of ya ta behave while I am gone and when I come back I expect ta find the house in order and all of ya in one piece. And that includes ya," and he pointed at Hannah. Then he asked for kisses from all his children including Hannah. He had to laugh when he saw her blush but she willingly kissed him on his cheek.

Abby was plopped onto her mare and in less than a minute, Gabe was mounted and they were on their way. As usual, Abby rode just behind Gabe flanked by Simon and Joseph and followed by Colm, Dougal and Cookie. The rest of the twenty men followed in a row of two by two which included her three sons.

The men were all concerned for Abby. She was still not acting herself and she did not need another problem. Gabe was sure that the Wikings would never bother her again after seeing what they thought was death. He believed the pirates were no longer a threat either, but there were highway men to look after and they were plentiful in route to London. All the clan including Gabe was heavily armed. Abby was made to carry a dirk under her skirts. As usual she protested adamantly, but Gabe just lifted her skirts and slid a knife down into her stocking. Then he reached a little higher and pinched her bottom, which made her squeal. She heard him chuckle when he mounted his stallion.

They had to camp out three nights before they reached the Scottish King's castle. Gabe kept Abby right next to him at all times. He positioned the men around their bedding and posted three guards as well. He was not feeling very safe for some reason. Maybe it was because trouble seemed to follow Abby everywhere she went or maybe it was experience, but after she was taken from him by the Wikings, he was being more protective.

Abby, for some reason, who was always nervous when they traveled seemed to be at peace. She hummed when she rode and glowed when she smiled. She seemed to be so relaxed and happy. Gabe did not want to spoil this for her. So when she excused herself to tend her needs, Gabe allowed it but watched her from where he was sitting. He also sent two men to flank her from a distance in case she had trouble.

Abby walked into the wooded area to take care of needed duties. She walked a little way in by the fir trees. It was so beautiful in here with the smell of pine strong all around her. She was humming to herself not paying any attention to the strange group that was watching her. She finished her needs and turned to go back to the group. "Are we finished now missy?" a man said holding a knife at her belly.

Abigail gasped to see, standing in front of her were seven dirty, nearly toothless men, wearing faded kilts and heavily armed. All smiled at her with scared faces. They were clearly interested in more than her funds. "Donna even think of warning ya friends. We will be through with ya shortly and then ya can return. Ya be liking what we have in mind. So donna scream if ya know what is good for ya," he said in a low hoarse voice almost at a whisper.

Abby stepped back, but there was nowhere to run. "I am sure that whatever you have in mind for me sir, I will most certainly not like. So step aside before my men come looking for me and kill all of you," Abigail demanded trying not to let her voice shake. At this remark the thieves started to snicker.

"Relax lass, they will not be looking for ya for at least ten minutes and by then two of us will have had the chance ta mount ya," the man with the knife said.

Abby had always taken her time to tend her needs in the past. She had wanted to escape after leaving James and was hoping that Gabe would not let her dally now. But the man was right. Gabe would not be coming after her for at least ten or so minutes. She kept telling herself to think and not panic, just stall.

He reached up and grabbed a hand full of her hair and brought it to his nose and smelled her. "Ya smell right nice and I will enjoy this." He pulled her close to him still holding the knife at her stomach and licked her face. Abby could smell his foul breath and feel his warm wet tongue slide up her cheek. She made a disgusted sound and pushed him away. "Unhand me this instant," she ordered again saying it a little louder in hopes someone would hear her.

Then from behind her a man reached around and grabbed her around her neck. The man with the knife slit her dress from the neck down to her knees exposing her breast and part of her belly. She gasped with the feeling of the knife sliding down her flesh and cutting her slightly enough to bleed. The man with the knife reached up and parted her dress ripping it opened further. Bending down he licked her breast while roughly squeezing the other. Abby let out a squeal when he pinched her but the man behind her put his hand over her mouth muffling the scream.

The other men watched quietly encouraging their leader on and laughing at Abby helpless struggling. Then from the edge of the trees Gabe called down to her, "Abigail ya are taking ta long. It is time ta leave lass."

The man behind her put a knife to her throat and said, "Answer him but donna be stupid. I will kill ya before he can get ta ya and then I will kill him."

"I will be another moment Joseph. I am sorry to be taking so long," Abby called hoping Gabe would get her message.

"Alright, Abby," was all he said and then there was quiet as the men in the woods watched him walk away.

Tears started to flood Abigail's eyes. She was in real trouble again and alone. The man with the knife at her throat threw her to the ground and stepped on her hair so she could not move. The first man started to lift his kilt and the other men gathered around to watch. Someone stuck a dirty cloth in the mouth which made her gag. Two other men pinned her arms down to the ground. She started to scream but the gag would not let her make much of a noise. The man in front of her dropped his sword belt and knelt down in front of her smiling.

Then he fell on top of her with an arrow through his head. The other men jumped up to see Gabe and his men surrounding them, swords drawn and ready to fight. The men that held Abby pulled out their weapons and the fighting began. The arrow that protruded from her now dead assailants' head, landed next to her right extended arm pinning the fabric of her gown to the grown leaving her helpless to get free. His legs were twisted in the lower fabric of her ripped gown rendering her completely imprisoned by his dead body. From her unspeakable position she could see the men fighting. Swords flashed in the sun and the sound of flesh being slice, seem to echo through the trees as she continued to struggle to get free. But her ripped gown held her firmly in place beneath the dead highwayman.

Gabe was relentless. His swing was fatal and unforgiving. Abby watched as his expression was full of hate and focused on the job at hand. Joseph and Simon worked by his side with the same skill and expertise as their older brother. The other men were also just as focused. The highwaymen were not as skilled as the McKenzie men and soon there was not one left alive.

Stepping over the dead, Gabe came to aid Abby as fast as he could. With one strong push, Gabe freed Abby from her dead assailant. Abby reached up with tears in her eye. Her dress still pulled apart exposing her chest, which was slightly bleeding from the knife wound. She wrapped her arms around Gabe's neck. He took his plaid off and covered her. Picking her up he carried her from the woods leaving the dead thieves to be eaten by the wolves. She cried in his chest hysterically having a hard time to catch her breath between sobs.

"It is over Abigail. Are ya alright? Did they hurt ya?" Gabe asked while carrying her back to camp. All Abby could do was shake her head yes and no. She could not speak and could not stop crying. She just shook all over. There was so many of them. Abigail could not imagine what would have happened to her if her clan had not come after her.

Gabe rested her on the plaid in the tent that they had made up for her. He called to get some water to wash her wound. In all the excitement, Abby had forgotten that she was bleeding from the knife wound. He laid her down and opened her dress to tend her. Abby resisted she did not want him to put her down for a moment.

"Abby I will not leave ya but ya are bleeding and I need ta dress the wound before ya get an infection," Gabe said gently.

Joseph handed Gabe some fresh linen for the wound and water. He had also brought a fresh gown for her from Gabe's saddle bags. Abby could not stop the tears. "Alright lass," Gabe said comforting. "It is alright. They will not hurt ya ever again. Luckily this is only a slight flesh wound. A little salve and it will be gone in a few days."

Abby lay in their tent refusing to come out. She was so ashamed and could not seem to face the men. Gabe could not even get her to eat. That is when Cookie took her dish and stomped into Abby's tent. When he came out it was empty and he was not wearing it. He smiled at Gabe and said "she is asleep and her belly is full." Then he walked away with a content smile on his face. As he was walking away Gabe asked him, "how in the hell did ya do that?" Cookie just said, "I told her if she did not eat I would never make her my rabbit stew ever again," then he chuckled.

When morning came Gabe took her to tend her needs. She was still having trouble facing the men. Gabe noticed her apprehension and said, "Abby ya have no need ta be ashamed. Ya did nothing wrong and my men do not hold a grudge against ya."

"Someone could have died because of me," was all she could whisper.

From behind her Joseph said, "We are happy ya are alive, Abby. We lost ya once and it was bloody hell. We all want ya ta know that we would fight for ya and give our lives if we need ta."

"No one is to die because of me," she said weakly. "But I am so thankful you came to help me," then more tears spilled from her eyes. Gabe reached out and hugged her. She was so special and he wasn't the only one that knew that.

They broke camp and headed out to the King's castle. During the ride, each man took his turn to ride next to her and assure her they were not disappointed with her. By the time they reached their destination, Abby was much happier and ready to greet the Scottish King.

When they finally reached the castle the King was waiting for his cousins and Abby. “Welcome my dear,” he said addressing Abigail. “I have been waiting for the time I can get ya alone for a moment and now is as good a time as ever.” Then he looked at Gabe and said, “I will return her for dinner. Make ya selves at home. My servant will escort ya ta ya chambers.” Gabe wanted to protest. He did not want to leave Abby alone for a second especially now that she had survived a brutal attack but he had to obey his king.

The King escorted Abby to a large room filled with books from the floor to the ceiling with a large fireplace on the outside wall next to a large window bordered by red velvet curtains. A dark green and yellow carpet covered a large wood planked floor and a dark highly polished walnut desk sat in the far corner with a high back leather chair.

The King walked to the front of the fire and motioned Abby to join him. When the door was shut by his servant he finally addressed her the way he had intended. “Empress Abigailia Analexia Tersa Foxonia McKenzie I am so pleased ta be able ta addresses ya as ya should be addressed. I have a lot of questions for ya.”

Abby’s eyes opened widely and her mouth dropped in surprise. She asked, “You knew who I was all this time or did you just figure it out?”

“I knew from the moment I met ya. I had my suspicions early on of course but after talking ta ya there was no doubt. But I promise I told no one including my cousin. Ya can imagine how pleased I was when I heard he wanted ta take ya for his wife,” the King said holding her hand and kissing it.

“How in the world did you know?” Abby asked pulling her hand back.

The King just smiled and pointed to the large painting above the mantel. Abby looked up to see the man she knew as her grandfather but now her father staring down at her. “Ya look just like ya Da, Empress, ya cannot hide that.”

Then he pointed to the painting. “I have been looking at this painting ever since I was just a wee lad. Your father and my father were best of friends. He spent many winters here with us and spoke of ya often but he kept ya hidden and would not let anyone see ya. The man standing next ta your father is my father." Then the King went around to the back of his desk and pulled out a small green box from the drawer. "Come and sit down Empress. We have business to discuss. I think this may help ya with the English. I want ya ta know that I had every intention of keeping ya in Scotland and then I remembered this and decided against it. I donna know what England wants of ya but this will help ya."

Abby watched as the King opened the box and reached inside and pulled out a set of documents. "Your father wanted ya ta be able ta go ta any country and plead for asylum. He came ta my father and paid generously for your safe passage into Scotland at any time. This here is the document signed by our fathers on your behalf. It states that failure ta allow safe passage will result in the return of the payment offered. It is a sizable fund. A copy of this agreement was given ta England and Italy. Similar agreements for safe passage where made with England and Italy as well. And I just happen ta have the documents here. Did ya know that ya own property in all three countries?"

Abby looked at the King and shook her head no. "Well ya do and ya have managers who have taken care of them for ya. Ya father's favorite place was here in Scotland and this is the deed ta your property. I believe it is just north of Gabe's land in fact ya border ta his property. The McDough laird is just north of his. Ya are a McDough."

"Are you suggesting that I ask for my father's funds back from England?" Abby asked still shocked with this new information. The King just smiled. He and the English king had been at odds for some time and he would love to see anyone vex his enemy. "England loves it treasures. Ya have been arrested, imprisoned and sold into white slavery. I think ya have every right ta request ya dowry back," the King answered. Then he reached into the box again and handed her another document. Abby's face went white. "I own this?" she asked surprised.

The King smiled and said, "Aye ya do and I am sure ya manager will be most surprised ta finally meet his employer."

"I can't believe this," Abby said putting the document on the desk. "What am I was supposed to do?"

"Ya will do what ya need ta when it is time. But I will tell ya donna let these documents out of ya sight. These are the only ones I have and without these ya have no proof of ya holdings. I cannot help ya anymore than this. I must stay neutral of this affair or it may lead ta more hard feelings between our countries. Ya must promise me that ya will not tell anyone where ya obtained these documents."

Abby gave her word. "Does Gabe know and can I tell him at least?"

"Gabe doesn't know any of this and he doesn't even know that I know who ya really are. He is ya husband and ya have the right ta tell him. I trust Gabe with my life and I know he would never betray me. It is your call, but let me say this, your father lived with secrets and because of that he gave up the only person he really loved and that was ya. It is fine with me if ya choose ta confide in Gabe and if ya still wish ta hide your identity I will keep your secret."

The King and Abby walked out of his study an hour later and found Gabe. Abby was feeling a little nauseous with all that the King had discussed with her and wanted to go lay down, which is where she stayed until dinner.

Gabe had a little surprise for Abby when she woke up the next morning. "Abby, how would ya like ta sail from here ta London on the Lady Fox?" Abby smiled and put her arms around his neck she kissed him gently and asked, "When do we leave?"

"Today, but I have given those sons of yours strict instructions ta not anchor in the harbor. They are ta let us off and then go back up the coast where I will send word when we are ready to return ta Scotland. I donna want ya ta change my plans behind my back now." And he gave her that look that said "*Do not dare.*" Then he said, "Ya sons are fine lads and I like them very much, but they are not skilled in fighting with a sword yet. I donna want ta take any chances with their lives. I want ya ta back me on my decision and not let them come with us."

"You are worried about this trip to London aren't you?" Abby asked surprised.

"Aye, I am not sure what is in store for us. But my cousin said he gave ya some help." Then he gave her a look, which was just asking for her to tell him, to trust him.

"I will not interfere with you and my sons. I know for a fact that they respect you and will not defy you. You have only known them for a few months, but you are more of a father to them than their own ever was and I want to thank you for that. Now we have a lot to talk about and we need to be alone. Is it alright if we wait and talk on the ship?"

"Aye lass it is. Ya donna have ta if ya donna want ta," Gabe said with a loving smile.

"I want to and I trust you as well as your opinion. For once I cannot do this alone and I do like having my big handsome husband on my side." Then she gave him a smile that was so sexy, he almost took her right there and then, but they needed to sail with the tide and they had to get ready.

CHAPTER 34
ALL LOOSE ENDS TIED UP—ALMOST

They delayed the sail until the next day to the delight of the Scottish King. The King kept Abigail very busy with questions about her childhood and how she finally decided to come to Europe.

"My grandfather," Abby started to say and then corrected herself. "I mean my father always talked about taking me to his home in Scotland, but we never took the trip. He always said I needed to be older. When my first husband died, I needed to go. I could not explain it, but I was going even if I had to swim. I never thought he still had holdings here. Hopefully Gabe will be pleased."

"He should be," the King said. "That land borders his own anyway and I know your father was very wealthy and had many treasures as well as secrets. As far as I know his properties have been run very well. You should be most pleased."

Gabe joined the two of them at dinner time only. The King insisted that he be alone with her. When Gabe saw them together laughing a little part of him wanted to hit his cousin. But when the king took Abby's hand and kissed it that was just too much for Gabe to ignore. He walked over to her and put his arm around her waist and gently encouraged her back to the table where he was sitting. "Tomorrow we will be sailing," Gabe announced as the King sat on Abby's left. "It looks like the storm has blown off to sea."

Abby smiled at her husband. He had such a scowl across his face. "Are you ill husband?" she asked with her hand over his.

"No why do ya ask?" Gabe answered.

"You don't look very happy that is all. Have I done something to displease you?" Abby asked hoping he would say no.

"I donna like another man touching ya in any way. My cousin knows that and he is trying ta make me angry. He is the King and can have ya if he wants and I have no say in the matter." Then he looked into her eyes. "He hasn't asked ya ta bed ya yet has he?"

"No he hasn't and I am not about to let him," Abby said with a little giggle. "I have one lover and that is you like it or not. Remember husband I will not allow it. This is one time when being an Empress pays off," she said with a smile and then under her breath she said, "I hope."

Early the next morning, Gabe and Abby got up and ready to leave. As usual the King was waiting to speak with Abby. He greeted her and Gabe as they came down to break their fast and as soon as Gabe was alone he said, "I did not bed her Gabe, but I would have liked to. It is a very good thing ya are married ta her or I would be." Then the King winked at Gabe making him think he was just pulling his leg but Gabe was still not sure. "Abigail is a fine woman and ya did very well ta marry her and ya have my blessing cousin," the King said to Gabe finally.

The McKenzies left shortly after but, had to promise the King that they would return for another visit down the road.

Abby's sons had The Lady Fox ready to sail when they arrived at port. Gabe did not want to wait another minute. He wanted this visit to England to be over as soon as possible. Abby was acting more uneasy as they sailed closer to London. She was reliving her first landing when she was arrested and put into prison. Gabe watched as she twisted her hands and paced the deck getting more anxious the closer they got

Waiting until they were close to docking in London, Abby asked to speak with Gabe in their cabin. "Your cousin gave me this," and she showed him the documents. Gabe was as shocked as Abby when she showed him the holding she owned in England. "Is this correct?" Gabe asked after reading her deed.

"Yes it is and I have every intention of doing something about this. But I have no idea what to do, any ideas Gabe?" Abby asked.

Gabe and Abby put their heads together. It was decided unanimously that Abby was to get rid of it as soon as she could, or put it to good use, but not keep it the way it is. Then they talked about what to do in the English court. As before Abby would not let her ship dock in the harbor. She, Gabe, and some of his men would go to shore and the ship would return to the sea. The Lady Fox would dock up north a ways and wait for word from Gabe. The ship would stop back in a day or two in case they were finished early.

Abby was sure that Jennifer was the reason she had been summoned, but Gabe did not agree with her. They did agree that Abby would do what she needed to and he would not stop her. "Are ya sure ya are willing ta show ya true identity?" Gabe asked just before they reached the London harbor.

"I am sick of hiding," Abby said. "I have you now and that means I can be me without being afraid of being attacked. My father always lived in fear and I am not going to do that. I have no country and the treasure is safe so there is no need to hide anymore."

"Ya always hated being an empress," Gabe said lovingly.

"I do hate it. But in order to deal with this holding in England, I will need to prove my identity and then we can go home and never come here again. I am just sorry I need to bring you in on this, yet again."

"I am here because I want ta be and ya did not ask me if I recall right," he said holding her chin in his fingers lifting it to make her look into his eyes. He loved her more than life itself and he knew she loved him, but this adventure would test their love yet again.

***

When Abby put her foot on the dock, a welcoming committee was waiting. This time she was not arrested, but escorted in a very fancy carriage with all her escorts including Gabe. The carriage brought them to the palace where the English King would have an audience with her. She was dressed in baby blue again adorned with pearl buttons and French lace but this dress was more beautiful than the one Elizabeth Shaw helped her buy.

Why she was thinking of Elizabeth at this moment; she did not know. Elizabeth was the reason that she had arrived in Boston so soon after Roy's death. She also had arranged for Abby have to her father's ship. She should be grateful to her, but she was not. Elizabeth had used her to get to the treasure and made her go through hell in the mean time. Although she did not wish her dead, Abby was not sorry she died either. But oddly it was Elizabeth's death that freed her from the Wikings forever.

Then Abby started to think about Jennifer. She had wanted revenge after Abby had totally exposed her to a room full of people and servants. Although Abby felt justified in her actions, she wondered if she had to go to that extreme. Jennifer needed to be taught a lesson in humility, and she got it. Abby only hoped that her lesson would not come back to haunt her.

Abby held on tight to the documents and a small satchel in white linen while the carriage made its way through the English streets. This time, the people were not throwing rotten food at her but instead watching calmly as she passed. She did not like this city. It seemed so full of trouble and problems. Abby hated seeing the poor in the streets and children running around without supervision. She wondered if they even had parents to care for them.

Then the carriage pulled into the palace and all changed. The grounds were exquisite. Flowers lined the road leading into the palace and the trees where all groomed expertly. Abby could see ladies walking under parasols and men with britches and jackets adorned with ruffled shirts and black gold buckled shoes. The English men were not anything like the rugged highlanders. They reminded her more of women than men.

Servants were everywhere. The royal palace was beautiful and full of treasures just as the Scottish King had told her. Every inch was adorned with something from gold leafing to fancy carved furniture to mosaic floors and fresco ceilings.

Abigail and Gabe and the others were led through the halls and up a large marble stairway to a room where she was to wait until the king called her.

"You are to stay here until summoned," the servant said that led them here. "It will not be long, the king is most anxious to talk to you. Your men will follow me."

Abby gave Gabe a frightened look. She knew what happened the first time and did not want to be separated from him.

The servant asked, “Who is Laird Gabriel McKenzie?”

Gabe stepped forward. “I am.”

“The King wishes to see you first and then her. Please follow me.”

Abby did not want to be alone. She was frightened for herself as well as for Gabe and the others. Gabe just nodded toward her and followed the man without looking back. Abby was left alone in the room while she waited for her turn. She paced the room looking around to keep her mind busy and then looked out the window, which was where she was when the servant returned for her a few hours later.

When the servant entered the room, he stopped dead and did not say a word. He was looking at Empress Abigailia Analexia Tersa Foxonia McKenzie. There by the window was Abigail standing in the most beautiful gown she owned wearing her crown jewels, the real crown of the Empress of Mania. The man stepped back and did not say a word.

“Tell your King I am ready to see him and I will not wait another minute. Is it the custom of this country to make an Empress wait?” The servant ran from the room as fast as he could. Five minutes later he returned with another man wearing similar clothes resembling the men she saw in the garden with more adornment of gold silk.

“This cannot be,” the man said. “I saw you die.”

“What you saw sir, was not me, but someone who wanted you to believe it was me. I will explain this to the King and only to the King. But if I have to wait much longer I will take my men and leave.” Abby was acting like the empress she had been trained to be. She hated it but this was going to be the one and only time.

The man in gold bowed low to her and introduced himself as Captain Jon Martin of the royal navy, the captain that sunk the pirate ship and the Wiking ship.

Abby would not even acknowledge him, but looked straight out the window. Finally the Captain said. “It would be my honor to escort you to the King, Empress. Please follow me.” Again without answering him, Abby straightened her shoulders and grabbed the documents in her white gloved hands and walked toward the room exit. Captain Martin brought her down the stairs and then to the doorway of the throne room. "We must wait until we are called Empress." the Captain said hoping he could get her to calm down, but Abigail had her feathers ruffled one too many times by the English and she was fuming. Separating her from Gabe and the men was bad enough, but making her wait in the room alone was too much.

Until this point she had not decided what she wanted to do with the documents the Scottish king had given her. Gabe and she had discussed this in length, but in the end Gabe wanted her to make her own decision.

The King was sitting on his throne, when Gabe was called into the throne room. The highlanders did not disappoint the King. He was expecting large rugged kilted men armed with swords and ready for whatever was coming. Captain Martin who was with Abby in the hall was also called in. His face was white as if he had seen a ghost and was terrified to hear his fate.

The King addressed the Laird McKenzie and his men. "Come forth Laird," he said. "It is an honor to have you in my home again. My captain here has told me that it was you and your men who helped defeat the pirate Black Dog. On behalf of myself and my country I thank you and wish to reward you. Please kneel."

The King stood as Gabe and his men knelt. "I now dub you knights. You will have my protection as you protected my country from the pirates, rise and except this sword as my appreciation for your gallantry." Gabe was given a large sword with a jeweled handle while the other men were given swords of lesser magnitude but still impressive. He took the sword and nodded to the King.

"Now I wish to speak to your wife. I am told that she is very special. I would like you to leave while I speak to her," the King said, but Gabe shook his head no.

"I will wait for her ta the side if that is acceptable your majesty." Gabe was not about to leave. Abigail had little trust when it came to the English and Gabe felt the same way. The King did not want to make a scene by forcing Gabe, especially after he had just honored the highlanders.

The King called for Abby.

Abigail was standing out of the hall waiting for her name to be called. When it finally was she would not come in until they announced her properly. Finally, the herald asked her how she would she like to be announced. Abby told him exactly what to say. Reluctantly the servant called in his very loudest voice. "Make way for the Empress Abigailia Analexia Tersa Foxonia McKenzie of Mania."

The entire room fell silent with surprise from the announcement. A moment passed and then Abigail finally entered. She was magnificent in her pale blue gown with the pearl buttons and French lace. Gabe had it made special for her. It resembled the first dress she wore when she arrived in England, but so much lovelier.

She stood in the entrance with shoulders back and her head held high portraying the empress she really was. From where Gabe stood he could see her clearly and she was breathtaking.

On her head she wore her crown jewels, the ones she had carried wrapped in the white linen. It felt strange to her to be announced as Empress. She had always tried to hide this fact about herself but now here she was standing tall and proud with her crown placed delicately on her head.

It was a simple crown in a pale gold color with red ruby stones. The crown rose from her head into a hill top shape over her forehead then declining toward the back of her head. In many ways it resembled a large tiara but the rubies dangled in their place as she walked.

Stopping in the center of the room she waited until she received permission to approach the thrown. Through the corner of her eye she could see Gabe looking at her with his arms folded and his legs spread apart. He was so handsome in his highland finery that she just had to look his way and nod her approval. On the other side she spotted Jennifer and James standing side by side with a very surprised expression across their faces.

The King was standing by now and was as in disbelief as the rest of the room. "This cannot be true," he bellowed. "Can someone please tell me what is going on here? She is supposed to be dead, killed in front of my captain. Yet here she stands."

Abby waited for him to address her. She did not move or let on that she was terrified inside. The king finally looked at her and said, "This cannot be, are you trying to deceive me?"

"I am who I say I am Your Highness. If you want answers, then please, allow me to speak." Abigail again waited for him to acknowledge her. Remembering her last time in an English court, she would speak her peace and he was going to listen.

"Do you have proof that you really are the Empress Abigailia?" the King asked.

"I do," was all she would say.

"Do you know the name of person that my faithful captain saw murdered?" he asked.

"I do," she said again. The king whispered something to one of his servants and then the servant left the room. A few moments later the servant returned and whispered something to the King. "Bring them in he bellowed." From the side door, four men wearing shackles and hand irons entered.

"Do you know these men?" the King asked Abby.

Again she answered, "I do," trying not to act surprised to see who they were.

"Would you kindly enlighten us and introduce these guests of mine to all in this room including myself?" the King ordered with a smug look on his face.

Abby walked right over to face each man and said, "This man here is known to me as Mr. Howard Pinkerton the owner of the Riverton bank in the colonies where I lived for twenty three years." Then she addressed Mr. Pinkerton, "It is so nice to see you wearing the proper attire. I am glad to see you finally getting what you deserve for the crook you really are. I hope the King is not making you wait too long."

Then she addressed the next two men. "Here you have George Webber and Jon Washburn from the W & W Shipping Company of which I was affiliated for a short time. It seems that these two men owe the country of England a large debt and you must know that the head operator in this company is neither of these two men, but Mr. Pinkerton himself."

The crowd in the throne room began to buzz with this information. Again the King whispered to a servant and again the servant left the room.

"Shall I continue, Your Majesty, or shall we wait for the confirmation of the information I have just given you?" Abby asked the King who was beside himself by now. She had correctly identified the first three men without hesitation and the crimes they were accused of.

As fast as the servant had left the chamber, he returned with a little white haired man holding a large ledger, which confirmed the debt owed by the W & W Shipping Co. All three accused started to stammer at the same time trying to deny all charges and calling the words Abigail had proclaimed a lie. They in returned blamed her for their crimes and demanded her arrest. Before things could get out of hand, Gabe and his men surrounded Abigail.

"Silence," the King bellowed. "I want to hear what this woman has to say. Anymore interruptions and I will have this room emptied and you all punished." Then he ordered, "I want those three men gagged. I am not interested in their lies or accusations toward this woman." Immediately the three where silenced, which made Abby feel a little better.

While they waited Gabe leaned over and said in a whisper for only Abby to hear. "I love ya and ya are doing just fine." Abby returned his whisper with a small smile just big enough for him to see.

"You may continue, Empress. Please go on and enlighten this court of the identity of the fourth man," the King ordered.

"This is not who you think it is, Your Majesty," Abby said waiting for his response.

"Oh," the King said now sitting back on his throne. "Who do I think this man is?"

"Black Dog," Abby said without hesitation. Again the room broke out into rage and did not stop talking for Abby to continue.

"Guards," the King ordered. "Stand in front of this audience and whip anyone who opens his or her mouth." With that command the room fell into silence again.

"If this is not Black Dog then please enlighten me to his identity," the King demanded.

"This is Niles Shaw, the husband of Black Dog," Abby said not showing any emotion.

Gasps spread throughout the chamber, but no one spoke a single word.

Abby continued before the King could ask another question. "Didn't you think it odd that you could never catch Black Dog and the pirates always knew just which ships to attack? That was because you where looking for a man not a woman. Elizabeth Shaw was Black Dog and the same woman your captain saw killed by the Wikings that day.

When her ship started to sink from the expert aim of the English vessel, Elizabeth disguised herself as me and rowed to the Wikings in hopes to escape. But what she did not know was the Wikings were interested in the contents of my box and me. When they found the box empty and the ship sinking, it sealed her fate. Her throat was slashed and her body dumped into the ocean in front of three ships for witnesses. One was your vessel, Your Majesty. The other belonged to Niles who was overtaken by my husband and his good men and the third was another smaller Wiking ship which rowed away.

Elizabeth had me tied to the helm dressed in black britches and shirt in hopes that you would think Black Dog went down with the ship. Your captain hit the helm with a cannon ball, which made a hole in the deck. When I fell through it, my bindings were released and I was able to later swim away."

"How can that be?" the Captain interrupted. "There were no survivors."

"You were only looking for the men swimming to the shore. I swam out to the ocean. A warm current swept me back to the island far from your ship where I found my husband's ship hidden away."

"Then this is true. Can you prove you are who you say you are?" the King asked.

"I can," Abby answered waiting for him to motion for her to go on, but he had one more question to ask.

"What should I do with your partners and Mr. Pinkerton?"

"I really do not care, Your Majesty, but if you kill them you will never get what they owe you. I would think that making them work off their debt would be much more satisfying than just killing them. Although that very thought had crossed my own mind from time to time especially when I was put into prison and then sold into white slavery because of their crimes."

"Who has done such a thing to you?" the King asked mortified to hear what had happened to her.

"England," Abby said waiting for the murmuring to quiet down. "When I reached your shores the first time, I was arrested before I could step foot on English soil. They took me in chains to the courthouse where I was tried for a crime I did not commit and sentenced to life in the debtors' prison. I spent sixty days there before I was bought by James," and she motioned to James standing on the side, "who brought me to my own house and made me work like a slave and live in a crate filled with rats."

Then it was James who spoke out of turn. "This cannot be. You do not own the manor."

Abby did not wait for him to go on, but held up the deed to her property. The king put his hand out for her to give it to him. "She is telling you the truth James. The manor is hers. She is your employer."

James stepped back waiting to hear what she was going to do with the manor and him as her manager. Abby, however was not interested in what he wanted at this moment. She was more interested in what the King wanted.

When the King handed back her deed, Abby handed him the next parchment. "This is a document stating the return of my dowry if any of the contracts between my father and you have been violated. I think this is the proof you are looking for to prove my true identify. It is my understanding that not one of the agreements has been upheld. Therefore, I am demanding the return of the dowry my father gave you." Abby stood her ground not flinching a bit.

The King just said, "Where did you get this?" As he reviewed the document in his hands.

"It has your signature on it and you signed it. You should know that my father put it in a safe place for me to retrieve in case you did not uphold your end of the bargain."

"Surely you will let me fix this mess. I had no idea that you were taken into custody and imprisoned," the King said apologizing.

"I was told by James himself that you knew all the members he took out of the debtors' prison. Is this now a lie?" Abby asked not showing any mercy.

"This is not a lie Empress. He does show me all the names of the people he buys. I was not looking for Abigail Fox, but I do confess I did not pay much attention. I am the King of England and I will take full responsibilities for my actions. Reluctantly I will return your dowry without a fight. I really liked your father and I am ashamed that I did not live up to his expectations."

Abby was shocked with the King's confession, but he was a smart man and she was not sure he was just saying words she wanted to hear too get on her good side.

"I wish to know why you summoned me to come into this country which has been so cruel to me?" Abby asked still holding her Empress attitude.

"Yes I did summon you and it is in the regards to the treatment of Lady Jennifer. You have been accused of unfair treatment to a member of the royal family. Obviously there has been a big mistake as well."

"She speaks the truth," Abby said with a smile. "I did treat her unfairly just like she treated my family and clan. I do not believe in hitting children, or humiliating servants, or making outrageous demands of my clan. I treated her like she treated all of us. Apparently she did not like what she received."

Gabe gave Abby a quick glance and a quick smile.

Jennifer stepped forward and said, "I am sorry Majesty. I did not realize that the woman I accused of this deed was the Empress. I had no right to be so critical of her. I would like to rescind my complaint against her."

"Now Jennifer that is not all true is it? I told you I was royal you just did not believe me," Abby said with a sweet smile on her face which enraged Jennifer. Then Jennifer lost control of her temper and lunged at Abby screaming, "He was supposed to be mine. You do not deserve him. I will kill you for what you have done to me."

Before Jennifer could reach Abby, Gabe stepped in front of her and restrained her by twisting her arm behind her back. Abby did not move or try to fight back. She acted her part as the perfect Empress wrongly accused and let Jennifer seal her own fate.

"Is this true Gabriel?" the King asked watching Gabe hold Jennifer in place.

"My wife does not lie Majesty. She is telling the truth and ya can see by Lady Jennifer's behavior that there is truth ta what she says."

"What do you think I should do in this matter Gabriel?" the King asked not really expecting an answer.

"Lady Jennifer has made some serious accusations against my wife and against me. She has disgraced your royal family with her behavior and demands. It is not for me ta say what ya should do about this, but if she was a member of my clan I would surely give her what she deserves."

"And what would that be exactly?" the King asked.

Gabe gave him a little smile and said, "Lady Jennifer needs to understand what it is to be a servant and work for a living and have her belly hungry once in a while. She needs to learn to respect the people that she mistreats."

The King nodded with this suggestion and then smiled.

James now stepped forward, "Begging your pardon, Majesty, but I need to know what the Empress has in store for me."

Suddenly at the side of the room Niles Shaw tried to escape. Men started shouting and the attention in the room shifted toward the prisoners. Guards were running through the throne room and swords were drawn. Gabe and his men surrounded Abigail ready to defend her. Both Abby's partners were now face down on the floor still bound and gagged. Some of the King's guards stepped in front of him to defend and to keep him safe. The pirate Niles Shaw had somehow loosened his irons and was now running for his life. He almost made it to the gate when he was finally apprehended and his restraints returned.

When all the commotion was finished, Gabe turned around to find Abigail lying motionless on the floor.

CHAPTER 35
You Get What You Reap

Abby awoke to find herself in the arms of Gabe lying on the throne room floor. Gathered around her were all the Scots as well as the King of England. She could hear Jennifer's and James' voice just in back of the Scots.

"Abby are ya hurt lass? Speak ta me." Abby heard Gabe say as she started to come to. The entire room thought that she had been physically hurt. Gabe had a look to terror in his eyes just thinking that Abby may be harmed.

She pushed herself up and out of Gabe's arms holding her head. Her stomach was turning around as fast as her head was and just as before the room went black. The next time she awoke, she was in a bed chamber resting on a large canopy bed with Gabe sitting in a chair next to the fireplace watching and a large round red faced man looking over her.

Abby jumped and gasped to find a strange man touching her forehead. "Relax Empress. I am not here to hurt you. Sounds like you have been through enough without me adding to your list. Let me introduce myself. I am the King's personal physician. My name is Henry and I was called to see why you keep passing out. I do believe that it has nothing to do with the bump on the head that your husband has told me about is it?" Then he raised his eyebrows at her as if to scold her for keeping another secret.

Abby just looked at him and shrugged her shoulders looking a little guilty.

"Well let me confirm what you, I am sure you already know. I will let you tell your husband and then we, Empress are going to have a long talk. You must start taking better care of yourself and if I need to talk to your husband about your care I will. You are going to take care of yourself from this minute on starting with a meal and warm goat's milk. You are much too thin."

Then Henry stood up and motioned to Gabe to come and get the news from his wife. Abby squirmed in the bed trying to tell Gabe hoping he would not be angry with her. "What is it lass?" Gabe asked holding her hand. Abby waited for the doctor to leave the room before discussing her fainting spells.

She started with, "Please do not be angry with me." Then she looked at him with misty eyes.

"Abby tell me now or I will become angry at ya and that is a promise," Gabe growled at her trying to be patient.

Abby cleared her throat, pulled the quilt over her head and said, "I am pregnant." Then she waited for Gabe to respond. She held the quilt over her head refusing to come out and refusing to look in his eyes.

"Abigail," Gabe finally said still waiting for her to come out from under the quilt. "We need ta talk and I am not going ta talk ta ya through the quilt."

"Just yell at me and get this over with," she blurted. "I don't care if you do not want anymore children. I do and I will not give this child up even if there is a physician here."

Gabe could not believe what she just said. She really believed the doctor was here to abort the child. Gabe knew right away that her first husband might have done this to her before. So he asked her, "Abby did your Roy yell at ya when ya told him ya were pregnant?"

"Yes", she said with a small sniff. "He yelled at me for hours then he brought a doctor to abort my child, but I ran and hid. I would not come out until the doctor left and my husband left. And I will not let you take my child. I am having this baby even if I have to go and hide from you, and this is your child I have not been with anyone else. I am not a whore."

Gabe heard enough. He stood and ripped the quilt from her hands and stood over her with a stern look on his face. Abby covered her face with her hands, tears streaming down her cheeks. "How far along are ya Abigail? I want an answer now."

"Four and a half months, I think. Please get this over with. But I warn you anything you say will not change my mind."

"Abby," Gabe said sitting down on the bed next to her. "I want ya ta look at me."

Abby slowly lowered her hands with tears still coming from her eyes and looked at Gabe. He reached out and touched her cheek. "I love ya Abigailia Analexia Tersa Foxonia McKenzie and I will never ask ya ta give up a child. In fact ya have made me so happy."

"Really? You're not going to yell at me and call me names or deny it is yours or ask me to give it up?" Abby asked surprised to hear what he just said.

"First, I know ya are no whore and ya would never sleep with another man willingly. Second, I know this is my child and last it makes ya happy and that makes me happy. Ya are a wonderful mother and I am so proud ta have ya for my own children. Your boys are fine young men and your daughter is lovely. I want them ta accept me as their stepfather even though they are grown and do not need a father anymore. I love the fact that ya are having my child and that ya want it and are willing ta fight for it, even against me."

Abby sat up in bed and threw her arm around his neck and kissed his cheeks, and then kissed his cheeks, and then kissed his cheeks until he had to pull her off him. "I love you so much," Abby blurted with more tears and sniffs. I only wish that you were my children's real father they missed so much."

"Now tell me, is there anything else ya have been keeping from me and I want to know. No more secrets," Gabe demanded.

Before Abby could answer Gabe's question, Henry returned carrying a tray of food. When Abby did not answer right away, Henry said, "I will tell him if you do not so you best get on with it."

"You cannot be sure it is too soon," Abby said trying to get out of telling Gabe her other secret. Henry turned to Gabe, "After she has your *TWINS*," and he really accentuated the word twins. "Put her across your knee and give her a good paddling." Then he turned to Abby, "Now you know as well as I do that you are having twins and you are now going to eat all of this if I have to feed you myself."

Gabe liked Henry and his bedside manor, but it took the two of them to get Abby to finish all that Henry had brought her to eat. "No more please I cannot eat another bite," Abby protested. "Oh yes ya can," Gabe said and shoveled in another bite. When the tray was finished, and Henry was satisfied with her performance, he talked to Gabe about keeping her healthy and what to give her to eat to keep her from passing out.

"Now this is what I want you to do from now until she gives birth," Henry said facing Gabe. "She is to eat three meals every day with at least three cups of milk. Do you have goat milk or cow?"

"Goat," Gabe said watching Abby make a face of disapproval.

"Good, I prefer goat milk," Henry said continuing his orders. "She is to have a cup of warm milk every night before she sleeps and I want her to take a nap or at least a rest everyday in the afternoon." Both men turned to look at Abby when they heard her gasp at this demand. Then Henry went on, "As I was saying Gabe, she is to nap at least one hour everyday. She has been through too much. I am surprised that she has been able to carry twins this long with all the trouble she has gone through. To me, that means that she is very healthy and I plan on keeping her that way." Then he looked at Abigail with his eyebrows lowered and shaking his finger.

"Next," Henry started to say when Abby interrupted. "Next? I think that is enough." But Henry simply ignored her and looked at Gabe.

"I think you have a spoiled brat here. You will have to be a little stronger with her after she has given birth. I personally liked making my disobedient wife stand in the corner, but I must admit giving her a good paddling once and a while worked as well." Then he winked at Gabe so Abby could not see he was teasing her. When they heard her gasp in disbelief the two men burst into laughter.

"She needs vegetables and fruit. At least six or so a day and I want you to make sure that brat eats them." Then Henry turned to look at Abigail with a sweet smile across his face. "I don't care if you are an Empress. You will do what I say or you will have me to contend with." Gabe liked this physician. He was too much like a highlander not to.

"Are ya sure ya are not Scottish?" Gabe asked Henry.

"How did you know?" Henry answered with a huge grin. "I was born from a Scottish mother, but my father was English and insisted I be brought up in London and schooled here but my mother was a highlander and she insisted I know my Scottish relatives. I will be going to see my cousin Laird Murray in the next few months. He, I believe is your neighbor. Mary, his daughter has been found and I just got word about it. My cousin insists I come and visit." Then he leaned over to Gabe and said just under his breath, "This is when you invite me to come and stay so that I can check on your wife."

Gabe smiled and nodded. "When ya are in Scotland why don't ya stop by and stay as long as you would like. Even if the babies have not come yet," Gabe said following up on the Henry's prodding.

Finally Abby had enough of the two men. "I know just what you are up to, both of you, and I do not need to be checked up on. I can have these babies just fine."

"So just when can we expect ya?" Gabe asked ignoring Abby once again.

Henry walked over to Abigail and sat down on the side of the bed. "I have teased you enough," he said holding her hand. "I do not want anything more to happen to you. I want your promise that you will do what I say and I am coming to check on you." Then he looked at Gabe. "This is where I have to threaten them because if I don't their men let them get away with murder." Henry then turned to her and said, "I will be the one that makes you stand in the corner when I come to visit you if everyone of my demands are not carried out to the fullest."

Abby had to smile at him. He wasn't there to take her babies like she thought and she needed to tell him that. "When I woke up I thought you were here to take my babies. I am sorry for my behavior. Please accept my apologies."

The doctor was shocked with this confession. He was a rough and tough physician, but this kind of practice he frowned on. Henry knew that such abortions were being performed, but never in his thirty years of practice did anyone ask for such a thing.

"You thought I was here to abort your babies?" He asked shocked.

"Yes," Abby admitted.

"Why did ya think that?" Gabe asked still in shock as well.

"Because it has happened to me before," Abby confessed with her head down unable to look at either man.

Henry gave Gabe a disgusted look. "I would never do such a thing and I am not about to now," Gabe said a little too loudly.

"Who Abigailia, would do such a thing to you?" Henry asked.

Still not able to look either man in the eye, Abigail started to tell them her story.

"My first husband was an evil man. At first he seemed to be a gentleman but as the months went on, his true self came out. My family thought he would be a good match and believed him to be a traveling salesman. He really only wanted the land the marriage gave him and his inheritance. He did not care an ounce for me.

When I became pregnant the first time, he yelled at me for hours. He told me he wanted children but when I was with child, he was furious which is why I did not tell Gabe. I did not know how you would react.

I was so happy to be with child when I was married to Roy, but that changed fast. We fought for hours and then he left and came back with a physician who could fix everything. Those were his words.

The doctor had a black bag and ordered me to go into the bedroom. I went in and climbed out the window to the roof and then climbed down and ran into the wood where I hid until they both left.

I had friends in a nearby Indian tribe who took me in for a short time until they knew it was safe for me to return. Roy left on one of his so called business trips and did not return until Ellery was born. He stayed just long enough to get me pregnant with my first twins and then left again. I never told him I was with child so he was most surprised when he returned to find three little boys.

He was an awful man and would not allow the boys to carry his name. That is why they all use mine. Roy did not think any of them were his but they were, everyone of them. When he found out I was pregnant for Hannah, I thought he was going to kill me. But I was really good at walking across the roof and took the boys and ran again.

After that he rarely came home, and when he did I would have to hide the children because he would beat them for no reason except to get back at me.

That is why I did not tell you Gabe and I am so sorry. You have never acted like Roy and I am ashamed I thought you could ever be a part of something like that." Abby lowered her head more and did not look up. The two men were speechless. Gabe came to the other side of the bed and reached out and drew Abby into his arms hugging her like he did not want to ever let her go.

Henry could not believe what the Empress had just told him. Silence filled the room which was finally broken by a knock on the chamber door.

When Henry answered the door, he found a servant from the King asking for Empress Abigailia to return to the throne room if she was able. Henry looked at Abigail.

"I don't want to postpone this any longer I wish to have this done with so that I may return to my home in Scotland," Abby sputtered.

"I will permit you to go only if you allow me to be with you and only if you promise to leave if this gets to be too much for you," Henry said sternly.

Abby nodded and Gabe helped her out of bed. He offered her his arm and whispered, "Do not even think of letting go of my arm while we are in that room. Do you hear me?" Abby nodded again and the two men started to walk her down the stairs to the throne room.

As they entered, Niles Shaw had been returned. This time he was well chained and heavily guarded. The partners and Mr. Pinkerton were also in chains in the front of the thrown where the King was waiting. Jennifer was now standing between two guards and James was waiting to hear what Abigail had in store for him.

He was shocked to find out that she was the Empress whose estate had been funding him all these many years. It had been so long that he had decided that she would never come back and he owned it. Now he would have to be accountable for each year he had managed the property for her. He would need to pay her the amount he owed her. While she was out of the room being examined by the physician, James had time to calculate her earnings. It was sure to break him. He had enough to pay her, but it would take every penny he had. James might even have to sell his own townhouse to do it.

When Empress Abigailia entered the hall, the crowd stood. She had returned to her pink self and was wearing her crown jewels. Gabe held onto her as tightly as he dared and Henry walked at their side.

"I wish to know if you are able to continue Empress?" the King asked.

"She is Majesty," Henry said. "But she is still a little shaky and I think she should have a seat." The King nodded and a white high backed chair with a bright red cushion and cushioned back was promptly brought in for her to sit. Abby did not protest which surprised Gabe.

The King rose from his throne and said, "I wish you to tell me again if this is the pirate Black Dog's husband."

"To my knowledge he is, your Majesty," Abby answered.

"Why do you say it this way?" the King asked.

"I met Elizabeth Shaw and Niles Shaw when I was still in the colonies. They introduced themselves as husband and wife, but Niles never was allowed to ride with us in the carriage and when we stopped for the night they took separate rooms. I do know, Your Majesty, that he was indeed one of the other captains of the pirate ships."

"You talk like there was more than two," the King said now walking to the top of the stairs where his throne rested.

"I believe there were three," Abigail said with her head held high waiting for the next round of questions. Gabe squeezed her arm a little when he heard her blurt this information. As long as he lived Gabe was afraid that Abby would have a secret or two still in her pocket. He looked down at her as if ready to throttle her. Abby cleared her throat waited for the King to continue.

"Three ships, you say. Well please go on so that I may understand," the King said sitting down now.

"Elizabeth Shaw was indeed Black Dog and I am certain of this without a doubt. She even confessed this fact to me when I was on board her ship before your vessel attacked it. Niles was the captain of the vessel my husband overpowered. The third ship, now owned by my husband as well was The Lady Fox."

"Are you certain of this fact?" the King asked.

"Yes I am."

"And just where is this third captain?" the King asked again.

"Dead and buried of which I was a witness to as well." Abby said hoping this was it and she could leave.

"Then the pirates have all been dealt with and I can now have safe shipping waters again?" The King asked with an approving smile.

"I cannot say that for certain, but you will not have any more trouble from these pirates again," Abigail said with the air of the Empress she was.

"Then our business is over Empress. I will give you your dowry and reward you and your husband for this fine day. In the future, you will always be welcomed in England even though you have been treated poorly thus far. Maybe as the days go by you will grace England with another visit and this time I will greet you in the manner you so much deserve."

The King then faced the prisoners. "You Niles Shaw will be flogged and then hung to your death one week from today along with all your fellow shipmates. Take him away."

As for you Mr. Pinkerton, Mr. Webber and Mr. Washburn you can thank the Empress for saving your worthless lives. You will work off your debt to England as she suggested, but first I will have the three of you flogged as well. Then you will return to me and I will assign you work fitting for the animals that you are. And make no mistake about this, gentlemen, those chains will be yours until you are debt free or die whichever comes first. All properties owned by the W & W Shipping company and Mr. Pinkerton will now become property of England as partial payment toward your debts."

Abby was pleased to hear the punishments dished out by the King and even more pleased when Mr. Pinkerton broke down and cried like a little baby as he was carried out to receive his punishment.

There was one more item the King needed to finish. "Lady Jennifer, please step forward and receive your punishment," the King ordered. Like Mr. Pinkerton, Lady Jennifer was putting on a good show with big tears and begging for the King's mercy, but the King was not moved by her display and ordered her to be silenced.

"It is a privilege to be born into royalty and a responsibility. Commoners need to be respected as well as royalty. They are the backbone of our country and must be treated honorably. You however have taken advantage of your station causing the royal class to have a bad reputation. I agree with the Empress. You need to be common for a while and maybe you will not be so critical of them. So until I deem you punished enough and it will be a long time before that happens. You are stripped of your title and station. You will become one of the servants in the winery where you will stomp grapes and serve wine at the royal tavern where your backside will be pinched and your breast that you so enjoy showing, handled whenever the men please. And finally you will also receive the beating you well deserve and expected the Empress to suffer."

Jennifer screamed as if she had been stabbed in the back, but the King just motioned for the guards to take her away. The crowd in the chamber cheered as she was taken out of the room.

"You Empress and Laird McKenzie are welcomed to stay in my home until you are strong enough to leave," the King said not waiting for an answer. He rose from his throne and exited the room at the back of the chamber.

Abby was helped to her feet by Gabe and escorted from the throne room to the carriage Gabe had waiting out in the courtyard. Gabe gave the order for the Lady Fox to reenter the harbor and plans were made as soon as she docked to leave.

Before Abigail could reach the carriage, James was standing there waiting for her. "Empress," James said bowing low. "When may I have an audience with you? We need to discuss my employment. I am prepared to give my notice if that is what you require." Abby was not ready to face James. She hated the man for what he had done to her knowing that she was innocent and still he was planning to kill her. If she had run the day Gabe bought her debt, she would be dead now. She was sure Gabe had saved her life and when they finally reached home she would thank him properly. Abby question the fact that James did know who she really was and wondered if he was trying to kill her so he could claim the manor for himself.

Gabe sensed her apprehension with this encounter with James.

"James," Gabe said. "Now is not the time. Abby has not decided what to do as of yet. Continue what you are doing and we will let you know as soon as we decide."

"You have taken very good care of the manor and for that I am grateful, but I do not approve of how you have achieved it or the fact that you were trying to kill me." Abby said as Gabe helped her into the carriage. She sat down and then looked into the eyes of James. "You will hear from me in the near future. I will give you time to get the books in order. Do not try to run or cheat me. Debtors' prison and crates are less to be desired. I guarantee you will not enjoy rats feeding off you."

Gabe tapped on the ceiling of the carriage, signaling the drive to take off and they exited the palace leaving James standing alone.

Gabe sat in the seat next to Abby and pulled her onto his lap. "I am sorry I did not trust you Gabe. Are you angry with me?" Abby asked as she put her head on his shoulder.

"No just disappointed that ya still do not trust me," Gabe said hugging her.

"What can I do to make it up to you Gabe?" Abby asked holding back tears.

"No more secrets between us would be a good start Abby. I donna want ta talk about this anymore today, but I have a few questions I need ya ta answer and we will talk on the way back ta Scotland," Gabe said still holding her tightly.

"You still want me?" Abby whispered in his ear.

"I will never let ya go and ya know it. And aye I do want ya, but I want all of ya. Not the secrets but I am not so sure that is what ya want." Gabe held his hand up and would not let her answer. They rode in silence from this moment on.

CHAPTER 36
No More Secrets

The Lady Fox had not gone too far out to sea. She returned the next day on the chance that Gabe, Abby and the men were ready to return home. The crew was thrilled to have everyone back on board and ready to return to Scotland. But Abby just greeted everyone and went to their cabin and did not come out.

The first few meals on board, Abby took in her cabin and Gabe did not join her even at night. The crew was beginning to feel uncomfortable with the distance Gabe had taken with Abigail. He would not let anyone talk to him about Abby not even Joseph.

On the third night out to sea, Abby joined Gabe on the deck. It was way past midnight and the ship was lit by the full moon. The night crew was on deck and watching as she came out of her cabin. "Husband," she said as the night crew watched. "I need to speak with you please." Abby twisted her hands together nervously hoping Gabe would not deny her.

Gabe noticed her apprehension, but he was still disappointed in her. Not because she was giving him two more children, but because she had been secretive again. He wanted her trust, but she still could not seem to give it to him. She was so beautiful and he loved her so that he was not about to deny her a chance to talk to him. Gabe doubted that she could say anything that would make up for the secrets, but he was willing to give her one last chance.

When they were on their way to England, she had finally confided in him and this pleased Gabe but after the events at the palace, Gabe knew she had not been completely honest with him after all.

Gabe did not answer her, but just nodded for her to continue. Abby was a little nervous with the night crew looking on so she asked if they could be alone but Gabe would not follow her back to the cabin. He just pointed to the helm as the crew scattered to give them privacy.

When all was clear of the crew, Gabe took over the helm. Abby started, "I am doing my best Gabe. I know you are disappointed with me and I understand why. So please let me talk and do not interrupt me and if you have any questions when I finish than I will answer them and hold nothing back." Gabe just nodded again. Abby twisted her hands trying to say the right words.

"I don't know where to start," Abby finally admitted.

"Why donna ya start by telling me who the other dead captain was and why ya did not tell me before we were in the throne room," Gabe ordered not making it any easier on her. She was going to learn to trust him and she deserved this attitude he was giving her.

"Very well," Abby said still twisting her hands. "I always thought it was strange that Elizabeth and Niles knew who I was. No one knew who my box belonged to until I produced the proof to take it. Yet there on the sidewalk when I left the bank was Elizabeth Shaw. Someone had to suspect who I was and tipped them off. I ruled out Mr. Pinkerton, but I could never quite rule out his cousin Roy Pinkerton, my dead husband. You never asked me my husband's full name and I led you to believe that it was Fox, but that was my maiden name and as you heard in the bedchamber my children all go by my maiden name because he refused to claim them as his own."

"Did ya kill him Abigail?" Gabe asked before she could continue.

Abby lowered her head and took a very deep breath. "Yes."

Gabe did not show any emotion and kept looking into the dark sea waiting for her to go on.

"I had not seen him in over ten years and then he showed up. He was his usual self, angry with me and ready to do me as much harm as he could. Ellery was home fixing the fire with a poker and thank goodness the twins and Hannah were away.

Before Ellery could do anything, Roy hit him over the head and knocked him lifeless on the kitchen floor. The hot poker still lay in his hands. I really did not know if Ellery was dead or alive. Roy started coming at me threatening to scar my face and cripple me forever if I did not tell him about the treasure. He was so angry to have discovered the very person he had been searching for all these years was living in his very own house.

I always thought it strange that Roy was suppose to be a salesmen, but he never had any merchandise and he would leave and come back in the spring all bronze in color like he had been in the warm sun all winter. He made comments like a sailor and as careful as he was I picked up on it many times. He always addressed the ocean as a woman and constantly used nautical knots when tying his horse. I knew he was not a salesman. He was a sailor and not just a sailor but a captain and the captain of the Lady Fox.

He kicked the chairs over in the kitchen and I ran behind the table. He picked up the hot poker out of Ellery's hand and started after me. There was a kitchen knife on the table that I had been using to carve a roast. I picked it up and threw it at him hitting him dead in the chest. He staggered and fell dropping the hot poker onto Ellery's leg burning him.

Roy lay on the floor still holding the knife that was protruding from his chest motionless. Not showing any signs of life. I ran around the table and pulled the hot poker off Ellery's leg before too much damaged was done and helped him get out of the house.

When Ellery was up to it, we put Roy on his horse and took him down the road and left him to look like he was attacked by bandits. No one questioned it, but I needed to get out of Riverton in case they did, even though my children protested vehemently.

We had a funeral and acted upset but not one of us cared that he was dead. Everyone threw a rose in his grave but I threw in the last letter from his mistress. It was just signed with a big letter 'E'.

I needed to get out of Riverton and Elizabeth needed to get the Lady Fox to me and then let me lead her to the treasure. I thought it strange how fast the Fox was mine and how fast I was on my way. I was so thankful to Martin. He and I figured out so much about the partners, but not everything. It wasn't until I was captured by Elizabeth that I realized who 'E' was.

I recognized her handwriting. It was the same handwriting on the letter and when I confronted her, she laughed and admitted that Roy and she were lovers while she was still married to Niles and Niles knew it. She told me that the Lady Fox was Roy's ship."

Abby had enough she did not want to talk anymore. She sat on the side of the rail and put her hands over her face. Now he knew everything. Gabe knew she had killed Roy and she was sure he would hate her, but she did not want to live with secrets any longer and this was the only way. Abby hated the look he had given her when he found out she had kept the babies from him and she would never do that again even if it meant losing her one true love.

Every time Gabe thought Abby could not shock him anymore she would come out with another surprise. He turned his gaze from the sea to Abigail. She was miserable and he started to feel sorry for her. Abby had every right to protect herself from Roy but there she was feeling guilty for killing him and saving her own life and probably Ellery's. Gabe asked, "Why did ya not tell me that ya killed ya first husband?"

Abby look up from her hands and said, "I was in prison, and a white slave. I did not want you to know I was a murderer as well. Believe it or not I was a very good person at one time. I would never do anything to hurt anyone. Roy was so cruel and I had no choice just like when I was thrown into prison or sold. I did not want you to know that I was capable of doing such a thing. You must not want me near your family or your children now and I understand that. So if you want me to go somewhere else I will and I will not fight you about it."

Abby was sure he was going to cast her out somewhere, but she thought he would wait until his children were born she thought. She was hoping he would put her in a cottage on his land or his father's until the babies were born. "I could stay in one of the empty cottages on your land and no one would know until the babies are born and then you can do what you want with me." Her head was bent and Gabe could hear a sniff. She was crying but did not want him to know it.

Gabe loved this woman. How in the world could she think he would cast her out especially now that she was with children? He shook his head and motioned for one of the men to come and take over the helm. Gabe wanted to finish this conversation, but not on deck. "Follow me Abigail," was all he said and he walked off the deck and down to their cabin. Holding the door open for her he watched her walk in slowly with her head down.

When she was in the cabin, he shut the door and said, "Is that what ya think I should do with ya? Ya want me ta lock ya up in some cottage and leave ya there until ya have my babies?" Abby just shook her head yes, but would not look up at him.

"Well I have a much better idea and ya will not fight me on it will ya," Gabe said sternly. She had done it again, surprised him with what she was thinking.

"I will not fight you, but I ask you to be gentle that is all," Abby said with tears running down her cheeks.

Gabe walked over to the door and bolted it. Then he turned and said, "I guess ya are determined that I should punish ya then? After all ya are a real murderess now and a criminal, but I feel ya have paid ya debt back ta me, so I cannot call ya a white slave anymore, not that I ever thought of ya that way." Gabe was going to teach her a lesson and this was not going to be easy, but she needed to trust him and he was going to make sure she did from now on.

"Very well then lie on the bed and lift ya skirts and let's get this over with," Gabe said as he removed his sword belt.

Abby gasped to think he was going to strap her. "I thought…" she started to say but thought better of it. She stood up and walked to the bed, lifted her skirts and lay on the bed. Before Gabe could get the first swing in she buried her head in her arms and cried uncontrollably.

He sat down on the side of the bed and removed the rest of his clothes. When she did not feel his strap across her bum, she picked her head up to see what was taking so long. Gabe was sitting on the bed naked waiting for this very moment. "Are ya finished feeling sorry for ya self?" Gabe asked with his hands folded across his chest.

Abby could not believe what she was looking at. He had no intention of hitting her. She sat up and said, "I thought…," but before she could say anymore he said, "You thought I would act like ROY."

Then Abby realized what she was doing. She was keeping him away from her just like her father had done and she had done her whole life. Gabe always accused her of not trusting him and here she was doing it again not trusting him. He had tried so hard to show her and now she finally saw it for herself.

"I don't know what to say anymore. You have never acted like Roy. I don't know what you want me to do," Abby said softly.

"I want your trust and your love and I will not take anything less. When ya hide things from me is the same as lying. Ya hurt me when ya do not trust me enough ta confide in me honestly. I have been patient with ya, but I am at the end of my rope. I would love ta strap ya right now ta knock some sense in that head of yours, but I will not strap my wife especially now that she is pregnant. It angers me ta think ya thought I would."

"But you did before," Abby said trying to understand.

"I did but that was before ya were my wife. I told ya I would not treat ya any different than my clan. I warned ya what I would do if ya ran. I was doing my job as laird. We do not abuse our women and it is not allowed ta hit. If I must punish a woman in my clan it is because she has broken our laws and I must follow our law. Ya broke my law and left me no choice."

"You are not going to strap me ever again?" Abby asked not believing what she was hearing.

"Never but I may put ya in the corner however," then he gave her the slightest smile.

Abby threw her arms around his neck and kissed his cheeks. "I am so sorry Gabe I really didn't mean to hurt you. I was so afraid to tell you what I did. I didn't want you to change your opinion of me."

"Abigail ya were protecting yourself and your son. He would have killed ya in the end after ya told him. Ya had every right ta defend yourself and I will not condemn ya for that," Gabe said looking into her red swollen eyes.

"Then you do not think I did wrong by killing him?" Abby asked.

"Abigail that is what I have been trying ta tell ya all this time. I donna think ya have done anything wrong. Killing Roy was your right ta defend ya self. Prison was because ya were at the wrong place at the wrong time and punished for someone else's crime. Ya are guilty of jumping into a situation ta quickly and ya are guilty of not trusting the one that would give his life for ya, me, but that is all."

"I'm so sorry Gabe," Abby said still wiping tears from her eyes.

"And donna even think of living anywhere but with me from now on. Do I finally make myself clear in that head of yours? What we discuss stays between us and no one needs ta know but ya and me. I do not want ya ta tell anyone else about Roy including a priest in confession. I know ya are innocent and that is all ya need. From now on this subject is closed unless there is something else ya are not telling me."

Abby finally smiled, "Oh there most likely is but at this moment I cannot think of anything."

"Good, now take that gown off. Ya have made me want ta bed ya flashing that beautiful round bum at me, serves ya right."

Abby did as she was told and Gabe made love to her as only he could do making her feel like she was his Empress, queen of his life.

When morning came a few hours later, the couple did not come out of the cabin. The crew was thrilled to find both Abby and Gabe in the same cabin again. But Cookie was fuming. Gabe had left strict instructions on her care and it was way after ten a.m. and they still did not come out. Abby needed her meals and her milk. Cookie had a goat on board special so she could stay healthy. He was going to give her husband a good lecture when they finally came out.

The news of her pregnancy had spread through the ship like wildfire. The crew all had questions to when she was due and if it was true she was having twins.

When Gabe came to the deck without her he was bombarded with concerns for her. "Relax lads, Abby is fine and ready to break her fast. I am sure that she will answer all ya questions when she comes up on deck but first she is still bathing and will be up soon. Woman seems ta take a little longer than men I've noticed." That explanation satisfied the men and Cookie went to the galley to get her morning meal.

When she came out into the sun she was beautiful and for the first time the men noticed that she did have a little belly. Cookie scolded her for not eating sooner and sat and watched her eat every bite. Abby and Cookie had developed a good friendship and he was the only one she would take that kind of scolding from. Throughout the day the other men put in their opinions and let her know how foolish she had been to try and hide her pregnancy from them. Abby had to apologize to each man one at a time and promise she would not cause them any more worry especially her sons.

When they reached Scotland, they stopped at the King's house to get their horses, and tell him the happenings in England, and of the new babies. Gabe's cousin was so pleased to see Abby and Gabe. Staying however was not an option. Gabe wanted to get Abby back home safely. With Abby's pregnancy they would be traveling at a much slower pace. The King insisted on sending a few more men with them after hearing of Abby's attack. Gabe was not too thrilled with this but he could not say no to his cousin. Once they made it to Gabe's land however the extra guards returned to the King.

Abby, Gabe and the other men were greeted favorably by the clan especially when Gabe announced the news of the babies. Abby was immediately treated like a fragile flower. She was waited on hand and foot despite her protests.

Even Gabe treated her special which she hated. "I am not an invalid," Abby protested. "I can do chores and take care of myself. I do not need to be reminded to eat or take that damn nap and I really hate warm milk." Without answering Abby, Gabe called for Emily.

"Emily it is time for ya nap," Gabe ordered to his six year old daughter.

"Da I am ta old ta have ta take naps now that I am six," Emily complained.

"I know but your mother really needs ta take her nap and if ya donna take her with ya she will not take hers. So ya are doing me a favor by taking good care of ya mother while she is pregnant." This satisfied the six year old and she went and took her mother's hand.

"Da says it is time for our nap Mom and he will not hear any complaining from either one of us so we best get on with it," Emily sputtered not really wanting to go. Abby gave Gabe a disapproving look as well. Neither one of the ladies liked their naps but Gabe would not let either one of them get out of taking a daily rest. And when he checked on them daily, he would find both of them sound asleep despite their reluctance.

As Henry ordered, Abby had her glass of warm goat's milk before bed every night.

"Abigail, ya are going ta drink this milk and that is final," Gabe ordered watching Abby hide under the quilt so she would not have to drink it.

"I hate warm milk and I do not want it. I have the other milk all day without complaining, but I really hate warm milk it is enough to gag a maggot," Abby said with a very childish expression. She then asked, "Are we going to do this every night until the babies are born? Because if we are you are really going to hate warm milk as much as I do by the time they are born."

Gabe was not going to let her get away with not taking her milk. Henry was a very good physician and it did help her sleep even though she would not admit it. So he just held the glass in front of the quilt until she finally gave in and took her milk. "Abigail that was a very good girl," Gabe said treating her like a child after the way she had just acted. Abby gave him a dirty look and rolled over. "If ya are going ta fight me every night than it is ya that is going ta be rolling over ever night angry. Now, how about meeting me half way about this?" Gabe said picking up the quilt and looking under it at her.

"What did you have in mind?" Abby said still upset he made her drink that milk.

"I will let ya skip a nap once a week if ya take ya milk without complaining once during the week," Gabe said.

"How about three naps?" Abby asked trying to get out of more naps.

"We do not have ta do this at all," Gabe said not willing to let her off.

"But on the day ya do not take a nap ya will spend the afternoon with just me," Gabe added. Abby smiled and said, "Done," and from that day on and until she gave birth, Abby skipped one nap a week and spent the day with Gabe alone. Each night she drank her warm milk without complaining, but she always made an ugly face when she finished it and stuck her tongue out.

A short time later, Gabe received word that James wanted to see Abigail and finish the business between them. The last thing Gabe wanted was to upset her especially now that she was getting closer to delivering, but they were having no more secrets so he called her into his study. When Abby walked in, refreshed from her nap and handed her James' note.

"Abby this came the other day and I did not know what ta do about it. It is from James."Gabe said.

When she finished reading it she said, "I hate that man with every breath I take. I have never hated anyone, but I just cannot stop thinking of all the cruel things he did to me and the others. I wonder how many people he killed because he had no more use for them and he justified it because he was dealing with criminals. Sometimes I think he is no better than Elizabeth Shaw. I realize that he helps you with your business so if you really want to let him continue managing my manor then I will not interfere."

"Abby I own three ships now. Did ya forget? Your sons and my baby brother have already started making a good profit better than James ever did. I do not need James any longer but I think ya should really think of not selling the manor and do something constructive with it."

"He wants to come and see me," Abby said with her head bent.

"I will not let him be alone with ya if that is what ya want," Gabe said. Finally Abby agreed to meet with James one last time. So Gabe sent a messenger off the next day and made arrangements for James to come without Jennifer in three weeks.

Gabe and Abby were in his study when Joseph came to announce that James had arrived. Gabe had him shown in immediately.

As James entered the room, Abby began to shake. Gabe put his arm around her and let her sit down behind his desk. He whispered. "It's alright lass. He cannot hurt ya anymore." Abby just nodded as she watched him enter.

Abby noticed a difference in James. He was not the cocky arrogant man he once was at the manor. He brought with him the profits he had raised for her over the years managing Abby's estate along with his letter of resignation.

"Gabe," James said as he entered the study. Then he looked at Abby and said, "Empress, I have come to finish our business and to resign as your manager. I also took the liberty to hire a temporary manager who will be honest. He will take good care of your property until you decided what you are going to do with it. If in the case you decide to hold on to it, he will stay on as manager."

Abby looked at him and said. "I will more than willingly accept your resignation. I am sure a man with your unique talents will have no problem finding employment somewhere else." Then James handed her his ledgers, all in order with ever entry neatly written and every penny accountable. He had not cheated her. He had only taken his agreed pay, but had managed her funds expertly making Abby a very good profit.

James waited patiently for Abby to finish looking through the ledgers. When she was satisfied with what she had seen she closed the book and looked at James. He no longer appeared as the confident cocky business man she once knew. He now had the persona of a defeated man, completely ruined financially, a fate worse than death in his eyes. Even his body showed the toll. He was now thin and his once rosy cheeks, pale and sunk in.

"Everything seems to be in order sir. I am pleased." Then she asked, "Did you have to sell your townhouse to pay me?" James looked surprised that she would even ask him such a thing. How did she figure that out by just looking over the ledgers?

James only nodded. Abby then asked, "What exactly did you get for it?" James looked at Abigail with a baffled look on his face, unwilling to discuss his ruination with her, but Gabe nodded his way and so he blurted out how much he sold it for.

"When I was in the colonies, I had my own house but it was in my husband's name. I was the one who worked the land and paid all the bills. My first husband never gave us much to live on and so I raised my four children myself and made a good home for them. When he died, his estate was sold to pay off his debts and we were all put out of our home before he was even buried. I will admit that you are the last person I ever wanted to see in my home but I do thank you for the expert job you have preformed as my manager. No one wants to lose their home and I will not be responsible for taking yours away from you." Then Abby gave him back the exact amount he received for his townhouse and said, "Consider us even." She did not wait to see him leave but started to walk out of the room leaving the two men behind. It was not until she stood up that James realized she was with child.

"For what it is worth, Abigail," James said as her back was facing him. "I did not know that you were the Empress."

Abby turned to face him. "And if you had, would it have made a difference?"

"Yes. Despite what you think of me. I have only acted honorably. I know that you do not agree with my ways but I have always done what I believe is fair and just," James said trying to apologize.

"You knew I was innocent but yet you kept me in that crate and treated me worse than an animal. How sir is that honorable and just?" Abby said with the air only a true Empress could have.

"I am ashamed to say that it is not and that is why I am handing in my resignation, Empress. I was wrong and for what it is worth. I am truly sorry," James said with much conviction.

"Are you expecting me to accept your apology sir?"

"No Empress, I do not expect anything or ask anything of you," James answered.

Abby had never seen him like this. He had always portrayed the perfect persona of a confident man with the world at his feet. Standing here in front of her was half the man she once knew. As much as she wanted to forgive him she could not. "You took from me a time in my life that I can never get back. I still wake thinking I am chained and in that crate fighting to get free from the rats. There is nothing I can say to you to make you feel better about what you did to me. I do not wish you harm and I do hope that your next business adventure will be successful but I cannot forget or forgive you for what you have done to me." Then Abby turned and left the study leaving the two men to speak alone.

When Abby was gone, Gabe asked, "How long have you been in love with her?"

James turned to look at Gabe surprised he knew that he loved Abby. "Since the day she sang that awful song to my guests. I still have to laugh when I think about it."

"How did you know she was faking?" Gabe asked with a small grin on his face.

"No one could ever sing that badly," James said with a smile. "I do wish you and Abby much happiness and if I could not have her, then there is no better choice for her than you. I know that you will treat her with loving hands and much better than I ever did."

"Why James, why did ya do that ta her if ya loved her?" Gabe asked trying to understand.

"Abby was the first woman I could not control. I hated the fact that she could weasel her way around me and vex me whenever she wanted. She would not cower in front of me or show any fear. I wanted to break her and make her mine but she was too strong and she would never concede to me. I knew she would never come to me willingly. It was my plan to take her to my townhouse in London but not as my whore but as my wife. You bought her before I had the chance."

"So ya were willing ta kill her so no one else would have her?" Gabe said through gritted teeth.

"Yes, I am ashamed to say. If she had tried to escape, I was going to kill her. She deserved better than I. I am happy she found you and that it turned out so good for you in the end. Hopefully down the road we can still do some horse trading, but for now I will take my leave." James tipped his head forward and left the study and Gabe's land.

Gabe found Abby in their bed chamber after James left. He took her into his arms and hugged her. "I am so proud of you Abigail McKenzie and thankful that ya are mine."

CHAPTER 37
Never Leave

Christmas would be coming soon and Gabe's whole family would be arriving. None of his siblings, or father had missed a Christmas yet and Gabe refused to let anyone miss it now. Christmas day was always spent with his children all ten of them now, soon to be twelve plus Abby.

The day after Christmas, Gabe's siblings and their families started to arrive. Every chamber in every wing was filled to capacity. Before they all arrived however every inch of the laird was made ready. And Abby was right there to help even though she was kicked out from time to time when heavy lifting was involved. Gabe especially made sure that each chimney was cleaned so that he would not catch Abby up one. Every bed was aired and every quilt washed and returned to the beds. Floors were washed and curtains cleaned and re-hung.

Eva, the cook, baked and cooked in preparation for the huge meals to come and again Abby was there to help. Having Abby in the kitchen made Eva's job a lot easier and unlike the cleaning, Abby was rarely kicked out of the kitchen.

Abigail was growing rounder by the day and Gabe love to watch her. She would waddle back and forth as she walked constantly rubbing her belly. But when Gabe would ask her if she was in pain, she would just smile and say the twins were just sparing. She never complained about being pregnant and seemed to beam when he looked at her.

Cookie and Eva kept Abby eating healthy and Emily made sure she was not the only one that had to take a nap. Abby had become very fond of Cookie's rabbit stew and wanted some every day. She never seemed to get sick of it. Cookie kept a pot of his stew on the stove simmering so she could help herself even in the middle of the night. Abby would laugh when Cookie would brag that his stew was good for the blood and it would make her strong enough to live through anything.

Gabe was hoping, Henry, the English King's physician, Henry, would be dropping by soon to check on Abigail. She was almost full term and his house would be full of his family. Although she looked healthy, giving birth was very risky and many women died in childbirth. Gabe had Eva and Martha who were midwives, but he wanted Henry as well.

Gabe's father was here already to help for the Christmas season along with the friar from the abbey who came once a year to bless the entire McKenzie household.

Christmas day came and went and the very next day the family started to arrive. Abby was thrilled to see Bess and Teddy. Teddy was still bragging about the peace offering Abby showed him how to cook along with the apple pie and sticky buns. Bess was surprised to see Abby in her condition, but very happy for her and her brother. The rest of the family drifted in as the days went on until the whole McKenzie Clan was together. Abby was thrilled to meet all of them. Gabe's family were thrilled that their brother was happy and obviously well loved.

Gabe's father finally lifted Abby's punishment of kissing each family member in the room except for himself. He still insisted she kiss him. Stories of the family were plentiful and Abby sat and listened to all of them while the children were in the designated sponge war room. Gabe had to tell the story of the sponge war and even recruited some of his brothers to join him in a game or two.

The last person to arrive was Henry, the English king's physician. As promised he arrived just before the twins arrived. Gabe was thrilled to have him in his home but not Abby. All the constant fuss and care finally got to her and she decided to take off for a while on her own.

Gabe was in his study with a few of his brothers when Ellery poked his head into the room and asked, "Laird have you seen my mother?"

Gabe did not think too much of this and just answered, "no."

A few minutes later Hannah poked her head in and asked, "Da have you seen my mother?"

Again Gabe answered, "no."

When Stephan and Daniel did the same and then his little children he became a little concerned.

Gabe excused himself from his brother's company and went to find out why everyone was looking for Abigail. He found Ellery again who was still searching for Abby. Gabe asked him, "Why are ya looking for your mother?"

Ellery just stood in front of him not saying a word. When the twins came in and asked Ellery if he found her yet and then the other children came in and asked the same, Gabe had had enough. "I want to know just what is going on and why are ya looking for your mother?"

Hannah was the one that finally answered him. "We have been trying to keep our eye on her now that she is so close to delivering."

"Aye so has everyone but now will ya please tell me why?" Gabe asked with his arms crossed over his chest and giving that very serious look he was so known for.

Little Emily said, "Because of the Indians, Da, of course."

"What do Indians have ta do with finding your mother and I want a straight answer right now." Gabe ordered.

Ellery answered, "Mom was brought up next to the Indians and practices many of their customs. When an Indian woman is to give birth she leaves the tribe and goes off into the woods and returns when the baby is born. Many times the woman dies in the woods during childbirth."

"Are ya telling me that your mother may be off in the woods somewhere having my twins by herself?" Gabe barked loudly.

"We really don't know," Hannah said trying to reassure him. "But we have looked all over the laird and we cannot find her anywhere. Was she with you this morning when you woke up?"

Gabe's eyes opened wide, realizing he had not seen her all day either.

"NO! She was not with me this morning but sometimes she gets up and walks early when she cannot sleep," Gabe said exasperated.

He was trying not to panic, but she was so close to delivering. He became worried that maybe she could not get back from her walk or maybe she was in the woods somewhere in labor like an Indian woman. He ordered everyone to find her. The entire laird, which included all the servants, and Gabe's family and the clan began a frantic search to find Abigail.

Four hours later there was still no sign of his wife and Gabe was beginning to become very worried. It would be dark soon and if she was out in the winter weather she could freeze to death. Earlier, Gabe had sent out search parties and they started coming back empty handed. Every room had been searched twice, as well as the barn and other buildings but she was long gone.

It was now well after dark. The entire clan and family were gathered in the great hall to discuss what to do about Abigail. Gabe was beside himself and trying to keep from panicking more.

He questioned everyone, but no one had seen her since the day before. Gabe was the last one to have seen her when they retired for the evening. No one had seen her leave this morning and she did not tell anyone where she was going in case someone needed her. She always let someone know where she was but not today. Gabe didn't know if she had come into trouble. He was very strict with where she could go and how far she could wonder alone from the laird and until today she had not disobeyed his orders once.

While all were in the hall, Abby returned after dark and waddled through the back kitchen door. She was so hungry and as luck would have it, Cookie had a pot of his rabbit stew waiting for her on the stove simmering. She helped herself and wondered where everyone was. The kitchen was empty and there was no one on the wall when she entered the laird. Abby was exhausted. She had a wonderful day without anyone watching over her. So she decided to just go up to her bed chamber and have a hot bath, eat her favorite meal of rabbit stew and go to bed. It was a wonderful day with no problems and no one hovering over her. Sleep would be a good ending to a perfect day.

Gabe had a pot of water heating in the fire of their bed chamber when she entered their chamber. She just had to fill her tub. The water was just the right temperature. She dumped rose water in the bath, which made it smell so good. Abby was happy she made it to her chamber without meeting anyone in the hall. It seemed strange not to see anyone in this huge house full of company. She finished her bowl of stew and dressed in her night gown and slipped into bed falling asleep before her head hit the pillow.

She woke to a full room of people looking down at her furious. It was way after midnight and why they were in her room she could not imagine. She sat up in bed from a sound sleep keeping the covers up over her chest. "What is going on?" she blurted out after seeing the entire room full.

"Just where have ya been all day might I ask?" Gabe asked trying not lose his temper with her. She looked so innocent lying in their bed clueless to what had happened all day.

"I went for a walk and then spent the rest of the day with Granny Isabella. I had promised her I would stop in now that she cannot get out so much because of her gout. Why are all of you looking at me like that?"

"Why did ya not tell anyone where ya were going?" Gabe asked through gritted teeth. "We did not know where ya went and we have been looking for ya all day long and that would include all of us."

Abby realized why they were upset with her. "So you missed me?" she said with a sweet smile on her face trying to calm the crowd down, but when no one returned her smile she said, "I thank you for your concern, but I am fine and I am sorry if I have caused all this commotion. I promise I will not leave without telling someone where I am going again."

"Ya will not be going anywhere from now until those babies are born and that is final," Gabe ordered. "I will not be looking for ya and my babies in the woods like an Indian woman. If I have ta post a guard on ya I will."

Abby had had it. "I am very tired and a pregnant prisoner needs to have her rest so thank you for your concern, but I really want to go back to sleep." She plopped back into bed and pulled the quilt over her head and started to cry. Normally this kind of thing would not bother her but she was pregnant and overly emotional these days.

Gabe motioned for everyone to leave but stayed to talk to her some more. She was in no mood to talk and would not even look at him.

"Ya will talk ta me right now," he ordered but Abby just stayed curled up and said nothing.

"Do ya want something ta eat lass?" Gabe asked frustrated. She had a lot to contend with and had handled it beautifully but he understood why she needed some time to herself. "Abby I am sorry. I was just so worried about ya. All I could think of was losing ya and the babies. I pictured ya out in the woods alone and cold or hurt or attacked."

"But I wasn't, nor did I disobey you. You are always asking me to trust you but here is one time when you did not trust me and I am sick and tired of all this constant fussing. I cannot even use the chamber pot without someone wanting to help me. I had a wonderful day until now and you just spoiled it for me." Then she broke out with tears. She jumped up out of bed and put her robe on and left the room.

The halls were deserted again as was the kitchen where she ended up. When she was upset she liked to cook and that is just what she did. She pulled out flour, lard, sugar, cinnamon and apples and started making pies. Lots of pies one after another all perfectly made. By the time she had finished the last pie it was sunrise.

Eva came into the kitchen surprised to find her there and more surprised to find over fifty pies all cooked and ready for dinner that evening. The kitchen was cleaned and all the dishes washed. Abby was sitting in the corner with her legs folded up under her rubbing her belly.

"Abigail are you alright?" Eva asked when she saw the look on her face.

"No Eva I think I over did it and I cannot seem to move," Abby said trying to breathe through her pain.

"Are you in labor?" Eva asked feeling Abby's forehead which was very hot and sweaty.

"I really don't know. This is different from anything I have experienced before." Then Abby let out a small grown and a gush of water spilled on the floor from under her skirts.

"I think your water has just broken lass. We need ta get ya up ta ya room. I will get some help." Before Abby could say a word she was off and out of the kitchen leaving Abby to go through another strange pain. Abby looked down on the floor to see just how much of a mess she had just made to see blood on the floor not just water. She was hemorrhaging. For the first time since she found out she was pregnant, Abby was frightened. This wasn't normal and the pain was excruciating. Abby tried to stay calm but she wasn't doing a very good job of it.

Henry came running into the kitchen shortly followed by Gabe, her sons, Hannah, Dunkin, Joseph and Simon and Philip. They found her sitting in a puddle of blood with her face as white as a ghost. "Take her to your study. Not to your bed chamber. We do not have much time before she bleeds to death.

Gabe picked her up and carried her to his study and laid her on the floor next to the fire. Henry ripped her gown open and examined her. The head of the first twin was crowning which was good news.

"Abby you are going to push now and we will have babies very soon," Henry ordered trying to keep her calm. Gabe knelt by her head holding her hand talking to her, encouraging her, trying to keep her with him.

Abby had worked all night and she was exhausted. She was much too tired to even push, but Henry was not about to lose her or the babies and ordered her to push and not stop until he told her.

"Get behind her Gabe and hold her up. It will be easier for her to push." When Gabe was ready Henry ordered her to push. "Now, Abigail push or I promise I will not leave ever," Henry said which made her smile. She started pushing through the pain feeling warm liquid spilling out of her. Abby could not tell if it was her water or blood but she was not about to lose these babies.

It took three pushes and Gabe watched his newest son born. This was the first time he had witnessed any of his children born and he was overwhelmed.

Henry let Abby see her new son and then handed him to Martha to be cleaned.

"Time to work again Abby," Henry said waiting to see the next little head coming into view. "Push Abigail," Henry ordered and again Abby gave all she had and pushed her new daughter into the world. Henry held her up so Abby could see her just before the room started to get fuzzy and then it was dark.

....She was walking in the clouds. It was sunny and warm. She could not see any snow or Fuchsiall. She was not sure where she was. She kept calling for Gabe, but he was no where around. She was looking for someone anyone but no one was looking for her. Then off in the distant she could see a sailor walking her way. He looked familiar, but she could not tell who he was. He kept coming closer, but she was not afraid. Then she could finally make out his face. It was the man she knew as grandfather, but really her father, walking toward her with a huge smile on his face. She started to run to him, but she could not run fast. Her legs would only move in slow motion. He kept motioning to her but she could not quite see what he was doing. The clouds were becoming thicker...

"We are losing her. Gabe hold her. I need to stop the bleeding," Henry said pulling the afterbirth from her carefully. "She is bleeding too much."

"Donna let her die Henry," Gabe ordered.

Martha and Eva came in from washing the twins and bent down to assist the physician. Martha, Eva and Henry worked as fast as they could to get the bleeding to stop. Abby was getting whiter by the second and Gabe watched helplessly praying for her to live.

Blood spilled over his study floor worse than anything he'd seen in battle. Gabe feared for Abby's life.

The entire clan had gathered in the hall waiting to hear some news about Abigail. Silence came over the entire room as they waited for news. The friar said his beads hoping he would not be called in. Finally Martha entered the hall. She had tears in her eyes. Her head was bent and she could not speak.

"Martha," Joseph said, "tell us what has happened. Are they alive?"

Martha had her head buried in her apron which was covered in Abby's blood. Joseph took hold of her shoulders and shook her. "Martha tell me now."

The entire room looked on as Martha raised her tear covered face from her apron. "The babies are fine. We have a perfect baby boy and a beautiful baby girl, but it is Abby. We did the best we could. There was so much blood."

"Is she alive?" Joseph asked with his eyes misting.

Martha shook her head yes, but then said, "Barely. Gabe is calling for the friar. He took her up to their room."

Before anyone could stop them Abby's four adult children ran from the room and up the stairs hoping to see their mother still alive one more time. The Friar followed as did Joseph, Simon, Cookie, Dunkin and Philip.

When they reached the door they found their mother lying in her bed, eyes closed, covered by a quilt with Gabe kneeling at her side holding her hand. She was colorless. Not a spot of color was left in her and she was barely holding on.

The friar came to the bed and pulled out his oils to administer the last rights. Hannah broke into tears as did her bothers. The room was filled with onlookers hoping and praying for the best, watching helplessly as Abigail fought for her life.

...She could hear his voice. Her father was saying something to her, but she could not make it out. She was so happy to see him. He was smiling at her waving his arms in the air. He was trying to say something, but it was not clear. She was starting to become colder for some reason and then he was standing right in front of her...

"Abigail what are you doing here?" her father said now as clear as could be.

"I don't know father." she said "Where am I? Am I dead?"

"I have waited my whole life for you to call me father. I love you daughter and there is nothing I want more than to have you with me, but it is not your time. Do you want to leave those new babies alone without a mother?" Then her father pointed behind her. She turned to see her pink castle on the hillside next to the ocean. "There it is." Her father said, "It is your dream. Don't give it up."...

Abby's breathing was getting slower and slower. They were losing her.

Emily pushed her way into the room before anyone could stop her. She jumped on the bed and said, "Donna leave me Mom take with me with ya donna leave me." She reached out and hugged Abby holding on to her around her neck. Gabe had to pull her off. He was having all he could do to hold his tears back. Emily kept calling for Abby as she cried helplessly. Hannah came over and took her from Gabe's arms.

.....She could hear Emily calling for her, "I have to go back father. It is the right thing to do but I don't know how. Will you take me I want you to meet Gabe, you will really like him, he is just like you, father."

"I cannot go Abigail, but I will help you. Do not tell Gabe about the map in the trunk until the twins are at least one year old..."

Then she heard Gabe whisper in her ear. "Abigail, donna leave me. Ya are my whole life I cannot make it without ya."...

Then to the surprise of everyone in the bed chamber, Abby opened her eyes, "I am not going anywhere Gabriel McKenzie and don't you forget it. You are stuck with me and that is that. I think I could eat some of Cookie's stew however."

Gabe's head shot up and looked at Abby to see her looking at him with a sweet smile. She reached up and stroked his hair lovingly with her hand.

"Abby, you are alive?" Gabe whispered with a smile. "I thought ya were dead. I thought ya left me forever."

"I gave you my word, I would not leave without your permission." Abby said with a grin. "I almost did leave but my father sent me back. He sent me back to my pink castle on the hill overlooking the ocean with my twelve children and my husband who I love and adore."

"And your husband loves and adores ya," Gabe said and he kissed her as only he could.1.....2.....3.....

THE END

ABOUT KAREN A. FAY

Karen is a native Vermonter. Her package plan contains one husband of 35 years, two sons and a daughter, one daughter-in-law and a six year old grandson. She owns her own craft business and in her spare time tortures her husband by trying to learn to play the bagpipes.